THE
KINGDOM
AND THE
POWER

A THRILLER

PETER ALBRECHT

AUTHOR'S NOTE

Thank you for choosing to read *The Kingdom and the Power.* Throughout the book, in an attempt to add flavor and authenticity to the story, I utilized words and phrases from various different languages. While I believe this enhances the characters, and I have made every attempt to allow the reader to garner the word's meanings from the context of either the dialogue or text, I understand that some readers may desire a literal translation.

Therefore, I have included in this Author's Note, a glossary which translates most of the words or phrases used. I hope this aids to your reading enjoyment.

Happy reading!

Peter

GLOSSARY

Kirche - *(German) Church*

Schweineschnitzel – *(German) A thinly pounded pork cutlet*

Ja - *(German) Yes*

Ach ja - *(German) Ahh, yes*

Nein - *(German) No*

Mein Gott - (German) My God

Auf Wiedersehen - *(German) Good bye*

Scheisse - *(German) Shit*

Wacht am Rhein – *(German) Watch on the Rhine. German code name for their counter-offensive in the winter of 1944 commonly known as the Battle of the Bulge*

Grosse licht - *(German) Big Light*

Grasslich – (German) Ghastly, horrible

Inspectore - *(Italian) Inspector*

Dirignete - *(Italian) Director/Manager*

Gendarmerie - *(French) A military force with law enforcement duties. The police force for the Vatican City State*

Strasse - *(German) Street*

Hauptsturmfuhrer - *(German) Nazi Party paramilitary rank equivalent to a captain*

Brigadefuhrer - *(German) Brigade Leader*

Oberleutnant - *(German) First Lieutenant*

Oberst - *(German). Colonel*

Hauptscharfuhrer – *(German). Chief Squad Leader. Second highest non-commissioned officer Nazi Party paramilitary rank*

Schutzstaffel - *(German) Protection squad*

SS Fuhrungshauptamt – *(German) SS Main office. Often used to force conscription on the populace*

Ja wohl - *(German) Yes indeed*

Burgermeister - *(German) Mayor*

Herr – *(German) Mister*

Was sind - *(German) What are*

Oekuk-saram – *(Korean) Derogatory term for a foreigner*

Cementerio – (Spanish) Cemetery

Dein anderer - (German). Your other

Rasen - *(German) Lawn*

Sieg Heil - *(German) Hail victory*

Opa - *(German) Familiar form for grandfather*

Kommt – *(German) Comes*

DPRK – *(USA) Abbreviation for Democratic People's Republic of Korea (North Korea)*

Danke - *(German) Thank you*

Bitte, hilf mir - *(German) Please, help me*

Amerikanisch - *(German). American*

Frohliche Weihnachten – *(German). Merry Christmas*

Immediatamente mi lider – *(Spanish) Immediately, my leader*

Hermana, hermano, hermanita – *(Spanish) Sister, Brother, Little sister*

Wo sind die plane fur das grosse licht - *(German) Where are the plans for the big light*

Der mann fragte er wo ist das grosse licht - *(German) The man asked him where is the big light*

Ich lieber dich – *(German). I love you*

Das grosse licht ist das kreuz das unsere familie tragt - *(German) The big light is the cross our family bears*

Ich kahn nicht sagen - *(German) I cannot say*

Kein plan überlebt die erste Feindberührung - *(German) No plan survives the first contact with the enemy*

Schnapp dir einfach das grosse licht und lass uns hier raus - *(German) Just grab the big light and lets get out of here*

PROLOGUE

THE HUMAN CONDITION, and humankind's interaction with the environment has always been synonymous with the search for power. As a species, a more developed brain and opposable thumbs were the only evolutionary adaptations that prevented the human animal from being at the bottom of the food chain. As animals go, Homo Sapiens did not possess sharp claws or fanged teeth. His coat provided only the thinnest of fur for protection, and the two legs on which Homo Sapiens ran, achieved an average speed of a mere ten miles per hour. Without those opposable thumbs and larger brains that enabled our ancestors to build tools, as a species, Homo Sapiens would have become extinct long ago.

One of the greatest early tools was humankind's first source of power. Fire. Fire provided both heat and light. Fire could scare away most predators. And as we learned to use this power more effectively, fire could help us build other, less primitive tools that would further assist us to survive and flourish as a species. As our first power source, fire was a pretty good start.

For millennia, most of our technological advances centered around how to create, use and store the energy created by fire. But as humankind evolved, so did our need for power and the ability to store it. By the late 17th century, German scientist Otto von Guericke invented a device that created static electricity. Then in 1752, Benjamin Franklin flew a kite during a thunderstorm to prove that lightening was actually a form of electricity. A new power source was emerging as we dismissed our old friend fire, and used our more developed brains and opposable thumbs to harness this "new" source of power; electricity.

The late 1800's saw great advances in both electric power generation and storage. The "Current Wars" between Thomas Edison's Direct Current and George Westinghouse's less expensive Alternating Current dominated all discussion around power at the end of that century. England built the first electrically powered lighthouse. Paris saw the first electric street lights, and the entire city of Buffalo, NY was powered by hydroelectric generators at Niagara Falls. As our ability to harness and put our new power source to work improved, it allowed our species to develop even more complex machines. With the advent of the internal combustion engine, the ability to now convert fuel into power accelerated other forms of technological advancement as well.

As the now, dominant species of the planet, we no longer needed to use our big brains and thumbs to build tools just to survive. No longer concerned by creatures with sharp claws or fangs, our focus changed to building tools that allowed us to improve the overall human condition. And with this change of focus, we also saw a change in our motivation. Enhancement of the human condition often brought with it financial reward. Advances in technology created financial opportunity, which often then motivated further advancement, and even greater financial opportunity. And financial opportunity brought with it a different type of power.

This new power inspired us to build tools that would help us retain this power, and defend ourselves from other humans who coveted it. We would use power to gain even greater Power, often by force or aggression. Unfortunately, across all of human history, war and human greed have often led as catalysts for some of our greatest advancements.

The first half of the 20th century saw the dawn of the nuclear age and all of the blessings and suffering that came with it. In 1917, German scientists, Kohlschutter and Haenni, performed extensive studies on a material known then as graphite oxide paper. This material, later studied by Hans-Peter Boehm and renamed "Graphene" was an allotrope of carbon, consisting of a single layer of atoms arranged in a hexagonal lattice. The material which was 200 times stronger than steel, had the ability to store electrical charges nearly 400 times that of present-day Lithium-ion batteries, conduct electricity over great distances with near zero impedance, and re-charge 33 times faster than any other battery.

Then in 1927, two Austrian scientists, Kurt Peters and Friedrich Paneth, reported turning hydrogen into helium by nuclear catalysis when the hydrogen was absorbed by finely divided palladium at room temperature. Their report of "cold fusion" was quickly retracted however when they reported that the helium found was from background air.

With these discoveries coming from a Germany struggling to rebound from the results of the first World War, it would be easy to see how both advances could have helped propel Hitler's dreams of European conquest. However, Peter's and Paneth's results were unable to be reproduced, and because of the extreme costs and inefficiencies associated with the mass production of Graphene, there is still no wide-spread commercial use of this amazing material. To date, there is also no accepted theoretical model for cold fusion to occur either.

Had these discoveries been able to be exploited, the results of the Second World War might very well have been different. Had they been available, it might very well have changed the balance of power.

PART 1

CHAPTER 1

**RAF Lindholme
Near Doncaster, England
September 12, 1944**

"Get those Lancasters in the fucking air, NOW!" Wing Commander Derrick Smythe shouted across the field. Ducking back inside the radar shack, he turned to the sergeant manning the radar scope. "Where are they now Sergeant?"

"One Hundred and fifty miles and closing sir." Came the immediate reply.

"Buggers going to mess up tonight's raid." Smythe said as he thought out loud. "Do we have any word on the fighters yet?" he said, turning to the corporal sitting at the radio.

"Not yet sir. They said they would be launching straight away when we had put out the call." Said the Corporal in a thick cockney accent.

"Get back on the radio and make sure to turn those

bombers south as soon as they are airborne. The last thing we need is for them to run headlong into the fighter cover from this incoming raid." Smythe commanded the corporal.

"On it sir." Came the Corporal's reply. Wing Commander Smythe had the reputation of being a fair if not easy-going commanding officer, but he expected what he referred to as *unparalleled professionalism* when duty called. And an incoming air raid was as loud a call as one could receive.

"Sir, I show what looks like a wing of fighters coming out of the south, headed on an intercept course." Shouted the sergeant. "They are bloody well movin' their arse too sir."

Walking over to look at the screen himself, the Wing Commander started performing some mental math as he calculated if the fighters would get here in time. "It's gonna be bloody close." He said to himself as much as to the men in the room. Sticking his head back outside, he watched as the last of his seventy-four Lancaster bombers taxied into position for takeoff. Turning back to his radio operator he said, "Get back on the horn to operations and get them to launch the rest of the strike force. They can still work with the original rendezvous and way points. They just need to get in the air sooner than planned. That should put the strike over target somewhere around twenty-three hundred hours. Make sure that operations also updates the fighter coverage. I'd hate to see us save these planes now, only to have them shot down because someone forgot to inform everyone of the change of plans."

"Yes sir" the Corporal replied as he began dialing in the new frequency.

"Once that is done and you have confirmation, get to a shelter. I have a feeling we may see some damage from this one." Smythe said as he looked back outside and searched the sky for signs of the approaching danger.

Of the fifty German Junker JU86 bombers sent against the Number One Group, RAF, only one bomber was able to persecute the target, cratering the recently built concrete runway and destroying two of the airplane hangars. Of the seventy-four bombers launched early, all were able to complete their mission and diverted to Wellington on their return until their runway was repaired.

St. Elisabeth Kirche
Stuttgart, Germany
September 12, 1944

The white and gold alter stood in stark contrast to the charred timbers that had once supported the roof. Blackened puddles of water sat haphazardly distributed across most of the floor, a reminder of the heroic efforts of the city's firefighters to save the church from the errant bomb that hit mere yards away only two nights before. As a cool fall breeze came in through the leaded frames of what once supported magnificent stained-glass windows, you could almost smell the fear and growing desperation in the air from a city subjected to nearly four years of allied bombing.

Two men sat in the dark, huddled together in one of the front pews, away from most of the puddles and charred wood. Leaning forward as if in prayer, they spoke in hushed tones despite the apparent lack of any other worshipers or listeners.

"So, if you are giving these plans to the Americans, why do I also need to take them?" asked the man wearing the collar of a Roman Catholic priest.

"I am not giving *all* the plans to them." Replied the elder of the two. "I can't give the Americans the formulas or plans for my discovery, only the ones for the metal. That could be bad enough. I fear their intentions to be only slightly less evil than the Fuhrer's. With what I am giving them, they can build nearly indestructible super weapons. There is no way that they get my research too."

"Ja, I understand." Said the priest. "But with the war hopefully ending soon, don't you think they will see the benefits to all of humanity by building on what you started?"

"That is my hope, and that is why I am going over to work with them. Giving humanity this gift is what I always wanted to do. But if I give them the plans and formulas, then I do not control it. The Americans could use it as a weapon, just as the Fuhrer did. We are only lucky that Hitler or his science lackeys never saw the full potential for what I found. If they did, the results for the world would have been devastating. That is why I must control the research. I can ration out what I know when I am more certain the world is ready. Just because man has invented a new technology does not mean mankind is ready for it. In the meantime, you keep the papers hidden and I'll keep the rest in here." The older man said tapping two fingers to his head.

"What time are you meeting the American?" Asked the priest.

"Our meeting is scheduled for 11:30. He plans to

get me out of Germany to the south. There are American troops near Strasbourg. Once we are across the Rhine, we should be safe. And you must be sure to be out of the city before midnight. That is when the British spies are scheduled to blow up the factory. The tanks are still being staged there. Once the factory and the tanks are destroyed, and with me gone, it will be next to impossible for Hitler to rebuild. I am hoping that even if the Fuhrer does not see it, his generals will see that victory is impossible and they will call for an end to this war."

Nodding his head, the priest said, "I have tickets for the last train to Munich, and will be continuing on from there." He paused and put his arm around the other man. "I am going to miss Sunday dinners with my brother." He said. "Your schweineschnitzel can make my mouth water."

"Just as your apple strudel and home-made pastries do for me. Ach ja, we will see each other again Georg. Maybe you come to America and we will do Sunday dinners there."

"Ja, Peter, I think that maybe my flock will need me here more than my brother in America will. There will be much to rebuild when this war is over... Both in buildings and in lives. But before we can start thinking about the end of the war, you must get out of Germany and I must get these plans safely out of the city."

"Where are you planning to hide the plans? I know you said you had some ideas when we had first discussed this."

"There is a small monastery up in the mountains. Very old. Very secluded. Almost forgotten by the Church and the town it overlooks. I am good friends with the Abbot. He has assured me that he can safely hide these plans and will tell no one about them." The priest replied, tapping the black leather covered tube sitting between them. "When you are ready to retrieve them, you will let me know, and I will contact the Abbot. He has promised that he will not give them to anyone except me."

"Georg, I know this is involving you in something that could be very… dangerous. I just cannot think of any other way to…"

Wrapping his arm around his older brother, the priest interrupted, "Ja Peter, it is all good. We do these things because we must. Our Lord Jesus walked in danger most of his life."

"And he ended up on a cross. I do not want anything to happen to you." Peter replied.

"Ach, you should not worry yourself. I walk in the way of the Lord. He will protect me. Besides, only you, the Abbot and myself know of our plans. And the Abbot does not even know what he is hiding for us. He is not fond of the Nazis and only knows that I want to hide this from them. I promise you Peter, I will make sure these plans remain safe."

Peter nodded as the two men faced each other in silence. The priest was the first to move, wrapping his arms around his brother. "Auf Wiedersehen Peter. Be careful." He said.

"Auf Wiedersehen Georg." Peter replied, returning the embrace. "Once this war is over, I will contact you. And thank you."

"Ja, it is nothing. I like spending time with the Abbot. They make the best beer in his monastery. This gives me a good excuse to visit."

The two men stood and the priest turned to leave, while the older man remained in place. "You are not leaving?" the priest asked.

"Nein. I have some time before I need to head to my rendezvous location. I thought I would stay and actually say a few prayers."

"Ja, so now my older brother begins to take my advice." The priest said as he waved at his brother while heading toward the altar. "What other miracles will this night bring?"

As the priest slipped through the doorway behind the altar, the older man sat back down on the charred wooden pew. Folding his hands in prayer he knelt down on the slate floor and began his recitations. After some time, deep in prayer, he looked up, performed the sign of the cross and sat back in the pew. Surveying the damage to this once magnificent church, Doctor Peter Wagner became even more resolute and certain that his course of action was the right one.

Born in 1890 in Bremerhaven Germany, Wagner's father was the captain of a merchant vessel that sailed from that port city. The oldest of three boys, Wagner's father expected his sons to follow in his footsteps in the maritime trade. However, with the death of Peter's mother during the birth of their third son, Wagner's father was forced to leave the youngest with relatives and enroll his older children in boarding school so he could return to sea. At boarding school the two brothers showed an amazing appetite for learning. The oldest, Peter, was fascinated with learning about the natural world, and the interactions of the elements, while the younger brother, Georg was consumed by the spiritual. Only the third child, Hans, decided on a naval career, and it cost him his life during WW I in the Battle of Jutland.

Having completed his initial university studies at *Ruprecht-Karls-Universität Heidelberg* by the start of the first World War, Peter enlisted in the Chemistry Section of the Ministry of War and worked under Fritz Haber. There he saw first-hand how the combination of elements can be used both for the benefit of humanity as well as in the making of instruments of mass destruction.

After the war, Wagner returned to Heidelberg and completed his doctoral studies. Remaining at the university as a faculty assistant, Wagner focused his research on catalyst development and their applications in compound generation. By 1936 Wagner was Chair of the Department of Applied Chemistry at the university, and was considered one of the brightest researchers in Germany. With the start of the Second World War in 1939, it was "strongly suggested" that he dedicate his research to the needs of the Fatherland, and he joined a cadre of other academics at the IG Farben research facility in Stuttgart. The only saving grace of this assignment would be that his brother Georg's church was nearby and he would be able to see him more often.

As luck, either good or bad depending on one's viewpoint would have it, Wagner was able to make a breakthrough discovery three years into his work. Testing a new metal with amazing properties as a catalyst Wagner was able to facilitate the growth of anhydrous salts. Amazed by the way the metal behaved during the electrolysis of water, he began a systematic analysis of what else this *graphene* could catalyze. When Wagner substituted the water with heavy water, the repeated experiment resulted in a flash of light that while lasting only milliseconds, was so bright that had Wagner been looking at the tube, he would have been blinded. Peter Wagner had succeeded in bonding two hydrogen atoms into one helium atom, and the resulting light was the discharge of energy created by the reaction. Wagner had succeeded in creating cold fusion.

For the next year and a half, Wagner worked tirelessly on modifying his formula and methodology to deliver a sustainable reaction. While initially interested, his higher-ups were disappointed by Wagner's inability to produce a continuous sustained reaction. Despite all of his efforts and modifications, the electrical charges produced by the reaction prevented the metal from sustaining the reaction. It seemed that the graphene absorbed and held the charge preventing further electrolysis. It wasn't until a chemical engineering student working in the lab recognized that graphene's ability to store a charge could be further used to absorb all of the energy created by the reaction. That information brought an immediate reaction from Nazi leadership who now recognized some of the immediate applications of this new discovery. By building graphene batteries, charged from Wagner's cold fusion reaction, the Third Reich was on the verge of being able to produce and store electricity without a hydrocarbon-based fuel source. The only problem was that graphene was nearly impossible to efficiently produce in mass quantities.

This problem was solved by Martin Schulthies, the same chemical engineering student who discovered graphene's electrical storage properties. Rather than start with graphite oxide paper, and work to extract the single layer of atoms, Schulthies boiled coal in a solution he developed and used a mechanical method of binding a single layer of the carbon allotrope to aluminum, thus creating the perfect storage medium for use in a battery.

The resulting development and tests of this new paired technology delivered a battery that could power an automobile for nearly 600 miles, and be fully recharged in under 5 minutes, or power a tank for 300 miles with the same recharging capabilities. Battery construction and the corresponding retrofitting of tanks, trucks and cars began immediately. Hitler now had the means to launch his counteroffensive

Despite being the same color, the crisp black uniform of the approaching SS officer was a stark contrast to the soot covered surroundings of the bombed-out church. Lost in his thoughts and prayers, Wagner did not hear the darkly clad man until he spoke.

"You appear to take your evening prayers very seriously, Herr Doktor." Major Max Schwarzkopf said in a voice dripping with distain. "There have been some recent developments that require your immediate attention back at the laboratory, and I must insist you accompany me there immediately."

Startled out of his private thoughts, Wagner did not immediately reply. "What…What sort of developments?" he finally stammered as he began to regain his composure.

"It seems that several copies of the plans for the graphene and battery production, as well as your fusion reaction have gone missing." The Major said as two similarly clad soldiers appeared by his side, sub-machine guns at the ready. "We have locked down the facility in the hopes of preventing any further theft or sabotage by this spy or traitor. We are gathering up all of the senior scientists and will be taking them… somewhere… for their safety. You will please accompany these gentlemen out to the truck."

Wagner glanced hastily around the church. There was nowhere to run. He wondered if any of the British spies were already caught, or if they had not yet even begun their plan to blow up the building. Standing, he retrieved the leather briefcase that held the plans he was bringing to the Americans and walking slowly toward the SS Major. "How did you know I was here?" he asked.

"We had someone come and speak to us, informing us about… well, that you were here. It seems that your earlier conversations disturbed his prayers. Our patrol saw your car parked a few blocks down and confirmed that indeed, you were here. This is your brother's church, is it not? Where is your brother, by the way?" the Major asked.

"I do not know. He was not here when I had arrived so I just…"

"Started praying." Schwarzkopf interrupted. "Yes, we saw you doing that. We will locate your brother in short order as well, so it does not matter. I wonder if he was one of the men whose conversations disturbed that parishioner earlier this evening. So, I also find it strange that you parked several blocks away. Almost as if you had done a bad job of hiding where you were going."

"No. With the bombing I was not sure if I could actually park closer to the church, and it was now not a far walk." Wagner said as he finally stood before the Major and his two guards.

"I'll take that Herr Doktor." Schwarzkopf said holding out his leather gloved hand.

"What?" replied Wagner

"The briefcase Herr Doktor. What is in it? I would like to see."

There was a brief moment of panic and Wagner felt all the blood drain from his face. Once the major opened the briefcase and saw the plans, he knew both he and his brother were dead. The SS would stop at nothing to find Georg, locking down the city and searching house to house if they had to. Taking a deep breath, Wagner regained his composure, and time seemed to slow. He cared less about himself than he did his brother, and knowing his brother would be hunted, found and executed prevented Wagner from just giving in to the building feeling of dread inside his entire body. Looking around the church, Wagner looked for an avenue of escape as he mentally reviewed his options. There were two guards and the Major standing in front of him, all three of them armed. Looking past the three men, Wagner saw another guard standing by the entrance to the church. He had not seen anyone go past him since the Major had approached, so he assumed that there was no one yet stationed at the rear exit of the church. Despite this one point, his avenue for escape was slim.

Wagner quickly reviewed the possibility of surrender. They had not seen him with his brother, and unless they had also captured the American he was scheduled to meet, he might be able to say he had taken the plans in order to review them at home to double check on a potential problem he had discovered earlier that day. Wagner had authorization and access to the plans any time he needed them. Despite the prohibition on removing them from the facility, this story might be believable. He could say that he was exhausted and wanted to go home and get a few hours rest before looking over the plans. But then he remembered the Major saying that multiple copies were missing, and he only had one copy in his briefcase. He had given the others to his brother. The story that he just happened to take one copy when others were missing was a coincidence he knew they would never believe. This conclusion was driven home when Wagner looked into the Major's eyes.

Schwarzkopf stood before Wagner with his arm still outstretched beckoning for the briefcase. A cross between a sneer and smirk graced the major's lips, but it was his eyes that caused a shiver to run down Wagner's spine. Schwarzkopf's eyes had the look of a predator eyeing up its prey. And while predators hunt and kill to survive, this man hunted for the joy of the kill. His eyes displayed the pure evil nature of the man, and Wagner knew in that moment, nothing he could ever say would prevent this monster from killing him and his brother.

"Herr Doktor, the briefcase, please." The Major repeated.

Wagner noted the musical chime of a clocktower in the distance. If he could escape and hide for a half hour, he still had a chance of meeting the American and escaping. He knew he now needed to act.

BONG… the clocktower chimed out, counting out the evening's hour.

"Now, Herr Doktor…". Schwarzkopf said, his right hand sliding down to his sidearm.

"Certainly." Wagner replied.

BONG… Stepping forward, Wagner feigned handing the case over, but instead he swung the case directly at Schwarzkopf's head with all his strength. The case struck the major in the left temple sending his hat sailing midway into the adjacent pew, just as the clocktower chimed for the third time. Staggering sideways into the guard, the major totally lost his balance just as the two men made contact, sending them both to the floor.

BONG…Without waiting to see the results of his attack, Wagner swung the case backhanded to the right, striking the second guard in the jaw and sending him back three paces. The second guard however would have remained on his feet if not for the partially burnt and weakened pew that caught the back of his knees and collapsed as he stumbled into it. Like his companions, the second guard fell over backwards to the ground, striking his helmeted head on the slate floor as the fifth chime rang.

Wagner wasted no time surveying his handiwork as he made his escape, turning immediately toward the altar and the doorway to sacristy and the rear exit of the church.

BONG… With adrenaline coursing through his veins, and the pounding of his heart drowning out the chiming bell tower, Wagner moved as fast as his aging arthritic legs would allow. He barely heard the guard by the door shout for him to stop. However, he clearly heard the report from the guard's rifle as the bullet flew past him and buried itself in the church altar. With his back to his pursuers, Wagner was unaware of the Major pulling his sidearm from a kneeling position and taking careful aim.

BONG… As Wagner mounted the steps to the altar,

he heard the second shot from the guard at the rear of the church, and this time immediately felt a burning pain in his right leg, sending him stumbling to the ground.

Had he not stumbled, Schwarzkopf's first shot would have killed Wagner. Instead, the bullet grazed his right ear as it whizzed past him. *BONG*...Summoning all of his strength, Wagner lifted himself off the ground and limped toward the doorway. The burning in his leg was nearly unbearable, and Wagner found he was getting lightheaded as he tried to move forward. The doorway was a mere fifteen feet away now. If he could just round the corner, he would be out of the line of fire and he may have a chance to escape. He wasn't sure what his next move would be once he was clear of the church, but he would take one step at a time. He just needed to get to the doorway.

BONG... Schwarzkopf had thought his first shot would have ended the fleeing academic. Having won multiple target shooting contests, Schwarzkopf was an expert marksman, and he had taken carful aim and not rushed his shot. It was only through bad timing that Wagner had collapsed and the shot had missed. As Wagner stood and began limping toward the doorway, the Major took aim again and slowly squeezed the trigger,... only to have his sidearm jam. "Scheisse!" he swore as he manually cleared and rechambered his next round.

BONG...Looking up, Schwarzkopf saw his quarry was now only a few feet from the doorway. There was still time, so he once again took careful aim... and slowly squeezed the trigger...

The sound of the eleventh chime was drowned out by the explosion caused by the first bomb impacting the roof of the church. RAF Bomber Group Number One had just arrived on target and began unleashing a torrent of high explosive ordinance on the city of Stuttgart.

Allied high command had deemed it safer to destroy the labs and factories from the air, rather than risk personnel, and had nixed the plan to send in spies to plant the bombs. Launched early because of the attack on their base, the bombers lined up on the church spire as they began their bomb run an hour sooner than originally scheduled.

The first bomb impacted on the remaining roof of St. Elisabeth Kirche, instantly killing the five men inside along with incinerating the plans for a cost-effective means of mass-producing graphene. In total, over the next half hour, 217 planes leveled the western part of the city killing 957 people, injuring another 1,600 and destroying the factory that was retrofitting Hitler's electric tanks. In one half hour, all Nazi evidence of cold fusion, graphene, and the breakthroughs in electric vehicles were wiped from the face of the earth, and all personnel associated with its development, save the German High Command were killed.

Hitler proceeded with his plans for a counter-offensive, code named *Wacht am Rhein*, sending the Fifth and Sixth Panzer Army through the Ardennes in an attempt to seize the port of Antwerp and cut off the Allied supply lines. Unfortunately for the Germans, they ran out of fuel and were defeated in what was to become known as the Battle of the Bulge. Seven months later, Hitler was dead and the Nazis officially surrendered a few weeks after that.

Peter Wagner's dream of peace eventually came true, while his nightmares of the dawning nuclear age were only temporarily averted.

CHAPTER 2

Stuttgart Central Station
Stuttgart, Germany
September 12, 1944

GEORG WAGNER MOVED swiftly through the quiet streets of the city. What was once a city with vibrant night-life, Stuttgart now huddled in collective fear of the night time bombing raids. Arriving at the Stuttgart train station a little after ten PM he boarded the 10:23 to Munich with connections on to Rosenheim and southern Bavaria. Finding a seat next to a middle-aged woman and across from an elderly couple, he placed his small rucksack and the black leather covered metal tube in the rack above his seat and settled in for his three-hour train ride. Despite the late hour, since this was the last scheduled train out of the city this week, his car was fairly crowded with Nazi Party faithful looking to make the pilgrimage to the Bavarian Alps and the towns adjacent to the Berghof, Hitler's vacation home.

As pastor of his church, Wagner had the ability to travel

regularly on church business, so he had little concern about his travel documents. However, upon pulling into the Munich station Wagner noticed what seemed like an unusual number of regular troops and SS officers waiting on the platform. Sensing a problem, Wagner collected his rucksack and tube even before the train came to a halt, and while the elderly couple was gazing out the window, Wagner grabbed the old man's hat and tucked it under his arm. Making his way to the train lavatory Wagner quickly ducked inside.

Once safely inside the lavatory, he removed the papers from the black tube, folding the smaller pages, he stuffed them in his backpack. After shredding one of his undershirts, he removed his trousers, securing the schematics and blueprints around the lower portion of his leg by tucking the one end inside his sock, and tying the other off at the knee with the shredded T-shirt. Removing his sweater, Wagner quickly stripped out of his clerical garb, opting for a plain white button-down shirt from his bag. Finally, he donned the stolen hat, pulling it low over his eyes. Leaving the tube in the corner behind the door, he grabbed his rucksack and exited the lavatory.

Wagner noticed that most of the passengers had already departed the train and were being approached by soldiers on the platform. Trying to think quickly, Wagner saw his opportunity as he approached the train doors. Seeing that no one was looking in his direction, Wagner quickly descended the steps and exited the train on the track, rather than the platform side. Reaching the ground, he saw that luckily, the 10:23 had pulled into the Munich station on the last track. The rail yard and tracks in front of him were damaged from prior bombings and therefore not in use. With abandoned freight and passenger cars stranded on demolished tracks sitting in front of him, Wagner hunched over and ran to the cover of the nearest one. Climbing into the damaged passenger car, Wagner peered across the rail yard at his train and platform to see if his movements had been spotted. Observing the scene for several minutes, Wagner confirmed that he had been able to get clear of the train without arousing anyone's suspicions, but noted that now several of the troops and SS officers were making their way through his train looking for anyone who may not have gotten off.

Lying on the hard floor of the abandoned train car, Wagner began to think of how he was going to get out of the city and make his way to the monastery. Assuming that the search currently going on in the station was for him, he considered heading to Saint Paul's church in the Ludwigsvorstadt-Isarvorstadt quarter, but quickly dismissed that idea fearing that, the church may be guarded. Knowing he needed to come up with a plan quickly before the search expanded beyond the station, Wagner took inventory of his resources and options. He knew the city fairly well, so whatever option he chose, he wouldn't be wandering the city streets aimlessly. He assumed that the troops were looking for a priest carrying a black tube, and by outward appearances, he did not currently fit that description. However, he knew that anyone found walking outside this evening would be stopped and questioned, and travel papers identified him as who he really was.

What he needed was a place to lay low for a while and potentially an alternate form of transportation out of the city. As the level of adrenaline dissipated in his bloodstream, Wagner began to think more clearly. After a few moments of thinking about his options he finally landed on reaching out to an old friend.

Johann Hasselmeyer was Wagner's friend from his boarding school days. Growing up together, Hasselmeyer moved to Munich after his time at the University and had become a successful business owner. Wagner still corresponded with him regularly and had visited numerous times prior to the start of the war. Wagner knew that Hasselmeyer was no friend of the Nazis, but he worried about the dangers he would be subjecting Hasselmeyer to by asking him for assistance. With all that this city had been through, he also wondered if his old friend would be willing or even able to help. Since there were few other options, and while it was still dark, Wagner figured the only way to find out was to go and ask. Verifying that his documents were still secured to his lower legs Wagner slipped out of the abandoned train car and made his way into the city proper headed for Hasselmeyer's home.

The night sky was giving way to the first gray light of dawn as Wagner approached Johann Hasselmeyer's home. The normal half hour walk from the train station to Hasselmeyer's street took Wagner over two hours as he picked his way through the shadows and across the rubble caused by Allied bombing. Walking through the abandoned streets and past mountains of broken stone and half burnt timber, it seemed like more than half of the city had been either destroyed or damaged from the repeated bombing raids. Between what Wagner had seen in Stuttgart and what he was now witnessing here, he wondered how many more

Germans would need to suffer because of this war, and if there would be any towns or cities left when it was all over.

After repeatedly having to duck into concealment with the approach of a vehicle or roving foot patrol, Wagner finally arrived at the heavily damaged building that was his friend's home. Knocking on the door, Wagner hoped to not attract the attention of others living in the area. Wagner knocked again, and still there was no answer. He wondered if Hasselmeyer had possibly moved out of the damaged house. The building had suffered fire damage from the burnt-out home to the left, and from the looks of it, part of the roof and back had also collapsed, either from fire damage or another bomb.

Wagner knocked a third time, and finally he saw some light emerge from the windowless frame of the second-floor front room. Looking up, Wagner saw the familiar face of his friend hanging out of the window, peering down at him.

"Johann, it's me, Georg."

"Georg? What are you doing here at this hour?" Hasselmeyer said.

"Hoping to be let in, and not have to shout up to you." Wagner replied.

"Come in. There is no lock on the door. No reason at this point. There is barely a door. I'll be right down."

Wagner entered the house and was greeted by the all too familiar smell of burnt wood and smoke. The couches on which Wagner had sat numerous times conversing with his friend late into the evening were now stained by smoke and water. The half empty curio cabinet adjacent to the stairs looked sad and broken. All but one of the windows were gone and the area rugs all displayed stains and water damage.

Hasselmeyer came limping cautiously down the stairs carrying an oil lamp dressed in undershirt and slacks. His right leg was bound to a padded board that stretched from his ankle to just under his armpit, holding his leg straight and ridged. Placing the lamp on the end table next to the couch, Hasselmeyer reached out to embrace his long-time friend.

"It is so good to see you. I had written you twice since your last letter and not hearing back, I had assumed the worst."

"I had written you numerous times as well Wagner replied. "I guess the mail is no longer as efficient as it once was."

Johann said, "Ach, Ja. Unless it is a war communiqué or something to do with the party or the government, it is no longer important. So, what brings you to Munich, and why are you here knocking at my door at this hour of the morning?"

"I wish I could say I was here on a social visit or to check on my old friend but that is not the case. I need your help. The Wehrmacht and the SS are after me. I am in trouble, and I need a place to hide." Wagner said with near panic in his voice. "I am sorry, Johann, but I have nowhere else to turn. I have been on the run all night, hiding amidst the rubble. Now I see your leg, and what has happened to your home, and I don't want to impose on you and Dorothy but I have nowhere else to turn…" Wagner buried his face in his hands. "Mein Gott…"

When Wagner looked up, he could see tears welling up in his friends' eyes. "Dorothy is gone." Hasselmeyer said. "The last bombing raid. We were returning from the market, and we're unable to get to the shelter. We ducked into a building right before a bomb hit. She died in my arms, and I injured my leg. My hip and leg were broken in four places. I spent several weeks in the hospital, but the doctors said there is not much more they can do. I use this for support." Johann said, tapping on the padded board. Otherwise my leg cannot bear my weight."

"Oh Johann, I am so sorry. And what of Otto?"

"Otto is fine. He is upstairs sleeping right now, although I am sure he will be down momentarily hearing our voices. Ja Georg, what has become of our beautiful country. Why has God forsaken us?"

"This is not God's doing, Johann. It is…"

"I know, I know. The workings of a madman…And yet people still follow him. Why?"

"Some believe we can still win. The military certainly thinks so."

"And those that do not are visited by the Gestapo in the middle of the night. Speaking of which, why is all of Germany after you Georg?"

Looking around the room as if he needed to see if anyone else could be listening, Wagner said, "I was given schematics by my brother. Plans he said were for creating a big light. A light that could change the world, but could also be used for great evil. I am on my way to a monastery to hide the plans until after the war when my brother feels it will be safer to reveal them."

"Your brother gave you these plans here in Munich?" Hasselmeyer asked.

"No. in Stuttgart." Wagner replied. "I came to Munich last night on the train.""

And They followed you on the train?"

"No, they were here already when I arrived at the station." Wagner replied. "Somehow they knew where I was going… that is assuming they are looking for me."

"You don't know if they are looking for you?"

"Not for sure, but I was not going to take the chance to find out." Wagner said.

"That is a smart move. I suggest you stay here with me for a few days. Lay low. I doubt they will go from house to house looking for you or whomever it is they are looking for. The city is in shambles. Some houses like this…" Hasselmeyer said waving his arm around his home, "… are occupied. Others are abandoned. It depends on if the occupants had somewhere else to go… or if they are… still alive."

Looking at his longtime friend, Wagner put his hand on Hasselmeyer's shoulder and squeezed. "Thank you Johann. Thank you old friend."

"Good Germans like us need to stick together. Now, let me see what I can get us for breakfast. You must be starving after all that nighttime activity, and I think I still have some of that dark bread and some bacon lard."

Schutzstaffel Regional Headquarters
Munich, Germany
September 13, 1944

Hauptsturmführer Dieter von Hilengard stormed into the office of the SS regional HQ and slammed his fist down on desk. "How does a priest evade an entire division of troops?" he screamed out rhetorically to the soldiers and officers in the room. "I just finished a telephone call with Brigadefuhrer Doring. He said that his orders come directly from Himmler himself. We are not to let this man escape. Oberleutnant!" he called out to the army field officer assigned to assist him.

"Yes sir." Came the immediate reply of the lieutenant as he entered the room and snapped to attention.

"What is the status of your patrols?" Hilengard asked.

"Sir, we have had our troops patrolling the city all evening, however we have not found anyone fitting the priest's description. Perhaps he was not on that train. I understand that Stuttgart sustained heavy bombing this evening."

"Perhaps lieutenant. Or perhaps your men are not looking hard enough."

"Sir, they are doing everything short of a house to house search, and that is nearly impossible."

"He is correct in that assessment, Herr Hauptsturmführer." Max Lubba, the highest-ranking non-commissioned SS officer added. "With all of the damage this city has sustained, performing a house to house search would not be realistic."

"No, I agree with you, Hauptscharführer." Hilengard said. "Since we have been unable to intercept this priest at the station or with a sweep of the streets, perhaps it is time to conduct ourselves more strategically. Our informant said the priest was headed to a monastery in the mountains. We know he had purchased a ticket to continue on to Rosenheim. That would mean he is headed to one of the monasteries in either southern Bavaria or northern Austria. It would make more sense for us to wait for him there."

"But sir, do you know how many monasteries there are? There must be hundreds." Said the lieutenant.

"Only sixty-three, to be exact." Hilengard replied. "You do not have to trouble yourself with this assignment Oberleutnant. You and your men will continue to search the city. Pay special attention to the roads leading out of the city and any trains and busses that are departing. Hauptscharführer Lubba, you will assign two or three of our men to each of the monasteries. They will head out immediately. Once they arrive, they will question the monks… rigorously, and then they will remain there until relieved, or our priest shows up. We should be able to arrive before he does, assuming he is able to avoid the Oberleutnant's patrols. We will then have our man, and recover the things he stole from us."

"Ja, wohl, Herr Hauptsturmführer." The men shouted in unison.

Kossener Strasse
Munich, Germany
September 19, 1944

After several days of waiting and watching, Wagner and his hosts noticed a decrease in the roving patrols. While they were still present, the intensity had diminished over the past few days. Hasselmeyer and his son Otto went about their normal daily business. They would rise in the morning, dress, then head over to the bomb-damaged building where Hasselmeyer had his leather import business. As did many of the remaining residents of Munich, Johann and

Otto spent most of their days, repairing what they could and working tirelessly at restoring their city.

Wagner would spend his days secreted away in Hasselmeyer's home. Much of the time he spent in prayer, but he also reviewed maps that Hasselmeyer had, and worked on planning a route out of the city and to the monastery. Upon arriving home that evening, Johann greeted Wagner with a look of desperation.

"Georg, I have news. I ran into Bishop Meiser today on my way to the market. He is the Lutheran bishop and he has a church,… ahhh it is St. John the Baptist in Garmisch-Partenkirchen. I have known him for years as he uses my business for the leather coverings on their hymnals. He has no great love of the Nazis. In fact, he organized resistance in the city against Hitler's plan for the Reich Church." Hasselmeyer said breathlessly.

"Yes Johann, I have heard of him. What of him. What is the matter?"

"He said men from the SS Fuhrungshauptamt are back in the city and are conscripting youth as young as sixteen. He told me that I needed to leave the city and take Otto or they would take him off the street if they saw him. Georg, he is sixteen years old. He should report in next year. If they find him, it will not be good for him or me."

Wagner thought for a moment, then said, "Then we should all leave together. When I head out to the monastery, you and Otto will come with me. We can remain at the monastery until the war is over. We can all be safe there."

"Ja, we will see Georg. In the meantime, he is coming here to help us."

"What? Who?" Exclaimed Wagner.

"The Bishop." Hasselmeyer replied.

"Have you lost your mind? I cannot be seen here. How do you know you can trust him?"

"He already knows you are here. And he told me they are definitely looking for you."

"What? How does he know that? Johann, what is going on?"

"They went to his church and questioned him. They told him that there was a Catholic priest who is a traitor to the Reich who is hiding out in the city. They searched his church and asked if you had contacted him at all. They are going to all of the churches that remain in the city. They are seriously trying to find you."

"So, what did you tell him."

"Meiser knows you and I are friends. He is a long-time customer and I have spoken of you to him several times. He can be trusted. He wants to help."

Wagner paced the room nervously. He considered gathering his things and leaving before the Bishop, or worse, the Nazis were at the door. But then he considered the fact that it was still too light outside, and now armed with the fact that there were patrols looking for him, he decided that remaining in the house and trusting his friend would be the better choice.

"Johann, I hope you are right." Wagner said.

"Trust in the Lord, Georg. And those that serve him."

It was well past ten PM when Bishop Meiser arrived at Hasselmeyer's home. With the drumming sound of bombs dropping off in the distance, everyone in the house was on edge. Sitting in a back room, illuminated by a single candle, the three men huddled around the scarred kitchen table.

"I do not know what you did, and honestly, I do not care to know." The Bishop began. "But I have not seen SS officers and troops behaving this franticly in… well, ever actually. The officer who came to my church was Wehrmacht, not SS, but I have seen the SS activity by their headquarters. Troops coming in, receiving orders, then hastily heading out again. The officer in charge of the men who searched my church stated that Himmler himself delivered the orders to find you."

"Mein Gott." Hasselmeyer said.

"Ja, so… I am here because I want to help." Meiser said. "Heinrich Himmler has to be one of the most evil human beings on the planet. While Hitler wants to unify the church under his control, Himmler wants to do away with all religion. That man serves Satan. I believe as men of the cloth, we must put aside our denominational differences and fight against evil. As badly as Himmler wants you, Father, you must be doing a good job of that."

"I am just… Wagner hesitated, "…just trying to keep a promise to my brother, and at this point, stay alive and away from those people who are after me."

"Well I want to help with that. And keep my friend's son off the front lines." Meiser said as he nodded in Hasselmeyer's direction.

"So, you can help us get to the monastery?" Wagner asked.

"Monastery? No, no… You cannot go there." Meiser replied. "That officer who searched my church was rather chatty. He said he was a devout Lutheran before the war began, but had been unable to attend services since. I think he was almost looking for me to grant him some form of absolution while he conducted his search and questioning. He acted very humbled to be speaking to his Bishop. Anyway, he said that he did not expect to find the priest…, you…" Meiser said nodding at Wagner. "…in my church, but he had to do his duty and perform the search. Then he mentioned that he expected the priest would be caught when he got to his destination at the monastery. It seems they have some form of a trap set for you."

Leaning back in his chair, Wagner placed his hand on his forehead in dejection. Letting out a slow and deliberate sigh, he said, "So now what are we supposed to do. How am I supposed to get out of the city, and where am I going to go to hide till after the war."

Meiser said with a smirk, "I am going to help get you out of the city by having you become a Lutheran pastor."

"What?… How are…?" Wagner started in confusion.

"I have drawn up papers identifying you as the Reverend Georg Schmidt. He and his son Otto will be traveling to Fussen to take over as the pastor of the church there. It is out of the way and up in the mountains. I doubt anyone will come looking for you there."

"Schmidt and his son Otto…?" Wagner questioned. "What about Johann?"

"My friend, I was never going anywhere." Hasselmeyer answered. "The cover works for the two of you. Not for a party of three. Besides, with this leg, I would only slow you down."

"No." Wagner said resolutely. "Either we all go or I am not going. I will not leave you here. I will…"

"Georg, please." Hasselmeyer interrupted. "Do this for me. Do this for Dorothy. I cannot lose both my wife and son to this war."

Meiser said, "Father, Johann is not in any jeopardy from the SS if he remains here. You and Otto on the other hand are. You both need to leave and I have a way to get you out. You hide out in Fussen until the end of the war, then Otto will return to his father, you can return to your church and things can return to normal." Sighing, Meiser continued. "Look, the Soviets are steadily advancing in the east. Despite the propaganda, I am hearing reports from wounded soldiers returning from the front. We are losing this war. The British and Americans are amassing their troops for a push from the west, and even the Italians to our south have switched sides. I cannot imagine this war will go on for even another year. And we are far enough to the south and west that we will not be occupied by those Soviets. They are a Godless bunch and are not much better than the Nazis. Father, if not for yourself, do this for your friend. Shepherd his son to safety. If you do not, I guarantee the SS Fuhrungshauptamt will get him in short order and he will be sent east to be cannon fodder."

"Georg, please..." Hasselmeyer said, tears welling up in his eyes.

"How will we get Otto past any patrols or the Fuhrungshauptamt?" Wagner asked.

"Ah so... he will be a wounded soldier who already served, and has been recently discharged for medical disability." Meiser replied.

"Medical disability?" Wagner asked.

"I have a parishioner who is good at… well, he can copy certain documents so they pass for the real thing." Meiser said.

"What kind of medical disability?" Hasselmeyer asked. "They only discharge you if you have lost a limb or something equally as serious."

"I should think a head wound that has left him impaired would work." Meiser said. "We can shave and bandage his head to make it look more realistic. Otto would have to act a little.. You know, not speak, drool, make awkward noises. I doubt anyone who stops you would contest this. In fact, it would actually distract them from you a bit, Father. Especially if Otto makes more noises the more they question you."

"I know Otto could do that." Hasselmeyer stated.

Thinking about the plan, Wagner could see the logic in it, and for the first time in days, he was actually beginning to feel optimistic. He still was not comfortable leaving his friend, but everything Hasselmeyer and the Bishop were saying made sense. "When would we leave?"

Nodding his head and smiling at Wagner's decision, the Bishop said, "Give me another day or two to finish the papers. I will need your original documents, Father. We need to speak to Otto and explain everything to him."

"I will wake him after you leave and speak to him. He will be ready." Hasselmeyer said.

"Ja, so as I said before, we need to stand together and fight this evil together. We need to be soldiers for the Lord."

Standing and shaking the Bishop's hand, Wagner said, "I already am, Herr Bishop. I already am."

Reichsautobahn 95
Just north of Ohlstadt, Germany
September 22, 1944

Wagner and Otto had traveled for nearly two hours without seeing any patrols. As luck would have it, contrary to the damage to Hasselmeyer's home and business, his vehicle remained in good working order. Now loaded with clothing and some of Hasselmeyer's personal belongings, as well as some of the Bishop's liturgical texts, the pair was traveling south on the Autobahn toward Fussen. Having been stopped twice as they headed out of the city, the combination of Otto's acting, disguise, and Meiser's paperwork had allowed them to continue without a problem. As they approached the latest roadblock just outside of Ohlstadt, Wagner was confident in his ruse.

"May I see your papers please?" the sergeant asked Wagner as he brought the vehicle to a halt.

Handing over both his and Otto's documents, Wagner smiled at the troopers while Otto began his previously successful charade.

"Where are you headed?" the sergeant asked.

"We are being relocated to Fussen. I am to take over the church there."

"Grrrooonnkkk!" exclaimed Otto.

Startled by the outburst, the corporal standing next to the sergeant asked, "What was that?"

"I'm sorry. My son was wounded outside of Wroclaw. He had some shrapnel from a mortar penetrate his brain. The doctors were able to remove it, and saved him, thank

God, but I'm afraid he has some limited faculties. It is all in the papers there…" Wagner said waving to the documents.

With drool dripping from the side of his mouth, Otto shouted, "Moouarrrrkkk.." Then with a repeated twitch of his neck, he began an incessant chant, "Ner…, ner…,ner…,ner,,,, newaaaak."

With just a cursory review of the paperwork, the sergeant looked clearly uncomfortable as he tried to address Wagner. "There is an escaped spy, and some Catholic priest who is wanted by the SS in the area. Unfortunately pastor, the road south of here is closed."

Over the new chants of "Hee…, Hee…, Hee…, Haaa…" the sergeant said, "You can take this road west.." pointing to the intersecting roadway and then find another path south toward your destination."

"Hee…, Hee…, Heee…, Heeee…" Otto's chant grew in volume and intensity.

"HEEEEOOOONNKK" Otto shouted, punctuating his performance with a loud and odiferous fart that backed the soldiers surrounding the vehicle up two steps.

"Sergeant, I apologize." Wagner said as the horrified soldier stared at Otto in disbelief.

Handing Wagner back his papers, the sergeant said, "Pastor, I think your son just had an accident."

Fighting to keep his composure, yet choking from the smell, Wagner collected his papers and thanked the sergeant. Starting up the car, the soldiers enthusiastically waved the pair through to the detour. Once through the roadblock and out of the soldier's earshot, both men began laughing hysterically.

"What in the name of all that is good did you eat?" Wagner asked.

"I guess that is why they are called deviled eggs." Otto replied. Because when they come out, they smell like Hell.

CHAPTER 3

**St. Matthew's Lutheran Church
Eschenberg, Germany
November 22, 1944**

Despite being abandoned, the church was in less disrepair than Otto's home in Munich. The roof was intact, and while the building needed to have the rodents and cobwebs cleared out, structurally it was sound. With a small rectory building situated behind the church and a barn across a small field adjacent to both buildings, this location appeared to be the perfect spot for Wagner and Otto to hunker down to ride out the balance of the war.

Because of multiple detours which extended their drive, Wagner and Otto were forced to abandon their vehicle when it ran out of fuel. Then, facing bridges blown up by previously retreating troops, they were unable to cross the Lech River. After traveling on foot for more than a week, the pair made their way into the town of Eschenberg, some fifteen kilometers north and east of Fussen.

Hungry and tired, they sought out the local Lutheran church with the hopes of finding shelter for the evening and possibly some food. Finding the church abandoned, and seeing how quiet the town was, Wagner damaged the papers from the Bishop to render the location of his assignment unreadable, and presented himself to the local Burgermeister as the town's new Lutheran pastor.

Wagner and Otto were welcomed immediately by the local populace. The pair would spend their days repairing the old church, and would visit with parishioners in the evening to introduce themselves, often managing a free meal in the process. On Sundays, Wagner would hold services, and since the Lutheran church service deviated only slightly from the Roman Catholic Mass, he had no difficulty fitting into his new role.

Otto, despite his "handicap" had a talent for carpentry. With his skills and the help of some of the local town folk, they repaired the barn, built a chicken coop, and penned in some of the surrounding field. Wagner received chickens, dried beef and produce as payment to officiate at weddings or funerals, and the money collected from the Sunday offerings, more than covered the rest of their needs. Overall, the pair were settling in to a quiet life, somewhat removed from the stresses they lived with while inhabitants of one of Germany's cities.

Somewhat isolated, Eschenberg rarely received news of the war. As an occasional traveler or a refugee from one of the cities would pass through they would be able to provide an update, but other than that, there were no German troops stationed nearby, nor did they see any patrols. Both the Soviet and American armies were concentrating their assaults north of Wagner's new little home, and any action in Italy was too far south to matter.

Based on what Meiser had told him before they departed, Wagner did not expect this war to drag on much longer, and he began to formulate plans in his head for how he would return to his life once that happened. His first order of business would be to deliver his brother's plans to the monastery. Still believing this to be the safest repository for the documents, Wagner wondered how long the SS would keep troops stationed there waiting for him to arrive. After three months he doubted they were even currently still there. But once the war was over, SS troops would either be going home or fight to the death. Either way, they would not be waiting for some priest who had never shown up.

Once free of the documents, Wagner could then reunite Otto with his father and then reach out to his bishop to discuss his disappearance. With all of the bombing and chaos this war had caused, he was pretty sure that the Church hierarchy would be understanding of clerics who had become refugees. For now, though, Wagner would continue to serve the Lord in other ways, and safely wait out the war.

Wagner and Otto had settled in to a regular routine. About every few days, either Wagner or Otto would take the two wheeled push cart, and head into town to purchase or trade eggs for the other food they would need for the next few days. If Wagner made the trek, he would also spend time visiting sick or elderly members of the church. If Otto went, he would carry a note outlining the goods they needed since he still maintained the ruse that he lost the ability to speak. While he no longer needed to twitch and honk as he had when they left Munich, he would still remain silent and presented himself with a vacant a stare and the occasional drool.

On this particular day, Otto was returning home when he saw something moving in the tall grass by the side of the road. As Otto approached, the movement stopped, but his curiosity was already piqued. Lowering the handles of the cart, Otto stepped over the small drainage ditch into the tall grass and immediately almost stumbled over the body of a man lying stretched out on his side.

"Bitte hilf mir." The man weakly asked for assistance.

Startled, but regaining his composure quickly enough to remain in character, Otto grunted at the man, then leaped over the ditch and ran back to the church as fast as he could.

"He was in a uniform, and he looked like he was injured, but I did not want to touch him to see how badly. I ran straight here." Otto explained to Wagner.

Grabbing his coat and a blanket, Wagner ran out after Otto. Arriving at the field, Wagner could immediately see the injured man was bleeding from a wound to his shoulder. The man wore the uniform and insignia of a major in the Luftwaffe, and he was covered in dirt and mud. His trousers were ripped in multiple places and despite the cold, he was missing the leather jacket worn by most aviators. It was obvious by his pallor that he had lost a decent amount of blood and his leather boots were barely containing the swelling in his left ankle.

Eyes closed, in a state of semi-consciousness, the man just kept repeating, "Bitte... Bitte"

"Herr Major, we are going to get you to a doctor." Wagner said as he bent down over the injured man. "Otto, grab the legs and help me carry him to the cart. We can then wheel him down to Doctor Blaumann."

"Ja… Bitte… Bitte…" the man just pleaded softly over and over.

"On my count of three… " Wagner said as he bent over and wrapped his arms under the Major's shoulders.

Otto bent down and grabbed the legs, halfway between the knees and ankles. "One… Two… Three…" Wagner counted and on three, both men simultaneously lifted the wounded man.

"Arrrghhh, Motherfucker" the man groaned in pain at the sudden movement.

Startled by the Major's exclamation, Wagner lost his grip and he dropped the man, causing his injured shoulder to slam into the ground, and his swollen ankle slide forcibly up and catch in the crook of Otto's elbow.

"Fuck!!" the Major bellowed out with his eyes snapping open from the jarring pain in both his shoulder and ankle.

Looking up at Wagner, he raised his hand in outreach as his eyes glazed back over. "Bitte… Please, I…" he managed before passing out.

Looking from the Major to Otto, and back again, Wagner asked, "Did you hear that?"

"Ja, Amerikanisch." Otto replied, his eyes wide and mouth open in shock.

Looking back down at the unconscious man, Wagner said. "We have to help him. We cannot just leave him here by the side of the road. But we cannot take him to Doctor Blaumann." Thinking for a few moments, Wagner continued, "Help me get him into the cart. We will wheel him back home. We can take him down into the basement and try to care for him there. Hopefully no one comes down the road while we are wheeling him down."

Carefully, Wagner and Otto lifted the injured man and placed him as best they could in the cart, with his legs and head dangling over the sides. Grabbing the man's rucksack and throwing the blanket over him, they each lifted a handle of the cart and started heading home as quickly as they could manage without dumping their cargo back over the road. Arriving home, they wheeled the cart around to the back of the house, opened the rear door to the rectory, and carried the unconscious soldier down the cellar stairs, placing him on the long work table stored in the corner of the room.

"We need to try to stop this bleeding. Go upstairs and get me whatever bandages we have as well as the spare sheets and a pair of scissors. We will also need the bottle of hydrogen peroxide from the bathroom to clean that wound. Finally, get the extra blanket out of the closet as well. I want to get these wet and filthy clothes off of him and wrap him in clean dry blankets."

Otto went upstairs and collected everything as instructed, returning as Wagner was performing the sign of the cross as he kneeled before the wounded man. Since we cannot use the doctor's help with this, I was asking for some other assistance." He said to Otto. "Now, help me get this filthy uniform off of him and let's get him bandaged up."

After getting the soldiers, dirty uniform off and cleaning him up, it became painfully obvious that his wounds were more serious than Wagner had originally thought.

It also became just as obvious that he was not a German Luftwaffe officer since he continuously spoke English in his semi-conscious state. The man's shoulder injury was clearly caused by a bullet with both an entry and exit wound through the upper portion of the shoulder. The crunching sound that occurred whenever he moved his shoulder, also meant the bullet fractured the man's collarbone.

The injury to the ankle also appeared to be a fracture, as the swelling almost prevented Wagner and Otto from removing the man's boot. Based on the puss that oozed out of the shoulder wound, and the man's fever, Wagner assumed that these injuries were sustained several days ago. Despite Wagner's best efforts in cleaning and caring for the wound, after three days the man's fever had not gone down, and he seemed to be unconscious more than semi-conscious and mumbling in English.

Knowing the man needed more aid than he was currently providing, Wagner hatched a desperate plan to get some antibiotics. Taking Otto see Dr. Blaumann, Wagner claimed Otto had a sore throat with what looked like white patches in the back. When the doctor attempted to look in the back of Otto's throat, Otto clamped his mouth shut, nearly biting off the tongue depressor and one of Dr. Blaumann's fingers, and refused to open it. Since this was not uncharacteristic behavior for Otto, and he would not open his mouth, the doctor trusted Wagner's assessment and gave him a supply of penicillin. And while the doctor was not looking, Wagner emptied more pills into his pocket. Now, armed with the antibiotic, Wagner in addition to cleaning the man's wounds, would force the pills down the man's throat as if administering medication to a dog.

Finally, after ten days, the wounded man's fever broke, and slowly if he began to regain control of his faculties. As his level of consciousness improved, so did his ability to speak only German.

"Danke. I owe you my life." He said in flawless German.

"We could not very well leave you on the side of the road." Wagner replied.

"No, I guess not, Father…?"

"Pastor. Pastor Georg Schmidt. You are on a work table, lying in the basement of my rectory here at St. Matthew's church."

"Well, thank you again, Pastor. When I was shot down…" Wagner was standing directly over the man's face, leaning both hands on the table shaking his head.

"…What? Why are you shaking your head and looking at me like that?" the man asked.

Wagner replied, "Because it is not good to lie to your priest."

St. Matthew's Lutheran Church
Eschenberg, Germany
December 25, 1944

A little more than a month had passed since Wagner and Otto had found the American by the side of the road. Despite the care the two men provide him, he maintained the ruse of being a Luftwaffe pilot for well over two weeks.

It wasn't until Wagner told the "pilot" that he was going to telegraph Luftwaffe headquarters the next time he was in town to let them know that their missing man was safe that the American finally told the truth.

His real name was Colonel Robert Castle and he actually was an American aviator assigned to the Office of Strategic Services, the intelligence agency of the United States. He was supervising several other agents in country when he got picked up by the SS as they were making a sweep for men of military age in the town in which he was operating. Given a rifle and loaded on to a train headed to the eastern front, he made his escape and managed to steal a small reconnaissance plane that he planned to fly to liberated France. However, the theft did not go un-noticed and he was shot down by two fighter planes about 20 kilo-meters north of Eschenberg.

Wounded in the fighter attack and subsequent crash, Castle tried to put as much distance between himself and the plane as possible. Heading south with the hope of reaching an extraction in the Tyrol section of Italy, he suc-cumbed to his wounds in the field where Otto found him, and would probably have died if not for the care provided by Wagner and Otto.

Staring out one of the rectory windows toward the mountains, Castle sat on the small living room couch watching the snow fall across the village and fields. His previously infected shoulder wound was finally healing nicely, however his fractured collar bone and ankle were causing him problems. Unable to actually set the bones, Wagner splinted and immobilized both as best he could. And while the bones were mending, they were significantly out of place causing what would be permanent deformity and loss of function.

Hearing the door open, he turned as Wagner and Otto entered the residence.

"Fröhliche Weihnachten, Herr Oberst." Wagner called out upon seeing the Colonel sitting by the window.

"And to you as well Pastor." Castle replied. "I take it that Christmas morning service went well."

"It did indeed. The church was packed and we certainly created a joyful voice in praise of our Lord."

Castle said, "Well that is good to hear. We will certainly need to rely on good institutions like the church to help heal the scars and wounds once this war is over."

"Were you a church going man before the war Colonel?"

He replied, "Not as often as I probably should have been. I was raised a Methodist, and my parents took me to church every Sunday in my youth. But after the First World War, I remained in the Army Air Corps, and it was not as easy… or honestly not as important to go every week. I'm sorry I couldn't attend your service today."

"Well, you could have, but then I think it would have raised some questions from a handful of people in the congregation." Wagner said.

"What seems to be the consensus of your congregation, Pastor? Do they support the war and what Hitler is doing?"

Wagner replied, "There doesn't seem to be so much support anymore. I think most people are still patriotic… If they knew who you were or what I am doing with you here, they would have a problem with it. But I think only a handful still support Hitler or the war. I said prayers for peace and the safe return of loved ones during the service this morning, and I still had a few folks come up after the service and tell me I should have prayed for our victory or for Chancellor Hitler as well. But then you will always find a few zealots in every group."

"So true, Pastor, so true. It's when those few turn into a mob, which then turns into a movement that you wind up where we are today."

Nodding his head, Wagner changed the topic of conversation. "Ja, so… What was Christmas like back in America, Herr Oberst."

"You know, in many ways it was similar to here. People sharing time with family. Going to church, exchanging gifts. It's a time of goodwill."

"In many ways, our cultures are not all that different." Wagner replied.

"America is the great melting pot." Castle said. "We have immigrants from all over the world living in the States. In many communities with a heavy German popu-lation, I would bet you would be hard pressed to find any differences from your customs here. Yet I believe our great strength comes from our diversity melding together for one greater common good."

"That sounds idealistic." Wagner said.

"Oh, don't get me wrong. There are many things wrong with America and our society, but our strengths and ultimately our unity far outweigh our weaknesses and differences."

"It sounds like a place I would like to visit once this war is over."

"When this is all over, I would be honored if you

would be my guest and come for a visit. After all you have done for me... You saved my life."

"Ach, ja. We couldn't very well leave you lying in that ditch where we found you." Wagner replied.

"No, but you could have turned me in." Castle said.

"And you'd have been shot as a spy. That would have been the same as leaving you in the ditch."

Shaking his head, Castle said, "I still can't wrap my head around why you have done all you have for me. How did you trust I wouldn't have tried to kill you? Despite my ruse, you never really believed I was a German officer."

"Two reasons, Herr Oberst." Wagner replied. "The first was that until we both came to terms with who each other was, you were effectively secured to that table in the basement."

Nodding his head in acknowledgement, Castle asked. "And second?"

"I did not need to trust you, Herr Oberst. I trust in the Lord and was doing his work by administering to you. Remember, Jesus said, *Inasmuch as ye have done it unto one of the least of these my brethren, ye have done it unto me.* Matthew, 25: 40."

"I have to remember and try to live by that one a bit more often." Castle replied.

Wagner said, "Ja, so... Otto was able to get some beef, and has been in the kitchen preparing his delicious goulash. Let us see how he is making out and then let's plan for an early Christmas dinner."

Town Square
Eschenberg, Germany
February 25, 1945

Word of the failed German counter-offensive in the Ardennes had reached the town of Eschenberg, and people began to openly talk about losing the war. While still off the beaten path and lacking any strategic significance, the village had yet to see any significant German or Allied troop activity.

Wagner was walking to the market on this warm, bright, late winter day when he saw the troop carrier pull up in front of the market and several regular soldiers along with an SS officer emerge from the truck. Going first to the market, the troops confiscated everything in sight. They then proceeded to the town hall where the officer and two soldiers entered while the rest loaded the truck with what they had just taken from the market.

Emerging from the town hall several minutes later, the soldiers all climbed back in the now fully loaded truck and drove away. Burgermeister Henkle came out of the town hall a few moments later trembling, with the pallor of a death mask. Stumbling to the town square he leaned back against the crossroads monument for support, placing his hands on his knees.

Wagner was one of the first to reach the Burgermeister. Placing his hands on the shoulders of the mayor to help steady him, he got the man to lift his head and make eye contact.

"Erich, what is it?" He asked. "What did they want?"

"They want us… All of us." The mayor replied.

"What do you mean? What did they say?"

By this time, a small crowd of villagers had formed around the mayor and cleric. Looking in at the two men, they kept silent as the mayor spoke.

"The SS officer said that they are going from town to town, confiscating what food and materials are needed for the continued war effort… and recruiting additional troops for the defense of the fatherland."

"What does that mean?" someone from the crowd asked.

"They are giving us till noon on Monday… two days… Pastor, you are to announce this in church tomorrow and I am to spread the news throughout the town. All men between the ages of sixteen and sixty are to report to the town square for immediate service in the defense of the fatherland. This requirement is for all men regardless of current station or prior service."

"What did they mean by that?" someone else from the crowd asked.

Henkle replied, "That means they are taking every-one… all of us. You Pastor, your son, me.." looking across the crowd he pointed to a woman. "Your son and your husband Frau Schwannhauer… Every man between six-teen and sixty."

"What if we do not report?" asked a man who looked every day of sixty years old.

"They have SS troops coming and plan to perform a house to house search. If they find you during the search, you will be considered a traitor to the Fuhrer and will be brought to the town square… where all of the traitors will be immediately executed."

By now, the Burgermeister had overcome his initial shock and was standing erect addressing the questions and concerns that were being voiced by his townspeople, with Wagner standing off to his left side.

"I can barely walk. How am I going to be able to fight?" Asked the same older man.

"The SS officer made it clear there would be no exceptions."

"We are being taken as cannon fodder." Said a man in a butcher's apron stained with blood.

The crowd had grown significantly since the mayor had first come out of the town hall. Word was spreading, throughout the village which was bringing more people out to the square. And as the crowd grew, so did the outcry.

"Where will they take us?" "Will we get training?" "Are they doing this everywhere?" "Why are they singling out, Eschenberg?" "I've already lost my husband, I cannot lose my son."

The Burgermeister raised his arms up and began waving them in an up-and-down motion for the people to settle down.

"People… People… Listen to me. Quiet down, please. Listen to me…" the mayor said with a raised voice. "Right now, I know about as much as you do. I suggest we all meet tomorrow morning after service at the church. Tell your neighbors." Turning to Wagner, Henkle asked, "Is that alright with you Pastor?"

"Of course, Herr Burgermeister. Tomorrow, immediately following service we can have a town meeting. In the meantime, I must return to the church and draft a letter to the Bishop. If they are conscripting me along with the rest of the town, I need to at least let him know."

"Yes, certainly, Pastor." The mayor replied, then turned to address the crowd again. "Ja, so everyone listen…

Wagner was already on the move. His and Otto's ruse was fine for this small town, but he was certain it would not withstand closer scrutiny by the SS, nor could he explain the "Luftwaffe" pilot hiding in his basement. Upon reaching the rectory, he grabbed Otto and they went into the basement to consult with Castle.

After hearing the news, Colonel Castle only paused momentarily before announcing, "So we leave for Italy, tonight."

"Italy? Tonight? Have you lost your mind?" Wagner replied. "We cannot leave for Italy tonight."

"If we wait until tomorrow, I guarantee you, the road will be crowded."

"What do mean?" Wagner asked.

"Look, Pastor. Most people when confronted with a situation like this are afraid to act. They will consider their options, then reconsider them, then think about them some more before making a decision. Then they rarely act on it right away. Most of the town right now is home wringing their hands wondering what to do. They will go to the meeting after church tomorrow, then go home and think about what to do some more. Those that plan to run will do so tomorrow. That is also when that SS officer will set up his roadblocks and patrols. He knows the worry and chaos he created today, but he also knows that since he suggested you announce this in church tomorrow, people will wait until after that to act. We need to move before that."

"But Italy? How do you expect to get there?"

"I have maps. It's only about 200 kilometers. It should take us about a week." Castle replied.

"But its winter, and we will have to cross the Alps, and you can barely walk." Wagner said in exasperation.

"I'm factoring all that in. Besides, I have a plan that should help us with at least the first part of the trip."

"I do not know Colonel." Wagner said shaking his head.

"Pastor, I am eternally grateful for what you have done for me, but you have to understand…I will be leaving tonight. I cannot be found here, and I will not wait until leaving becomes more difficult. If you wish to protect your son and not be forced into combat, I would suggest you come with me. To be honest, we both have a better chance of escape and survival if we go together, so I am not being one hundred percent altruistic when I tell you to come with me. But either way, I leave tonight."

Wagner paused to think about what Castle had just said. The Colonel's logic was sound, and he was experienced in things like this, however, crossing the Alps in winter was not something Wagner felt he could manage. Pacing around the room, he considered his options, and thought about all he had already been through to get to this point. Then he thought about the schematics and the formula for *The Big Light*. If he was forced into the Army, who would protect the plans. And if the SS learned who he was, then it all would definitely fall into Nazi hands, and everything he had done so far to protect them would be for nothing. He had made his brother a promise, and it was imperative he do everything in his power to keep that promise and protect the documents in his care.

Wagner looked over at Otto, who gave a discrete nod, then said, "Ja, so… It will be cold in the mountains. What do we need to pack?"

It was slightly after 3:00 AM when Wagner, Otto and the Colonel left Eschenberg. After convincing Wagner that the need for their safety outweighed the sin, Wagner and Otto broke into the Burgermeister's garage and stole his 1937 Opel Olympia, pushing it through town and down to the church barn where Castle was then able to hot-wire the vehicle and get it started. With the addition of the nearly full thirty-five-liter petrol container also found in the garage, Castle estimated they would have enough fuel to make it well into the Austrian Alps.

Loaded with warm clothing and a supply of food and water, the trio headed south, remaining primarily on dirt roads out of town until they reached Lechbrucker Strasse. Turning right on to Lechbrucker they continued until they reached Bundestrasse 17. Again, turning south, Wagner drove the little coupe through Halblech toward Fussen and the Austrian border.

Although rated at a top speed of sixty miles per hour, the little Opel was pushing its mechanical limits at any speed over forty. When taking on hills, Wager was forced to downshift to maintain any momentum, lending to both he and Castle's apprehension on the vehicle's ability to cross the Alps.

Castle estimated it would take a little over a half hour

to reach Fussen, and then it was less than two miles to the Austrian border and the next test of their escape plan. While Germany annexed Austria with the Anschluss in 1938, there technically was still a border just south of Fussen. If the crossing was guarded, it would be the first test of the trio's cover story. However, as luck would have it, the same units Castle and Wagner were running from in Eschenberg were focused on keeping the Soviets out of eastern Austria, and had moved the bulk of their personnel into Hungary in preparation for the planned counteroffensive at Lake Balaton.

Once across the border, the Opel drove through the quiet town of Weishaus and continued south on roads that basically followed the Lech River valley. Traversing small riverfront towns in the pre-dawn hours, the trio continued to their next hurdle; the mountains outside of Breitenwang.

As Wagner drove the Opel out of the valley, he noticed the vehicle's temperature climbing each time it would ascend a hill. Additionally, as the terrain became steeper and more mountainous, he would be forced to now downshift back into first gear to maintain forward momentum. With the mountains outside of Breitenwang topping out at nearly fifteen-thousand feet, he became more and more certain the car would overheat before making it over the mountain.

Turning to his companions Wagner said, "I think we will need to stop in Breitenwang. The engine temperature keeps climbing despite the cold weather outside."

"The radiator could probably use a topping off." Said Castle. "Let's go into the town and see if we can get some water. If not, there are some lakes and streams nearby that we could probably access."

"We can top off the petrol from the can and maybe eat a little something as well." Wagner said.

Castle said, "Let's see what the town looks like first. We have been lucky so far with avoiding troops. I'd like to keep it that way."

The trio passed the train station and railway yard, entering the slowly awakening town square via Muhler Strasse, and parked the car a few blocks past the square.

Wagner said, "I saw a bakery that looked open a few blocks away. I'll see if I can purchase some fresh rolls and ask if they can give us some water for the car."

"That sounds good. I'm going to look at the map and see if I can find us some other options for crossing these mountains." Castle replied.

"Otto, you stay with the Colonel. I shall return shortly." Wagner said before setting out back toward the town square.

Castle took out the maps and spread them out across the hood of the Opel. He had one map that detailed the highways, streets and railroads, while a second map displayed only the main roads, but indicated terrain features and elevations. Aligning the two maps he traced potential routes and weighed the options.

Twenty minutes later, Wagner returned carrying a bag of fresh rolls and a bucket of water. He said as he opened the door of the Opel and placed the bag on the front seat, "The baker said if we need more water just let him know."

"Were there any problems?" Castle asked.

"Not really. He asked us where we were headed and I

told him our father had passed away in Zwieselstein and we were on our way to officiate at the funeral. Most people do not doubt a man wearing a collar. So, what are our options?" Wagner asked pointing to the maps.

"Well, we can pick up Lechtal Strasse…" Castle said pointing down the road, "out of town and continue to follow the Lech River valley. While we are still going to be headed uphill, the gradient is less steep. However, that will take us miles out of our way to the west, and then we will still have to cross some of those big boys." His head nodded to the south and the mountains clearly visible over the buildings.

Castle continued, "The other problem is that route will take us through a bunch of little towns during the middle of the day. Our chances of running into people other than civilian villagers increases the more towns we encounter."

"What is our other option?" Wagner asked.

"We continue south, into the Alps and over the mountains and see how long our little Opel lasts. Every mile we make in the vehicle saves us an hour of walking."

"Then into the Alps we go." Wagner said enthusiastically. "And I need to add some things to my strategy as well."

"What strategy?" the Colonel asked.

"My prayers." Wagner replied. "I've been praying for forgiveness for us stealing this car. Now I need to pray for deliverance from these mountains too."

Fernpass Strasse
Austrian Alps
February 25, 1945

The Opel's climb over the first peak went off without an issue. Keeping the car primarily in first gear, Wagner coaxed the little four-cylinder engine up the steep inclines and over the mountain. Continuing south on Fernpass Strasse, the trio was able to relax a bit as the road followed a valley south, with only minor changes in elevation. Still, the car could only move at a little over five miles per hour, so the trek into Biberweir took nearly three hours.

Wagner thought it would be prudent to refuel the vehicle, top off the water and have everyone stretch their legs. Castle was inclined to press on, but another quick look at the topographical map showed the route getting significantly steeper after this. After taking care of the vehicle, Wagner, Castle and Otto walked over to the local inn where they ordered lunch. Thinking about the next part of the journey, Castle voiced an opinion of what their next steps should be.

"We have some fairly steep climbs over the next several kilometers." Castle said. And while the car is doing OK now, I would hate to have it die on the top of the mountain with nightfall approaching. This town seems to be fairly secluded and I haven't seen any military presence, so I'm thinking we get a room for the night and depart first thing in the morning."

Wagner said, "Considering we have all been up for more than twenty-four hours, I think that is a splendid idea."

That decision most likely saved the trio's life. As the

three men slept, a late season storm rolled in from the southwest, blanketing the entire area with nearly a foot of fresh powder overnight. Awakening to a snow-covered town, Castle hurriedly made his way downstairs and out to the partially buried car. Opening the hood, he unscrewed the bolts holding he car's battery in place, and disconnected the cables. Closing the hood, he cradled the battery under his arm and limped back inside the inn.

By the time Castle returned to the room, both Wagner and Otto were awake. "Where did you go?" asked Wagner.

"I'm from Colorado, just east of the Rocky Mountains. I've seen these mountain storms before. This is just the prelude. I'll bet we're in for two to three days of this weather, and unless I grabbed the battery out of the car, she would never start after being buried in the cold and snow."

True to his prediction, the snow and wind raged on for two more days, piling up drifts over eight feet in height and effectively imprisoning everyone at the inn. The three men spent the time safely cloistered away, playing cards, eating and drinking beer with the other guests. Sunday morning, Wagner led a prayer service for the inn's guests and employees. Finally, four days after the storm had stopped, the sun and wind melted or moved enough of the snow that they were able to get the doors open and get out of the inn.

With the mountain roads still impassable, the three men dug out their car, and watched as the town began to return to normal. Finally, after nearly a week of waiting, word came that the roads through the mountain passes were clear enough for cars to traverse. The three men began packing their things in preparation for leaving.

Looking uneasy, Wagner approached Castle and said

quietly, "Colonel, I believe we may have a problem. We have been here two weeks, and I had initially expected to only stay the one night. I do not think we have enough money to pay the bill, and if we do, our funds will be totally depleted. If we run into another storm or situation, we will have no money to secure lodging."

"Don't worry about it, Pastor. I'll take care of it." Castle replied.

"Look Colonel, I am still saying penance for stealing the Opel. I cannot condone skipping out on this bill or, doing anything illegal or unethical. I must insist that we stay and work off our debt or something similar if we do not have the funds to pay. I will not go along with…"

Relax, Pastor… I said I got this." Castle said cutting Wagner off. "Hand me my rucksack."

Hefting the backpack off the floor, Otto handed the bag to Castle who pulled a folding knife out of his pocket, then opened the bag. Removing his clothing from the bag, he turned the bag inside out, then slid the blade of the knife along the inner seam at the bottom of the bag. Reaching in, Castle removed two stacks of neatly bound Reichsmarks. "I believe this should be more than enough." He said flipping one of the stacks over to Wagner. "Why don't you go downstairs and settle up with the Innkeeper. Otto and I will get everything loaded in the car."

Twenty minutes later the three men were climbing the first hill out of town in the tiny Opel. While not totally clear, the mountain road was passable, and Wagner took his time steering through switchbacks up and down through the mountain passes. With Castle navigating, the three men descended the mountain into the town of Weisland, and then continued through the valley, entering the town of Osterstein just as the sun had dipped below the mountains.

Getting a room at the local inn, the trio ate dinner then retired to their room. With Wagner and Otto huddled around the maps spread out on the bed, Castle laid out his plan for the balance of the trip.

Pointing to the map and tracing out the route with his finger, Castle said, "Tomorrow morning we can follow this valley road south toward Zwieselstein. Most of the trip should be relatively easy, however the final third of the trip looks to be mostly up hill. After our first night's problems, we pretty much learned how to keep from overheating, but this next run will be one of the toughest for that little car, so we have to be sure to top off the radiator and not push it too hard.

We will stay overnight in Zwieselstein, and the next day we will prepare for the most dangerous part of our trip. We will need to get some supplies… Warm clothing, socks, gloves, face coverings. We should plan on bringing food and water, and we should make every attempt to purchase snowshoes for each of us."

Looking up at Wagner and Otto, Castle paused to get confirmation that they understood his plans to this point. He continued, "We will load the car, and then spend one more night in Zwieselstein. We will need to be on the road by five AM because we will need every minute of daylight to complete this next leg of the trip."

Pointing back to the map, he said, "Pastor, you will drive the car to a spot somewhere in this area, and we will keep our eyes open for a place to hide the vehicle before we are able to be seen by any guards at the border. Then, leaving the car off the road, we will don our snowshoes and packs and begin what looks like a three to four-mile hike across these mountains. Now, normally, a person can hike three miles in mountainous terrain in about three hours. However, we are walking in deep snow, and I am not in the best condition to make this trek. So, I estimate that it will take us double that time, but I believe we should be able to make this shelter, Timmelsalm before nightfall.

Then after a night's rest, we head out the next morning for our next destination, Rifugio Montanese. The next leg has us going about four miles to Moarerberg Alm. Finally, the last two sections will be tough as we go over two mountains, the first into Staudenbergalm, then two more mountains and three more miles to Malga Joggele Alm. Then it looks to be about five miles down through some pastures in to Ridanna. I am hoping to be in the mountains no more than five days, but with weather and terrain that I can't really see on the map, it could take longer."

The three men looked up from the map and Wagner began nodding his head. "That sounds like a solid plan." He said. "But I do have to admit that I am worried about hiking over those mountains... Not so much for myself and Otto, but for you. You still have difficulties walking up and down stairs."

"Pastor, you worry about yourself and Otto. I will rely on my training and I promise you, I will make it no matter what... Even if I have to drag myself to Ridanna." Castle replied.

The first part of the plan went off without a hitch. They arrived in Zwieselstein and checked in to the local inn. The next day was spent with Castle and Wagner visiting the local merchants and stocking up on their required supplies. Castle and Wagner were a bit nervous because for the first time in over two week they were seeing troops at various locations throughout the town. However, Castle said that this level of troop activity was not unexpected since they were so close to the border. This troop presence also gave credence to their need to cross the mountains and border on foot, rather than with the car.

Departing Zwieselstein before dawn, the three men abandoned the Opel off the road behind some snow drifts about a half mile from the border. With snowshoes on their feet, and oversized rucksacks on their backs, they set out on foot into the Alps on the three-mile first leg of their hike. Despite his injuries, Castle did fairly well keeping up with Wagner and Otto. True to his initial estimate, the trio crested a hill and saw Timmelsalm, their next shelter six hours into their hike.

The next day, despite his pain and stiffness, Castle plotted the course across the next set of mountains. However, by mid-day, Wagner could see that Castle was clearly in pain and having trouble walking. Refusing help, Castle pushed on markedly struggling with every step for the last mile. Castle's condition, along with a more challenging terrain caused the team to take a little more than eight hours to hike the same distance they covered the prior day in six.

The following morning, Castle's pain barely allowed him to stand. In defiance of the pain, Castle donned the snowshoes and his rucksack and headed out of the shelter. Wagner tried to persuade Castle to take one day to rest, but he insisted on pushing forward. Two hours into the hike,

Castle stumbled and collapsed. Wagner and Otto were by his side immediately. Stating he heard something "pop" in his injured leg, Castle said he found it next to impossible to put any weight on that leg.

Wagner consulted with Otto outside of Castle's earshot and came up with a plan. Putting Otto's pack on his chest, Wagner allowed Otto to pick Castle up and sling him across his back. Now with the two men carrying significant weight, and following Castle's wayfinding, the three men set back out for their third shelter.

Arriving as he sun was setting, all three men collapsed on the floor of the shelter. After laying on the floor for a while, recovering from the day's labors, Wagner had Otto fetch some wood from outside to light a fire in the shelter's over-sized fireplace. Once the fire was going, and a pot with water was boiling over it, Wagner sat down opposite Castle to discuss their options.

"I think we should rest for at least a day and see if your leg gets any better." He said to Castle.

"I would agree with you if I thought it would get better by resting." Castle replied. "I don't know if the bone was properly healed and all of the strain may have caused it to fracture again. Resting won't help, and I'm afraid if weather rolls in, we could be stuck up here. We really don't have the supplies to last getting snowed in."

Wagner said, "Otto and I can take turns carrying you, but it will significantly slow us down. You said the other day that these next two legs of the hike are the most challenging. I am afraid we will become stranded in the mountains in the dark. So, what do we do?" Wagner asked.

"We build a travois." Castle replied.

"A what?"

Castle answered, "A travois. Or more accurately, a travois with skis."

Wagner and Otto looked puzzled as Castle explained. "It is a type of sled developed by the Indians of the American Great Plains. We find two long poles, lash some cross beam supports to them and cover it with one of those blankets over there. Actually, I would bet there are some boards laying around in the barn back behind the shelter that can be attached to the bottom of the sled for it to kinda glide across the snow. Tomorrow, you fetch me those things and I can build one that will make hauling my butt around significantly easier."

"I think between that and some heavy-duty prayers, we may just make it." Wagner said.

Two days later, Wagner and Otto hiked off of the mountain on to the open pasture just outside Ridanna, dragging Colonel Castle behind them. As luck would have it, members of the Italian Resistance movement found them almost immediately and after exchanging code words, the three men were taken to a safe house where Wagner and Otto were able to get a hot meal, and Castle received some much-needed medical attention. After resting three days, they were informed they would be transported to where troops from the American 10th Mountain Division were stationed, and from there to the coast and a boat to America.

Believing their rescue meant they were safe, the men breathed a collective sigh of relief. Had they known what was yet to come, they would have collectively held their breath instead.

Apennine Mountains
West Coast of Italy
March 26, 1945

The journey from Ridanna south was as dangerous and difficult as any part of the odyssey Wagner had lived for the past six months. While Allied and Soviet troops secured almost daily victories in their march to Berlin, the Italian peninsula was still strongly under Nazi and Italian fascist control. When Castle was originally briefed in the spring of the prior year, it was anticipated that by no later than August, the German Tenth Army would have been surrounded and have possibly even surrendered, allowing Allied forces to move north through Italy and into Austria. The plan, as originally laid out for the Anzio landing, was for the U.S. Fifth Army and the British Eighth Army to trap the Germans in a pincer maneuver. However, U.S. General Mark W. Clark, concerned that the British would get to Rome before his troops, diverted some of his units toward Rome, thus allowing the Germans to withdraw to defensive positions in the north.

Named the Gothic Line, the Germans built a ten-mile wide belt of fortifications stretching from just north of Pisa on the west coast, to Rimini on the Adriatic Sea and through the Apennine Mountains. This German defensive line consisted of over twenty-three hundred machine gun nests with interlocking fire, nearly five hundred anti-tank positions, one hundred and twenty thousand meters of barbed wire and miles of anti-tank ditches. It would take the Allies till the middle of April before they would be able to break through these German defenses and move into northern Italy.

If not for the prevalence of Italian Partisans in the northern part of the country, the three men would have been safer remaining in Germany. The Partisans had an effective network of operatives who would fight the Nazis and fascists as well as hide escaping Allied POWs. A form of underground railroad was established to move people from occupied territories across enemy lines or to liberated France. Castle, Wagner and Otto were ferried through this network from one small town shop sub-basement to another, or from one barn hayloft to a wooded mountain encampment.

Over the course of the next several weeks, the trio moved in a mostly southerly direction, avoiding German strongholds and patrols. They slept primarily by day because most of the transportation was done at night. They were given food and water, and Castle's leg was well cared for, and by the third week, he was able to once again walk, although still with a pronounced limp.

After nearly four weeks of careful movements, the trio was finally able to link up with elements of the Tenth Mountain Division just outside of Ravenna. Castle was immediately taken to the unit's commanding officer, and Wagner and Otto were housed under the watchful eye of two privates. Castle had been presumed dead, so telegrams needed to be sent to the States immediately letting his family know he was still alive, and he needed to be debriefed. Otto and Wagner didn't see much of Colonel Castle for most of the next week. While they were not officially prisoners, both were restricted to the building they were housed in, and the restaurant turned mess hall across the street. All movements, including those to the bathroom were under the watchful eyes of at least one of the four GIs "escorting" them. Finally,

Castle came to see them and announced they were all headed to Marseille, where they would board a ship to America.

The trip to Marseille was easy compared to their previous trek. Loaded on to a troop transport and attached to a convoy headed west, the trucks took major roads and highways. Stopping to disburse or pick up supplies or wounded, the convoy made the trip in two days. As they got closer to their destination, Wagner began to think more and more about what might have happened to both his brother and his old friend Hasselmeyer. He wondered if both were still alive, and how he would even find out. He knew Otto was safe with him, and once they were in America, he could stop the silly ruse of being disabled, and become a fully functioning young man again.

He wondered what he would do in America. He was a Roman Catholic priest who abandoned his flock and his calling for what he still considered an even greater calling. Having served the Church long enough, he knew there would be punishment or sanctions when he let them know he was still alive and where he was. With the chaos of the war and his disappearance, he was sure he was presumed dead, just like Castle was. Knowing in his heart that he needed to still serve God, Wagner was concerned that the Catholic Church might defrock him or give him some missionary or other work as punishment. Ministering to a congregation was what he was good at, and what he wanted to do. He felt that despite this little detour in his life he still needed to fulfill this calling and serve in a church, just like he had in Stuttgart and Eschenberg… Eschenberg?… but there he impersonated a Lutheran pastor. The question he needed to ask himself was, did he still serve God, and despite the subterfuge, was he still true to Jesus Christ and his teachings? This would be something he would give greater thought to before making any decisions. There would still be time for greater soul searching, and planning next steps.

Arriving in Marseille, Wagner and Otto were once again transferred to some temporary housing. Given each a cot in one bedroom, the pair were informed that Colonel Castle was advocating on their behalf to get them passage to America, and they were to "sit tight".

The port city was busier and noisier than they had gotten used to. Ship horns could be heard throughout the day and night, and the noise from the constant truck traffic made it difficult for Wagner to sleep. With more time to think, Wagner contemplated his future. The more he thought about it, the more he was certain the Bishop would call him back to Germany to face punishment for leaving his church. And even with the end of the war in sight, there would still be plenty of people who knew he was protecting his brother's secret. He could not return to Germany, and he could not serve as a priest in America. He wondered if Bishop Meiser were still alive, and if he were, would he even consider the crazy idea he was formulating in his head. The only way to know, was to ask.

After a little more than a week, Colonel Castle returned to Wagner and Otto. Escorting them over to another building he said, "I apologize for everything taking so long." Pulling papers out of the inside pocket of his jacket, Castle continued, "I have your approval letters here. All you need to do is take these over to those two clerks who will process your Red Cross passports. The letters and paperwork just need to have your names printed on them and then attached to the passports.

There was a bit of difficulty initially since you have no forms of identification, but that was all fixed after I spoke to General Donovan and vouched for you. I told him I lived with you for several months after you saved my life… Twice actually. Once the Major General of the OSS gave his blessing, everything was fine. I also secured your passage to America. After everything you have done for me, there is no way I am leaving you here with the chaos that is coming."

"Danke Herr Oberst." Wagner replied.

"Once we get to America, I will help get you on your feet. It won't be easy for you, but it will be better than remaining here." Walking Wagner and Otto over toward the Red Cross table, Castle instructed Wagner. "Now these two gentlemen will get your paperwork processed, and then you can head on back to your cots. I need to check on a few things, but I will see you at dinner."

"Thank you Herr Oberst. Yes, dinner would be wonderful. I do have one other favor to ask." Wagner said a bit sheepishly. "Would it be possible for you to ascertain if Bishop Meiser from Munich is still alive. I need to get a message to him."

"Of course. I'll see what I can find out."

Shaking the colonel's hand, Wagner and Otto headed over to the two clerks at the desk.

"What are your names?" the first clerk asked.

"Was sind your namen?" the second clerk poorly translated to poorly pronounced German.

Pointing to the boy, then himself, Wagner said, "Otto und Georg…"

"What the fuck kinda name is that?" the first clerk asked in a thick southern drawl. "Gay – Oick?"

"Georg" Wagner corrected.

"Gay – Oick?…" the first clerk said again.

"It's Kraut for George, you stooge." The second clerk said chuckling and shaking his head.

Recording the names, first in his manifest, then on the passport papers, the first clerk asked, "OK Georgie… and the last name?"

"Dein ander name." the second clerk mis pronounced.

Wagner paused. He had just realized he had given his real first name rather than his alias. Currently exhausted, he had endured so much in the past 10 months and the stresses had definitely caught up to him. And while he now felt the safest he had since leaving Stuttgart, he was still concerned about covering his tracks. Leaving a paper trail may lead to someone tracking him down. He had promised his brother he would keep the documents safe, and so far, he had been able to do that. He was not about to slip up now. He still needed to protect the "Big Light."

"What was that? What did you say?" the first clerk asked.

Wagner hadn't realized that in his exhaustion, he was thinking out loud. In a daze, and focused on keeping his identity secret, Wagner said it again without thinking. "Grosse Licht."

"Grass lickt?" the first clerk asked.

Snapping back to the present, Wagner looked down at the two clerks with a confused look on his face. Based on what the clerk just said Wagner wondered to himself, "*What does he think is ghastly…?*"

"G-r-a-s-s-s L-i-c-k-e-d?" the clerk said again, this time very slowly in his southern drawl.

Assuming a mispronunciation, Wagner corrected what

he thought was the clerk's bad German. "Grasslich? Ja was ist grasslich?" He said still wondering what the clerk thought was so horrible. *Could he be referring to me?... to the way I look?...It has been several days since we have been able to bathe... Does this man think that I am ghastly?*

"Ich bin grasslich?" Wagner asked

The two men stared at each other in silence for a moment. The clerk was looking confused while Wagner was shrugging his shoulders and nodding his head.

Finally, the clerk broke the silence. "Well OK then..." he said, writing first in the manifest, then on the passport paperwork. "George and Otto Grasslicked it is. Here are your documents"

Wagner took the papers and stood there looking totally confused. *What just happened?* He thought.

"Ok, you can go. There are others waiting...Go on... Go away... Gehest vek." The second clerk said incorrectly in German. As Wagner and Otto headed back to their sleeping quarters wondering what just happened, the second clerk said to no one in particular, "Wow! I feel bad for those guys. Those names are ghastly."

The news spread quickly during dinner. Adolph Hitler was dead. He and a number of other high-ranking Nazi officials committed suicide at the Fuhrerbunker. While Germany had still not surrendered, the general consensus was that it would not be long now. Castle joined Wagner and Otto for dinner that evening.

"I have great news." Castle said grinning from ear to ear. "We are set to leave tomorrow on the transport ship bound for Brooklyn, New York. In two weeks, we will be on American soil. I understand there is a fairly large German immigrant population in Brooklyn, so you should be able to acclimate fairly quickly. And I promise, I will be available to help."

Pausing to reach into his pocket, he withdrew a sheet of paper. "I also made some inquiries about your Bishop. It seems not only is he still alive, he was instrumental in getting many of the cities defenders to lay down their arms."

Removing a letter of his own, Wagner handed Castle an envelope addressed to Bishop Meiser. "Is there any way you can see he gets this."

Taking the envelope, Castle replied, "It shouldn't be a problem. I understand he is working with our people in preparation for a smooth transition at the end of this war."

The next morning the three men boarded the transport ship and departed for the U.S. The fifteen-day journey was uneventful, and it gave Wagner time to craft a letter to *his* Bishop and sever the final ties to his old life.

Upon arriving in New York and clearing customs, Wagner and Otto were being escorted to the street by Colonel Castle when a man in a clerical collar approached the three men.

"Good day gentlemen." He said in German. My name is Hans Pritzki. I am the Pastor of St. Paul's Lutheran Church. Would you happen be Pastor Schmidt?

Surprised by the greeting, Wagner hesitated, but slowly nodded his head.

"Bishop Meiser telegraphed my Bishop and asked if we could assist you and help get you settled. He said you were a great asset to the Church, and since you needed to escape the

Nazi's because of the assistance you have given the Colonel, we should embrace you into the family that is the Lutheran Church here in America."

"He said all that in a telegram?" Castle asked. "That must have cost a fortune."

"No, actually he sent the telegram first, then he sent the rest of the message in a letter via air-mail. That arrived yesterday before your ship docked."

Laughing out loud, Castle turned to Wagner and said, "Well Pastor, it looks like you have already gotten off to a rocky start as a man of the cloth here in America."

Puzzled, Wagner asked, "What do you mean, Herr Oberst?"

"The first thing you did when you arrived was lie to this man."

"What do you mean?" Wagner asked, as both he and Pritzki had confused looks on their face.

"You said your name is Schmidt, didn't you Pastor Grasslicked?"

Holding his face in one hand in mock disbelief, Wagner replied, "Ach ja. Pastor Pritzki, we will have much to discuss."

Rather than go through the bother of getting his name changed, Wagner, assumed one alias was as good as the next and he kept the name Grasslicked. He and Otto settled in Bushwick Brooklyn and assisted Pastor Pritzki until 1955, when he accepted a calling to St. John's church in Perth Amboy, NJ. St. John's also served a predominantly German immigrant population, but Wagner's assignment was an interim assignment since the land was to be sold to developers and the synod had already planned to build a new church in the neighboring town of Sayreville.

Otto, who also retained the last name of his immigration papers, followed his passion for woodworking and went on to become an accomplished carpenter. He followed Wagner to New Jersey and eventually married and had a son of his own. Not long after arriving in Brooklyn, Bishop Meiser got word to Otto that his father had unfortunately died in a bombing raid.

Wagner retired upon the completion of the new church, and insisted that the original communion cup and paten, as well as the beautiful hand carved wooden cross that hung above the altar in the old church be saved and used in the new building. Made by Otto and originally presented to the church on the installation of his adoptive father as Pastor, the two-tone wooden cross while somewhat modern in appearance, served as a reminder of the German immigrant heritage in the area.

Pastor George Grasslicked lived and served the Lord until he was one hundred and one years old. While he wore the collar of a Lutheran minister, he remained true to his Catholic beliefs, never marrying and regularly confessing his sins to a priest in a Roman Catholic church in a neighboring town. Despite all the years of his life, the lives he saved, and the people he ministered to, Georg Wagner and his family's true mark on history had yet to be written.

PART 2

CHAPTER 1

**Headquarters, Gendarmerie Corps
of Vatican City State
Vatican City, Rome
Present Day**

THE HUMIDITY USUALLY seen during winters in Rome never seemed to leave this particular year, and the summer heat had come much earlier. Having just returned to the locker room of the Gendarmerie headquarters from his morning run, Director General John Nowalski sat on a bench opposite his locker dripping sweat. Trim and fit, Nowalski had yet to develop the paunch of many men his age, and his close-cropped salt and pepper hair did little to betray his age. Years in the field also did little to add to the few wrinkles around eyes that still revealed a wit not yet tempered by the years. Despite appearing much younger, at that moment however, Nowalski was feeling every minute of his 56 years on this earth.

"You don't look good boss." Stated Nowalski's second

in command, Vice Ispettore Antonio Febbaccio in heavily accented English.

"These runs seem to be getting harder and harder every day." Responded Nowalski.

"Well you need to get yourself cleaned up. You have a meeting with Cardinal Sentille in twenty minutes." Febbaccio said.

"When did that get added to my calendar?" Nowalski asked. "It wasn't there at Eight AM this morning."

"It must have been added right after you started your run, boss."

"That's the problem with working with all of these geriatrics." Nowalski quipped. "They wake up at four AM and think the rest of the world only needs three hours of sleep as well." It's all well and good if you can nap in the middle of the day the way most people in this country do, but poor working stiffs like me can't put in fourteen-hour days with a two-hour break in the middle of the afternoon. Not unless we want to work till midnight."

"You are just the hardest working man in law enforcement." Febbaccio sarcastically said in his heavily accented English.

"Will Pinocchio be there too?" Nowalski said, ignoring his colleagues remark.

"I hates when you call him that." Febbaccio said. "Some of these days I'm going to slip and either call him that to his face or say it in front of someone who really does not like me. Then they will go running to Pinnocci… Inspector General Pinochinio to tell him what I said."

"Don't sweat it Tony." Nowalski chuckled. "You are too smart and careful to slip, and anyway, I got your back."

"Lotta good that will do me. You might have my back, but who has yours?

"Yeah, I know what you mean." Replied Nowalski. "That list seems to be growing shorter every day."

Appointed to his current position by the former Pontiff, John Nowalski had an interesting career. Nowalski began his law enforcement career on a mid-sized police force in the U.S in his home state of New Jersey, but left to enter a monastery after the murder of his wife and son by Columbian drug dealers. When he was tapped to assist the Vatican investigate a series of church related murders, he was central to solving the case and preventing the Church from having to deal with some potentially embarrassing press. It was at the conclusion of that case that the late Pope Gregory XVII, the former Archbishop of New York, created the position of Director General for Investigations, Intelligence and Special Projects of the Gendarmerie, the police force of the Vatican.

In charge of a small, but well trained and loyal cadre of officers, Nowalski had proven his worth to the Vatican a number of times over the course of his twenty-one-year career, thwarting multiple attacks against the Church or its leaders. Despite not making the news, threats against the Church were very real and ever present. As an institution that dated back millennia, the Roman Catholic Church had created numerous enemies throughout its history, many of whom had an institutional memory as strong as that of the Church they hated. Some of these enemies actually acted on that hatred in attempts to extract their revenge.

In addition to protecting the Vatican, during John's tenure he had also finally been able to complete his college degree. He went on to earn a Master's in Criminal Justice with additional post-graduate work in anti-terrorism strategy and tactics. Considered an expert worldwide, Nowalski specialized in tracking down terrorist leaders who had gone into hiding. His men all said he had a sixth sense when it came to finding the tiny clues that led to solving difficult cases. In addition to serving the Vatican City State, Nowalski often consulted with Interpol and various other police agencies across both Europe and the U.S.

Despite John's track record of accomplishments, with the passing of Pope Gregory, it soon became evident that many in both the Gendarmerie Corp and the Holy See either disliked or resented John or the position he held. Where in the past he regularly updated members of the legislative body, the Pontifical Commission for Vatican City State, and enjoyed access to Cardinal Connavo, the former President of the Governorate, now Nowalski could rarely gain an audience with any of the seven members of the Commission. Any intelligence or updates on his division's cases were now sent only to his superior, Inspector General Pinochinio who disseminated the information as he saw fit. Likewise, requests for resources were now only funneled through the Inspector General's office, where those requests often died unanswered. And while Pinochinio had standing weekly meetings with the three other division heads, and permitted each of them unfettered access on an as needed basis, John was required to schedule time with his boss via the Inspector General's secretary. It was painfully obvious that the once golden boy of the Gendarmerie had fallen out of favor.

John showered quickly and donned his uniform. He considered running to his office and changing into either the civilian business suit he kept there for emergencies or his dress blue uniform, but opted instead to remain in the standard issue navy slacks and white shirt he wore to the department most days. Wearing either one of his other choices would be viewed as sending a message he was currently not willing to send.

John arrived at the prelate's office one minute early so that the announcement of his presence by the cardinal's secretary would be made exactly at nine. Taking a seat in the office anteroom he was advised by the young priest who served as the personal assistant to Cardinal Sentille that the Cardinal was tied up and it would be just a few minutes. The few minutes turned into sixteen which was pushing the obnoxious side of the requisite power statement that the Cardinals time was more important than Nowalski's and John should be at Sentille's beck and call. When finally escorted into the office of the President of the Governorate John saw that Pinochinio was already seated in the center of the couch to the left of the large oak desk.

A small cocktail table sat between the two couches that flanked the Cardinals desk and the leather wing-backed chair completed the rectangular configuration of the office furniture. The room was adorned with various ecclesiastical paintings and artifacts, some looking like they dated back hundreds of years or more. A fully stocked bookshelf occupied the wall adjacent to the office door while three large modern floor to ceiling windows filled a large section of the opposite wall. A large crucifix hung over a credenza behind the oak desk with the agony filled face of Christ on the cross putting the finishing touch on the overall atmosphere of the room.

Sentille sat in the large leather swivel chair behind the immaculately empty desk. The balance of the office was as impeccably neat as the desk, save for the couch opposite Pinochinio which held books and papers strewn across the seating area. John noted the juxtaposition of his couch with the rest of the room and the seating positions of the other two occupants. This configuration forced John to sit in the wing-backed leather chair that faced the desk and was furthest removed from Sentille's seat of power. John was forced to sit in the hot seat as it were.

Standing behind the chair John came to attention and saluted the two seated individuals. "Director General Nowalski reporting as ordered."

Without saying a word, the Cardinal rose out of his swivel chair moving to his right and extending his hand. John moved from behind the chair and table and approached the Prelate and his outstretched hand, taking the Cardinals hand, John genuflected and kissed his ring.

"Your Eminence."

"Have a seat my son." The Cardinal replied as he returned to his desk.

Half tempted to squeeze in next to Pinochinio, John smiled to himself as he returned to the wing-back and asked, "What can I do for your gentlemen?'

"To begin Director General, we were a bit taken aback when we reached out to your office this morning and learned you were not there." Pinochinio said.

John said, "Inspector General, I live a fairly monastic lifestyle, and my days are usually very similar. I awaken at five, eat a muffin with some coffee and am in the Oratory of San Pellegrino by six for my morning devotions. I arrive at the office around seven AM and review the overnight reports from both my division and the Corps as a whole. Usually around eight, I will either go for my morning run, perform a workout in the gym, or do both. I am back at my desk by nine, and unless I have a scheduled lunch meeting, have lunch around noon. I finish my day somewhere between seven and eight PM. After a light dinner, I will answer any late emails, catch up on any trade articles and be in bed by ten. I generally keep this schedule Monday through Friday. On Saturdays, I arrive by eight, skip the workout and work until around two, usually forgoing lunch as well. Sundays I attend Mass in the morning, and then spend the balance of the day taking care of any personal business, shop for food, and possibly visit with friends or colleagues. This of course is my normal routine when I am not in the field. When I am on an investigation or in the field I will often be required to work evening hours. In those cases, I will sometimes work forty-eight hours without a break if required.

Sir, I was on my morning run when you reached out to my office. I apologize to the Inspector General if he feels this schedule that I just outlined is insufficient for me to accomplish my required duties. However, I was unaware that at my rank and pay level, I was required to punch in and out on a time clock.

Glaring at his commanding officer John ground his teeth as he struggled to keep his face passive and maintain his composure and overall outward appearance professional.

"Director General," the Cardinal began, breaking the

uneasy silence. "Based on that narrative, it would appear you live a fairly monastic life which should allow you to be able to satisfactorily perform all your required duties in a timely manner."

"Excellency, that sounds like an accusation that my assigned duties are not being satisfactorily completed." John said. "Had I known this meeting was intended to be a performance review, I would have brought supporting statistics and detailed documentation to show that both myself and my division have been performing well beyond expectations.

"Dirignete General Nowalski," Pinochinio began. "This is in no way a review of your performance. I am sure there are some in the Holy See who would commend you on your service over the years to our beloved Church. That being said, we did summon you here today to discuss the future of your division with you."

"I see. And what would that future be, sir?" John asked.

Leaning backward in his chair, the Cardinal clasped his hands together with his index fingers coming to a point and brought his hands up to his lips before speaking. "We have been in consultation with His Holiness, and it is our consensus that your division be disbanded. Your men will be reassigned to other divisions as needed by the Corps, and while they will retain their rank, their duties will differ greatly from that of their current positions."

John glanced over at Pinochinio and saw what could only be described as an evil grin beginning to form on his face. John asked, "When will this plan become effective?"

"We are hoping immediately." Pinochinio replied. "However, because of paperwork and scheduling issues it may take four to six weeks before everyone is reassigned."

Nodding his head, John said. "I see. May I ask what precipitated this decision?"

The Cardinal replied. "It was not one specific event that brought about this need for a change. His Holiness does not feel that there is that much of a need for what you do any more. He believes that through dialogue and Christian outreach, the Church would be better able to mitigate future threats, and right any wrongs of the past. By doing this, certain groups that may harbor feelings of ill will for the Church will be less inclined to act on old feelings of animosity. Additionally, as we look at the budget, it makes good fiscal sense to manage our expenses judiciously. Worldwide church revenue has been in decline for the last several years as you know, and cost cutting is just good stewardship."

John sat in stunned disbelief. He knew that politically, he had fallen from favor, but he had not recognized the depths to which he had fallen. While he always had assumed that the new powers at the Vatican would do something to marginalize his position and relevance in the Corps, he never expected the Holy See would jeopardize overall security of the Church just to get to him. "You are making a big mistake." John finally managed. "The threats you are looking to mitigate through dialogue don't want to talk. Some of those groups have had centuries to stew and bring their hatred of our Church to a boil. And the best way to protect both this institution and the lives of the people in it is to be proactive. Learn their plans, and take steps to shut them down before they act. What you are proposing will get people killed."

His Holiness the Pope does not see it that way, and

neither do we." Sentille replied. "Disbanding your unit will be viewed as a sign of peace. As a sign that the Church would rather talk than put more people out there with guns and badges who believe they can do whatever they want. The "Defund" movement is gaining traction around the globe. We should be on that forefront. Fighting and killing is what we did in the Dark Ages. We do not do that any longer."

Pinochinio added, "And besides, this institution survived very well for the thousands of years before the well-intentioned but misguided creation of your division. It will continue on for thousands more without you."

Shaking his head in silence, John processed everything he had just heard. Finally, he asked, "And what do you see as my role after this reorganization?"

Pinochinio replied with a grin, "Again, there are processes and procedures that address situations such as this. Therefore, unless you are found derelict in your duties, you will not suffer a reduction in rank nor pay. However, since we no longer see the need for your particular skill set, and someone at your level does not neatly fit into the current organizational structure, I see your function being primarily administrative. I can imagine your reporting to and assisting one of the existing Dirignete, primarily as I said, in an administrative capacity.

"So effectively I would be working as a secretary to some other director. It would seem like I am receiving a three-level demotion in rank."

"Or you could retire." The Cardinal replied. "You have served the Church well for more than twenty years Director. You are still a relatively young man. Perhaps there are other avenues available to you that would be a better match for your specific set of skills."

"Is this your way of asking for my resignation, Excellency?"

"Not at all. I was simply pointing out some of your options should you decide that your new role does not fit with your… well, your self-image." The Cardinal replied.

"I see." John said, nodding his head. With dozens of thoughts swirling in his head, John just sat in the wing-backed chair trying to decide his next course of action.

Standing to signify the end of the meeting, Pinochinio spoke before John would have a chance to continue the conversation. "Well Director General, we will be getting the paperwork started this morning so we can make this all happen as quickly as possible. I would assume you have some serious thinking to do, and you will need to inform your men. In the interim, until the reorganization is complete, I would expect your division to maintain its current level of effectiveness and for you and your team to remain focused and professional. You can liaise with the other division heads to develop a comprehensive plan to wind down your operations. They will be expecting your call. I would hope that I would be able to see a draft of that plan before the end of the week so that I can provide my input. Thank you for coming in."

Seeing that all avenues for discussion were closed, without saying another word, John stood, came to attention and saluted Pinochinio and the Cardinal. He turned to leave and had taken a few steps toward the door when Pinochinio called out to him. "Director General Nowalski…"

"Sir?" John said turning back toward the two men.

"I am curious about your Saturdays."

"Sir?" John repeated in confusion.

"Well, you gave a detailed accounting of your life from morning till night earlier. You fully outlined every day except Saturday. You failed to inform us what you did with the rest of your day. You said you are in work by eight, but you leave at two, and did not provide us with any other details. I just wonder what is so important that you leave work by two, and what you do with the rest of your day?"

Eyes growing wide in disbelief at what he just heard, John blurted, "You gotta be fu…" Before catching himself. Taking a deep breath to calm down, John stood motionless glaring with distain at his boss. The two men stared at each other silently before John came to attention and rendering another crisp salute, never breaking eye contact. After several moments Pinochinio finally returned the salute and broke eye contact. Spinning on his heels, John once again headed for the door, wishing he could actually say out loud what he was mumbling under his breath. "What do I do with the rest of my day? What the fuck do you think I do, you sanctimonious prick… snort coke and whack off to Pornhub, like you?"

Aryphon Corporate Headquarters
Montevideo, Uruguay
Present Day

The mahogany conference table was so highly polished that it seemed to reflect the early morning light streaming in from the windows overlooking the Rio de Plata. Located on the 11th floor of the corporate headquarters of Aryphon Industries, SA, the seven men and four women seated around the table this morning made up the company's Board of Directors and represented a cross section of the executive leadership of a myriad of multi-national corporations.

Seated at the head of the table, Aryphon Chairman and CEO Hermann Alvarez was eager to get this meeting started. Though privately held, Alvarez owned more than 75% of the Aryphon stock and the Alvarez family was in its second generation of company leadership. With the recent appointments of his daughter Emma and her younger brother William to the Board, Alvarez was proud that the family legacy would continue into the next generation.

"I would like this meeting to come to order." Alvarez said after clearing his throat loudly to silence the side conversations.

"We have a number of items on this morning's agenda, and several of them will need exploration in greater detail. Miss Kim, the lights if you would please."

Entering some commands on the keyboard at the podium at the front of the room, Joon Min Kim, Alvarez's Executive Assistant prompted the computer to dim the room lights, darken the windows and illuminate the projector that would display the PowerPoint presentations. Bowing her head, she said, "If that will be all sir?" and began backing toward the door even before receiving Alvarez's nod of acknowledgement. With Kim gone, Alvarez began the meeting in earnest.

"We have had a few recent setbacks and I would like to review the causality as well as actions we have taken to rectify the situation." Alvarez started. "Mr. Lopez, if you would?"

In addition to serving on the Aryphon board, Edwin Lopez was the Executive Vice President of Timbore Mining, a wholly owned subsidiary of Aryphon. Stepping up to the podium Lopez began. "Our overall lithium production is up 35% year over year, and despite the setback we experienced in Afghanistan, we are still on target to meet our goals for this year." Lopez said proudly, pointing to the graphs displayed on the screen.

Alvarez interrupted, "I am not concerned about this year's production Edwin. We invested great sums of money to quietly acquire controlling interests in Albermarle, the leading producer of lithium in the world. Our expectation was that once we did that, Albermarle would be able to secure the exclusive rights to mine lithium in Afghanistan. The U.S. president pulls out just as he was instructed, and our man in country winds up getting killed? I find this failure nearly inexcusable."

"Sir, our liaison had met with the Taliban leadership and had negotiated a deal even prior to the American's departure. We believed everything was in place. There was no way to know some blood thirsty regional warlord would kidnap him and behead him as a show of authority."

"The fact our man was not properly protected, and then the Chinese were permitted to swoop in before we could get another representative there with the proper protection speaks to your lack of proper planning and foresight. Edwin, you know what those people are like in that part of the world. You should have taken extra precautions up front." Alvarez said.

"I thought we wanted to keep a low profile and security teams would…" Lopez began.

"You obviously thought wrong, Edwin." Alvarez said cutting off the younger man. Shaking his head while letting out a sigh, Alvarez continued, "Alright. Well. We cannot change the past. All we can do is learn from it. Hopefully you have done that Edwin. So, continue with your presentation. Please tell me you have a plan in place to recoup the lost production we were expecting from Afghanistan."

Lopez continued, "We are realigning the management of Albemarle which will allow us to modify the company's operations. The new people we have already put in place have negotiated additional mining rights in Chile and have contracted with Timbore to begin pulling deposits from the new claims. As this next slide will show, this will unfortunately set our plans back by two to three years. We are looking at other potential resource streams, but I did not want to share those with this body until my teams have had a chance to better assess their viability."

Still shaking his head, Alvarez replied. "This news is unacceptable Edwin." Getting up and walking around the table, Alvarez stopped behind Lopez's chair. "This is truly unacceptable. You know, when my father founded this company he personally selected many of your parents to be part of his vision. He personally asked your father to help found this company, Edwin. Both of our parents had such great expectations for you when you took over your father's seat on this board. That is why you were tasked with such an important component of our plan. Lithium ion battery production is key to the reshaping of the transportation systems in our new green world. Without lithium ion batteries we will be forced to power our cars and buses and trains with hydrocarbon fuels. And without lithium, we cannot produce our lithium ion batteries. That is why your role is so vital. Edwin, I am sure that you will direct your teams to re-double their efforts and find a way to meet the projected lithium needs to keep us on schedule."

"I will get my teams on it immediately." Lopez replied

Returning towards his chair, Alverez stopped at his son's seat, bent over and whispered into his ear. "We need to find a contingency plan in case Edwin fails us again. There is too much riding on this to allow a mistake to dramatically alter our plans."

Nodding his head, the younger, Alverez replied, "I understand father."

Sitting back down, Alverez once again returned his attention to the podium. "Oh, and Edwin, if you haven't already done so, please see to it that those warlords that killed our man are properly dealt with. We wouldn't want the Taliban leadership thinking that you are weak as well as ineffective."

"Inmediatamente mi líder." Lopez, quickly replied.

It took John most of the day to figure out how he was going to tell his team the news. He had reached out via email at lunchtime advising everyone of a mandatory meeting at 5 PM that evening. Dreading the inevitable, the intervening hours dragged on for the rest of the afternoon. John felt an immense sense of guilt, for what was happening. No one on his team has done anything to deserve this reassignment, and while none of them would suffer a reduction in rank or pay, being reassigned in this fashion carried a certain stigma. No matter what their tenure was, they would be considered *the new guy* and subjected to the lousy assignments and crappy shifts usually relegated to fresh recruits.

Additionally, being a small department, the Gendarmerie had an overactive rumor mill. With the dissolution of his department, people would begin to wonder what they messed up, or if there was any corruption or wrongdoing on the part of its members or their leader. And while this couldn't be any further from the truth, the negative effects of this political play would have long term implications on the members of his team.

As 5 PM approached, John headed into the team's conference room. It was from this room that this team had planned some of their most successful actions. Whiteboards surrounded the outside of the room and multiple projectors hung from swiveling brackets in the ceiling. There were three desktop computers and a dedicated server, with multiple monitors stored in a control panel in the front right corner of the room. Each team members however, had a laptop connected to the server and able to control any of the projectors in the room.

The first to arrive, John looked around the room,

reminiscing about both the work they had done here, as well as the good times celebrated. John was never one to let a birthday, work anniversary, or personal life event go unrecognized, believing that blurring the lines slightly between work and personal life built a stronger, more cohesive team. The fact that the only turnover on his team came from retirement or promotion, and there was a long waiting list to join this division proved John's theory correct.

The men began filing in and taking seats around the foldable conference table set up in the center of the room. Looks were passed around, but no one spoke. After ten of the twelve men who made up the Division for Investigations, Intelligence and Special Projects were seated, Tony Febbaccio, John's second in command spoke up.

"Vito and Michael are out on assignment, boss. They are on overwatch on that suspected satanic cult terrorist group. We expect that group to be making a large purchase of C4 any day now and did not want to take the chance of missing it when they made their move."

"Good choice." Replied John as he began pacing around the room.

"Besides, they already know what's going on." Victor said.

"What? What do you mean they know what's going on?" John said spinning toward Victor.

"Pasquale's sister-in-law works in Personnel." Tony said. She said the paperwork all came through this morning. She called Pat right away, and he… well he let everyone know."

"And you waited until now to… Why didn't anyone come to see me? John asked.

"Well, sir, your door was closed, and, well, it rarely

ever is, so we assumed you did not want to be disturbed." Another team member chimed in.

"Well you could have knocked. It would have saved me the time and trouble of writing this speech." John said as he crumpled two pages of paper together and tossed them in the trash.

"Any idea why, sir?

"Ideas, yes. Good ideas or facts, no not really. For some reason, Pinnochi..." sighing, John corrected himself. "... Inspector General Pinochinio never liked me. I mean from day one. I tried to be cordial, and then when he got the promotion, I tried to be respectful, but after a while, I found that my professionalism was being met with hostility, and it was impacting my ability... our ability to do our job. So, I just went around him. I think that made things worse. Everyone else here kisses his butt. I never did that. I never thought he was a very good cop, and I thought he was an even worse leader. When Pope Gregory passed, I guess it was just a matter of time."

"So how will this affect us?" one of the men asked.

"Well no one will receive any reduction in pay, nor lose any rank. However, despite most of you being seasoned veterans to the Corps, transferring to a new division or team will mean you may lose some seniority. So, you can expect to have lousy shifts for a time, and probably some bad assignments too."

"What about you boss?" Pasquale asked.

"I don't know what my new assignment will be. I was told that until everyone is reassigned, I must maintain full operational readiness of this division, so I have a feeling that the longer it takes each of you to get reassigned, the tougher things will be. Those of us still here may have to pull some double shifts or all-nighters."

"Whatever it takes sir." Tony replied.

"Look everyone… I want to say… I'm sorry. I let you all down. If I'd have played the political game this wouldn't be happening. I should have swallowed my pride and done things differently. I'm really sorry."

Victor spoke up. "Sir, I think I speak for most of the team when I say, we would not have wanted you to do anything differently. You led this team with integrity and professionalism. You believed that your actions, not your words should speak for you, and when you do speak, your word is your bond. You taught us to always persevere and strive for perfection. You taught us what it means to love and serve both Christ and our fellow man and how to protect that which we love. I will take those lessons with me wherever they send me."

Choking back tears John said, "Thank you Victor. What you just said means a lot to me."

Tony said, "Is there nothing you can do about this boss? I cannot believe you do not have one last trick up your sleeve to change this situation."

Nodding his head, John said, "I do have one person I can speak to. But I don't want you guys holding out hope that I can change this. In the meantime, we continue to strive for flawless performance of our duties, just as we always have. Just because some bureaucrats feel we are not needed doesn't mean that there are no longer any threats out there."

CHAPTER 2

**Borough of Sayreville
Middlesex County, New Jersey
Present Day**

"Two DAVID TO dispatch. I am southbound on Jernee Mill. Can someone please get in front of these guys and lay a strip down?" Detective Adam Levy shouted into the microphone over the wail of the siren.

Getting a tip about a small-scale meth lab operating in town, Levy was staking out the location and waiting for back-up when two men came running out of the house and dove into the pick-up truck in the driveway. As Levy was about to step out of his car and confront the two, the house exploded, sending debris into the neighboring houses and across the street. It appeared that something went wrong in the highly flammable lab, and the two suspects were running for their lives.

Peeling out of the driveway, the pair took off down the street, with Levy in pursuit. Having already evaded two roadblocks, Levy was now asking for assistance by deploying spike strips across the road. Reaching eighty miles per hour, Levy thought he may have them when their car began to fishtail around the big curve just past Hartle Street. But safely navigating the curves, they once again accelerated past the concert venue.

"Six three one to dispatch." I just turned north on Jernee Mill off Bordentown. I will attempt to lay down the spike strip"

"Two David to Six three one. They are coming at you pretty fast. If you wanna set the strip, you better do it quick."

"10-4 Sarge." Came the officers reply.

But just as the officer was about to roll out the spike strip, the blue Chevy pick-up rocketed past, with Levy and his unmarked car two seconds behind. Luck was on the drug dealers' side as they reached the intersection and had the green light. Barely slowing down enough to make the turn, the pick-up turned left on to Bordentown Avenue.

The duo once again accelerated on Bordentown Avenue. Now hitting speeds up to ninety, they sped past the sports complex and ran parallel to the train tracks on the right. Knowing the road, and wanting to bring this chase to an end, Levy closed the distance between his car and the pick-up, causing the driver to floor the accelerator as they passed the township Water Department.

The driver of the pick-up miraculously saw the sign for the S-curve, and slammed on his brakes just as the truck entered the sharp right-hand bend of the curve. With the rear end of the truck swinging to the left and the tires squealing in protest, the pick-up managed to stay on the road, but was perpendicular with its nose to the right as it went under the train trestle. With the left-hand bend coming up, the driver attempted to swing the nose of the truck hard left to complete the turn when the laws of physics finally caught up to him.

As the front of the truck came around, the rear end had built up too much inertia and slammed into the side of the brick and concrete train trestle. Like a cue ball with English, the crumpled rear end of the truck now came back around and with the vehicle's momentum being perpendicular to its tires, the truck flipped over landing on its roof, then rolled on to the passenger side.

Pumping his brakes right after the pickup had accelerated, Adam called in to dispatch in anticipation of what was about to occur. "Two David to dispatch. Better roll fire and EMS." Ten seconds later, as he rounded the curve and saw the truck on its side he continued, "We have a roll-over with possible entrapment."

Getting out of his car, Levy approached the truck. Peering in through the smashed in front windshield at the two bloody and tangled bodies, he asked, "You two assholes alive in there?" Hearing both men moan in reply, Levy continued, "Good. You are both under arrest. You have the right to remain silent. Anything you say may be used against you in a court of law…"

Office of the Secretariat of State
Vatican City, Rome
Present Day

John waited patiently outside the office of the Secretary for Relations with States. As part of the office of the Cardinal Secretary of State, the Section for Relations with States was the Vatican office responsible for maintaining diplomatic relations with other nations, and assisting in assigning Bishops to postings around the world. As such, it is considered one of the foremost responsibilities of the office of the Vatican Secretariat of State. The section is always headed by an Archbishop, with the assistance of a Prelate, who serves as the Undersecretary for Relations with States, and numerous other Cardinals and Bishops.

A tall and lanky priest approached John and cleared his throat to get John's attention. "The Cardinal Secretary will see you now." He said in heavily accented English.

Entering the sparsely decorated office, John was greeted by the Cardinal with a broad smile and outstretched arms. "John, my old friend. It is so good to see you. You have been a stranger to this office for way too long."

Walking over and embracing John with a big hug, Archbishop Hans Dietrich greeted Nowalski before releasing him but holding him at arms-length by his shoulders and looking him up and down. "You are looking fit as ever." He said.

"Thank you, Your Eminence. I know, it has been way too long. I believe the last time we spoke was at the funeral."

"Ja, I think you are right. Come, sit. Let us talk." Dietrich said gesturing to the couches near his desk.

Settling in on the couches, the two men sat without speaking for a moment, sharing a bond that dated back over twenty years. Hans Dietrich was a priest serving in this office when he first met John. Dispatched to the United States to recruit and work with John on a series of murders with ties to the then Cardinal Flynn, John, Dietrich and a detective from New York City were able to solve the cases and ultimately saved Flynn's life before Cardinal Flynn was elevated to the papacy and became Pope Gregory.

Originally from Munich, Germany, Dietrich returned to a church in his home city as a Monsignor not long after, and with Pope Gregory as his patron, he was fast tracked through the church hierarchy. After being elevated to Cardinal, he returned to the Vatican and served as the Undersecretary for Relations with States, and was recently elevated to his new role by the current Pope.

With his smile fading from his face, the Cardinal said, "Ja, so… I take it your visit is not just a social one."

"No, your Eminence, I'm afraid it's not. I assume you have heard…"

"Ja. It is unfortunate, but not surprising."

"I had expected some fall-out,.. some changes after Pope Gregory passed, but I never expected this. Excellency, they are disbanding my entire unit."

"Ja, I know." Dietrich said with a sigh. "But to say you never expected this? John, how could you have been so naïve?"

"Naïve? What do you mean?"

"John, most of the Gendarmerie have hated you since day one. You were appointed to your position by the Pope, and his edicts are infallible so they could never be openly questioned. But that did not change the way people felt about you. You were an outsider. You were not Italian and you did not come up through the ranks.

In your twenty plus years here, I would venture to say you have only learned enough Italian to order food or find the bathroom. You have insisted on issuing all your orders and presenting all your reports in English. John, the Gendarmerie is an Italian corps, run by Italian officers. In fact, the majority of the Curia is Italian, yet you seem to have never recognized this and behaved as an ugly American. This is not America John. Unlike your United States, most Europeans make it a point to learn several languages. You have just been lucky that most of them have chosen English to be one of those languages."

John attempted to speak in his defense, but Dietrich held out his hand and cut him off. "I am not finished. Then you have never moved forward with your monastic discernment. You have not studied nor moved forward with temporary vows, let alone Solemn Vows. This is seen by the Curia as a lack of commitment. It is almost as if you view what you do as merely a job, and not a calling.

Finally, even after Gregory passed, you continued to treat Pinochinio with contempt. You could get away with that when you were under the Pope's protection. But once that was gone, you were just another one of his direct reports. And the one he hated the most."

John said, "I always thought my record… my results spoke for themselves. I thought that after everything my team and I did…"

"You would be judged on your merits?" Dietrich interrupted. "John, the Vatican is the world's oldest bureaucracy.

It is almost where politics were invented. You needed to play a smarter game."

Hanging his head, John said, "I guess you're right."

"I am right, John. You may know police work, but you have never been good at politics. With you, it is always straight ahead. John, you must learn that sometimes the shortest way to move between two points is not a straight line."

"Still Excellency, I would have thought that either Cardinal Sentille or the Pope would see the benefit of keeping my unit. With all we have done for the Church you'd think the Pope…"

"The Pope is a communist." Dietrich interrupted. "And Sentille is above all else, Italian, and the Pope's lapdog. I am sure it did not take much for Pinochinio to convince his fellow countryman to get rid of you, and then all Sentille needed to do was convince the Pope that you were a threat… a wild card, and like any good communist, he looked to consolidate power."

"The Pope is a communist?" John said in surprise. "I mean, Sentille did talk about defunding and other ultra-progressive ideas, and I know some of the Pope's ideas are left leaning and idealistic, but…"

"John, the man rose to prominence in Venezuela. A socialist country lead by a crazy dictator. You do not do that unless you carry the party banner."

John said, "I assume so."

"Ja, so… This is not all. They will not be satisfied with removing you from your position. They will want to embarrass and discredit you as well. If I were you, I would watch out for that. Remember, you are not good at politics."

"Discredit me? What do you mean?" John asked.

"Your troubles are not yet over. Things will get worse for you. If there were a gulag for them to throw you in, they would. Watch what you say and what you do. They will look for a way to make things even worse, so be prepared."

Nodding his head, John thanked the Cardinal.

"Now my friend, I must take your leave." Dietrich said. "I have another meeting to attend. Be careful. There is not much I can do to help you, but if you need advice, come and see me."

"Thank you, Excellency." John said as he stood from the couch. While he may not be good at politics, John was well versed at getting inside the head of adversaries with bad intent. He thought he would just have to put his bosses in the same category as the terrorists he usually hunted.

Police Headquarters
Sayreville, New Jersey
Present Day

"I hear you had a bit of excitement the other day." Captain Jake Benjamin said as he passed Levy's desk on his way to his office.

"Yeah. You would pick the one week we actually get some action here to go on vacation." Adam replied to his boss.

"Hey, excitement is highly overrated. In fact, that incident we had with the cartel kingpin twenty some odd years ago was more than enough excitement for my whole career."

"That was a bit before my time Captain." Adam replied.

Giving a 'follow me' wave to his second-in-command as he continued walking toward his office, Benjamin said. "C'mon in and give me an update on what else I missed."

Entering his office, Benjamin removed his sport jacket, unclipped his holster and sidearm from his belt, placing them in his top desk draw, and sat down behind his desk. "So where do things stand. I see you knuckleheads didn't burn the place to the ground while I was gone."

"Despite our best efforts to the contrary, no sir, we did not burn HQ down. Actually, other than the incident with the meth lab and those two assholes, it was pretty qui... Almost said it and jinxed us." Adam said referring to the emergency services superstition of avoiding the word "Quiet," or *The Q Word* as it is referred to.

"Where are we with those two."

"They are still in the hospital and the sheriff's department has taken custody. I have completed my report and passed it along to the DA's office. I think we are just waiting for the County CSI folks to finish their investigation on the meth lab."

"Suspected meth lab." The Captain corrected. "Get used to always using the correct terminology, even amongst your colleagues. This way you won't slip up when giving testimony, and you won't have to think as much on the stand."

"Copy that, sir." Adam replied

"What else is on our plate?"

"We are still looking for that dude that slashed his girlfriend. She is doing OK, and I've checked in on her a few times since the incident. She knows to call if he shows back up at her place."

Benjamin said. "When he shows up. These types of

domestic cases almost always go the same way. The dude goes too far, hides out for a while, then goes back and begs for the woman's forgiveness… Which nine time out of ten, she gives to him… Until he puts her back in the hospital, or kills her, or, we catch him."

"Or she kills him." Levy added.

"Yeah, that too." The Captain replied. "Stay on top of her. Build that rapport so she trusts you. Make sure she knows that her safety depends on calling you when he comes back. And go sweat the parents again. It's bullshit that they haven't heard from him. We don't have enough for a warrant, but I would bet my lunch that he's hiding out in their basement right now."

"Yes, sir." Levy replied.

"What else you got? The Captain asked.

"That's really about its sir. Still following up on some of our old cases, but nothing really new."

"Good… Good to hear. So where are you on your studying for the lieutenant's exam?

"I'm doing what you suggested. I'm taking that review course. I'm in a study group with some guys from different departments, I'm making sure I am blocking out several hours a week for additional review…"

"Good. Keep at it. You need to ace this test and come out on top. The position has been vacant for well over a year, and I'm getting some pressure to appoint someone from the last test before the list runs out. You need to get this position and get time on grade before you can sit for the captain's exam. Adam, I got more time behind me on this job than I do in front of me. You have a pretty clear shot at this desk, but you have to do your part and follow the path I've laid out."

"Yes sir. I am. And again, thank you for all your help."

"You are a good man, Levy. I know your background and I'm sure it can be tough when you… you know don't really have any family."

"I like to think of this department as my family, sir."

"And we are. But sometimes you need more. You need blood, you need your heritage."

"That might be true for you, boss, but it's different for me. In my case, my heritage doesn't want me."

Adam Levy was born into an ultraorthodox Jewish family and grew up surrounded by like-minded people of faith in Lakewood, NJ. Although he often pretended to be a police officer when he was a young child, his parents encouraged him to pursue and study the sciences. He attended yeshiva and went on to attend Rutgers University as a pre-med major. It was in his junior year, that Adam's life took a hard turn. Despite being in an arranged relationship with a girl from his community, Adam met Laura, a non-Jewish girl from Long Island who majored in criminal justice. Falling hopelessly in love, Adam informed his parents that summer that not only was he was not marrying the girl from his community, he would marry Laura, a girl outside his faith, and he was going to follow his dream and take the civil service exam to become a police officer.

After multiple arguments with his parents he was told if he were to pursue this path he would need to leave the house and he would be considered dead to his parents. Familial bonds and reason succumbed to youth and passion, and Adam grabbed some of his things and stormed out of his parent's house.

Cut-off, disowned and alone, Adam found a single room apartment near the campus, worked at a local convenience store and took classes part time while he studied for the civil service exam. His relationship with Laura came to a screeching halt when Adam caught her in bed with one of members of the school's football team. Despite this, Adam felt his direction had been set and he was determined to follow his own path for once in his life.

Taking the civil service exam, Adam scored extremely well and was hired by the Borough of Sayreville the following spring. He survived the police academy, and did well as a patrol officer his rookie year. After five years of solid performance, he applied for an open position in the detective bureau, and was accepted and taken under the wing of then Lieutenant Benjamin. Despite a bumpy path and now a fairly solitary personal life, Adam Levy was living the career he always dreamed.

Aryphon Corporate Headquarters
Montevideo, Uruguay
Present Day

Emma Alvarez stormed past her brother William as she left her father's office. Turning to face her brother she said, "Go on in baby brother. Maybe the golden child can get what *he* needs. Our father obviously doesn't give a shit about me."

Walking into his father's office, William found his father seated behind his desk still shaking his head. Looking up at his son, Alvarez gestured to the chair in front of his desk.

"What was that all about?" the younger man asked.

"Your sister is still upset about her company not getting the vaccine for the pandemic. She said she had promised her superiors that her division would be able to formulate something and be the first to get approval, and the first to market, but when we had to give the vaccine formula to the other companies, she said she was unable to come through on her promise. She said it was a serious black mark against her and that she missed out on a promotion because of it."

"Ahhh, that is the root of the problem. I'd heard the promotion was given to that Richards guy." William said.

"Wasn't he…"

"The guy Emma was fucking… Yeah. And from what she told me, it ended pretty badly. The fact that he got this promotion must really be a thorn in her side." William said.

"Your sister has got to learn to keep emotions out of these things. This is business and politics, not some college sorority drama fest. She wanted a seat at the big table. She has to learn to keep focus. We have much bigger goals than her petty paybacks against some lover who jilted her."

"You reminded her of the future plans?" William asked.

"Of course." Alvarez replied. "And I explained to her why we had to pivot the way we did. Our inside man was way too heavily invested in the other companies for us to go with your sister's firm. And we needed him to move things forward the way he did for this all to work. Initially he had the President's ear and he always remained a darling to the leftist media, even with his inability to keep to a prescribed narrative. Masks off,… masks on,… double mask… It sounded as if he did not know what he was talking about or he couldn't make up his mind. Regardless, we needed him and if we had not made the switch, he would not have gone along with the plan. Still, Emma is upset. She will just have to get over it or learn to live with disappointment."

"She has always been hot headed, papa."

"Ja, so… What is it you came to see me about?" The elder Alvarez asked.

"So, remember you asked me to look for a possible alternative should Lopez fail to reach our required quota?"

"Yes…" Alvarez said,

"So, I had our researchers looking through the archives to see if there were ever any references to previously untapped lithium deposits. As you know, during the war there was work done around the globe in search of mineral deposits and other natural recourses to support the war effort. I was looking to see if any of that prospecting found lithium deposits that are still untapped."

"And you found some?" Alvarez said eagerly.

"No, papa. But I found something else that is very interesting."

"Go on…"

"There were documents that talked about a graphene-based battery that could instantaneously be re-charged, and hold a charge longer than the batteries that were being used."

"Ja, so. Lithium-ion batteries do that now, and graphene cannot be mass produced efficiently. It would take twice as long and cost four times as much just to make the graphene as it would to mine, process and then convert the lithium into a battery." Alvarez said waving his hand dismissively. "I do not see how this will help us."

"No, papa. I think they found a way to efficiently and cost effectively manufacture graphene."

His eyes lighting up, Alvarez raised his eyebrows and wagged a finger at his son. "Now there, you might have something. If we could find and develop a comparable alternative to lithium ion, and be the sole producer of it, not only would we be back on track, but we would secure a stronger revenue stream than the one we were looking to establish with our original plan."

"Exactly my thoughts papa."

"Do you think this lead that you uncovered may result in something that substantial? What are your next steps."

William said, "I just uncovered this string. I am going to have my researchers keep pulling at. We will follow the trail of information to find these plans. Once we have them, our engineers and chemists can evaluate them. In the meantime, the researchers will also continue the search for unknown lithium deposits."

"That sounds like a solid course of action. I fear that Lopez is falling further behind, even on the production side. We may need this alternative plan sooner rather than later. Keep me informed, William." Alvarez said as he sat back in his chair, a giant smile forming across his lips.

CHAPTER 3

**Headquarters, Gendarmerie Corps
of Vatican City State
Vatican City, Rome
Present Day**

John paced back and forth in front of his office desk like a caged animal at the zoo. After his fifth attempt at providing an *"acceptable"* plan to manage operations of his division through its dissolution, he had finally received Pinochinio's approval to move forward.

Each time Pinochinio rejected Nowalski's plan he asked for more frequent reporting and insisted on greater micromanagement, to the point that now he wanted daily detailed reports on the division's activity along with a weekly threat assessment broken out by geographic region. Additionally, Pinochinio wanted weekly updates on the overall progress of the personnel reassignments. The level of detail required from the daily activity reports alone would take John several hours to prepare, and with an ever-shrinking team, maintaining an accurate global threat assessment was a nearly impossible task.

Now, three weeks in to this reorganization and new reporting requirements, John was becoming consumed by the pressures of meeting the minutia of his detailed reporting responsibilities and maintaining a comprehensive view of the true threats, and what was truly important in his mission to safeguard the Church.

With only five of his original twelve-member team remaining, John was finding himself hard pressed to properly follow up on the information his division received and gather good actionable intelligence on potential threats. His reorganization plan called for turning over some of the in-depth investigation work to other units of the Corps, but Pinochinio had already warned him that he didn't want the other divisions "chasing ghosts," as he called it, so John needed to carefully dole out those assignments. Those decisions were what was currently causing John to pace and talk to himself.

A knock on the door drew John out of his contemplations and back to the present. "C'mon in" he said.

Entering the room and looking a bit puzzled by John's location in front of his desk, Antonio Febbaccio tilted his head to the side quizzically. "You lose something boss?" he asked.

Confused by the question, John said, "No. Why do I look like I lost something?"

"Well, you are standing in front of your desk, with all your papers on the desk, so… I was expecting to see you sitting behind your desk, not in front of it."

"I was actually walking around. I sometimes think

better when I'm moving. One of the reasons I go for my morning runs. It lets me think and plan my day. But ever since this reorg started, I haven't had time to take those runs. I need to spend that time writing my daily report." John said, emphasizing the last two words in a sing-songie voice.

Walking over to the chairs by John's desk, Febbaccio sat down and said. "So, what are you thinking about?"

John said, "Which part of this caseload to pass over to other divisions to follow-up on. If I pass along a lead to something that turns out to be nothing, I'm gonna hear about it."

"Boss, I think you are going to hear about it no matter what. If I could make an observation, it seems that this whole reorganization thing was a set-up to get you to fail. They quickly deplete your team to where it can no longer properly function, then drag out the end forcing you to operate without adequate resources. Then they ding you if you follow up on something that turns into nothing, and ding you again if you miss something. You know how much of intelligence is following up on big nothings? But that is what we have to do. Pinocchio is setting you up to fail, Boss."

John sat back against his desk and rubbed his head as he nodded to his second-in-command. "First off, I thought you didn't like to call him that because it might get you in trouble." John said putting the last part of his sentence in air quotes. "Secondly, I have been so busy trying to meet all of these demands that I never really stopped to look at the big picture. It seemed like every time I would meet with Pinocchio, he would do something to make my life tougher…to make it more difficult for me to meet my goals. You know, when I met with Cardinal Dietrich, he said that they were going to be gunning for me. He said that they wouldn't be happy with just knocking me down and embarrassing me, they wouldn't stop until I was ruined.

In fact, when I met with Pinocchio and Sentille, they even said I would retain my rank and pay as long as I was not derelict in my duties. That is what they are trying to do…" John said as the thought was coalescing in his mind.

"They want to take it all. My job, my pension, my reputation… everything."

"How could people in the Church be such bastards?" Antonio asked.

"Dietrich said that the Church was like the inventor of politics. When something as twisted as politics is that imbedded in the culture, I guess it overrides almost everything else."

Febbaccio asked, "So what are you going to do?"

"I could retire." John replied. "But then what happens with you and Vito and the guys?"

"We would be OK. We are destined for reassignment anyway. I guess they would just speed it up."

"Yeah, maybe…" John said, looking off to the distance in thought. "Or I could fight. Maybe they want me to quit. The longer I stay and keep meeting their insane requirements, the more I drive them crazy."

"Boss, I hate to say this, but I am afraid this is a fight you cannot win. They have the upper hand. In the long run, they will make it simply impossible to perform your duties, and then they will hang you for that."

John said, "Perhaps you are right Tony. I don't know. This is something I need to give more thought to."

"So, more pacing I guess?"

Getting up and slapping his hand on the other man's shoulder, John said with a smile, "Yup… I guess I'm in for more pacing."

Established in 1948, Aryphon Industries started out as a steel manufacturing company. Riding the post-World-War Two economic wave of both industrial and residential expansion and reconstruction, the company thrived and built manufacturing sites in North and South America, as well as other locations around the globe.

Remaining privately held, Aryphon rode the steel wave to its pinnacle in the early '70s, then began diversifying into other growth areas before selling the steel business to a multinational rival in 1979. By this time, Aryphon had footholds in pharmaceuticals, banking, media and electronics. Now cash rich, they took advantage of a stagnant economy, buying up competition and consolidating their positions in those industries, emerging as a powerhouse multinational conglomerate in the late 1980s.

The '90s saw growth in chip sets and micro-processors, and Aryphon's electronics division was able to take advantage. Unlike most other banks Aryphon's financial institutions avoided the sub-prime mortgage frenzy in the early part of the next decade, and once again having surplus cash, they capitalized when the housing bubble burst in 2009.

Management at Aryphon seemed to always have a crystal ball and be positioned to take advantage of the next great industrial wave, and avoid the pitfalls to which so many other businesses succumbed. Now in the early '20s while still strategically positioned in their core businesses, Aryphon was branching out into AI, and green technology.

One of Aryphon's divisions that was instrumental in their success was its Research Division. Divided into two branches, one Application and one Academic, the two branches worked in tandem to keep Aryphon ahead of the curve. While the Academic research branch scoured the news then tied the present to history in order to find behavior patterns that may predict the next great wave or human need, the Application branch then took the information and worked to develop the technology or strategy to take advantage of that wave.

Led by William Alvarez, the youngest son of the current company chairman, the division had grown in both staffing as well as importance since William took over at its helm.

William had been groomed since his youth for a position of leadership in Aryphon. After earning a degree in engineering from MIT, William continued on to get a Ph.D. from Harvard in his true passion, Behavioral Predictive Analytics. Utilizing social media as well as the plethora of global online news sources, William and his teams were able to develop accurate behavioral algorithms from the endless data points available.

With higher education going through a consolidation, there were no shortages of recently minted doctorates looking for a job. And since Aryphon paid substantially more than most universities, he was able to frequently find some of the brightest researchers for his teams.

Having earned her doctorate in history only two years earlier, Mary Morrison had joined Aryphon after only finding adjunct teaching positions available. After accepting the fact that the job required relocation to Uruguay, Mary packed her belongings, said her goodbyes, and found a small apartment ten minutes from her new office. Settling in to her role as a researcher on the Academic team, Mary frequently was required to work on projects she felt were outside the scope of her expertise. Despite this, she could never complain about the salary, the collegiality of her teammates nor the management of her division. Unlike academia where bickering colleagues and rampant politics were the norm, Aryphon, and her division's head, William Alvarez put results first and were always fair and professional. With her most recent assignment taking her into an area she not only felt comfortable in, but passionate about researching, Mary felt that she had landed the best job in the world.

Now tasked with reviewing old Nazi documents in her search for hidden lithium deposits, Mary stumbled on correspondence that mentioned a new "super battery" made out of graphene. Bringing this to her supervisor's attention, she was immediately sent to present her findings to the division head, William Alvarez.

Alvarez was excited about what she had found, and said he needed to check on a few things before getting back to her. Then, two days later, she was summoned to Alvarez's office again, given a small team to lead, and access to additional private archived files stored in a sub-basement of the company's headquarters.

Initially, Mary and her team had some difficulty in

being able to locate useful documents. The taxonomy was not something any of them had seen before. To complicate matters even more, very few of the documents were in English. German, French, Italian and even Russian were the predominant languages of most of the files. And while Mary was fluent in German, no one on her small team spoke any of the other languages. This problem was solved by requisitioning to have one of the translating scanners the division used be brought to the sub-basement, a necessary move since none of the files were allowed to leave the basement repository.

Mary was amazed at the numerous and detailed primary source Nazi documents the archive held. There were orders of battle and personnel records dating back to nearly the start of the Nazi party. It was rumored that Hermann Alvarez was fascinated with the history of WWII, and that he spent millions of his fortune in securing Nazi relics and artifacts. This repository was proof of his obsession.

About two weeks into their research, the team uncovered the first mention of "Der Grosse Licht" or the Big Light. It was tied to one of the uses of graphene in the work being done by IG Farben. The researcher with a background in chemistry almost dismissed the notation when he mis-read the follow-up notes as the experiment results being unrepeatable. However, when re-read by the researcher with a Ph.D. in physics, the mis-translated note actually read unsustainable. In the report to his superiors, Professor Peter Wagner talked about a brilliant flash of light accompanied by the discharge of heat and electrical energy from a chemical reaction that the physicist said "almost sounded like an un-sustained cold fusion reaction."

Knowing that cold fusion has never existed, the team almost left it out of their weekly report to Alvarez. But when she was called back to Alvarez's office, Mary instantly knew it was good that she included it. The next day the size of her team tripled, and Mary was tasked with tracking down every lead to uncover any nugget of information on this Grosse Licht in addition to learning all there is about the graphene battery.

The restaurant's air conditioning was blowing full blast as it attempted to compensate for the hot sticky air that poured in from the front of the restaurant. Sitting in the overhead tracks like a raised garage door, the restaurant's walls that could actually help keep the facility cool, were elevated allowing the patrons to enjoy the ambiance of the mall parking lot.

Ludicrously asked if he would prefer a table inside or out, Adam replied that he didn't really care, not that it would make a difference for the couple's comfort. Taking a seat at the bar while waiting, the bartender asked what Adam and his girlfriend wanted, and although he wanted to say a comfortable place to eat, Adam replied, "A rum and Coke," to his girlfriend's coffee martini.

Grabbing a napkin from the stack behind the bar, Adam looked at his girlfriend and asked, "So how has your week been babe?"

"Well, to say that this is the highlight of my week so far, should give you a bit of an indication." Faith White, Adam's current girlfriend said as she waved her arms around the restaurant to exaggerate her displeasure with her current environment.

A bit distractedly Adam asked, "Oh, why? What's been going on?"

"Really?… OK. Well, for starters, I got reamed out on Monday for not completing that financial analysis my boss said he wanted by Tuesday. You know if he really wanted it Monday he should have just said so and not given me the erroneous information of saying it was due by Tuesday but hey, he's the boss, so I guess he can do shit like that. Then Tuesday night I lost power for about an hour and when it came back on it created a power surge that fried the computer in my stove and knocked out the whole apartments air conditioning unit. So, despite my numerous calls to the building management, since Tuesday night I have basically not been able to get much sleep because it is so freaking hot. I just lay there sweating. Then yesterday, my girlfriend, Susie calls me and tells me that I won't be able to go to the shore with her tomorrow because the house her boyfriend is renting is going to be full of his old frat buddies and there would be no place for me to sleep… unless of course I think one of them is cute and then want to sleep with him. And now, to top it all off, I get to go out with you and we get, this…" Faith said waving her arms around again.

"I am sorry babe. If I had known, we could have gone somewhere else. I didn't know you were living without air conditioning and had such a shitty week at work." Adam replied.

Faith let out a long sigh, and was about to reply, when the bartender brought over their drinks. Taking the glass,

Faith put her lips to it and took a large gulp of the martini, sucking down nearly half as if it were a shot.

Returning her glass to the bar, Faith looked over to Adam and said, "You know Adam, I think that's just one of the problems that exists with this relationship."

"What do you mean?" Adam replied.

"I mean that either you have the memory of a goldfish or you just don't listen to a thing that I say."

With a quizzical expression on his face, Adam went to reply, but was cut off when Faith said, "I told you about the shit with my boss on Tuesday and then I told you about the air conditioner when we spoke Wednesday. Weren't you paying attention?"

Set back on the defensive John said, "No… Yeah I was paying attention but I thought that you'd gotten the air conditioning fixed by now."

"So even if it was fixed Adam, you think that after me not being able to sleep because of this freaking heat you wouldn't take me to some sweatbox for dinner." Faith said, waving her arms around once again to emphasize her point.

"I'm sorry babe I didn't know it was going to be this hot in here. Adam said.

Taking another gulp of her martini, this time finishing the glass, Faith looked at Adam and replied, "You know, I guess it takes the intuitive powers of Sherlock Holmes to figure out that if a restaurant has no walls, the hot air from the steaming parking lot will cascade in, and no amount of air conditioning will make it comfortable enough to actually enjoy the meal… But then I guess while you may be a detective, you're not necessarily Sherlock Holmes."

She concluded while signaling to the bartender her need for another drink.

"Look, I'm sorry. Let's go someplace else. Adam said.

"I just ordered another drink, and if we leave, by the time we get there it will be late and you have work tomorrow. And that's another thing, Adam, you're always sorry. *I'm sorry babe, I forgot. I'm sorry babe, I'll make it up to you.*" She said in a mocking voice. "You have to be the sorriest guy I know."

Looking up from his feet, Adam said, "I'm..."

"What? Sorry?" Faith interrupted. "Jesus, Adam... really?"

Sliding off the high-top chair, Faith grabbed her purse. "I gotta go pee."

"OK, I'll be here." Adam replied.

The bartender brought the drink over and raised his eyebrows at Adam. Having overheard the conversation he said, "Sorry about the heat dude. I know it's friggin' stupid to have the walls up when it's this friggin' hot outside, but our GM insists. Says its policy to keep them up if it's above 75 degrees. Can I get you anything else?"

"Naa, man. I'm good." He replied just as his phone buzzed indicating their table was ready. Gesturing to his phone, Adam said, "Let me settle up. Our table is ready."

Adam pulled out his wallet and handed his credit card to the bartender to close out the tab. He had just finished signing the bill when Faith came back to the bar.

"Our table is ready." Adam said grabbing his phone as he prepared to head to the reservation counter. Sitting back down at the bar, Faith took another long sip from her fresh drink.

"Our table is ready, babe." Adam repeated.

"You know what your problem is, Adam?" Faith said without moving from her seat. "You're boring. You do everything the same way all the time. We have been going out for what, like six months now? Yet you behave like we've only been together for a few weeks. You talk to me the same way you first did. We go on dates the same way all the time, we even have sex the same way… There's never any variety. You're just freakin' boring. It's like you always have to play it safe."

Running his hand across his face, Adam replied, "I guess it spills over from the job. You have to do things a certain way to stay safe or else people can get hurt."

"And that spills over into matters of the heart?" Faith asked. Taking another drink, she continued, "Adam, we have been exclusive for six months now, or at least I have…"

Nodding his head vigorously, Adam said, "Yeah, me too, I…"

"And have seen each other pretty much every week. Yet in all that time, you have never said how you feel about me… about us. We text. We talk. We go out. Sometimes when you take me home you come up and we have sex, but even then, you have never spent the night. We have never gone away together for like a long weekend trip. You treat me the same way as you did two weeks into our relationship. I don't know if you are afraid of commitment, or you don't really like me, or if you are just plain boring." Taking the last swig of her drink, Faith continued, "I feel like our conversations are on auto-pilot… Our dates are on like, auto-pilot. Everything is… You also obviously don't listen to me…"

"No, Faith, I do…"

"No Adam, you don't. If you did, we would be sitting somewhere,… anywhere else but in this *fucking* inferno having a nice dinner. But this was just another date, another night on boring autopilot. This was not a… *Wow Faith, you had a really rough week, let me take you someplace nice, and maybe ask you to stay at my place till your air conditioner is fixed.* Adam, I just can't do auto-pilot anymore."

"Faith, I'm sorry, I…" Adam realized his mistake as soon as he said it.

Standing up from the chair, Faith moved in close to Adam and looked him squarely in the eye. "There you go Adam. You're either on boring auto-pilot or you're sorry… And I deserve more. Goodbye Adam."

Faith turned and began to leave. "Faith stop. Where are you going. Let me at least drive you home."

Stopping to look back at Adam, she replied, "Thanks, but I can call an Uber. Besides, I don't know if I'm even gonna go home."

"Where would you go?" Adam asked.

"I think I'm gonna go grab Susie and head down to the shore. If I'm going to be sweating all night in bed, I might as well be having some fun doing it. And that certainly won't be on auto-pilot or boring."

William Alvarez was thrilled with the results of Mary Morrison's team. Sorting through mountains of papers and Nazi records they were able to confirm that Peter Wagner had created a new, high energy source that was easily repeatable and inexpensive. Paired with a newly discovered process to mass produce graphene in a cost-effective manner, the Third Reich had planned to convert two full divisions of their Panzer tanks to electric vehicles powered by new graphene batteries and recharged by Wagner's new process. This was a key element of their *Wacht am Rhein* counter-offensive.

Morrison thought she had reached a dead end when her team discovered that Hitler's plans were thwarted by the British led bombing raid on the city of Stuttgart, wiping out both the lab where Wagner worked as well as the factory making the graphene batteries and the tanks. Additionally, it was confirmed that Peter Wagner along with all of his assistants perished in the massive bombing.

However, pulling on this historical thread a little further, it was learned that Wagner had passed the formula and schematics for both his "Big Light" power source as well as the graphene fabrication to his brother, a priest. From Nazi documents that recorded an interview with an informant, it was learned that the priest planned to hide the stolen plans in a monastery somewhere in either northern Austria or Bavaria. Copies of orders further showed the SS in fact had sent teams to a number of the monasteries to await the brother's arrival, but were unable to intercept Wagner's brother and obtain the plans.

Armed with this information, William forwarded his report and scheduled a meeting with his father to discuss next steps. Arriving at his father's office, William could hear the raised voices from the conversation taking place behind the office door. A few minutes later, the door opened and Edwin Lopez hurriedly left the office without even looking at William or saying a word. Entering his father's office,

Alvarez found his father calmly seated behind his desk, his hands folded in front of him, resting on the desk.

William said, "Lopez left in a hurry."

The senior Alvarez replied, "He says I expect the impossible from him, when in reality, all I expect is what was expected. If he had not made his judgmental errors, he would not have his current supply chain issues which are negatively affecting his production quotas. I fear our carefully planned timeline may be in jeopardy."

Sitting down in one of the chairs facing his father's desk, William asked, "Where are we with the other parts of the plan?"

"The gain of function research is progressing on schedule. The lab believes that everything should be completed by autumn."

"Are we using the same people as last time."

"No. That would not be prudent." The father replied. "There is too much scrutiny there. No, we have enlisted the help of some of our friends in North Korea."

"North Korea?" William asked in surprise. "Is that wise with such an unstable leader heading that regime?"

"They will comply… At least for the time being. Their need for hard currency will keep them in line. And they believe they will also have access to the vaccines. By the time they learn otherwise, it will be too late."

"Speaking about the vaccines, how goes the work Emma and her team are doing?" William asked.

"They are right on schedule. They have been working in lock-step with the North Korean lab, so we do not anticipate any surprises there."

William asked, "So if everything else is in place, what would be the harm in pushing back the timeline?"

The senior Alvarez stood up from his chair and began to walk around the room as he spoke. "It is imperative that we launch our plans in the warm weather months and before the U.S. Presidential elections. The full scope of our plan has been predicated on the meticulous adherence to a timeline. Work that was done ten years ago is only bearing fruit now, as scheduled. If we deviate from that timeline, things that were set in motion in the past will not happen when those results are needed to have the maximum effect on our overall objective. We cannot fully implement the Green agenda if every individual in the U.S. is negatively affected. And every individual will be negatively affected if they cannot drive to work, or to the grocery store, or to grandma's house. There needs to be the appearance of a viable alternative to the internal combustion engine for the left to hang their hat. That will create the infringement of liberties we desire along with spurring further division and turmoil. And the full agenda must be in place *before* the American Presidential elections."

Nodding his head, William replied. "I understand Papa."

"William, it's like dominos. Set them up carefully, and you know once you knock over the first, the rest will fall. But remove one, and the results become questionable. The plans for America are the key... the lynch pin. If those plans fail, the rest of our plans become questionable.

We must learn from history. Failure to learn from history means you are destined to repeat it. And we cannot repeat history. We will not get another chance at this."

William sat silently as he listened to his father. He knew his father was right. His team used historical data extensively when they built their behavioral algorithms because they knew most people did not learn from history, and therefore repeated it.

William said, "And producing the necessary battery stockpile has the longest lead time of any of the plan's other components."

"Exactly." replied the senior Alvarez. "That is why I was so excited to read your report. So, the Third Reich was able to develop these batteries, began building them and then outfitted their tanks in less than a six-month period. Even with Edwin's failure, if we could find those plans we could do the same by adjusting our manufacturing to incorporate the new process for producing graphene and therefore, remain on schedule."

"And the charging system… Father, I think it may be referring to cold fusion."

"I know… And adding that to our arsenal would give us limitless possibilities." Alvarez said.

"So, what are our next steps, Papa?"

"I think we send some of our specialist teams to Austria to start going through the monasteries. You get your researchers to identify which ones were previously watched by the SS, and cross those off our list. This priest Wagner never went there. Then have the ones that are no longer operating searched thoroughly, and send one team to start interviewing… aggressively interviewing the monks in the monasteries that are still active. Keep your research team working to see if there is any way to narrow down our search, and I will reach out to our contact in the

Vatican and see if he can assist us. If Wagner's brother was a priest, there may be information they have that would be pertinent. Perhaps some of your researchers could comb Church records for additional information."

"I will get on this right away, Papa"

"In the meantime, I want you to also take over the lithium procurement and battery production from Edwin. I have lost faith in his ability and I plan to seek his removal in our next Board meeting. Make sure you fully explain to his direct reports the importance of reaching established goals."

"I can do that Papa. And what about Edwin?"

"I think his talents can best serve us over in Afghanistan working to re-establish some of the trade deals he lost for us. He should also make sure he maintains a low profile similar to when he sent our representative in without a security contingent. We wouldn't want any potential new partners to view our actions as intimidating."

"Don't you think that might be a dangerous assignment, Papa?"

"I am hoping it is my boy. I am seriously hoping it is."

Gertrude Elfmann was a second-generation spy. Her father Reinhardt was a young SS officer at the end of the Second World War, when the Stasi recruited him for a distinct set of skills that he possessed. From the age of 16, Gertrude was trained by the East German secret police in all manner of spy craft, and when not officially training, she was tutored by her father. By the age of twenty-two Gertrude had already completed a handful of covert assassinations, and was considered a star asset by the East German government.

Then in 1987 Gertrude was chosen for a special mission. Teamed up with a with a young North Korean operative, Kim Yoon Shin, the pair were sent to the United States as a couple to gather intelligence for their respective countries. Both countries believed that U.S. counterintelligence would never suspect that East Germany would work cooperatively with North Korea, and therefore the team would have a stronger cover.

This belief held true, and for a number of years Elfmann and Kim provided solid intelligence to their respective countries. While their marriage was initially a sham, working closely together over time created a strong bond of mutual trust that grew into love. With the fall of the Berlin Wall in 1994, Gertrude's services were no longer needed and the new government disavowed her, leaving her out in the cold. So, in 1995, after the birth of their daughter, Gertrude returned to spy work for her newly adopted nation, North Korea.

From a young age Mr. and Mrs. Kim taught their daughter, Joon Min about the *Dear Leader* and how it was every North Korean's duty to serve and obey him. They taught their daughter from an early age that as a family, they had an obligation to work in the land of their enemy and she was not to believe the lies that would be taught her in school. When her father passed away from a heart attack a few weeks after her fourteenth birthday, Joon Min was told the enemy had discovered who he really was, and poisoned him at work.

Gertrude and Joon Min's life would dramatically

change two years later when the Dear Leader passed away. The power void that accompanied the purge that followed, left Gertrude without a handler and a means of reporting. Once again out in the cold, her reporting network dissolved, Gertrude and Joon Min turned their tradecraft to corporate rather than governmental intelligence.

Joon Min enrolled at Georgetown University and earned her degree in International Relations in three years, and her MBA in International Finance two years later. Recruited right out of graduate school by Aryphon, she managed to work her way up to her current position in less than two years.

Now sitting in her small apartment overlooking the ocean, Joon Min listened to the tapes made from the listening devices she had planted in Hermann Alvarez's office some time before. After hearing the conversation between Alvarez and his son from earlier in the day, Joon Min decided she had enough information, and it was time to act.

"Darling… It is wonderful to hear from you."

"Hi mom." Joon Min said to the Facetime image on her computer screen. If I gave you some possible contacts in our home country, would you be able to re-establish some connections? I have some information that I think they would be interested in hearing."

CHAPTER 4

Cementerio del Buceo
Montevideo, Uruguay
Present Day

Joon Min Kim had just found the third gravesite she was told to visit, and seeing the mark on the right side of the tombstone, she knew the meeting was still on, and she headed to the final grave. Arriving as instructed at the gravesite of Juan Carlos deSilva, she placed the flowers in front of the tombstone, then sat on the marble bench opposite the grave.

Despite all of the training her parents had given her, she never heard or saw the man now standing behind her until he spoke.

"It was a shame it took until now to re-establish contact with your mother." The ghost said in perfectly accented Spanish. "She and your father performed good work for us for many years before she succumbed to the lure of the capitalist pigs."

"My loyalty to the Supreme Leader and my country are surpassed only by my love for my mother." Joon Min said. "You will please refrain from speaking of her that way."

Sitting down on the bench facing the opposite direction with his hands tucked into his sportscoat, the man replied, "You would be wise in the future to not say such things to true patriots. Your love and loyalty to the Supreme Leader should surpass all, even your love of your family, hermana. I am surprised your father did not teach you that."

"What I was taught and what I believe are two different things."

"And what is it that you believe?" the man asked.

"I believe that right now you are wasting my time. You arranged for this meeting when I could have given you the tapes via a dead-drop. What is it that you want?"

"I wanted to meet you face-to-face." The man said without actually turning to look at her. "I wanted to get a better feel for the asset I might be working with. I need to know whether or not I can trust the intel you are delivering."

"I could have sold the information I collected, but instead we chose to give it to you." Joon Min said.

"Yes, I suppose you could have done that hermana… You could have sold it just like you have for the past eleven years. What I don't understand is why change now? Why has your Oekuk-saram mother decided now to stop whoring herself to western capitalist corporations and re-establish contact with us?"

Struggling to maintain her composure, Joon Min replied, "First off, my mother may not be native born to Korea, but you do not have the right to use derogatory slang to point that out. She and my father were loyal. It was you who left us out in the cold. Secondly, I warned you about insulting my family…". Standing up, Joon Min turned toward the man on the bench. "Thirdly…"

"Sit down Miss Kim." The man said without moving or even looking up. "You do not want to make a scene in such a public place, or didn't your whore mother teach you that either?"

"That's it. We're done here." Joon Min said as she prepared to turn and leave.

"I said sit down." The man demanded in a more ominous tone as he finally looked up at Joon Min and displayed a silenced pistol pointed at her. "You never asked me what my name was, hermanita"

Sitting down slowly, Joon Min kept her eyes trained on the gun. "Why do you keep calling me that? She said. "Hermana. Why do you keep calling me that?

"Because that is who you are, Miss Kim. My sister." The man replied. My name is Kim Joo-Won, and I am your half-brother. Your father, Kim Yoon Shin was a major in our intelligence service when he was chosen for a special mission as a deep cover operative in the United States. He was to be paired with an East German spy, your mother, and set up to work in the aerospace industry securing missile technology for our country. He left his wife and baby behind because, as I said before, we put The Supreme Leader and our country before all else. He was to remain in this role for no more than ten years, and then was to return home.

Then in 1994, with the fall of your mother's government, he was ordered home, but by this time your mother was already pregnant with you. He convinced his control officer that both he, and now your mother were still an effective team, and together, they could continue to deliver quality intelligence. His control officer agreed, and my father remained in America."

Finally turning his head and looking at Joon Min, Kim continued. "He abandoned me and my mother. It is one thing to do your duty for your country, but he chose you and your mother over us. My mother loved him. She mourned his death… She mourns for him still. So, to answer your initial question, I guess I also wanted to see what was so special to him that he abandoned his family."

With genuine compassion in her voice, Joon Min said, "I am so sorry. I had no idea."

"I am not looking for your pity, hermanita. I am looking for a reason to trust you and your mother."

"My mother never had the connections my father had. After his death, she continued to report to her control officer, and she provided some pretty damn good intel. But after the change in leadership, and the loss of her control officer, she had no good way to make contact… at least not without blowing her cover. So, we made the best of the situation and used what we knew to make a living.

Then when I learned what Alvarez and Aryphon were planning, I was able to figure out who Alvarez's North Korean contacts were and we used them to contact you. We came straight home once we knew how to do it. Now, you can either believe me and we work together, or you can kill me and put me in one of those open graves I know you and your men have already prepared. But if you choose that option, it had better be a pretty big hole, because I will be taking some of you with me." Joon Min moved her arm slightly revealing her own silenced pistol pointed at Kim.

Nodding his head, Kim switched from Spanish over to Korean. "I have to hand it to you little sister. If nothing else you have style and guts."

Responding in flawless Korean, Joon Min said, "Career decision time, big brother. Do you let personal feelings of hatred and envy derail what could be a major intelligence victory, or do we work together to collect the prize before they do?"

"Based on what your mother already told us, we have dispatched teams to Austria. One will begin searching the abandoned monasteries, and the other will begin searching and interrogating the monks in the monasteries still occupied. Your job is to let us know if your employer develops additional information that may narrow the search, and keep us appraised of the work their teams are doing. If they locate the plans first, we must be prepared to intercept those teams and secure the plans for ourselves."

"Are your teams any good?" Joon Min asked.

"Our people are trained to go up against the best from any imperialist nation. A few corporate security goons will be no problem."

"It's good to be in from the cold, hermano." Joon Min said switching back to Spanish.

Replying, this time in English, Kim said, "Welcome home comrade sister."

Tony Febbaccio came running in to the divisions offices and ran directly into John as he emerged from his office.

"Boss, I am glad I caught you." He said breathlessly.

"Tony, what is going on, what's the matter?" John asked.

"Not here, sir." Tony said gesturing towards John's office with his head. John turned back to his office removing the keys from his pocket and opening the door. As the door opened, Tony rushed in and moved in to the center of the room. "Were you headed to Pinochinio's office? He asked.

"Yeah," John replied with a quizzical look on his face. "Tony, what is going on?"

"Two things, boss. Pasquale grabbed me first thing this morning. He said his sister-in-law, the one who works in personnel, said that our new part time admin girl is a spy. She is Pinocchio's cousin and she reports back to him every day she works."

"I kinda figured that out for myself." John replied. "No one could be as stupid or screw up as much as her. She messes up everything she touches and requires me to re-do all her work myself. I think she is hoping I fly off the handle on her, and she will then report me to HR."

"So, about that. Not only is she trying to do that, but Pasquale got word from his sister-in-law, who heard it from one of the other division's admins that Pinocchio is really going to stick it to you in the hopes you will do something that can be considered insubordinate. That is why I ran down here. I needed to catch you before you headed up."

John stepped forward and embraced his second in command. "Tony, you are the best. I could never have been able to do this job without you. Thank you for everything you've done, and continue to do."

"Sir, I have learned so much from you. You are the best boss anyone could ask for."

"OK, well enough of this lovefest. I gotta get up to Pinocchio. I'll make sure to keep my cool. He's not getting rid of me that easily."

After sitting outside Pinochinio's office for nearly an hour, John was finally allowed in to meet with the head of the Gendarmerie.

"Director General Nowalski, is this what you try to pass off as a detailed update?" Inspector General Pinochinio said waving around several sheets of paper.

Having been prepared with Tony's information, John made sure to keep his tone level, and his answers respectful. Still, he couldn't resist the opportunity to jerk his boss's chain just a bit.

"Sir, I don't know what it is you have in your hands. The reports I send you are sent in a digital format so those papers are..."

"Do not get cute with me Nowalski." Pinochinio snarled, cutting John off. Throwing the printed pages at his subordinate he continued. "You know very well those are the printed copies of your last report... the report from yesterday, I might add. I asked for you to give me a detailed daily report, first thing in the morning, yet here it is..." Pinochinio looked at his watch "...nine AM and I still do not have today's report. Could you explain to me why I do not have today's report yet?"

"Sir, as talented and efficient as I am, I am unable to be in two places at the same time. If I am summoned to your office first thing in the morning, and then spend nearly an hour waiting for you to become available, I am unable to be in my office compiling the information necessary to prepare your report."

Smirking as he formulated his response, Pinochinio said, "Then perhaps you should arrive to work earlier in anticipation of my potential need to see you before nine AM in the morning"

Sighing in exasperation, John struggled to maintain his composure and responded "Yes sir."

"And that report from yesterday… You call that complete and detailed? It did not tell me anything."

"Sir, thankfully, there was not much going on yesterday."

"According to what you told myself and Cardinal Sentille, Director General, there are always things going on. Did you not say that bad actors are always looking to do harm to our beloved Church? That was the argument you made when we told you about our plan to dissolve your division."

"Yes sir, I did say that."

Smirking again as he saw that he had John clearly on the defensive, Pinochinio said, "Then were you lying to me and the Cardinal when you said that, or are you lying now to cover up your dereliction of duty… Your inability to properly execute your orders."

Seeing the logic corner Pinochinio had just painted him into, John took a deep breath, and exhaled slowly before answering. "I have never lied to you nor the Cardinal sir. I meant what I said back then, and I still believe it. As for being derelict in my duties, I can only report on what I see. I stand by what I report and categorically deny that I am derelict in my duty. If you are planning to file a formal review of my performance, please let me know so I can prepare the required documentation to support my dispute of your assessment."

Glaring at Nowalski, Pinochinio moved back behind his desk and opened the report file that John had sent the day before, then decided to try a different approach.

"Director General, in your report you mention a number of monasteries that have recently been vandalized. A number of them are no longer owned by the Church, they are tourist attractions and one is even a…" he scrolled through the report "…a brewery. I do not see the relevance or the potential threat to the Church. Can you explain what you were thinking?"

Forcing back another sigh of exasperation, and concentrating on not rolling his eyes, John replied. "The vandalisms go to a pattern. While they may no longer be part of the Church, they once were, and since it doesn't appear to be an isolated incident, I wanted to explore the full extent of these acts. Over the last week, there have been sixteen."

"So, who is committing these crimes?" Pinochinio asked.

"I do not know sir."

"Director General, do you not think it is your job to know these things. If you feel this is a threat, you should not just report the crimes, but you should determine who is committing them and put a stop to them."

"Yessir. I am working on it."

"Well since the rest of your report is just some

innocuous information about things in the middle east, I would expect you to be able devote your attention to this matter and get some results."

"Yessir. I will get right on it." John replied.

The two men stared at each other in silence, each waiting for the other to make the next move. Finally, John asked, "Will there be anything else sir?"

"No. You are dismissed." Pinochinio said waving his hand as if shooing a fly. "But I expect to see today's report in my in-box within the hour, and there needs to be an update on these vandalism cases. I expect results Director General." John left the office wondering if it might just be easier to slay the Nemean Lion or steal the Golden Fleece.

Mary Morrison had never flown on a private jet before. As she and her team climbed the stairs leading into the tastefully decorated cabin, she wondered if she had packed enough clothing and toiletries for the upcoming trip. It was less than three hours earlier that she had received the phone call from William Alvarez directing her to return home, grab her passport, and pack for at least a two-week trip to Rome. She would have one hour to pack before she was scheduled to be picked up from her apartment and driven to the airport. During the intervening time she was not to discuss this with anyone outside her team. Now boarding the company jet, in addition to her packing concerns, Mary wondered what new research tasks lay ahead.

Once airborne, a flight attendant approached Mary with a manila envelope and handed it to her. Opening the envelope, Mary saw there were instructions from Alvarez on what they would be doing once they arrived in Rome. They would be met at the airport by a representative from the Vatican who would escort them first to their hotel, where they would drop off their luggage, then on to Vatican City where they would be given access to files and records from the second World War.

Mary was informed that a Cardinal had pulled some pretty hefty strings to be able to secure her team unfettered access to the files and records needed to continue their research, and that everything was strictly confidential. While scholars and historians had actually been allowed access to the Vatican Secret Archives since the early 1800's, certain records, particularly those relating to church personnel after 1922 remain classified. If Mary were to be able to uncover any information regarding Peter Wagner's brother, it would most likely be found in these classified records.

After seeing that Mary had returned the instructions to the envelope, the flight attendant approached Mary and asked if she wanted a drink before dinner. Having previously only flown on commercial flights, and then only having been able to afford coach, Mary was surprised by the question and asked what kind of drink could she have, and what was on the menu for dinner. To the delight of herself and her team, the dinner choices consisted of three different gourmet meals, previously prepared and loaded into the plane's galley. Additionally, the galley had a fully stocked bar.

After Mary finished a rather delicious meal and two potent cocktails, the cabin lights were dimmed and the flight attendant came around to show the passengers how their leather seats could recline and become rather comfortable full beds. The flight attendant advised the team that the eight-hour flight directly into Leonardo da Vinci International Airport would have them arriving around Eight AM local time, and they would be expected to begin their work immediately, so it would be a good idea to try to get a few hours of sleep.

While initially believing she was too excited to sleep, Mary found that the combination of the wonderful meal, strong cocktails and comfortable bed soon had her yawning. As Mary dozed off to sleep, her mind was filled with visions of the scores of books, scrolls and documents she was about to see. Smiling to herself as she drifted off she thought she truly had a dream job.

The air in the unmarked patrol car was thick with the smell of spilled Mexican food, cigarette smoke and coffee breath. Unwilling to run the engine, thus allowing the vehicles air conditioning to both cool and filter the stale air, Adam sat with another detective outside a suspected burglary suspect's home.

The department had received a tip that a known fence who also operated a legitimate pawn shop two towns over was coming to meet the burglary suspect to possibly view some of the merchandise. The fence was known to never conduct business in his shop so that his security surveillance systems were always clean of him purchasing any stolen items. Since Adam and his partner didn't have enough evidence to get a search warrant, they needed to actually catch the suspect with at least some of the stolen merchandise.

Unsure where the stolen goods were being stored, Adam parked the car several houses away but still close enough to observe if someone came or left the building.

Drumming his fingers on the dashboard, Adam beat out the rhythm to the song running through his head. As his partner for the evening, Detective Steve Tortorice reached for the pack of cigarettes sitting on the dashboard, Adam looked over and said, "Do you have to light up another one? I mean, the air is fucking thick enough in here and you just freakin' finished one."

Looking over at his supervisor, Tortorice said, "Well excuse me if you find my habit so fucking offensive." As he threw the half empty pack back on the dashboard.

"I mean it's hot as balls in here already, even with the windows open, Steve. Every time you light one up I can't fuckin' breathe."

"Alright, alright, I'm sorry." Tortorice replied. After a minute of silence, he said, "Can you believe this summer? I think it's the hottest one we've had in years."

"I know. All you hear about on the TV or radio is how hot it's been and global warming. Global warming, global warming. They always gotta make a big disaster outta something. Yeah, it's fuckin' hot. But last winter, it was fuckin' cold. Adam said.

"They say that was because of global warming too."

Adam shook his head. "That doesn't make any sense. How can global warming cause cold winters? It either gets too hot, or it doesn't."

"So, you don't believe global warming is a real thing?" Tortorice asked.

"No, I do. The hole in the ozone is real. But I think

politicians with their hands in the pockets of special interests are exaggerating and exploiting it for financial and political gain. If you wanna see where things are headed, you gotta follow the money."

"Not that I don't agree with you Sarge, but that's a rather cynical point of view."

"It's merely an observation of the world we live in, Steve-o."

Picking up the night vision binoculars from the center console, Adam scanned the street and the suspect's house. Setting the binoculars back down, he let out a long sigh.

"Anything?" Tortorice asked.

"Nah. Nothing. But it's still early." Adam replied.

The two men sat in silence for a while, watching the house and contemplating their thoughts. Tortorice reached for his cigarettes again, but caught a look from Adam out of the corner of his eye and decided to forego the smoke. A car drove past the stakeout vehicle and house, and Tortorice grabbed the camera with the night vision lens and snapped several pictures, making sure to capture the license plate. After the car turned the corner, he called the plate in to dispatch.

"So how did you do on the lieutenant's test?" Tortorice asked.

"I think I did OK. I only have to score better than Lucas. Francone doesn't have barely enough time on the job, so unless I bombed, I don't have to worry about him."

"It would suck if Lucas got the job. He has no experience in investigations. He's spent his whole career in patrol." Tortorice said.

"Yeah, but he's a bit of an arrogant prick. He thinks

he's super-cop and can fix things…" Adam said making air quotes, "… in the detective's division."

"It would really suck for you, Sarge. Everyone knows there is no love lost between you two."

"We came up together. He always looked at our relationship as a competition rather than a collaboration. He outscored me on the Sargent's exam, and got that opening in patrol. I moved over to detectives and then got the supervisor spot when Mercer retired. Now any time there is significant interaction between our divisions he always gives me shit about it. He says the detective division couldn't find their own asses with both hands and a road map."

"Yeah, he's a dick…" Tortorice opined.

"Yeah, well hopefully he dicked himself, this time on the test. He was signed up for the review class with me but never showed up, and I heard he rarely attended the study group."

"Well he's got that hot new girlfriend that I hear has been taking up a whole bunch of his time… and money." Tortorice said. "They went away to some all-inclusive down in the Caribbean, and then like a month later they spent a week up in the Finger Lakes doing wine tours."

Chuckling and shaking his head, Adam replied, "Someone once told me when it comes to women, you will always have to pay one way or another to get your dick sucked."

"Speaking of which, I haven't seen or heard of you spending much time with any female companionship, Sarge."

"Yeah, me and Faith broke up a few weeks ago. She said our relationship was… how did she put it?… on auto-pilot and that I was boring."

"Wow, that sucks." Tortorice said.

"I know." replied Adam. "But you know what Steve-O, I think she was right. I was boring. I mean look I was raised in an ultra-orthodox family where you didn't mingle with kids of the opposite sex. I didn't really date in high school, and from my senior year on, I was told that my marriage was already arranged and that once I finished college, I would be married to a girl my parents picked out for me. So, my experience with women is somewhat limited. And then, when my college girlfriend broke my heart I guess I just, I don't know, threw up this wall. Now, whenever I go out on dates I guess I keep the girls at arms-length. I don't know how to let them get close and I don't know how to avoid having my heart broken."

"Wow Sarge. Did you figure that shit out yourself or did your therapist tell you all that?" Tortorice quipped.

"OK wiseass." Adam replied. "I open up a little bit to you and this is the shit I get. Fine."

"No Sarge… I get it. I'm just bustin'. I mean, I don't think you're boring.

"Yeah, but I'm not looking to go out with you, Steve. You're not quite my type." Letting out a long sigh, Adam adjusted himself in the car seat, then said, "No actually, boring has become my middle name. I mean look at us here. It's a Friday evening… we're sitting in front of this dirt bags house waiting for shit to happen… I mean 99% of everything we do is just routine boring crap."

"What, like you want to be shot at or something? Tortorice asked.

"No that's not what I mean." Adam replied. "But I don't know… Working more interesting cases than nailing some stupid burglar and his fence. Shit, I mean, I just wish once in a while, we would get something that… You know, something that makes a bit of a difference."

"You know Adam I used to think like that too. And then my first supervisor, Sergeant Franks told me that we do make a difference every time we return a woman's wedding or engagement ring… Every time, we find a bicycle that was stolen from some little kid… Every time we put some scumbag drug dealer behind bars we're making a world of difference. At least to the people whose lives have been affected… The people who have suffered the trauma or had their lives violated. They deserve the closure we bring. They deserve justice.

Nodding his head Adam replied, "Yeah I guess you're right, Steve-O. Maybe my outlook will change if I make Lieutenant. My responsibilities will be different and it'll give me that variety that I might be looking for."

"Be careful what you wish for, Sarge. What you may call variety today, you'll be calling a headache tomorrow… Hey, is that motion down there by the house?"

Adam picked up the binoculars and looked through them in time to see a solitary figure turn off of the sidewalk and head up to the suspects house.

"Well, it looks like our friend might have some company." Adam said. "Let's give them a few minutes and then see if we can come up with anything. I'll stroll past the house while you stay here in case they leave to head to where the stuff is stashed. Stay on the radio. I'll call if I need anything. Remember, since we couldn't get a search warrant we need to have probable cause."

"Copy that." Tortorice replied.

After several minutes, Adam opened the car door. "I'm gonna head down that way and see if I can see anything."

Walking casually down the sidewalk toward the house, Adam heard the sound of two men's voices as he got closer. Walking past the front door, Adam saw the house remained dark, but the voices were clearly coming from outside the house, by the driveway. As he reached the end of the driveway, Adam saw the suspect and the fence, standing outside in front of an open garage door. Inside, illuminated by the garage's interior light and in plain sight was a garage full of stolen goods.

Surreptitiously bringing his radio to his mouth, Adam quietly called to Tortorice for back-up. Walking toward the garage, he casually called out to the two men, "Good Evening…"

"Who the fuck are you?" the taller of the two replied.

"I wonder if you guys could help me?" Adam said in a polite tone as he continued down the driveway toward the garage.

"You need to get the fuck out of here." The taller man said, now squaring off to face Adam as he approached.

"OK, OK…" Adam said holding his hands out in front of himself and gesturing for the man to calm down. "You live here?" Adam asked nodding his head in the direction of the taller man.

"Yeah, what's it to ya? I told you, you need to get the fuck out of here, NOW." The man replied in a more menacing tone.

"OK, I heard you, but first I need to ask you…Did you really think you could get away with stealing all this shit?"

The realization that Adam was a cop and they were in

trouble came a split second before Tortorice came racing up the driveway in the unmarked stakeout vehicle, red teardrop, grille strobes and high-beam lights flashing. Effectively blinded, the two men instinctively stepped backward and shielded their eyes. By the time they were able to re-focus, both Adam and Tortorice had their weapons drawn and pointed at the suspects, and Adam was commanding them to get down on the ground with their hands above their heads.

With both suspects safely in custody, Adam turned to Tortorice and said, "So, I'll flip you for who goes back and starts the paperwork on these two idiots."

"You're senior officer, Sarge. I'll do the paper work. You go home."

"You misunderstand me, Steve-O. Winner doesn't go home." Turning toward the garage with a sweeping motion he continued. "Loser gets to stay here and inventory all this shit."

Shaking his head at the sight of a garage full of stolen goods, Tortorice replied, "Looks like it's gonna be a long boring night for both of us, Sarge."

Adam replied, "Yeah… Like I said. Boring is my middle name."

CHAPTER 5

**Residence of the Under-Secretary of State
Vatican City, Rome
Present Day**

THE PRIVATE APARTMENT residence of the Cardinal Undersecretary of State was the very definition of opulence. Not that Cardinal Dietrich had any more lavish a residence than any of the other two hundred and twenty-one prelates. However, compared to most of the other lay and clergy employees of the Holy See, the homes of the Princes of the Church were exceptionally impressive.

Having been invited into the sitting room, John sat on one of the two French Provincial couches awaiting his host's return from the kitchen. Moments later, Cardinal Dietrich emerged from the hallway with a mug of hot tea in his hand, and as John went to stand, he gestured for John to remain seated.

"I want to thank you for seeing me Your Grace. I needed to speak to someone and get some advice." John said.

"What can I help you with, old friend." Replied Dietrich.

Getting up from the couch, John began to pace around the room.

"I think I'm at a crossroads in my life. I am being set up for failure by Pinochinio, and I believe Sentille supports this. They keep demanding more and more oversight to the point that I am buried in reporting requirements. Pinochinio regularly questions the content of my reports, saying I am raising too many alarms when I note things that are happening, and questioning the thoroughness of the reports if they are not chock full. Then every day, I am called to his office to review these reports…" John said putting air quotes around the last part. "…where I sit for at least an hour waiting for him to be available so he can berate me for like another hour. Like I actually have the time to just sit there not being productive. They have been slowly taking my resources away so that I am at a point where I am doing the work of five people just to keep my head above water."

As John continued his monologue, pacing around the Cardinal's sitting room he began speaking faster and faster as well as gesturing with his hands.

"And yet he expects me to maintain complete operational effectiveness. It's impossible for three individuals to operate effectively when the tasks require the work of a dozen. Then yesterday, I get called to Pinocci… Pinochinio's office and he begins saying I'm derelict in my duties. That's what this whole thing is about. They want to either get me to fly off on someone and be insubordinate or mess up and then they will claim I'm derelict in my duties.

Eminence, I'm at a loss. I don't see how I'm going to win this one."

"John, first of all, please sit down." The Cardinal said. "I am nervous that you are going to have a heart attack with all your gesturing and pacing."

As John took a seat on the couch again, the Cardinal continued. "I need not remind you of my warning the last time we spoke. This place invented bureaucracy and perfected the cut-throat politics that go with it. You are now paying the price for taking a position some considered above your station, and then having the audacity of actually being good at it. Had you failed, all of your nay-sayers would have been right, and you would have been quietly removed without malice. But by being as effective as you were, you upstaged the life-long bureaucrats and they cannot suffer their own misjudgment. Hence, you will be made to fail, and your failure will be highlighted in the most spectacular fashion."

John weighed what the Cardinal just said, layering it in with his own assessment and possible options. Looking over at the Cardinal he said, "So you are saying I have no hope and I should just quit."

"I am saying John that you have no way to win in this situation. Quitting denotes giving up and allowing them to do whatever they want. I think you still may have options that remove you from this no-win situation, yet give you a semblance of control."

The Cardinal took a sip from his tea and thought for a moment before speaking. "John, I will never be Pope. I do not have the right political connections, nor do I have the necessary pedigree. I am not Italian, and none of my political capital comes from the real ruling class of the Holy See. I was elevated to Prelate by Pope Gregory, and while his very elevation to Pope was the perfect political expedience for that time, he far outlasted what the powers that be thought was his usefulness. And then, to top it off, he enacted a whole slew of changes they are still working to reverse.

No John, I comprehend that I was groomed from the start of my career to be a worker bee. Like so many worker bees, it was expected that I would rise to the level of my incompetence, but never achieve greatness. And it was never expected that I would achieve what I have. So, like you, I am living above my station. However, unlike you, I have not been a superstar. I do my job. I do it correctly and with efficiency. But I make it a point to not stand out. I do not draw attention to myself nor my department. I remain to most observers, a worker bee. I may be a very lucky and highly placed worker bee, but a worker bee nonetheless.

John, my true political power comes from what is not seen. It comes from the quiet deals I make behind the scenes. It comes from the alliances I've made and the assistance I've given over the years that now in turn, allow me to better do my job. And while these all elevate me well above the status of worker bee, my appearance will always be the happy little member of the hive."

John was a bit shocked by what Dietrich had just told him, but the admission of how he managed the politics of the Holy See gave John perspective on the inner workings of the world's oldest bureaucracy. Despite this insight, he still was unsure how to manage his current problem.

John said in reply, "Your Eminence, I am a bit surprised

by what you just told me, but looking at it in light of what has happened to me, I can see how your strategy could be…"

"Beneficial?" The Cardinal said cutting John off. "It is more than beneficial my old friend, it is essential."

John said, "OK. But I still don't see how knowing this now will help me in my current situation. I have proceeded over the last twenty-some-odd years believing that superior performance, and giving my men credit for that performance was the way to go. Changing gears now won't do me any good. I still don't know what to do."

"John, I believe your days here are limited, and you are right in your assessment that there is not much you can do to change that now. Your thoughts now must focus on where do you go next and what do you do. Do you return to the monastic life? Can you quietly accept a lesser role in the Gendarmerie? Are there other paths for you to follow? You want that choice to be yours, not one that is forced upon you. To achieve that, you must try to think what would a worker bee do. If the hive wants you to feel defeated, you must act like you are defeated, all the while, working behind the scenes to plan your escape. You must use your connections and rely on your reputation. Allow the work you have done in the past to bear you fruit now. Then, when the moment is right, you leave, but on your terms, not theirs. Remember, they want to destroy you, and they will not stop until that is fully accomplished. But if you act defeated, they will slow down the process because they will want to bask in your misery. And that will give you time to find your way out."

"Eminence, this whole thing sounds incredibly Machiavellian."

Dietrich replied, "My old friend, why are you so surprised? If you remember your history, the Medici family ruled most of Italy for over three hundred years, except for a period from 1494 until 1512. Then, in 1512, Giovanni de Medici re-conquered the Florentine Republic, which happened to be Machiavelli's home. The following year Giovanni became Pope Leo X and Machiavelli wrote *The Prince*. Based on Machiavelli's position in Florentine politics, which now seems interlaced with the Vatican, I'd say that is too much of a coincidence for the two to not be related, wouldn't you?"

The black clad figures entered the ancient stone building by silently opening one of the first-floor windows. While some medieval monasteries were more fortress than friary, the monastery in Bludenz was primarily a four-story building that looked more like a church with dormitory wings attached than the castle-like structures seen throughout central Europe.

Immediately heading to the sleeping quarters, the six-man team moved with practiced precision, sweeping for threats and providing cover despite the obvious lack of combatants at this target.

Arriving outside the sleeping quarters, the team split into two groups, each group taking one side of the hallway. With two men entering the room and the third man remaining outside, the teams made short work of gagging and binding the hands of the sleeping occupants with zip-ties, then dragging them out to be unceremoniously deposited on the hard, slate floor of the hallway.

With all seven of the monastery's occupants lying bound and gagged outside their bedrooms, the team leader was finally confronted with the surprising fact that all seven of their prisoners were not monks, but nuns. While this probably would impact the ultimate results of his team's mission, the process still needed to be followed nonetheless.

"Who is the head nun?" the team leader asked in poorly pronounced German. "Who is in charge here?"

The heads of several of the whimpering women turned to look at the Mother Superior, now sitting upright with her back against the wall.

"Who is in charge here?" the team leader demanded again in an even louder voice.

The older woman the others looked at was struggling to say something through the gag. Walking over to her, the leader removed the gag from her mouth. "I am Mother Mary Elizabeth." The woman said.

As one of the soldiers brought a chair out from one of the bedrooms, two other men grabbed the Mother Superior under the arms and irreverently sat her in the chair. Cutting the zip-ties, they then bound her arms and legs to the arms and legs of the chair. Drawing a knife from its sheath on his ankle, the team leader brought his face menacingly close to the woman's and placed the tip of his knife under her chin so she was forced to look into his eyes.

"Wo sind die Pläne für das Grosse Licht? The Big Light… Where is it?" he repeated in poorly pronounced German.

The team leader could tell almost instantly when the woman's face went from displaying terror to confusion that these interrogations would be fruitless. However, the parameters of his mission dictated he move forward.

"Where are the plans for the Big Light?" he yelled at the older nun, then slapped her backhanded across the face.

As her right cheek began to swell, the nun managed to squeak out that she had no idea what the man was talking about, which was immediately met with a punch to her face splitting her lip as the team leader yelled "LIAR."

"Perhaps you would be more forthcoming if it would protect one of your flock." The man said as he turned away and pointed to one of the women sitting on the floor.

Dragging the chosen nun by her hair to a chair placed in front of the Mother Superior, two of the team sat and bound her to the chair in the same fashion as the older nun. Before the two team members could leave, the leader leaned in to the closer man. "Leave me two to help here. The rest of you begin tearing this place apart and see if you can find anything. Use the GPR equipment. I highly doubt these women know anything, but we need to be thorough."

"Yes sir." The other man replied as he turned to leave.

Now turning his attention to the younger nun bound to the chair in front of him, the team leader took his knife and opened a six-inch gash across the woman's inner thigh. Letting out a shriek of horror and pain, the younger nun began to sob uncontrollably.

Turning back to the Mother Superior, the team leader said, "You can stop this. Just tell me where the plans for the Big Light are."

Between sobs of her own, and through swollen lips the older nun said, "I swear... I don't know what you are talking about."

"Wrong answer." The team leader said, and withdrawing his silenced pistol, he shot the young nun between the eyes.

As the two remaining men removed the dead nun from the chair and replaced her with another, the team leader again placed his face in front of the Mother Superior and asked so softly he almost whispered it. "Where are the plans for the Big Light?"

Hanging her head with tears streaming down her face, the Mother Superior said, "Please… I don't know what you are talking about."

Leaning in close to the woman's ear, the team leader whispered, "I know you don't, sister, but I still have to do this just to be sure."

Four hours later, with the pre-dawn light just cresting the mountains to the east, the six-man team was climbing back into the black cargo van parked off the road a quarter mile from the monastery. With the building in shambles from the search and the bodies of the seven nuns strewn across the floor outside the dorm rooms, the team left without their prize or any additional clues where it could be hidden, save for the fact that one more monastery could be crossed off the list.

Headquarters, Gendarmerie Corps of Vatican City State
Vatican City, Rome
Present Day

John was actually surprised that he was directed in to the office of Inspector General Pinochinio without having to suffer the usual hour long wait. Upon seeing the two other divisional Directors General there, John understood that Pinochinio did not want to waste his other officer's time. Standing to the left of Pinochinio's desk was Aldo Costanza, chief of the patrol division, and to the right, Director General of Administration Stephan DiClemente.

Coming to attention, John saluted his superior officer and was again greeted with Pinochinio waving papers he held in his hand at him.

"What is this, Nowalski? Again, is this what you try to pass off as a detailed report?"

Assuming the pages were the report he had distributed to Pinochinio, the Gendarmerie leadership and key members of the Holy See at three AM that morning, John replied, "It is an Interim Emergency Action Report, sir."

Still waving the pages around, Pinochinio said, "And why is it so lacking in information?"

"Sir, because…" John began to answer, then realized that in all the years of sharing these reports, Pinochinio had never actually read one before. But now that he was pouring over every action John was taking as he looked to find fault, he actually read this one.

"… because this is still a developing situation. We only became aware of it around midnight."

Pinochinio placed the papers down on his desk, then placed his balled fists on the desk and leaned over it as menacingly as he could toward John and said, "And how could this happen Director General? How could two of our places of worship be attacked on the same day without your knowledge?"

"Sir?" John asked questioningly.

"Are you hard of hearing? How could ten of our brothers and sisters be tortured and murdered on the same day, when you knew that monasteries were being targeted and viciously vandalized. And do you even have the slightest clue who is responsible?"

"Sir, to clarify, these two attacks did not occur on the same day. The monks were killed first, but because of their cloistered nature and fairly remote location, they were not discovered until yesterday. The nuns frequently hosted meditative retreats and welcomed tourists and guests, so their bodies were found yesterday morning.

And to answer your questions, there was no indication that the vandalism was in any way a precursor to physical violence. In fact, I believe you even initially said that the vandalism bore no threat on the Church. So, there was no way to forecast an escalation in violence based on what we had seen. As for your second question of who is responsible, sir, I do not have an answer to that, yet. This investigation just started. I have yet to go see the crime scenes, there is forensic evidence that I need to verify has been collected, I have to liaise with the Austrian authorities, check for potential witnesses and about a million other things before we can even begin to develop a suspect list."

"Well Director General, that is where you are wrong." Pinochinio began. "*You* will not be doing any of that. You are being relieved of your command, effective immediately and are charged with dereliction of duty. You were correct in saying I initially did not believe the vandalism was a threat to the Church, but if you remember, I changed my mind after *YOU* convinced me otherwise. I then gave you a direct order to identify and apprehend those perpetrators. An order that you have either chosen to ignore, or are too incompetent to follow. In either case, Director General DiClemente will now take over your administrative duties."

John looked over at DiClemente who was having difficulty hiding his obvious discomfort. While John believed DiClemente was a good guy overall, his long-time position in administration had left him lacking in many of the current practices of policing and investigations. His people had already assumed the role of staffing the Operations Centre, and despite Tony's best efforts at coaching, they struggled at best to manage the technology and the flow of information.

"Director General, I will convene a hearing board at the earliest possible date, but in the interim, you are officially suspended without pay and I must ask for your gun and your badge."

John suspected this would be what Pinochinio would do when he had received the message of the attacks last night. A situation like this was just what he was waiting for, so John was not at all surprised. But then, being the consummate professional, John began collecting data and working the case with Tony as he followed protocol and prepared the Emergency Action Report. When answering his superior's questions, John almost forgot where he knew this would go.

Silently handing over his gun and badge, John's brain shifted between this case and his present situation. He knew DiClemente was in over his head, and any chance of solving this lay in he and Tony getting the resources to follow where the leads took them. He thought that this move by Pinochinio was unfair not only to him, but the poor monks and nuns that were killed. They deserved justice, and this political move was robbing them of that chance.

John's mind then moved to his present situation. He believed he had a better than even chance of beating the dereliction of duty charges. Despite what Pinochinio stated, you cannot be derelict in your duty if you fail to follow an impossible order. Given the current circumstances, Pinochinio's order to identify and arrest these suspects in such a short time frame without the necessary resources pretty much qualified as an impossible order. Even if the Review Board was stacked against him, John felt the facts supported the assertions he would use in his defense. Pinochinio had been too heavy handed in how he managed John's situation overall.

But then John remembered what Dietrich had said. These people were masters of the political game. Pinochinio knew he was being heavy handed, and that he had issued impossible orders. If they wanted him gone, this was not their best play. So, what was... And then it hit him. Pinochinio said he would convene the Board "at the earliest convenience." In the meantime, John was suspended *without pay*. If Pinochinio dragged this out, how long could John go without a paycheck. He did not earn that much, despite his rank, and he tithed a full thirty percent to the Church. If he were to resign while suspended, he would forfeit his pension. John thought he would have to research the rules regarding all of this. How long could he be kept in limbo? Could he legally work elsewhere while on suspension? What legal rights did he have? John stood there silently in front of the three officers oblivious to the surroundings and fully inside his own head.

"...said you are dismissed! Nowalski, are you there? You are free to go." Pinochinio was nearly shouting at John.

Snapping back to the present, John said, "Thank you sir." and turned to leave.

Pinochinio called after him, "John, don't leave town or anything like that. We may need to get in touch or have questions for you."

"Sir, if you have any questions or other concerns, you can either voice them at the review board hearing, or reinstate me. Otherwise,... you can go..." John paused and looked at the other two men standing there, shocked expressions growing on their faces, and decided to show how a true professional behaved. "... to your remaining division heads for answers. Enjoy your day, gentlemen."

The Aryphon private jet taxied to a secure private hanger in the southwest corner of the airport. As the jet's stairs came down, a black limousine pulled up to within a dozen feet of the plane. An attendant got out of the front passenger seat and held the door open as Hermann Alvarez stepped from the jet to the waiting car.

Ignoring the outstretched hand with the Ecclesiastical ring, Alvarez said, "You said this was urgent. I certainly hope it is good news about the research being conducted in your archives. I have important business in Dubai for which I cannot be late, and a stop in Italy impacts my schedule."

The Cardinal shifted in his seat so he could better see and address his companion. "So, did you think that offering me a seat on the Board would buy you cover from your atrocities? I will not be used as one of your other lackeys or minions. I am a Prince of the Church and you will show me the respect due my office."

Annoyed, and believing the Cardinal was speaking only of Alvarez's failure to kiss the Cardinal's ring, he said, "I don't have time for this." Performing a mock bow, he continued, "If this was just to show me how big your ecclesiastical balls are, then fine… Yes, your Eminence…" he said in a mocking sarcastic tone… "Your balls are big and hairy. Now you can either try to keep wasting my time, or tell me what it is that was so imperative that I needed to divert my…"

"Why did you kill those nuns?" the Cardinal interrupted.

"What?… What are you talking about? What nuns?"

"The nuns in Bludenz. It was bad enough killing the four Capuchin monks in Imst, but that monastery fit the description and I understand the importance of finding these plans. But there was no way those nuns could have had any knowledge of where the plans were hidden, yet they too were tortured and killed."

Alvarez paused for a moment, then pulled out his phone and pressed a number on his speed-dial. "How many active monasteries have been interrogated? He asked when the other party answered. "You sure? Nothing in Bludenz? OK. It would appear we have other teams in the field. Yes. Let our teams know. I will advise you when I have more information."

Hanging up the phone, Alvarez turned to the Cardinal and said, "It would appear we have other players interested in our prize. We did not hit Bludenz. I just confirmed it. Thank you for letting me know."

Not expecting this information, the Cardinal said with a surprised expression on his face, "So, that's it? If we didn't do it, then who did?"

"That, I do not know, your Eminence. But I think it best if we work together to figure it all out, and find our Big Light, rather than cast aspersions and accusations. This news only heightens our need to quickly gather more intelligence and locate where those plans are hidden. I would hope you see this need as well and are committed to assisting in any way you can."

"Yes, of course." The Cardinal replied.

"Good." Alvarez said, then lowering his voice he continued. "Because further outbursts like the one you just demonstrated are counterproductive and will not be tolerated. I understand and appreciate your current position in the Church, and I do respect it. If not for that and our shared worldview, I would not have offered you a seat at the table. Eminence, we are changing the world. Together, we can make that happen faster. All that being said…" Alvarez's eyes bore into the Cardinal with malignant intensity and his voice grew harsh and clipped. "…you will *NEVER* speak to me like that again, and you *WILL* address *me* with the respect I deserve."

Alvarez continued, "Cardinal, you come from a strong family… a solid bloodline and fine heritage. You would be one of the few Board members selected from outside of Aryphon's founding families. It would be a shame if your insolence brought not only shame, but harm to your family. Do we understand each other?"

Nodding his head while trying to suppress the look of shock and fear, the Cardinal replied. "Yes… Yes, I… I clearly understand."

Smiling like a shark right before he sinks his teeth into you, Alvarez said, "Good. Now go see if you can help uncover some information that will allow us to identify who else is looking for those plans, or better yet, find out where they are hidden."

CHAPTER 6

**Headquarters, Gendarmerie Corps
of Vatican City State
Vatican City, Rome
Present Day**

Two weeks after his suspension, John received the phone call from Director General DiClemente that his presence was requested in Pinochinio's office at nine AM the next morning. When he asked DiClemente if this was his disciplinary hearing, and was told it was not, John was very tempted to tell his replacement that he would not be attending, and any future requests be funneled through his attorney. However, since he did not actually have an attorney, he did not think it wise to be antagonistic. And, despite being more of a bureaucrat than a police officer, DiClemente was never anything but professional in his dealings with John, so he had no real cause to snap at his former colleague.

John's problems were with his boss and the petty behavior displayed by members of the Holy See. While he wanted nothing more than to have things return to the way they were, he was swiftly coming to fully understand that those times were behind him and any attempt to return to the way things were, was simply an exercise in futility. In the days since his suspension, John came to terms with the fact that he needed to do whatever possible to protect his reputation and figure out the best way to prepare for his new future.

Arriving at Pinochinio's office right before nine AM in his best suit and freshly pressed and starched white shirt, John was surprised when he was ushered into Pinochinio's private office immediately. The immediate admittance gave John a moment's pause since the last time he was brought right in he was given his walking papers. Seated around the room were not only Pinochinio, but DiClemente, Costanza and Cardinal Sentille. While still technically an employee of the Gendarmerie, John was no longer receiving a paycheck, had no official position within the Corps, and had no powers of arrest. His days of even technically being employed were limited only by Pinochinio's desire to string John along and make him suffer by waiting. Acknowledging this reality, John embraced a different perspective to govern his interactions with the men currently in the room.

"So, you dragged me away from another scintillating morning of early daytime TV. What is it you want." John asked.

"The monastery case has taken on additional significance. In addition to being on the national news in Austria, it is getting play across the globe." DiClemente replied. "The Holy Father has asked us to make this a priority and bring it to a resolution as quickly as possible."

John smiled to himself, first at the answer, then at who

actually responded. DiClemente was in over his head, and clearly, not only did he know it, but the others in the room recognized it as well. Secondly, Pinochinio was still trying to play power politics and would only speak if absolutely necessary. Whatever request for help they were about to ask for would come from an underling and not the Inspector General or the Cardinal. If they were to make the request they would be lowering themselves to John's level.

"So, it looks like you have your work cut out for you Stephan." John replied.

DiClemente continued, "Yes, well,... you have been summoned here today because, well, as a good Catholic, the Holy See would like you to lend your services to the Corps to support the Holy Father's wishes for a speedy resolution to this case."

"By lend my services you would mean...?"

"Myself and my team would grant you access to the information we develop, and you can give me recommendations on how best to proceed." DiClemente replied.

"So I would be assisting solely on a consulting basis?" John asked.

"Yes." DiClemente answered, then taking a deep breath continued, "It is his Holy Father's hope that you would agree to volunteer your services in support of our Holy Church."

A bit shocked, and then actually amused by the request, John started laughing.

"You know, Stephan...I thought at first old Pinocchio there was playing a power game by having you address me, rather than he do it himself." John began nodding his head in his old bosses' direction and purposely using the derogatory nickname. "But now I see I was mistaken. It's not a power play at all. He simply does not have the balls to present such an audacious request himself."

"John, I must…" DiClemente began before John cut him off waving his hand.

"No, no… It's OK Stephan. Save your breath. I refuse to waste any more of my time standing in this room and being insulted. I had to do it when I worked for him…" John said waving a hand in the direction of Pinochinio, "…but he made it abundantly clear that he was changing that." Looking over to Pinochinio and Sentille, he continued. "You gentlemen either have the biggest set of balls this side of the Atlantic or the biggest case of entitlement that I have ever seen. First you treat me and my team like shit, then you set me up for failure by giving me unachievable goals. Then when I fail to reach those goals, you fire me and now, when you realize that you can't do what my team and I did, you invoke a papal decree and tell me I need to volunteer my services? You guys are fucked in the head, and right now, I have no duty or obligation to play these games, so I'm leaving."

John turned and began walking toward the door, ignoring DiClemente's sputtering protests. He had gotten about four steps away when he heard Sentille say, "Director General Nowalski, please,… stop. Let us try this again."

"Eminence, You can't address me in that manner. I don't hold that title any longer." John said in reply.

"I know John. And we can rectify that immediately." The Cardinal said.

Pinochinio started, "Eminence, before we go down this road perhaps you and I should confer and…"

"No Inspector General! I knew he would never go for your plan."

Pinochinio said, "But my team can still resolve this. They just need a little more time. Going this route is a mistake that…"

"ENOUGH." Sentille shouted. "We tried it your way, and the results are the same as those we are seeing from your people's investigation." Turning back to John, the Cardinal continued. "John, please.. Come back and sit down. You are right. That was insulting, and I apologize. We do need your assistance and need for you to return to work."

"In what capacity, your Eminence?" John asked.

"In your former capacity, of course. We will reinstate you immediately to your former rank and command. All disciplinary charges will be dropped, and we will even get you your back pay for the days you have been on hiatus. We need you to get started on this case immediately. The Holy Father fears there may be more attacks, and the sooner we learn who is perpetrating these horrors, the sooner they will stop."

John had walked back toward Pinochinio's desk and now was sitting in one of the leather wing-backed chairs. Leaning forward, he stroked his chin in contemplation, then said, "Eminence, I cannot work for that man." Pointing at Pinochinio, John continued. " He is devious, malicious, and a poor excuse for a law enforcement officer. There is no way I can effectively do my job if I am subjected to his micro-management. He had me spending more time writing reports than actually doing my job. If my choices are to return and be subjected to his bullshit, or face the Disciplinary Hearing Board and possible termination, I would choose the latter."

The Cardinal replied, "For this case John, you can report directly to me. I don't necessarily believe that a permanent breaking of the chain of command would be a good thing, but we can re-visit that after this case is closed."

"And I'll need my team back." John said.

"I don't believe we can make that happen without too much disruption at this point. However, we can reassign back to you the team members who were with you when you were suspended."

"So, then you are saying that once this case is closed, my division will still be disbanded."

"I am saying that we cannot bring your team back together right now without significant disruption. We can re-evaluate the situation once this case is resolved."

John sat thinking about the offer for a few moments, while everyone in the room just watched him. He remembered Cardinal Dietrich's warning about appearing like a worker bee until the right moment. Based on this conversation, John felt he was back in the hive, but his moment had not yet arrived, so therefore it was time to play the part of the worker bee. Looking over to the Cardinal he said, "I will probably need some help from both DiClemente's and Costanza's divisions."

"This case has the highest priority, John. Whatever assistance you need, I guarantee you will receive it."

"OK. So, I'm in. What now?"

"Why don't you head on down to your old office. Aldo and Stephan can accompany you and bring you up to speed with where things currently are. I will have someone bring you your gun and shield. I am closing your suspension case and will have a disposition typed up and sent to you. Thank you, John. Welcome back."

"Thank you, Eminence. I will keep you posted." John said as he stood and left the room with DiClemente and Costanza in tow.

Waiting a few moments after the inner office door closed, Sentille turned to Pinochinio and said, "I think that went rather well."

"He is un Idiota! For someone with the years of experience that he has, you think he would have been able to see through our *"good cop – bad cop"* play."

Sentille said, "He desperately wants to come back. It is all hinged on the fact that he has nothing else in his life. He needs this job. He will work this case like a demon as he always has, and he will want to show how invaluable he is. His effectiveness is the only thing larger than his ego."

Pinochinio asked, "And once the case is closed…?"

"You will find another reason to let him go. I'm sure there will even be something that happens in this case that can be spun to his detriment."

"Or if not, I will find something." Pinochinio said, a grin forming across his face. "Either way, the days of John Nowalski as part of this Corps are numbered."

St. Luke's Evangelical Lutheran Church
Sayreville, New Jersey
Present Day

The Multi-Cultural Peace Parade was a brainchild born of the 1960s. Beginning as an ecumenical rally for peace during the Vietnam war, the parade and accompanying fair remained a well-attended staple in the Borough each Labor Day weekend. Over the years, the focus of the event morphed away from ending the war to combating hate and racism.

Groups from all over Middlesex as well as surrounding counties participated in both the parade and fair. With the opening of the town's recreational complex, the fair was moved to larger grounds thus accommodating even more groups. While still organized and run by the Borough's churches, the Peace Parade and Fair had become more about fund raising for area non-profits and exposure for local businesses than promoting peace and cooperation.

Each year, one church took the lead in organizing the event. They would coordinate various committees that would manage every aspect from group registrations to the interactions with the Borough's officials. This particular year, the local Lutheran church was slated to run point on the event, and Adam Levy was running late to meet with the church's pastor to discuss security and police coverage.

Parking his vehicle in the church lot, Adam jumped out and raced up the walkway toward the church. Arriving at the door, Adam pulled the door open, then remembered he had forgotten to lock the vehicle. Pulling the keys from his pocket, he turned and aimed the key fob at the car and clicked the lock button, receiving the acknowledging beep from the horn in return. Without looking, Adam swung around the open door and collided with the woman emerging from the church.

Grabbing the woman by the shoulders to prevent her from falling, Adam said, "Oh, I am so sorry. I didn't see you coming out."

The woman was tall and slender, with shoulder length brown hair. She looked to be in her mid-thirties with deep brown almond shaped eyes. "I thought you were holding the door for me, so I went." She said.

Recovered from the initial shock of forcefully bumping into someone, Adam chuckled and said, "Being a gentleman, I should have held the door for you, but I was looking at my car. I forgot to lock it and was turned and…"

Looking directly at Adam, the woman smiled. "That's OK. I guess we should both be more careful."

Adam became lost staring into the woman's deep brown eyes. Almost afraid to look away for fear the moment would disappear, he stood there staring and still holding on to her shoulders.

"Ah, I'm OK now…" the woman said looking down at Adam's hands still firmly holding her shoulders. "You can let go."

Realizing he was still holding on and coming back to reality, Adam apologized. "Oh,,,, I'm sorry. I didn't realize. I guess I should just pay more attention all around."

"That's OK. Well, take care. Be careful." She said stepping around Adam and walking toward the parking lot.

Opening the door, Adam stepped into the hallway that

connected the church to the church's fellowship building. Pastor Lembrich was standing by the inner door to the fellowship building, and Adam walked over to greet him. Extending his hand, Pastor Lembrich said, "Sargent Levy, so good to see you again."

"Pastor. Long time no see." Adam replied.

"So how long have you known Janine?"

"Excuse me?" Adam said.

"Janine Wagner. The young lady you were just embracing and talking to." The Pastor said.

"Oh, no. We'd never met. I just bumped into her by the door and almost knocked her over. That's why I was holding her up."

"Ah, I see. From a distance, it looked like you knew each other. Like there was a connection."

Thinking about those eyes and that smile, Adam smiled at the thought of a connection, but said. "No. Just me being clumsy. So, do you want to go over the plans for the parade and fair?"

An hour later, the two men had most of the details ironed out. Since the event was held each year, most of the plans were well established and just needed some tweaking. Wrapping up the documents, Pastor Lembrich looked up at Adam and asked, "So, will you need anything else Sargent?"

"Do you have a few minutes Pastor?" Adam asked.

"Sure, what's up?"

"I have a personal question to ask you."

Looking a bit concerned, Pastor Lembrich asked, "What is it?"

"Do Lutherans believe that God is a vengeful god?"

"Wow… That's some question. Why? What's going on Adam?"

"I'm not sure if you know this, but I was raised in the ultra-orthodox Jewish faith.

"I assumed you were Jewish, but I didn't know your background." Lembrich answered.

"I turned away from my faith back when I was in college. I fell in love with a Catholic girl and told my parents I didn't want to marry the girl that was arranged for me to marry, and I didn't want to continue with my studies in medicine."

"That must have gone over well." The pastor said sarcastically.

"Yeah, I was ostracized by the community and I am dead to my parents."

"So how did that decision work out for you?" Lembrich asked.

"The girl dumped me less than six months later, and I wound up becoming a cop."

"There are worse jobs you could have ended up in." the pastor said.

"No, it's not the job. That was what I wanted to do. I never really wanted to become a doctor. That dream was my parents, not mine. No, it's the relationship part. According to my community, I should be married and have a bunch of kids by now. Yet, ever since I left the faith for that girl, I have not been able to maintain a steady romantic relationship. I think this is my punishment for abandoning my faith. I am to die a lonely old man."

"You know Adam, you said several times you abandoned your faith…"

"Yeah…"

"But did you really?"

"What do you mean, Pastor?"

"Do you still believe in God?"

"Yes." Adam replied.

"Do you still believe the Torah is the word of God? Do you believe that God gave Moses the Ten Commandments, and do you follow those laws?"

"Of course." Adam said.

"Then I put it to you, that you have not abandoned your faith, you have just left your religion. Adam, religion is a set of rules devised by man to address how we should interact with our Lord. In some cases, these rules may be divinely inspired, but if you study the history of religion, you will find that there are just as many rules to control the masses as there are that are truly divinely inspired."

"You sound more like a cynic than a man of the cloth." Adam said.

"I like to think of myself as a well-informed realist. A true cynic doesn't believe in anything but himself. I still believe in God and our Lord Jesus Christ. Adam, things like the Ten Commandments are the divinely inspired word of God. The practice of tithing, and things like the Catholic practice of abstaining from eating meat on Fridays, those are the things invented to control the masses. I have a feeling that arranged marriages were something developed by people who wanted to do some early forms of social engineering, rather than divinely inspired rules given by God. Adam, God is love, not vengeance. If you followed your heart, you were listening to what God was telling you. He wouldn't be angry about that.

Adam, God gave man the gift of free will. While throughout history He has taught us how to love him and each other, free will means that just because he taught it, doesn't mean we have to have learned it. Blaming God for your problem is an escape… it's the easy way out. You have free will. You need to learn what He has been teaching. And sometimes learning is hard, so we try to shift the blame on the teacher. But ultimately, our happiness… our ability to love and be loved is our responsibility. We've been given the tools and the lessons. We just have to learn how to apply them."

Adam sat and thought about what the Pastor had said for a few moments. He had been living his life under the shadow of the guilt he felt for letting down his parents and leaving his community and religion. What this Pastor was saying was something brand new to him. This was not what he had always been taught by the rabbis and his parents. According to them, God was vengeful, punishing those who defied his rules. But despite what he was taught, what Pastor Lembrich was saying resonated. It seemed to feel right to Adam. Perhaps a more optimistic perspective could make a difference.

Adam said, "You know, I never thought of it that way. I was always taught that if you break God's laws, you get punished."

"Adam, I'll go back to what I initially said. Which of the laws are actually God's laws, and which ones are man's? You will find that throughout history and across cultures, the more dogmatic a belief system is, the more rules they will have. When you couple unquestioning belief with a myriad of rules, you get total control. And that, my friend, erases the greatest gift God gave us. The gift of free will."

Getting up from the table they were seated at, Adam extended his hand to the Pastor.

"Pastor, thank you so much for your time and insights." Adam said. "I have a lot to think about. Would I be able to reach out to you if I have any additional questions?"

"Of course, Adam. I am available to help whenever you may need me."

"I'll be in touch once I have the Department's plans for the fair all worked out too."

Lembrich said as he escorted Adam toward the door. "I look forward to working with you on the fair and continuing our conversation."

After nearly three weeks going through the documents in the Vatican archives, Mary Morrison's team got its first break. Focusing first on personnel files, it had taken the team more than ten days just to locate the old file for Georg Wagner. When they opened it, like most of the personnel files in storage, it contained information pertaining to Wagner's receipt of the Sacraments, his assignments and postings, and a note stuck in the back stating that he was missing and presumed dead after a bombing attack on September 12, 1944 leveled his church in Stuttgart.

Not willing to give up, Mary had her team cross reference the files of both the Bishop and Archbishop of Stuttgart that Wagner served under. While the Bishop's file did not contain any relevant information, tucked into the file of the Archbishop's was a note from a Monsignor in the

Stuttgart diocese asking if "… in light of the new information, should he begin the process of excommunication?"

Pulling the file of this Monsignor yielded no additional leads, but it led Mary to wonder where the correspondence was kept. Using the date on the note from the Monsignor and working backward, the team was eventually able to locate the source of the "new information" on Georg Wagner. The letter, dated May 11, 1945, but postmarked in Bedford Stuyvesant Brooklyn on May 18th read:

"Your Eminence,

We have lived through tumultuous times, with these past few months being especially hard on all children of God, but especially those personally touched by the brutality of war. While neither my faith nor my calling have waivered during this time, events have caused me to follow a different path. I have been tasked with protecting a secret that can either bring great joy to mankind, or unleash great evil. And while I neither consider myself a saint nor a martyr, I believe God in his infinite wisdom, chose me for this task.

Therefore, I am advising you that I am leaving the priesthood. While I understand the normal process and paperwork can take a considerable amount of time, I am now living in New York and will not be in a position to move through the normal channels. Please accept my most sincere apologies. This is not a choice made lightly.

May God grant you the peace that surpasses all understanding, guard your heart and thoughts in Christ Jesus.

Your humble servant in Christ,

Georg Wagner

Formerly of St. Elisabeth Kirche

Stuttgart, Germany

Wagner, and most likely the missing documents were in Brooklyn, New York. Mary was ecstatic. While she did not believe the Vatican could provide any further assistance in tracking down Wagner's exact location, this new information significantly changed the direction she and her team were looking. Now it would be a simple matter of obtaining passenger manifests from early May to the eighteenth to see when and where Wagner landed and who was his sponsor. From there, the trail should be fairly simple to follow.

Mary would need to contact William Alvarez and let him know of their findings and see if he could get the team to the U.S. where any hard copies of manifests would be stored. In the interim, she and her team would begin scouring the internet to see what data was available. With these new developments, Mary wasn't sure if she was more excited about the prospect of finding Georg Wagner, or going home to America.

The four monks sat huddled on the hard tile floor outside their bedrooms, staring in fear at the black hooded men guarding them. Having identified the Abbot, the team leader had already bound the old monk's hands and feet to the chair. As he had done in the past, the team leader had already dispatched half his team to begin their search of the monastery. Unlike their last assault, these men and this monastery may actually hold the plans they were looking for. Also, unlike the last time, this monastery was fairly remote and was not known to be a tourist attraction. If the team needed to extend both their search and interrogation, they did not need to be concerned about visitors interrupting them.

After a few well-placed punches to the solar plexus, the team leader began the questioning of the Abbot, while brandishing a large hunting knife. "Where is the Big Light?" he asked.

With a look somewhere between abject terror and confusion, the Abbot replied that he did not know what the masked man meant. This answer was met with a few well-placed and painful cuts by the team leader's knife. While these cuts would have required stitches if the Abbot were to ever receive treatment, none of them would produce any life-threatening level of bleeding.

"Where did Georg Wagner hide the plans? The team leader asked.

"I don't know anyone named Georg Wagner, the Abbot replied.

Deciding to try a different approach this time, the team leader sent one of his men to find some buckets and some towels. Filling the buckets with water, two members of the team lifted the bound Abbot, chair and all, onto a nearby table and tipped the Abbot and the chair backward. While the team leader placed the towel over the old monk's nose and mouth, he leaned down close to the Abbot's ear and whispered, "You know, it's a little ironic. Your church used this method extensively during the Inquisition to elicit the truth from their prisoners. They say that the feeling you get is like you are drowning. It produces uncontrollable feelings of panic and terror, and you experience extreme physical suffering. If I do this correctly, you will wind up with a bit of water in your lungs, but not enough to cause you to stop breathing. Each subsequent session creates even greater terror and suffering until you eventually pass out. However, I am not going to let that happen. I will not let you pass out because if you do not tell me what I need to know from these little sessions, we are going to go right into the next phase of our interrogation, and so on and so on until someone tells me where the plans are."

Whimpering with tears now streaming down his face, the Abbot looked with pleading eyes at the team leader shaking his head. "I do not know…"

The Abbot never finished his sentence as the team leader began slowly pouring water over the monk's towel draped nose and mouth. Sputtering and struggling to turn his head to the side, the Abbot was prevented from moving his head by the legs of the other two gunmen pressed firmly against his head.

When the bucket was finally empty. the two gunmen lifted the Abbot back into the sitting position. With the water-soaked towel falling into his lap, the Abbot spit out a mouthful of water, gasped twice for air, and then vomited into his lap and shoes. Shaking his head to regain some composure, the Abbot looked over at the team leader as he worked to catch his breath.

"That looked like it was pretty rough." The team leader said. "We can stop now if you just tell me where the plans are hidden."

Beginning to sob, the Abbot took a deep breath and replied, "I wish I knew what you were talking about. I don't know about any plans."

Without hesitation, the two other team members tipped the Abbot back a second time, placed the vomit and water-soaked towel back over his face, immobilized his head as before while the team leader began pouring his second bucket of water slowly over the old monk. The Abbot was subjected to two additional waterboarding sessions before the men removed the soaked and vomit covered monk off of the table.

While the two other team members grabbed the next monk and bound him to a chair seated in front of the Abbot, the team leader knelt down in front of the old monk and said. "You can make this all stop by telling me where the plans are."

Turning on his heels, the team leader stood and walked over toward the second monk now seated and bound to the chair facing the Abbot. He continued, "I understand you men of the cloth often believe in enduring suffering for your beliefs, but you also are duty bound to help ease the suffering of those less fortunate. Placing his hand on the shoulder of the younger monk, he faced the Abbot and repeated. "Where are the plans for the Big Light?"

Shaking his head vigorously, the Abbot replied. "I swear, I do not know."

Stepping around behind the young monk, the team leader knelt down and calmly asked, "Would you know where the plans are?"

In a weak shaky voice, the man replied, "No. I do not know anything about…"

Standing as soon as the young monk began to speak, the team leader pulled his QSZ-92 pistol from its holster and fired one hollow-point nine-millimeter bullet into the back of the young monk head. Mushrooming as it traversed the brain, the bullet exploded out of the front of the man's face leaving a gaping five-inch hole where his nose formerly was, and spraying blood, brains and bone onto the horrified Abbot seated in front of the young monk.

While the body of the dead monk was removed from the chair, the team leader paced in front of the Abbot and shouted "Someone needs to tell me where the plans for the Big Light are in order or this to stop."

Another young monk was secured to the chair, then taken over to the table where he was subjected to a half hour of waterboarding before he aspirated vomit into his lungs and passed out from the subsequent coughing. He was unceremoniously removed from the chair, and at the unspoken direction of the team leader, deposited at the feet of the Abbot.

"Why do you insist on holding out?" the team leader asked the Abbot.

"I am not holding out. I do not know about this Big Light."

Nodding his head, the team leader said, "OK… We'll

see." And shot the unconscious monk lying at the Abbot's feet in the head.

The third monk was subjected to a beating with a blackjack that fractured both his eye sockets, his jaw, and knocked out several teeth, before being hoisted on to the table and waterboarded. Throughout the entire time, the team leader just kept repeating, "Where is the Big Light… Where is the Big Light?"

When the third monk finally passed out, he too was removed from the chair and dropped unconscious at the feet of the Abbot. Standing over the man at the Abbot's feet, the team leader said to the Abbot, "We have been at this for hours, and we are still not closer than when we started. I am going to give you one more chance to tell me, and then it will be your turn to go back on the table."

With his breath already labored from the water in his lungs, the Abbot resigned himself to his fate. Hanging his head, he said, "I cannot tell you what I do not know, so do what you feel you must."

Firing two shots into the body of the monk lying on the floor, the team leader focused his gaze back on the Abbot, and pistol-whipped him across the face. As the two other team members removed the monk from the floor, the team leader said, "We have one more person who may be inspired to tell me something before I get back to you." Turning to his teammates, he said, "Grab that last one and put him in the chair."

The Aryphon assault team became aware that they may not be alone as they performed their reconnaissance before entering the monastery. Seeing the removed window, and then finding the front door unlocked, it became fairly evident that the other team of operators they were warned about may actually be on site.

Hand chosen and led by Dieter von Alpiner, Vice President of Operations for Donner Global Security Services, the seven additional operators were recruited from various elite special operations units around the globe. As a wholly owned subsidiary of Aryphon Industries, Donner Global provided security and protective services to key personnel who worked at high risk locations around the world. Additionally, they were rumored to perform certain "off the books" operations for countries needing to solve problems in a less than diplomatic fashion, yet remain anonymous and protected from any political fall-out.

Hearing the shouting and cries coming from the direction of the dormitory, von Alpiner was about to send his team in that direction when he noticed lights shining across the center courtyard from the chapel, with voices and hammering noises echoing from the hallway to the right. Signaling two of his men to remain in place to protect their rear flank, he took the remaining five across the open courtyard toward the chapel.

The monastery, if viewed from above, was shaped like a cross with a wider cross piece framing the open courtyard in the center. With the main entrance at the base of the cross, and the chapel at the peak, the left side of what would be the cross piece held the dormitory wing, while the right side held offices and meditation rooms. A hallway ran around the perimeter of the building separating the dorm, office and meditation rooms from the exterior walls.

A set of doors across from the main entrance led into the courtyard, while similar doors sat on the other side of the courtyard, across from the entrance to the chapel. While the hallway was open from the end of the dormitory wing past the front entrance, around to the office wing and then finally around to the chapel, a locked door prevented people from taking the short route directly to the chapel from anywhere in the dormitory area.

Approaching silently through the courtyard and remaining in the shadows, the team approached the entrance to the chapel in two by two cover fashion. Arriving at the entrance, von Alpiner carefully peered in to assess the situation. The room was in shambles with pews overturned and gaping holes in the walls. A ground penetrating radar device was sitting halfway up the aisle to the altar, and there were two locations where the wooden floor had been torn up, exposing steam heating pipes.

Three men stood around the altar, facing the front of the church with their backs to the door. One had his weapon slung over his shoulder, while two other Sterling Submachine Guns lay on the first step to the chancel. All three men were attempting to push the altar over onto its side. The three targets all wore body armor and similar black clothing and face covering. From what von Alpiner could see, they had sidearms and other weapons attached to their utility belts, and aside from the helmets and night vision goggles worn by his team, they could have easily passed as members of his unit.

Von Alpiner decided his best course of action would be to take out these men here, then move on to where he had heard the cries and shouts. Signaling to two of his team, they took up position by the entrance to the chapel and illuminated their laser targeting devices. With each man taking aim at one of the targets head, the plan was that each of his team would double tap, or put two shots in quick succession into the heads of the men by the altar on von Alpiner's signal. Whispering into his headset, von Alpiner quietly counted out, "One… Two…"

The Korean operator on the left turned his head to the right just in time to see the red laser of the targeting device slicing across the chapel toward him and his teammates. Yelling out in warning, he dropped to the floor drawing his sidearm in the same motion. Von Alpiner and his team fired simultaneously, but the warning had already been issued and the other team's reflexes were lightning fast. Two of the shots missed totally, while the third hit the target in the Kevlar vest, knocking the man to the floor and breaking a rib, but not putting him out of the fight.

All three of the targets were now returning fire. Two were using their sidearms while the third with the Sterling had unslung the submachine gun and was laying down cover fire as his teammates moved to better firing positions. Immediately upon missing their shots, von Alpiner sent the two members of his team guarding the rear flank in toward the dormitory area, and sent one of the men outside the chapel to cover them. The final member of his seven-man team was told to find another way into the chapel and flank the three men firing at them from the front of the small church.

The team leader of the Korean assault team had just resigned himself to the fact that these monks did not know where the plans for the Big Light were. He had intended to perform a quick, intense interrogation of the final monk, possibly set the Abbot up for one more waterboarding session, then assess the status of the rest of his team before departing.

His men had just finished securing the final young monk to the chair facing the Abbot when the report of multiple gunshots echoed down the hallway. More curious than concerned, the team leader sent his two remaining men toward the chapel to investigate the sounds. Headed down the hallway in a slow trot, the two Koreans almost ran headlong into the two Aryphon men moving in from the monastery entryway.

With all four operators diving for what little cover they could find, a second gun battle ensued near the front of the dormitory hallway. Seeing the situation unfolding before him, the Korean team leader drew his QSZ-92 pistol and put a bullet in the head of the young monk sitting in the chair in front of him. About to turn and do the same to the Abbot, the team leader took two errant bullets to his Kevlar vest fired by one of the Aryphon team. Figuring the Abbot could wait until he dealt with the threat in front of him, the team leader used the young monk's body for cover, and began firing at the Aryphon assailants.

Emptying his magazine, the team leader ejected the spent cartridge and slammed in a fresh one. Firing into the shadows of the dimly lit hallway at muzzle flashes, the five men filled the hallway with smoke and the echoing cacophony of gunfire. The chaotic life-and-death scene playing out in front of the team leader left him oblivious to the threat coming up from behind him.

The man von Alpiner's sent to back up the men at the dormitory opted to try to gain access to the dormitory hallway through the locked door nearest the chapel, rather than circumnavigate the entire building. Shooting through the lock, he quietly entered the hallway behind the team leader. Stepping to the side to be clear of the Abbot, the Aryphon mercenary aimed his laser sighted Heckler and Koch MP5 at the back of the team leaders head. Squeezing the trigger, he put a three-round burst of hollow point 9mm bullets into the back of the team leader's head, blowing the majority of his face, brains and skull across the face and chest of the dead, young monk.

Turning his attention to the other two Koreans in the hallway, he switched his MP5 to full-automatic and sprayed the rear of the Koreans positions, putting them in a nasty crossfire. Realizing their untenable position, the Koreans waited until the man at their rear expended his magazine, then taking advantage, dove out of the hallway into the nearest bedroom. From there, they immediately smashed through the bedroom window into the courtyard.

Once in the courtyard, the two Koreans saw their comrades pinned down in the chapel. Running toward the doors adjacent to the chapel entrance, the Koreans began firing at the Aryphon team. Now caught in in a crossfire themselves, von Alpiner had his men move behind another set of overturned pews for cover. As the two Koreans in the courtyard advanced on von Alpiner's position, the Koreans pinned down behind the altar saw the opportunity to run for the chapel exit. While their teammates provided covering fire, the three men that were ransacking the chapel, ran for the exit while continuing to fire as they ran.

Reaching the courtyard, all five men began running toward the front door. Pulling flash-bang grenades from their vests, one of the Koreans tossed one through the open window of the bedroom they escaped through, while the other threw one toward the entrance to the chapel. Both sets of Aryphon men were caught unaware by the sudden explosion and flash of light, and were temporarily blinded and disoriented.

Rather than re-engage in an attempt to recover the body of their leader, the Korean second-in-command ordered the team to head straight out of the monastery, into the surrounding woods, and make for their vehicle. Upon reaching the nearby wooded area, the team leap-frogged down to the road, leaving one man behind at each waypoint to cover their escape. Upon reaching their vehicle, the team quickly stashed their weapons and gear in the hidden compartment under the floor of the van, then donned civilian clothing and departed the area.

Von Alpiner and his team gathered in the courtyard. While they sustained no casualties, five of the seven men had bullet wounds in their arms or legs. Each member of the team sustained multiple broken ribs from shots taken to their body armor. Von Alpiner himself had a nasty bleeding gash above his right eye from a bullet that grazed his forehead, and a splitting headache from the other two bullets that were stopped by his helmet.

"Let's see if they left anything interesting behind." Von Alpiner said to his men. "I know, everyone is banged up, but I need you all to move with purpose. I want to be out of here in fifteen minutes or less."

Heading over to where the team leader lay dead on

the floor, they turned the now faceless body over as they checked his pockets for any kind of I.D..

"He look Asian to you?" One of the operators asked von Alpiner.

"Could be…" von Alpiner replied. Checking out the team leaders sidearm, von Alpiner continued, "QSZ-92 pistol… Standard issue for the DPRK Special Operations Force." Looking over at the Abbot, who had taken multiple rounds to his torso, von Alpiner said, "Too bad we couldn't have saved him. I wonder if he would have told us anything."

"He obviously didn't tell them anything. Why would you think he'd tell us?" the other operator said.

"Because we would have been his saviors. If he knew anything, he might have willingly given it to us… Oh well. Let's wrap up here and go lick our wounds."

Ten minutes later, the Aryphon team was in their van winding their way down the mountain. Von Alpiner was already writing his after-action report in his head. While they might not have found the prize, at least now they knew who else was after it.

It was nine AM when John arrived in the Salzburg office of the Austrian National Police, and headed straight for the office of Chief Inspector Wolfgang Altschuler. Once reassigned to the case, John had commandeered Tony from his current assignment and had him make inquiries as to who was working the case in Austria. Then he went to the Information Center to get print-outs of all the information the Gendarmerie had on both attacks. Finally, before looking for a flight or train to Austria, John met with DiClemente, to get his read on the information, and see if there were any insights his people developed that were not necessarily written down.

John was horrified, but not overly surprised that no one from the Gendarmerie had actually traveled to Austria to do any first-hand investigative work. DiClemente had said that Pinochinio had initially shot that idea down, saying that the Austrian National Police had the capabilities to effectively process the crime scenes, and we would just be getting in their way.

"Well, I have a lot to get caught up on, and then I need to find a ride to Austria." John told DiClemente. "You can tell your boss that despite his flawed directive, I'm going to look at the crime scenes myself."

After searching for flights, and finding none available, John booked an overnight train that would get him in to Salzburg by eight thirty the following morning. Buying the ticket online, John told Tony to reach out to the lead investigator in Austria, and let them know he was coming. He then went home and packed a small carry-on, grabbed a bite to eat and headed to the train station. After boarding the train at eight PM. John found his berth, settled in and reviewed all the material the Gendarmerie had on the case, along with his notes from his meeting with DiClemente. Once he felt he was as up to speed as he could be, John closed his eyes and got a few hours of sleep before the train pulled in to Hauptbahnhof station in Salzburg.

"I was wondering when you guys would show up." Chief Inspector Altschuler said as he extended his hand in greeting to John.

"Yeah, well, there has been some reorganization going

on in the Corps and that led to some overall confusion. I was not initially assigned to the case." John replied.

"Well I for one am actually glad you are here now." Altschuler said. "Between the ransacked and vandalized buildings that were a precursor to this, and now these gruesome murders, I fear we may have some terrorist group targeting the Roman Catholic Church. Your anti-terrorism reputation precedes you Director General."

"Well thank you… and please, call me John."

"Very well, John. What would you like to see first?

John replied, "Well, I have looked at a bunch of crime scene photos, and I have read your initial reports. I've seen a lot of the forensic reports. What I have not seen are any of the coroner's findings or ballistic reports."

"I can get you those. They both just came in yesterday."

"Great, you know, if there is any way I could speak to the medical examiners… sometimes there are things I can glean from speaking to them that you don't necessarily see in the report."

"I can see about setting that up." Altschuler said. "The bodies were examined by two different offices since the crimes happened about one hundred and fifty kilometers from each other."

"Speaking of that… I would really like to personally see the crime scenes."

"Ja, we can go now if you like since they are a bit of a drive away from each other. Maybe you could review some of the reports while we drive."

"That sounds like a good plan." John replied. "Nothing like good old Austrian efficiency."

Altschuler got one of his subordinates to drive while

John sat in the back and reviewed the reports. Looking first at the coroner's report on the nun massacre, John noted that all of the victims had undergone some form of torture prior to being shot in the head, although one of the nuns only had a six-inch gash on her inner thigh in addition to the bullet wound. All showed signs of having both their legs and arms bound, and John remembered that the Mother Superior was found bound to a chair in that fashion.

Based on the wounds sustained by most of the nuns, they had undergone an extensive period of torture, primarily with a knife, but from the bruising, most likely a baton as well. One of the nuns had been shot in both kneecaps, and strangled to death before being shot in the head. Of the nuns beaten with a baton, the coroner noted internal injuries ranging from fractured ribs to bruised spleen, kidneys and liver. This meant, John noted, that the attacker was most likely a man, and he possessed above average strength, and, or martial arts training.

Aside from the nun that was strangled, the official cause of death on all of the other nuns had been a single 9mm hollow point bullet to the brain. All of the shots had been delivered at close range, some close enough to cause powder burns. The toxicology report was unremarkable. As expected, all of the nuns had eaten the same thing for dinner, and none of them had any signs of drugs or alcohol in their system.

Opening the coroner's report on the killing of the monks, John immediately noticed vast differences in the murders. For starters, all of the monks were bound only by the wrists, and were found with their wrists still bound. There was no bruising, lacerations or burns, so none of the men had been tortured. While each of them had the same cause of death as the nuns, a single gunshot to the head, the monks were all shot execution style in the back of the head, while the nuns were facing the shooter.

Looking over the toxicology report, the monks also all ate the same meal, and while there was no alcohol in any of their systems, the toxicology screen of their blood came back positive for Sodium Amobarbital, a strong barbiturate that had been used extensively as a "truth serum" in enhanced interrogations.

Just by looking at the coroner's reports, John would surmise he was dealing with at least two sets of killers. But when he looked at the ballistic reports he noted one very large difference. While 9mm hollow point bullets were used at both locations, ballistics information from the INTERPOL Ballistic Information Network showed that the weapon used in Bludenz was not the same as the one that killed the monks. Unfortunately, the IBIN was unable to match the weapon in either case against any other crime or terrorist activity.

Arriving first at the Bludenz monastery, John followed Inspector Altschuler into the building. Other than the local constabulary guarding the building to keep the press or curious away, the building was empty. John noticed the smell of death immediately upon entering the monastery. Altschuler pointed out the window the perpetrators removed to gain access, then led John down the hallway to the dormitory area. Despite the fact that the bodies had been removed, the volume of blood on the floor still attracted swarms of flies.

John opened the file and began comparing the pictures

with the physical location. He stood behind the chair the Mother Superior was bound to and looked down the blood-stained corridor. The blood encrusted chair each of her sister nuns were tied to and then tortured sat in front of them. Looking down first at the photographs, then the floor to the left, John could see from the preponderance of blood stains where they had thrown the bodies of the murdered nuns. There were no shell casings or other physical evidence present, having already been processed by the National Police crime lab staff days before. But John knew that and still felt he needed to see the scene, touch the chairs, smell the decomposing blood in order to fully comprehend the level of evil depravity needed to commit such an act.

After several minutes connecting the physical site with the photographic images, John moved on. He looked at the dorm rooms, the offices, the gift shop and meditation rooms. He visited the chapel and saw the floorboards torn up in certain areas. While the destruction to the building may have looked random, to John, each room painted a clearer picture of what had occurred here. The destruction of the monastery was not random vandalism committed by a group of people seeking to harm the Church. Instead, these people were looking for something, and the nuns were tortured in order to get them to divulge whatever secret the perpetrators thought they were hiding.

During the ride to the next monastery, John asked Inspector Altschuler for his impressions and theories. The Inspector told John that his department was proceeding on the assumption that a terrorist group with an axe to grind with the Roman Catholic Church had committed these crimes. While he had reached the same conclusion that the two incidents were done by different people, they remained focused on trying to identify groups that may have issued some threats recently against the Church. Altschuler's discussions with DiClemente and Pinochinio supported his thinking, and the Vatican was attempting to find groups that may have felt they had been wronged by a monastic order in the past. Since many of these orders were centuries old, their research was taking a considerable amount of time to develop a suspect list.

Since the nuns were the first group found, and because of the shocking and gruesome nature of that scene, John could see how Altschuler may have gotten a case of tunnel vision regarding the direction of the investigation. It would be just as easy to support the terrorist premise based on the evidence. When you include the earlier cases of vandalism, one could easily say the perpetrators were escalating their violence against the Church. And if that line of thinking is also supported by another agency like the Gendarmerie, then your tunnel vision can become even narrower.

Arriving at the second monastery, John again went first to view the dormitory area where the monks were killed. While there was significantly less blood, the scene of the execution was gruesome in its own right. These monks however were not tortured. From the looks of the scene, which confirmed what John had seen in the photographs, the monks were taken individually into one of the bedrooms, where based on the toxicology report, they were drugged and then interrogated. They were then brought out into the hallway, and the next monk was similarly drugged and questioned.

When all four of the monks were done, someone walked up behind them as they sat on the floor and shot them once in the head. From the positioning, it looked like at least two of them made a feeble attempt to flee since their body was found fully stretched out and several feet from the other two.

The building was vandalized in a similar fashion to the nun's building, with torn up floor boards, and holes in walls large enough for a man to stick his head in between the beams and look for something stored between the framing. Every draw was overturned, every cabinet opened and the content emptied, every file cabinet opened and every bed stripped of linen and mattress overturned. The scene at this monastery screamed robbery rather than terrorism. These people were looking for something.

John was wrapping up his assessment in the chapel when Inspector Altschuler rushed in a little out of breath.

"There has been another attack about forty kilometers from here." Altschuler said. Four monks and the Abbot were savagely tortured, but from the looks of it, there was a firefight and one of the perpetrators was killed."

Turning and heading toward the doorway, John said, "So, what are we waiting for... Let's go. We have a fresh crime scene to investigate."

"But wait... Altschuler said. "One of the monks... he's in the hospital. He survived."

CHAPTER 7

Alvarez Family Compound
Montevideo, Uruguay
Present Day

IT WAS JUST after ten PM when William Alvarez stepped into his father's study. Most of the servants had already retired for the evening, and the balance of the palatial estate was dark. Walking into the room, William saw his father reading from the computer screen. Knowing not to disturb the elder Alvarez, William quietly sat down in one of the chairs across from his father's desk.

"This is some after action report." The senior Alvarez said to his son as he turned away from the screen to face the young man.

"I know. This confirms that someone else is looking for the plans." William said.

"Did you get to speak to von Alpiner at all?" Alvarez asked.

"Briefly. As he stated in the report, they did manage

to kill one of the operators, and von Alpiner has some suspicions who the other players might be, but he wants to confirm some things before he makes his final report. They took some shell casings and a DNA sample from the dead man. He hopes to be able to use that to learn who they are."

"Unfortunately, once again, nothing was found, and we didn't develop any other leads." The senior Alvarez said. "I fear we will not be able to continue these interrogations much longer. This is the third monastery that has been attacked. Both the Austrians and the Vatican will be planning to do something to stop these attacks."

"Well I have good news on that front." William said with a huge grin on his face. "We no longer have to search in Austria. Our researchers found a letter postmarked from Brooklyn, New York on May 18th, 1945, written by Georg Wagner to his Bishop in Stuttgart. In it, he advises the Bishop that he has escaped to America, he will not be returning to Germany, and he is relinquishing his priesthood. He actually just about admits in the letter that he has the plans and is hiding them per his brother's wishes."

"He says that in the letter?"

"Not in those words, but he alludes to it and knowing the story, you can see what he is trying to say without actually saying it." William said.

"Were they able to get any other information from the Vatican Archives?"

"No, unfortunately not. Dr. Morrison has asked to travel to the U.S. to try to track Wagner from immigration papers and transit manifests."

"Aren't most of those online nowadays? I mean I can

subscribe to that Ancestry website and get most of that information." Alvarez countered.

"Most of the records are online, however, not everything made it into electronic records. She actually already did an online search"

"And did she uncover anything?" the father asked with anticipation.

"There were two *Wagners* who emigrated during the time period in question. Both used a different first name. There was one *Georg,* and three *Georges.* None of them were priests, although one was a Lutheran minister." William replied.

"Do you think maybe…" Alvarez asked.

"We discounted that one because he was traveling with his son and was met by a Lutheran pastor"

"Mmmm… Alvarez acknowledged contemplating next steps. "What about the others?"

One of the *Wagners* was too young, and the *Georg* was too old." William replied. Dr. Morrison wants to take the team there to verify there were no other potential targets by reviewing the original documents, and then begin tracing the remaining ones."

Sitting back in his chair and stroking his chin, the senior Alvarez said to his son, "Lets come back to that in a few minutes. I understand von Alpiner's team is pretty beaten up."

"Yes Papa. The gun battle was pretty intense. Most of the team sustained at least one gunshot wound to one of his extremities. They will not be at full strength for a while."

"See that they get the medical attention they need. You know, I have been thinking… We may need to accelerate our timeline. I have been speaking to your sister, and things are ready on her end. And your brother claims that his part of the plan is progressing as well. Your latest report shows that battery production is back on target, and even if we cannot get the plans to mass produce graphene, there are two companies that have already found a commercially feasible method of producing it. Both of them are publicly traded, so worst case, we complete a hostile take-over of one of those companies. We continue to track down and obtain the Big Light, but that was never part of our original master plan. Compared to the master plan, we may be slightly ahead of our original schedule."

"You surprise me father. You were the one preaching to me about the importance of letting the plan work to full fruition."

"I know. That is what I would like to do, however, my gut is telling me something different." Alvarez replied. "William, I think we need to hold a Board meeting. There are forces at play that we did not necessarily anticipate, and I feel we need to advance our schedule in order to take advantage of those forces, before they turn against us."

"That is not a bad idea, father. We update everyone and can get some additional details into all that has been happening. That would give everyone a clearer picture to make the right decision."

Nodding his head in agreement with himself, Alvarez said, "I will get Joon Min to get something scheduled. In the meantime, it appears Dr. Morrison is a pretty insightful and talented researcher."

Nodding his head in agreement, William replied, "She is Papa."

"So, do you have other researchers who could go to America and pick up where she left off?"

William answered, "I do, father... What are you thinking?"

"Dr. Morrison and her team has been given access to many of our most inner sources of information. She has been given a glimpse of all that Aryphon is and can do... Yet she is not really one of... us. I would hate for her to see some of our plans begin to come to fruition, and because of her insight and access, predict where things are headed and then try to interfere."

"I can see your point, Papa."

"Then we need to utilize other methods to bring this prize home. When will von Alpiner have his team ready to work?"

"He said he wanted a week or so to finish tracking down his leads into who the other team is, and give his guys a rest."

"OK. In the interim, have von Alpiner make a quick stop in Rome before rejoining the team in NY. Once he is closer to where he will need to be, he can finish his investigation and the team can rest up and await further instructions. Send another research team to New York to follow up on Morrison's work.

William, I know you just promoted her, but the leader of that research team can no longer work for this company. She has way too much insight and any future exposure to our plans, even anecdotal exposure may have deleterious implications. I trust you can manage what needs to be done."

"I'll get right on it Papa."

Adam could feel the vibe the minute he arrived at police headquarters. Having parked out front, he entered through the visitor entrance in the front of the building, walking past the entrance to the municipal court over to the door to the right of the desk sergeant's window.

Sergeant Palmer, sitting at the desk looked at Adam for several moments without saying a word before he finally hit the door release button permitting Adam to enter.

"G' morning Joe." Adam said as he entered the hallway.

"Mornin'" Palmer mumbled without looking up from the papers he was reviewing.

Heading down the hall to the detective's squad-room, Adam passed a few other patrol officers who all gave him a sideways glance without any other form of acknowledgement. Entering the squad-room, Adam headed to his desk to the silent gaze of the other detectives in the room. Sitting down at his desk, Adam glanced up to look around the room and caught everyone's head snap away from him. Scanning the room, he watched as everyone there would take sideways glances to see if he was looking, but refused to make eye contact or even look directly at him. Adam was about to ask the room what was going on when Captain Benjamin shouted, "Levy, get your ass in here."

Getting up from his chair and walking toward Benjamin's office, Adam thought he heard a snicker come from one of the men sitting at their desk.

"Close the door and siddown." Benjamin said as Adam entered the office.

Following his Captain's directions, Adam closed the door and sat in one of the side chairs facing his boss's desk.

"Levy… you have been with this division for how long?"

Adam began to answer, but Benjamin waved him off. "That was actually a rhetorical question. You claim to be a detective, yet sometimes you can be rather… dense."

Adam sat silently, his mind racing to figure out what he had done wrong. Whatever it was, word of it had spread through the entire department based on the reactions he had received from the patrol officers he saw when he first came in this morning.

"Are you going to tell me, you didn't notice people behaving strangely towards you this morning?" Benjamin asked.

Nodding his head Adam replied, "Of course I did. I was trying to figure it out… I was trying to come up with what I could have done wrong to become a pariah in the squad-room and piss off all of patrol."

"So why didn't you come in here to ask me?" Benjamin said, raising his voice. "Do you think I wouldn't know what you did? Do you think you could have found out and hidden it from your boss? "I'll have you know, Levy, I was solving cases before you even learned how to jerk off."

With his back turned to the door, Adam could not see the other detectives all stand and begin moving closer to the entrance of the office.

Benjamin continued in a calmer voice, "You know Adam, you work with the same people every single day, and you think you know them." Benjamin stood and began to move around his desk toward Adam. "Sometimes, you think you see something… a spark, or a glimmer of something that could be extraordinary. You work to nurture that spark. You guide that person. You mentor them, you give them every opportunity for them to rise to the fullest level of their potential…"

Adam was now hanging his head in shame. He continued to run through all of his cases, all of his arrests… what had he done wrong that had now exploded to cause this. And then listening to Benjamin's words made Adam feel even worse. Benjamin had given Adam every opportunity. In many ways he had become a surrogate father for Adam, and now, whatever this was, he had seriously let the man down.

Benjamin was now standing behind Adam with his hands on Adam's shoulders. He continued, "…and if you are lucky, that person achieves what you always knew they could. And hopefully, they remember you and what you have done for them and they will take a page out of your book and pay it forward by doing the same with someone they see has potential. Do you understand what I am saying…Lieutenant?"

It took Adam a few moments to process what Benjamin had just said. Turning to now look at his mentor, he saw through the glass front of the office, all the other detectives standing just outside and applauding. Standing he took the outstretched hand of his Captain.

"Congratulations Adam." Benjamin said. "The results came in last night. You beat Lucas by one point. The chief already called me this morning and said that he supports your promotion. To make it official it has to go through the town council, but the chief knows this position has been vacant for a while and he will get it on their agenda for next week's meeting."

Putting his arm around Adam, Benjamin steered him out the office door into the squad-room where Adam was greeted by another round of applause. The detectives all came up to Adam and offered individual congratulations, patting him on the shoulder or shaking his hand. Chuckling, Adam said, "That explains why the patrol guys were so pissy this morning."

"So, in their case, it affects all of them…" Benjamin said. "The guys that love Lucas are pissed at you for beating him because he won't get that promotion and be able to 'fix' our division, as he so often says he would do. And the guys that hate him, are pissed at you for making sure he stays put busting their balls a bit longer."

Shaking his head, Adam looked out at the team of detectives still standing around him and their Captain. "You guys scared the shit out of me. I thought I fucked something up, and for the life of me, I couldn't figure out what I did."

"It was Tortorice's idea. He knew you had to do that car swap thing this morning, so you'd be in a little late, so he asked if we could jerk your chain a little." Benjamin said.

Looking over at the older detective, Adam said, "Thanks Steve-O. I know I can always count on you to bust 'em at every opportunity."

"Hey, think nothing of it." Tortorice replied.

"OK ladies and gentlemen, let's get back to it." Benjamin said to the team. Then turning to Adam, he said, "We can go back into my office and I can outline some of your new duties, but if you need a few minutes first… If there's anyone you want to call to tell the good news to…"

Shaking his head, Adam replied, "No sir, now is good. There isn't anybody I need to call."

As luck would have it, the trauma center where the monk was taken by helicopter was only 24 kilometers away from where John and Altschuler were investigating the murders of the monks. Arriving at the hospital less than a half hour after the helicopter had touched down, the pair rushed into the trauma section of the emergency department, bypassing both the local and National police who wanted to stop them to give a report. Finding the doctor directing the monk's care, Altschuler inquired about the patient's condition.

"I am amazed he is still alive." The doctor responded. He has two gunshot wounds and lost a lot of blood. He was also beaten up pretty badly. He's been in and out of consciousness, but the paramedics couldn't get him intubated because of the facial trauma. I'm currently holding off with the intubation because he is presently protecting his airway, and intubation will drop his blood pressure and it is already dangerously low. We are preparing him for surgery and will be taking him up in a few minutes."

John asked the doctor, "What do you think his chances are, doctor?"

Frowning and shaking his head, the doctor replied, "We can't be sure till we get in there and see the extent of damage. My concern is because of his blood loss and subsequent lack of perfusion, I don't know how his organ systems will respond. They may be irreparably damaged from the lack of sufficient blood and oxygen. Then again,

I've seen people in worse shape make it, and he should have the Lord on his side."

"Doctor, we need to talk to him before he goes up for surgery." John said with urgency in his voice.

Shaking his head again, the doctor said, "I don't know how responsive he will be, and we really need to get him to the operating room."

"Just two minutes doctor." John pleaded. He is the only witness to a string of very gruesome murders."

Like most Austrians, the doctor had heard about the terrorist attacks on the news, and weighed the need for information this monk may have against the needs of his patient. Reaching a compromise, the doctor said, "OK, come with me. If he is conscious, you can question him as we move him to the operating suite. But once we get there, you must stop."

Agreeing to the arrangement, John and Altschuler followed the doctor to the monk's bedside. Like most critical trauma cases, the monk's bedside looked like a ballet of controlled chaos. Nurses and doctors moved around the gurney, checking tubes and wires, pushing medications and calling out critical observations, while another team of people stood on the periphery documenting everything. Escorted to the patient's head, the doctor said, "OK, he looks like he's conscious. Go ahead."

As the doctor inquired about when they could head to the O.R., Altschuler and John leaned in toward the monk. While the doctor at the head of the bed responded they could move in two minutes, Altschuler softly asked the monk, "Brother, can you hear me. I am Inspector Altschuler of the National Police. Do you know who did this to you?"

The monk's face clearly displayed the signs of the beating it had received. His left eye was completely swollen shut, while his right looked heavy and bloodstained. His nose was swollen and obviously broken and the bruising on both cheeks went beyond purple to black. His cracked lips, and what could be seen of his teeth were caked with blood, and his jaw moved unsymmetrically as he tried to speak.

"Graaslikt…" he mumbled with a thick tongue in his native German. "Wo isht dash graaashlikt."

Looking over to Altschuler, John asked, What did he say?

"I think he said Wo ist das grässlich." Altschuler replied.

"That makes no sense…" John said. "Where is the ghastly? My German might be a bit rusty. Am I getting that right?"

"Der mann fragte er, wo isht das grushlisht?" The monk moaned to the Inspector.

"What man. Do you know who they were?" The Inspector asked in German.

"Graaaslikt… Wo isht dash graashli… graslikt. Wo isht.." the monk faded off into unconsciousness.

Standing beside the head of the bed, the attending physician called out, "OK people, we are moving now!"

As the stretcher started moving out of the trauma bay and down the hallway, the attending physician stopped John and Altschuler. "I don't think you are going to get anything more from him now. He sounded like he wasn't really there before he faded into unconsciousness anyway. We will do our best with him and hopefully if everything works out, you can question him in a few days."

Altschuler replied, "Thank you doctor. Please keep us informed on his condition."

"I will." The doctor replied, and left John and Altschuler as he turned to help push the stretcher on to the elevator.

Ninety minutes later, John and Altschuler were standing amidst the battlefield remnants that was once a thriving monastery. Shell casings were everywhere as were the bloodstains. With the volume of shells on the floor, John expected to see multiple corpses. However, aside from the monks and Abbot, there was only one body the investigators could label as that of a combatant.

John and Altschuler approached the dormitory area where all the bodies were found. Based on the report from the local constable, a local farmer would come to the monastery every Wednesday to deliver fresh milk and eggs. When he arrived today, finding the front door open, he entered and found the scene they were currently looking at. The farmer ran home and called the local police who arrived with an ambulance. Upon checking all of the bodies, the first responders found the monk John had just been with at the hospital, lying on top of two dead monks.

Surveying this area, John said. "From the looks of it, this faceless dead guy on the floor, used this poor monk tied to the chair as cover from whomever he was shooting at." Pointing at the monk he said, "With all the bullet holes in his back, he didn't last too long as a human shield."

Turning his attention to the Abbot, John noted the random spread of the bullet wounds. "I'll bet he was just hit with stray shots that were intended for this guy…" John said pointing at the dead Korean, "… but missed both him and shield monk."

Altschuler had been standing by the two other dead monks. "Both of these monks were assassinated." He said. "They have single gunshot wounds to the head, but it looks like each may have taken a stray round or two."

The dead Korean team leader lay on his back near the feet of the monk bound to the chair. John now turned his attention to him. "I have a sneaking suspicion that if you test the ballistics of that weapon over there, it will match the casings from at least one of the prior scenes. I'd bet the ones from the nuns."

"Because these victims were shot from the front…". Altschuler opined.

"Exactly." John replied. Walking back toward the end of the hallway, John saw the brass from the Aryphon shooter halfway between the door and the dead Korean and he said, "This is where his killer fired from." Walking a bit further to the open door between the chapel hallway and the dorm, he continued. "The shooter shot out the lock, approached from the rear and then took him out,"

Altschuler was now standing by the table in the hallway with the two full water buckets and the still damp towels sitting beside it. "Do you think they were waterboarding the monks? He asked.

Nodding his head, John replied, "It's a good possibility. We'll know from the autopsy report. If they were waterboarded, there will be water in their lungs."

The pair left the dormitory hallway and headed to the chapel. As they walked through the courtyard John said to

Altschuler, "Your forensics folks are gonna be here forever processing this scene."

"I know." Altschuler said. I've never seen anything like this. "So many bullets, and blood everywhere."

"They were probably wearing body armor like our faceless friend in there, and took hits in the arms, legs or abdominal area. Not enough to kill you, but certainly enough to leave these blood trails." John said. "Make sure the forensic folks get DNA samples of all this blood."

"They will. They are very thorough.

Arriving at the chapel, John could make out the locations of where the shooters had taken cover, While he needed to get a feel for the scene so he could mentally orient future photographs, John was more interested in the machine located halfway up the aisle to the altar. Walking over to the ground penetrating radar machine left behind by the Koreans, John asked Altschuler if he knew what it was.

"I haven't a clue." The Inspector replied.

"It is a ground penetrating radar machine." John said. "This confirms my suspicion that they were here looking for something. Same as in the other locations. The holes in the walls and floor were not random acts of vandalism. They were made to check if something was hidden behind or beneath where ever they made a hole. That is why these people were tortured. They were interrogated to give up the location of whatever these people were looking for."

"What could they be after that would have them do these… these things to people."

"I don't know." John replied. "What was it the monk at the hospital was saying?… Where is the ghastly? That makes no sense."

Altschuler said, "The nurse at the hospital thought he was saying the big light. Wo ist der grosse licht?"

"That doesn't make much sense either". John replied. I'll run it through our data base when I get back to Rome, and share what I find with you."

"And hopefully the monk pulls through and I can interview him again in a few days. He might be able to tell me more when he is more lucid."

"I'll include him in my prayers tonight". John said.

John and Altschuler spent the next hour examining the scene, and while Altschuler was focused on trying to piece together a chronology of events, John was already formulating his next steps. Based on everything he had seen and read, the key to this case was learning what the 'ghastly' was. Once he knew that, John assumed he could figure out who wanted it so badly that they would murder over a dozen people for it.

Mary Morrison and her team were waiting in the hotel lobby at six AM, per William Alvarez's instructions. Despite the early hour of their departure, she and the team had gone out the night before and celebrated their accomplishments. Now after too many bottles of red wine, and some amazing food courtesy of Aryphon and Mary's expense account, she and her team were sporting massive hangovers.

The limo arrived a few minutes later, and the driver escorted the researchers to the car and assisted them with their luggage. He apologized for being a few minutes late and explained that there was early construction going on, and that had also prevented him from stopping and picking up some water for the trip.

Mary had taken two Tylenol when she had awakened, but it had done nothing to relieve the throbbing headache she was feeling. One of her team members had asked Mary for some of her Tylenol, but without water, she was unable to take it. The driver assured the team that once they got to the airport and on the plane, they would be able to take their medication and also get some food that might help quiet any queasy stomachs.

As the limousine navigated through the early morning traffic, they reached the area that the driver had indicated was under construction. Coming to a complete stop, the car crept along for the next half hour moving only a few feet at a time. Finally getting clear of the construction crews, the driver apologized, and advised his passengers that they should be at the airport within twenty minutes. While powerless to change the circumstances, the incessant stop and go of the construction traffic did little to improve the condition of the hungover passengers.

Finally arriving at the airport, the team was escorted out of the car and directly up the stairs of the waiting Gulfstream jet. Directed to their seats by the flight attendant, Mary and her people were informed that they needed to leave immediately if they were to make their departure window. Mary and her team buckled up, the door to the private plane was closed and the engines spooled up to advance the corporate jet onto the taxiway.

The plane traveled along the DaVinci Airport taxiways for several minutes before it came to a stop. Getting on the intercom, the Captain advised the passengers that there was a ground-stop at their destination, Kennedy Airport, and they would need to hold here for a bit. Promising to keep everyone informed, the Captain shut down the engines while everyone waited.

After twenty minutes, as the temperature in the cabin continued to climb, Mary signaled to the flight attendant that she needed to speak to her.

"Unfortunately, my team and I celebrated a little too much last night. I was wondering if you had any water so we could take some Tylenol."

The woman Mary had given the pills to earlier said. "I can't find what I did with the ones you gave me earlier. I'm going to need more along with the water."

"Of course." The flight attendant replied. "Give me a minute."

Heading to the galley section, the flight attendant poured four cups of water, then donning latex gloves, took a pill container from the cabinet and went back into the cabin,

"Here, take two of these." The flight attendant said, shaking two pills into her gloved hand after handing Mary a plastic glass filled with water.

"What is it?" Mary asked, looking at the pills in her hand.

"It's a European pain reliever. The flight attendant replied. "It's similar to ibuprophen, but it doesn't upset the stomach. It works great. I take it all the time."

Popping the pills in her mouth, Mary washed them down with her water.

Distributing the water and medication to the rest of the passengers, the flight attendant returned to her seat, and pushed the intercom button twice, alerting the flight crew it was clear to proceed. Coming back on the intercom, the Captain announced they had received clearance to depart and would be taking off in a few minutes.

Mary sat looking out the window as the plane advanced to the runway, then accelerated down the runway and into the air. By the time the plane was airborne, Mary noticed that her headache was gone. Banking left as they climbed, then right, Mary watched the clouds float by the plane, and began to see them take the shape of animals.

Bunnies and squirrels were running alongside the plane as Mary watched them change from the white of the clouds to multi-colored creatures that smiled back at her through the window. If Mary had thought to look at the rest of her team, she would have seen each of them, relaxed in their leather seats, smiling at the drug induced trips they were experiencing in their heads.

Leveling off at thirty-thousand feet, the pilot signaled the flight attendant they had completed their climb out, and it was safe to move about the cabin. The Donner Global mercenary, substituting for a flight attendant went to the galley area, and prepared four syringes of a fentanyl based opioid and injected each of the passengers, completing the overdose of the fentanyl pills she had given them earlier.

Four and a half hours later, Gulfstream 2040 in-route from Rome to Montevideo declared an emergency, claiming hydraulic failure and the loss of one engine. Descending rapidly to five hundred feet, the pilot issued a Mayday stating that they were going to ditch the plane in the ocean. Giving the latitude and longitude coordinates, he manually shut off the transponder, then carefully banked the plane north and dropped below four hundred feet to remain below radar.

Crossing over land by the Oyapok River, along the border between Brazil and French Guiana, the pilot flew the corporate jet inland over jungle and rainforest to an abandoned airstrip deep in the jungle. Previously used by South American drug smugglers, Aryphon had purchased the land surrounding the airstrip and after forcing the drug smugglers out, used the site to clandestinely ferry people and materials around the globe.

Taxiing to a nearby building, the flight crew was immediately met by a crew of workers who removed the four bodies and began the task of changing the plane's registration markings and transponder. Within three hours, Gulfstream 2040 became a totally different aircraft, refueled and ready for takeoff, and Mary and her team were deposited in a mass grave in the middle of the jungle.

The Brazilian Coast Guard was unable to locate any survivors or the wreckage of Aryphon's Gulfstream despite an extensive search. Both the company as well as William Alvarez personally sent flowers and cards of condolences to the funerals for Mary and her team, lost in a tragic accident over the Atlantic.

After leaving Austria, John arrived back in Rome early the next morning and headed straight to Gendarmerie Headquarters. Grabbing Tony, they entered the Information Center in order to utilize the computers and databases to run down potential leads developed by the investigative work that had been done to date.

None of the ballistics evidence gathered at either of the first two scenes matched anything in any of the databases. The torture methods, while gruesome, were not unique, and matched literally thousands of other cases across the globe over the last twenty years. In order to help support his theory that the perpetrators were looking for something, John wanted to be able to disprove that the attacks were targeted against the Church by terroristic groups with a vendetta against the Church.

John and the Information Center team spent nearly three hours searching first for threats against monastic orders, then acts committed by monastic orders against other groups that may have precipitated an act of vengeance. While there were a handful of the latter done over five hundred years ago, unless you call eastern European witches an institution, and believe they are organized and possess an institutional memory, no one could realistically say there were any groups actively looking to deliver vengeance against monastic orders.

After taking a quick break for lunch, John and Tony returned to the Information Center to begin looking at the new information gathered from the latest attack. While none of the forensic evidence had been processed yet, John had written down extensive notes from his observations at the scene, along with what the survivor had said at the hospital.

While not confirmed by ballistic information, John quickly discounted the possibility that there was a mutiny of sorts by members of one team of operators. Based on what John saw, that just did not feel right. There were two teams at the monastery. One team was in the process of searching for something, while the other interrupted them, with the gun battle ensuing. Following this line of thought supported John's observation that the two prior attacks had been committed by two separate teams. While initially, it could have been argued that the two teams were both part of one larger group, based on the intensity of gun battle that took place, these were clearly competing teams looking to remove the competition completely.

John glanced at his watch and noticed the day was quickly getting away from him. He needed to meet with Sentille to give him an update before the end of the day.

John said, "Hey Tony, I have to see about getting an audience with Sentille. I want to go over the monk's statement next. Can you find an officer who is fluent in German? Mine is a bit rusty and I want to really dive into what he is saying."

Looking at his boss with surprise, Tony said, "Your German is rusty? I did not even know you spoke German."

"Tony, you should know by now... I'm full of surprises." Excusing himself John stepped out of the Information Center and reached out to Sentille's assistant to make an appointment. Informed that the Cardinal was tied up for the balance of the day, John was about to request some time the next day, when he overheard Sentille in the background speaking to his assistant, then the Cardinal got on the phone himself.

"Welcome back, my son. I understand that you were right there when the new monastery was attacked." The Cardinal said.

"Well, I wasn't there when they were attacked, but we were able to speak to one of the survivors, and I got to see the new crime scene first hand. I have an update that I wanted to provide you and thought it may be better to do it face to face rather than to just have you read it in a report."

"Yes, I am very interested in hearing your insights, and it may be more efficient if I were able to ask you some questions as well. I also know the Holy Father is looking for an update too. Especially since this is the third monastery that has been attacked." The Cardinal said.

"I am still processing all the information, and may not have all the answers you are looking for, but I am available whenever you need me."

The Cardinal said, "You know… I am dining with Cardinal Dietrich this evening at his residence. I believe you are familiar with him and know where he lives. Why don't you stop by there after dinner… Say around eight PM? "I'm sure he would be interested in hearing your progress so far as well."

"Eight PM it is. I will see you later your Eminence."

John hung up his cell phone and returned to the Information Center. Tony was still sitting at the computer station, and another officer stood next to him.

"John, this is Gendarme Angelo Boccio. Gendarme Boccio, may I introduce Director General John Nowalski."

The young officer snapped to attention and rendered John a sharp salute. "Relax Gendarme." John said as he returned the salute. "We need your assistance and if you are all stiff and structured, you might miss something we need you to catch."

Boccio stood at-ease while John took a seat next to Tony. "OK, we have a statement from a survivor of the attack at the monastery. I was there and heard it personally, but I recorded it on my phone so we could review it again here."

John took a cable from the back of the computer and plugged it into his iPhone. He then opened the file of the bedside interview and downloaded it to the computer. Tony handed each man a set of headphones he had set up earlier, opened the newly downloaded file, and hit play. The three men listened to the recording from start to finish before John asked Boccio. "OK… what did he say?

Looking a little sheepish Boccio said tentatively, "Wo ist das grässlich? I agree with the Inspector. I think he said, *where is the ghastly.* "

Shaking his head, John said, "See, now I hear a "T" at the end." Turning to his friend, John said, "Tony, see if the computer can clean this recording up a bit. There is a ton of background noise. Can we get rid of that?"

Tony began typing commands into the computer, and the soundboard wave began to move. After a few minutes, he said, "Let's try it now."

The three men listened to the recording again with the background noise removed and the sounds within the vocal ranges amplified. After listening intently, Boccio shook his head and said, "I still hear where is the ghastly."

"And I still hear the "T" at the end… not every time, but enough. That would make what he is saying Wo ist das grasslicht." John replied.

"That makes no sense." Said Boccio.

"And where is the ghastly makes sense?" John quickly replied in disagreement.

Tony sat listening to the exchange and said, "OK, I don't speak German. What does it all mean?"

"If the last word is *grasslich*, it means where is the ghastly. If the last word is *grasslicht*…" John said, emphasizing the "T" on the end, "…grasslicht, with a "T" on the end, it means where is the grass light."

Boccio responded. "But if he meant grass light, they wouldn't say it like that. They would most likely say *Rasen*. Grass or lawn light would be *rasen licht* in German.

Tony shrugged, saying, "Well I think it sounds like *Grass licked*. But what do I know. I don't speak the language." Then looking over at John said, "And until a few minutes ago, I didn't think you did either."

John just smiled at his old teammate, then turned to address Boccio. "Gendarme Boccio, you have been a huge help. We will take it from here and let you know if we need any further assistance."

Boccio removed the headphones from around his neck, stood up from the chair and saluted. John stood out of respect and returned the salute, then extended his hand to the junior officer. "Thanks again." He said.

Turning back to Tony John said, "We have a lot of work to do with this. My working theory is that we are looking for some kind of religious artifact or ancient relic that was either left at, or taken by some monastery some time ago. News of this may have surfaced and we now have competing groups looking for it. Whatever it is, it must have significant value if these people are willing to fight and kill for it."

"When are you supposed to be updating Sentille?" Tony asked.

"Eight PM." John replied. "So that leaves us a good four hours to try to get some solid information. We will need to run all of these possibilities through all of the databases… criminal, religious, legal, scientific,… everything we can come up with. Why don't you get started with *Grass or Lawn Light*, and I'll run down *Ghastly?*

After nearly three hours, the two men ran through multiple permutations of the words through multiple databases. There was nothing in any of the religious, legal or scientific databases. Other than some minor vandalism reports under Grass Light, nothing came up on any searches there. Trying the words in English or Italian had similar useless results… a Pokémon, a garage band in California, an author, a filmmaker, and of course, hundreds of ads for yard and garden illumination systems.

John had begun typing up his notes and reports so that he would have something to present to Sentille in addition to his personal update. Tony had just excused himself to take care of some other matters he was working on, leaving John at the computer. The fact that after all this work, and gathering of all this information, they still had no solid leads, ate at John as he typed. Taking out his phone, he hit the button to play back the recording one more time. Closing his eyes, John listened intently to the savagely beaten monk.

"Graaslikt…" "Wo isht dash graaashlikt."
" What did he say?"
"I think he said Wo ist das grässlich"
"That makes no sense… Where is the ghastly? My German might be a bit rusty. Am I getting that right?"
"Der mann fragte er, wo isht das grushlisht?"
"Graaaslikt… Wo isht dash graashli… graslikt. Wo isht.."
"Tony is right…" John said to himself. "He is asking

where is the Grass Licked. I wonder if they are not looking for a thing, but a place. I wonder…"

John switched over from his reporting program to Google. He typed in *GRASS LICKED,* and hit enter. Several images and links came up immediately. While the first several referenced a meme, and the next talked about why dogs lick and eat grass, about three quarters of the way down the page, the search began to return addresses. From what John could tell, there was a Grasslick West Virginia in the United States.

Now potentially on to something, John continued to scroll until one particular link caught his attention. A funeral home from his home town in New Jersey listed an obituary for Mathius Grasslicked. John opened the link and read the short biography…

..Survived by his two daughters, and father, Mathius was a custom carpenter who followed in his father's footsteps and provided his customers with "fine German craftsmanship."

John sat and thought for a few moments. Altschuler was following up on all of the forensic evidence and John could reach out and get regular updates. The Inspector would also follow up once the monk was able to answer questions, and John trusted the professionalism of the Inspector to do a thorough job. Other than follow up on what he had just found, there was little else for John to do right now. There was also something else about this line of inquiry that was nagging at John. His gut was telling him something, and John had learned through his years of experience, that his gut was not often wrong.

He quickly finished typing up his report, ending it

with a nebulous note about following up leads in America based on his database searches, then called Tony on his cell phone.

"Hey Tony. I need you to do me a favor. I uncovered a lead in some additional database searches I did after you left. I have to run to see Sentille, but I need you to go online and book me a flight to…"

John quickly debated in his mind whether he should go to West Virginia or New Jersey first. While the New Jersey lead was not as sound as West Virginia, his gut was saying New Jersey. However, if his gut was correct, it may take a bit of time to develop any leads there. It may be more efficient to go to West Virginia first and get that crossed off the list.

"… one of the airports near West Virginia, maybe one of the DC area airports."

Knowing his boss, Tony asked, "Is this a solid lead or a gut thing?"

"It's actually more of a gut thing, but at this point, until the forensics turns something up, we don't have much more to go on."

"OK boss." Tony replied. "But you know Pinocchio won't like this."

"I'm not reporting to Pinocchio on this, and if it doesn't pan out, I'm gone anyway. Might as well go big or go home. And in this case, I mean that literally."

"OK. I will text you the flight information. Good luck at Sentille's"

"Thanks Tony. I'll keep you posted."

CHAPTER 8

**Kobe-San Japanese Restaurant
Sayreville, New Jersey
Present Day**

ADAM HAD NEVER used a dating site before. Since none of his friends or co-workers had been able to introduce him to someone, they suggested he try one of the popular online dating sites used by so many people. Posting a few of his pictures and writing what he thought was an interesting bio, Adam received a number of "matches" right off the bat.

All of the women were in their late thirties, and based on their pictures, appeared fairly fit and attractive. Communicating through the site at first, Adam struck up conversations with several of the women, and exchanged phone numbers with two of them. After a handful of phone conversations, he was able to recognize that one did not seem to be a good match, while the other agreed to a date the next night at seven PM. Now sitting at the Sushi restaurant bar, Adam waited for his date to arrive.

A few minutes after seven a woman appeared at the door to the restaurant and scanned the bar area. Dressed in a powder blue polyester pants suit that looked like it came straight out of a 1970s-time capsule, her stringy shoulder length gray hair looked like it hadn't been washed in over a week. She was tall, even without the four-inch black stiletto heels with broad shoulders and a slim waist. Seeing Adam, she entered the bar area balanced on the heels and walked with a swishing sound of the polyester pants straight to Adam.

"Adam! So good to meet you in person she squealed extending her manly hand for Adam to shake.

"Joyce?" Adam replied questioningly. "Thanks for coming."

"You know, I wasn't sure about coming tonight." She said. "I mean, there are just so many catfish out there, I wasn't sure you were real."

"Oh, I'm real alright." Adam said, thinking to himself, '*Real what, I don't know.*' "Shall we get a table?"

The couple were taken to a table and the waitress brought over two menus. Looking over the menu, Adam asked, "Do you like sushi?"

"Oh, I just love it. I think it's just amazing how they put all that stuff together in those little rolls." Joyce replied.

"Well we could either get the sushi entrée, or do the hibachi and get some sushi as an appetizer. Whatever you prefer."

The waitress returned and Adam ordered the hibachi

steak while Joyce ordered a sushi appetizer and a hibachi chicken dinner.

"On the hibachi chicken, does that come with rice, noodles and vegetables? Joyce asked the waitress.

"Yes, Noodles, rice and mixed vegetables." The waitress replied.

"Would you be able to substitute the rice with extra noodles. I'm trying to watch my weight and don't want the extra carbs. Joyce said.

As the waitress left Adam said, "You know, the noodles probably have just as many carbs as the rice."

Smiling at Adam as if he were an idiot, Joyce replied, "I know, silly. But I'm already eating the noodles, I don't need the carbs from the rice too."

"But you're… Never mind." Adam started, as he shook his head.

The pair began eating their salads when Adam made the mistake of asking, "So Joyce, tell me about yourself."

Joyce smiled at Adam, then put her fork down and launched. "Well, I'm really the shy and quiet type, and I'm an Aquarius but I'm not cold nor unpredictable. I'm also not a free spirit. I conform. I'm very conforming. That's me, Ms. Conformity. But maybe I am very much like what an Aquarian is like 'cause I am philanthropic. I love to help other people and am always giving away money or my clothes or food. I give my old clothes to those veterans bins all the time, and then I can't help myself when I see a food bank I have to give them canned goods or pasta or like jarred stuff like pasta sauce. You know, you really can't just eat pasta without the sauce. Yes, I think I'm very philanthropic. I also love music. All types of music. Rock, punk, country, new age, classical, rap, hip-hop, even disco. Well, maybe not disco that much. I never liked the 70's That was just a bad decade. I mean I wasn't alive during that decade, but I saw movies and stuff from it, and TV shows, and then the music, I already said I hate the music. But other music I do like, I like show tunes and grunge. Yeah, I guess I like almost all types of music, but I don't like just music. I like movies,... but not all types. I like horror movies, love stories, dramas and some comedies. Not all comedies, 'cause I don't think they are all funny..."

The waitress brought out the sushi appetizers and some miso soup, which allowed for a pause in Joyce's monologue. Adam took a piece of the sushi, and went to ask Joyce if she wanted a piece of sushi, but was interrupted. "Ssshhhhh." Joyce shushed putting here index finger over her lips. "I wasn't done talking." She said, and then continued.

"Oh yeah, I really don't like all comedies. Like Jim Carey, I think he is hilarious, but I'm not a fan of Chris Rock. Like, his stand up is OK, but I don't like his movies...

Joyce had taken a piece of the sushi and put it on her plate. Separating the chopsticks, she began picking at the California roll with the chopsticks, separating the crabmeat, avocado, cucumber and seaweed from the rice. She then used the chopsticks to pick up and eat the crabmeat and avocado.

"What are you.. What are you doing?" Adam interrupted.

"Sssshhhh, I'm still talking." Joyce replied again, putting the index finger first to her lips, then wagging it disapprovingly at Adam.

"No, not shush. Seriously, what are you doing?" Adam insisted.

Letting out a sigh, Joyce said, "What does it look like I'm doing? "I like the crabmeat and avocado, but I already told you I don't want the carbs from the rice."

"So, if you don't want the rice, why didn't you just get the crabmeat sashimi?

Joyce sighed again. "Because… then I wouldn't have gotten like the avocado and the seaweed and stuff."

"So, you like the avocado and seaweed, but not the rice…"

"Oh God no." Joyce exclaimed. "I hate the seaweed. Who on earth do you know who likes the seaweed? So, do you want me to finish telling you about myself, or don't you care anymore?"

Stunned by the behavior, Adam just said, "I'm sorry. Please continue."

Joyce continued, seemingly without stopping to breathe for the next ten minutes. Finishing the appetizer, soup and salad, the waitress brought out the entrées. Joyce finally came up for air and asked Adam, "So what's your story?"

"Well, I don't know… as my bio said, I like camping and fishing and outdoors stuff. My favorite music is classic rock-n-roll, you know, the Beatles, Stones, Led Zeppelin… that kind of rock. I went to Rutgers… got a degree in Criminal Justice… I'm a cop. Been on the job for…"

"Wait… What? You're a cop?" Joyce interrupted.

"A detective actually." Adam replied.

"You're not one of those racist, blue lives matter abusive cops, are you? I could never be with someone who beat up poor minority people just because you think you can get away with it."

"No. I'm not like that, and in reality, most cops are not like that." Adam replied.

"Ohhhh yes they are." Joyce said. "My friend Angela is Black, and she said she is afraid every time she sees a white cop because they are all racist."

Becoming a bit defensive, Adam said, "That, Joyce, is the opinion of one person, not a proof of fact. I can assure you, I am not racist, I do not go around beating up minorities, and none of my cop friends or fellow officers are either."

"Well, I think we will just have to agree to disagree. Now let's drop the subject." Joyce said.

"Fine." Adam said.

The two began eating their entrees as an uncomfortable silence settled over the table. A silence that was broken by the chewing noises emanating from Joyce. With each bite, Joyce would open her mouth about half-way, making a loud, wet lip-smacking noise, then biting down forcefully enough that Adam could hear her teeth clack. When she swallowed, she emitted a gulping noise similar to when cartoon characters swallowed in fear.

With so much air entering the mouth during her chewing, then forcefully swallowed, every fourth or fifth swallow was followed by a burp that was only stifled by the food still in her mouth. Adam could not imagine farm animals eating any more loudly than his current date.

"Excuse me for a minute. I need to use the restroom." Adam said as he got up from the table. Walking toward the back of the restaurant, Adam found the waitress, handed her his credit card and asked her for the check. Adding another twenty dollars to the bill, then leaving a twenty percent tip, Adam paid the check and returned to the table.

Joyce was finishing up the last of her meal when Adam asked. "So Joyce, I have to ask you. Whose pictures did you post on the dating site?"

Looking up from her food, Joyce replied, "Huh? What are you talking about?

"You know, the pictures. The ones you posted on the dating site. Clearly they are not you. And who wrote that bio, because either you have a serious disease that ages you, or you are not thirty-five years old. The bio also failed to mention your obvious narcissistic tendencies or your aversion to socially acceptable hygiene practices."

Joyce's mouth fell open in disbelief at the way Adam was speaking to her.

Adam said, "Close your mouth Joyce, you got food hanging out of it." Pausing for a second, Adam continued. "I have already paid the bill, and added some additional money on in case you would care for desert or coffee. You have wasted enough of my evening, so I am going to go. Please delete my number and don't reach out because I intend to block you. Joyce, you are the complete personification of everything wrong with online dating, and why I will NEVER go on any of those sites again. I wish you well. Have a good rest of your evening."

Adam turned and left Joyce sitting in stunned silence.

John arrived exactly on time at Cardinal Dietrich's residence and was escorted into the living room. The two prelates were seated on the couch enjoying a cup of espresso after their dinner. Dietrich offered John a cup, but he declined and asked if he could begin the briefing because he had a plane to catch.

"Where are you going now Director General?" Cardinal Sentille asked.

"After this briefing, I am headed to America to follow up on some recently developed leads." John replied.

"America? Do you think that wise? I mean, I would think you would head back to Austria in order to be there to stop the next attack." Sentille said.

"Your Eminence, the Austrian National police is working with some of the local constabulary to set up protective postings around as many of the monasteries as possible. If we want to catch these perpetrators, we need to get ahead of them, and to do that we need to figure out what they are looking for."

"What do you mean looking for? Sentille asked. "These are terrorists, not robbers."

"I don't believe they are terrorists. And there's more than one group out there doing this."

"What? Director General, you have been on this case for less than a week and you have already come up with a completely different line of thought than both the Austrian National Police and your Inspector General. I find that discomforting and a bit self-aggrandizing. Why do you think you are right, and all the others are wrong?

"Based on the evidence and what I saw from the first two crime scenes, and what was then confirmed at the third scene. Please, allow me to explain."

John spent the next twenty minutes laying out the facts

of the case, the differing interrogation and execution methods, the ballistic differences, the ground penetrating radar machine and the body of the attacker. John concluded with the statements made by the monk, and vaguely alluded to his development of leads in America.

"There is not much I can do sitting here. We are waiting for the forensic evidence from the third scene to be evaluated, and for the monk to wake up enough to be questioned again."

Dietrich said, "Oh, so you haven't heard… the monk passed on an hour ago. It seems he had pneumonia and a massive infection in addition to the other injuries."

"Oh,… I'm sorry to hear that." John said pausing to incorporate this new information into his plan. Continuing he said "Based on that, I believe it is even more imperative to follow up on the information we currently have. I think the key to this is either around the Sayreville, New Jersey area, or Grasslick, West Virginia."

Cardinal Dietrich asked, "Isn't Sayreville where you are originally from?"

"It is , Your Grace." John replied. "But that has no bearing in why I need to go there. I am following up on information that may be very relevant to this case, and need to conduct some interviews to see what additional leads I can develop."

"I still think you should go back to Austria." Sentille said.

"Eminence, you promised you would not micromanage me on this case. I am providing you with the updates you need. Please, just let me do my job."

Sentille was clearly unhappy and agitated by John and

the report he gave. He turned to Dietrich and said rapidly in Italian, "You said he was an amazing investigator. Now the idiot wants to go off chasing this down the wrong road."

Dietrich responded in Italian, "Give him a chance. If he fails, he is only hanging himself."

Looking at John, Sentille asked, "When do you leave?"

"I am on the eleven fifty-five flight to Dulles in Washington, DC."

"Well, it appears your mind is made up. Good luck in America. Please continue to keep me posted." Sentille said.

"Thank you, I will." John replied. "And don't worry, I am not going down the wrong path. I wouldn't do this if I thought it would hang me or the investigation out to dry."

As Sentille closed the door after escorting John out, he asked Dietrich. "His response… Do you think he understood what we said?"

Dietrich replied. "I'm not sure. I always thought he only spoke English."

It late in the afternoon when Joon Min Kim knocked on the door frame of Hermann Alvarez's office.

"Sir, the Cardinal is on the phone. He says it's urgent."

"Very well. Put him through." Alvarez replied. Picking up the phone, Alvarez greeted the Cardinal. "Your Eminence, what can I do for you at this fine day?"

"I am following up on your last request of me." The Cardinal said.

"And what request was that?"

"That I help find the Big Light." Replied the Prelate.

"Oh… You have new information?

"I do, and I believe you will find this very helpful. We have assigned our best investigator to the monastery attacks. While he is not highly thought of in the Curia, he is brilliant at tracking down leads. Unlike the other fools here who still believe the attacks were done by terrorists, he has determined that there were actually two groups, and they were looking for something hidden at the monasteries. That is what led to the monks and nun's deaths. He has uncovered information that the items the people are looking for has been moved to America, and he is headed there now to track it down."

"Did he say precisely where in the States he was looking? Alvarez asked.

"One possible location was in Grasslick West Virginia. The other was near a town in New Jersey called Sayreville."

"This is wonderful information. We have already determined that the plans made it to Brooklyn, New York. We have our researchers attempting to track them from there. This new information will give us greater confidence in anything we uncover, and help us pinpoint where the plans are. My only concern regarding this is how good is this investigator?" Alvarez asked.

"As I said, he is the best we have. John Nowalski has helped thwart several attacks on the Church over the years, as well as two planned assassination attempts on the Pope. He and his team took the lead on the multi-national task force that tracked down and brought Khalid Al-Bagdona to justice."

Alvarez asked, "Do you think he will find these plans before we do?"

"It is a possibility, but he doesn't know what he is looking for. He thinks he is looking for some kind of priceless religious relic. He also trusts me, so I am privy to any information he uncovers. Therefore, what he knows, you will know."

"My other concern is if he is as good as you say, and his ultimate goal is to uncover who attacked those monasteries, will he be able to trace it back to us?"

The Cardinal thought for a moment before responding. "I can help steer him toward the other team, and help misdirect him, however, he is smart…"

"We will have to remain vigilant. Make sure you continue to get regular updates on his progress, and keep me or my son William informed. He is personally directing all aspects of our alternative energy initiative, and the procurement of the Big Light and graphene manufacturing plans falls under that vertical."

"I will make sure of it." The Cardinal replied.

Alvarez concluded, "I would love to use Nowalski's talents to augment our efforts, but if this goes sideways, we will need to take other action to safeguard our success."

"I understand." The Cardinal said.

"Thank you for your attention to this, Your Eminence."

"It is my pleasure to serve the cause." The Cardinal replied.

Hermann Alvarez sat in his study later that evening, sipping a tumbler of finely aged bourbon. He looked at his watch for the third time in the last fifteen minutes. So much of his future plans hinged on the information he was about to receive. Finally, his phone rang and he quickly picked up the receiver.

"This is Hermann Alvarez." He said, indicating to the caller that he was alone and able to speak freely

"Hermann, so good to speak to you again. How are things in beautiful Uruguay?

"It is hot, as always, Senator Conrad. Actually, this is our winter so it is quite a bit cooler than during our summers, which tend to be unbearably hot." Alvarez said in scripted reply. If either of the men had said anything different, the other would have known it was not safe to speak, and the remainder of the conversation would be about trade deficits or other innocuous topics.

"I am considering moving up the timeline. There have been a handful of developments that are causing me some concern and since they are out of my control I do not want to leave them to chance." Alvarez said.

"So, what do you need to know?" the Senator asked.

"Where do things stand on the political front, and how would you read the mood of the people?"

"Well, both houses of Congress are totally divided along ideological and party lines. There is very little, if any compromise going on, so ultimately, nothing is getting done. The immigration problem is totally out of control and is putting a major strain on both the finances and resources of a number of the metropolitan areas across the country. Despite this, the Administration is staying the course and not putting any controls on the border."

"Between what we and that idiot anarchist in New York are giving them, the Administration better be staying the course." Alvarez said.

"Because the Republicans control the House, we have not heard too much more about the Green New Deal. The

Democratic Socialists keep reintroducing the bill every year, but with a Republican majority, it will not go anywhere. However, the House majority is slim, and with both the Senate and Presidency under Democrat control, one more little push and we could see a cascade of restrictive legislation in response to the climate crisis."

"This all sounds like what we anticipated." Alvarez said.

"It is." Conrad replied. "Right now, it looks like our current president will seek re-election, and those idiots in the Republican party will nominate a convicted felon. I can't even imagine which way things will go if either of them gets elected. If the Democrats win, and they are able to flip the House back, you will see spending to reward their constituent groups and restrictive legislation like you have never seen before. They will be like kids with mommy's wallet let loose in a candy store… If the Republicans win, the chaos that the media and the Democrats will create will be like nothing ever seen before. And all this will have a negative effect on the psyche of the people."

Alvarez asked, "Eric, you are a student of history. Give me your thoughts… Are the American people on the verge of revolution?"

"I have never seen this country so divided. They long for someone to unify them, but all they keep getting from their leaders is more divisive rhetoric, and a media that broadens the divide… I wouldn't say they are on the verge of revolution right now, but as a nation, we are on a very slippery slope."

"And if a little gasoline is added to that fire?…"

"I could see the bottom falling out." Conrad replied.

Alvarez sat quietly for a few moments as he contemplated this recent report in relation to his overall plans.

"Dad?… Are you still there?" Conrad asked.

"Yes son. I'm just thinking. So, essentially, no matter the outcome of the 2024 election, you do not see much chance on repairing the political divide in the country, and despite Republican control of the House, the climate alarm is still ringing loudly."

"That is a pretty accurate assessment, yes."

"Good. This was most helpful… So, how is your mother?

"She is good. We miss you. We were able to see Emma the other day. She had a trip out to the west coast, and was able to make a stop to visit."

"I have this Board meeting coming up this week. I'll make it a point to come up and visit after that and I can fill you both in on where things stand."

"Sounds good. How goes the search for the cold fusion and graphene plans?" Conrad asked.

"We've traced the plans to America and our researchers are following up on where they may have gone. In the meantime, I plan to have one of our teams trail an investigator from the Vatican who seems to have uncovered some leads on the plans whereabouts as well. Currently the investigator is searching in West Virginia, but they may be looking up in New Jersey as well. I am confident we will find them, and when we do, it will put us in an even better place to see our plans to fruition."

"Very good. Well, keep me informed Dad. Let me know if you need any other help."

"I will son." Alvarez replied. "Give my love to your mother. Tell her I will speak to her soon."

Laura Conrad was a college freshman taking summer courses at Hertford College in Oxford, England when she met Hermann Alvarez. Ten years her senior, Alvarez was completing a graduate degree in Economics at Oxford before returning home to assume a senior leadership role in his father's company. Their brief whirlwind romance left them both smitten, and despite his father's objections, Alvarez wanted to pursue the relationship.

Spending all of his free time traveling to the States to see Laura, the couple grew closer and began planning a future together. Seeing that his son's relationship was not a passing phase, the senior Alvarez did a bit of investigating into who his potential new daughter-in-law was. It was at this point that the senior Alvarez saw an opportunity to satisfy both his son's desires as well as the family's plans for the future. Laying out his idea to Hermann, the senior Alvarez was delighted when his son agreed.

Laura's mother was a widow. Having had her daughter late in life, Laura's mother struggled financially after her husband had passed away from a sudden heart attack. Now sixty-five years old and wanting to retire, Laura's mom was forced to continue working in order to help put her daughter through college. Alvarez invited Laura and her mother to come spend the upcoming Christmas holiday with him and his family. If everything went as planned, Hermann would be married by New Years.

Hermann and Laura were married on New Year's Day

in a private ceremony at the Alvarez estate. Laura and her mother returned to the States and soon after, Laura's mother retired from her job and relocated to a nice waterfront apartment in Montevideo. Laura remained in college and visited her mother and her husband during summers, holidays and semester breaks. After completing her nursing degree, Laura would see Hermann often, but the couple maintained a clandestine, long-distance marriage with Laura living in the U.S. and Hermann remaining in Uruguay.

As time went by and their bond of trust grew, Hermann let Laura know of the family's plan. When Laura gave birth to their first son, Eric, he was to be raised in the States, primarily by his *"single"* mother. Their other two children were born and raised in Uruguay with their father as the principle parent. While the arrangement was unorthodox, Laura and Hermann made it work. From an early age, the children were told they were destined for great things. Eric entered the Naval Academy, and went on to serve as a naval aviator, attaining the rank of Commander. Leaving the service, he entered politics and went on to become a State Senator from his home state of Texas before being appointed to the U.S. Senate after the death of the state's senior Senator. Recently elected in the last general election, Conrad had quickly earned a reputation as a common-sense conservative who had a knack for negotiating compromise solutions while protecting his conservative principles.

There was talk amongst party insiders that the young senator from Texas showed great potential for higher office. And while Conrad made it clear his plans did not include a desire to be considered in the upcoming election, what the beltway crowd did not know was that his family's future plans were for Eric to achieve something even greater.

Joon Min Kim sat in the back row of the relatively empty movie theatre eating her popcorn and staring at the screen, but not paying the least bit of attention to the movie. Finally, after half the movie was over, a darkly clad figure slid into the seat beside her. Looking straight ahead, with his eyes in perpetual motion, Kim Joo-Won asked, "What is so important that we needed to meet. We received your last transmission relayed through your mother and have already sent the team to America. We are using some of our Mexican cartel connections and will have them across the southern border in two days. Once across, they will rent a vehicle and drive to New Jersey. There are only four *Wagners* living in that town Sayreville. We will start there, and see what else develops. If we turn up nothing, we can always follow that Vatican cop and see where he leads us."

"I understand one of the team members was killed at the last monastery they searched." Joon Min said.

"Yes, the team leader. It was a pity. He was a good man. I will be meeting the team in New Jersey and taking charge personally, so this meeting is delaying my departure."

"And his team was unable to retrieve the body before they exfiltrated…"

"Yes, unfortunately that is true. The report from the second in command stated they were taken by surprise by a force of superior numbers and lost the tactical advantage. They all sustained injuries and two of the team actually need to be replaced. I need them for the next phase of the operation, so any punishment for breaking protocol will be withheld until after this operation is complete."

Joon Min sighed, then said, "OK, so here is the problem. The other team took DNA samples and photographs."

"There is nothing for any western intelligence agency to match either of them to." Kim replied.

"No, but the DNA reports will say they were Korean." Joon Min said, the exasperation still coming across despite the whispered tone.

Looking confused, Kim said, "I do not understand."

"The problem with being a 'Hermit Kingdom' with a very homogenous population for multiple generations is that the genetic markers for a region are clearly discernable. I'm sure you never did one of those commercial genetic test things. One of the first things they can tell you is your genetic ancestry. I'm sure the more sophisticated tests they used on your team leader and any blood left behind by your wounded men will let them know with certainty that he was from the Korean peninsula."

"OK, so maybe they will find that out. How does that effect what we will do?" Kim asked.

"It will have little effect on what you do. It will have a dramatic effect on what happens to me." Joon Min said. "Alvarez has been acting a bit strange ever since our labs halted the gain of function research on the virus. I don't think he knows what is going on, but he has been more cautious, and has had more meetings with his key people, checking on the progress of their projects. Something is going on and once he learns the other team was Korean, I have a feeling I would not be working there much longer. In fact, I probably wouldn't be alive much longer."

"So, what do you propose to do?" Kim asked.

"I need some better tech. I want to plant a listening device in Alvarez's office and the Board room that I can monitor from a distance. I don't think it is safe for me to be there any longer. I am also going to need a safehouse to operate from."

"Joon Min, I feel you are being a bit paranoid. Since you were not professionally trained, you do not necessarily know when a situation presents real danger."

"Do not underestimate my training. I was raised by two of the best operatives either of their countries ever saw. I learned surveillance when I was five. My favorite game at age eight was counter-surveillance. Where other kids my age were playing hide-and-seek, I was learning how to disappear from my parents… operatives trained in surveillance."

"I just want to make sure you are not just getting scared as things get a bit more intense." Kim said.

"If they suspect me and grab me before I can escape because I was too concerned with proving to my control officer that I am brave and as professional as any of his other operatives, they *WILL* use enhanced interrogation techniques including drugs before they kill me. They did that with the monks, I don't think they would hesitate with someone they feel betrayed them. And I don't think you want me divulging any information, do you, brother?"

"You really feel like your life is in danger?" Kim asked.

"Immediate danger, no. But as soon as they learn the DNA results of your operator, I am as good as dead if I am still there." Joon Min replied. "Brother listen… My mother always told me that good operatives develop a sixth sense.

They instinctively know when to push and when to back off… and ultimately, when to run. I know you have those traits, because you are a good operative. Please give me the benefit of the doubt that I am one as well."

"OK, sister, I will. I have the technology you need at the safehouse. Meet me outside in five minutes and I will show you where the safehouse is, and give you the listening devices. When do you plan to deploy them?"

"I will go back to the office this evening and replace the one in Alvarez's office with this new one, and then find a place to hide the one in the Board room. After that, I will go back to my apartment and grab some things and take them to the safehouse. I will operate from there until there are further developments."

"The listening devices have a range of a little under a kilometer. You must remain in the general vicinity of your office to be able to monitor and record the conversations." Kim said.

"I plan to sit in my car a few blocks away. As long as I move every so often, I shouldn't draw attention to myself, and the company doesn't patrol its perimeter. All of their security is internal. I will continue to report through my usual channels. If anything changes, I will report that as well."

"You are doing well, comrade sister. Perhaps I was a bit too harsh with you when we first met."

"Its water under the bridge, brother." Joon Min said.

"What? Which bridge?… What are you talking about?"

"Brother, if you are going to America, you should brush up on some of the expressions. You wouldn't want to say the wrong thing and have someone think you were a spy."

The red-eye flight from Rome to Dulles International Airport got John to Washington at two AM. John would have started his five-hour drive to Grasslick right away, but the kiosk for the car rental company did not open again until six. Utilizing the one luxury he had always afforded himself, John made his way to the American Express lounge. With the global travel his job had previously required, whether for working on cases or delivering lectures, John had accumulated a wealth of miles, and his upgrade to the Platinum card was worth the cost on occasions like this.

Settling in to one of the comfortable leather recliners, John set his phone alarm for five-thirty AM, and dozed off to sleep. Awakening to the alarm, he made his way to the bathroom, splashed some water on his face, and addressed his beard with the electric razor in his toiletries kit. His short-cropped hair needed a little water and gel to get back into shape, and a fresh application of deodorant and cologne completed his morning emergency makeover. He counted on being able to shower once he had secured a hotel room.

John was first in line at the car rental counter when it opened, and after getting himself a comfortable car, and ensuring the rental agency knew this would most likely be a one-way rental, he set off for the Sheriff's Department of Jackson County West Virginia. Having gotten the Commanding Officer's email address from Tony during the flight, John had sent an email out last night informing them of his arrival today, and requesting some time to speak to one of the supervising deputies.

Arriving at the Jackson County Sheriff's office in Ripley, West Virginia, John parked his rental in a visitor space and went to see the desk Sargent. Advising the Sargent who he was and that he had requested to meet with someone, he was escorted back into an interview room and asked to wait for the lieutenant.

After a few minutes, the door opened and Lieutenant Darryl Hoskins entered and shook John's hand.

"Ya know, when ah was forwarded your email this mornin', ah went an' googled ya." Hoskins said with a thick southern drawl. "Then ah saw you are a reg-u-lar Wyatt Erp. Ah mean, you done caught that drug kingpin, then that Al-Bogdana terrorist guy. Ah mean, we got ourselves a real cee-lebrity here."

"I wouldn't say that, Lieutenant." John responded. "I was just doing my job in both of those cases."

"Well, shee-it... You still got yourself some track record. So, what are y'all doin' here in little ol' Jackson County, and how can I help ya?"

"This is going to sound a bit strange, Lieutenant, but I am not sure. I am working a case where a number of monks and nuns were murdered, and I uncovered some information that pointed me here."

"Ah saw that shit on TV. A bunch of terrorists attacked some monasteries, right?"

"Yeah, that's the case, but I don't think they were terrorists. I think they were looking for something... some religious artifact or ancient relic perhaps. I'm not sure."

"And y'all think these people are hiding out here?" Hoskins asked.

"No, I don't expect to find them here. I'm hoping I can develop some additional leads on what they were looking for." John replied. "Here...Let me play you the recording."

John pulled out his phone and cued up the recording of the monk. "This is a recording of a monk who survived the most recent shooting. It was taken at his bedside in the hospital emergency room, so there is a bunch of background noise. He is speaking in German, but listen to the last word in each sentence. Tell me what it sounds like he is saying."

John played the recording for the Lieutenant, who listened carefully, nodding his head at the end of the tape.

John said, "So he keeps repeating, Wo ist das, which in English means where is the…" John held his hands out as if cueing the Lieutenant to finish the sentence.

"Grasslicked." Said the Lieutenant. "But he sounds like he's got marbles in his mouth." Hoskins continued.

"He was beaten pretty badly, had lost teeth and had a broken jaw. He was also shot twice. It's a wonder he could talk at all. So, I did a Google search and came up with the logical answer to 'where is the grass licked?'… in Grasslick West Virginia."

Hoskins said, "Well alrighty then. That there makes sense. I guess we are all headin' down to Grasslick."

John accompanied Hoskins down to his patrol car and the two headed down the county road toward Grasslick.

"How you fixin' to handle this?" Hoskins asked.

"I thought I would just poke around a little. See if I could get the lay of the land. Check in on any of the Catholic churches in the area. Are there any old Catholic churches down around Grasslick?" John said.

"You aint been down these here parts much." Hoskins replied. "We got a lot of Baptist and Pentecostal and Evangelical churches down here. But not too many Catholics and not too many Jews."

"What about years ago. Any churches that maybe used to be Catholic churches?" John asked.

"Not that I can recall. But you know who you need to talk to?… Old man Brammer. He's like ninety-five years old but still sharp as a whip. He's got a lot of oral history of the county. I could have Fitzhugh back at HQ reach out to his grandson. Maybe we could take a run over and talk to him."

Fitzhugh got back to the Lieutenant and informed him that old man Brammer was in Charleston getting some medical tests done. If Hoskins wanted to go there on Monday, the grandson said he could speak to him. Hoskins suggested that maybe they could talk to some of the folks at the State Police. They patrolled this area as well, and maybe one of them might have an idea where John could look.

Grasslick was more like the name of an area in West Virginia than an actual town. There was a road that ran through the area that bore the name Grasslick, as did a creek. The residents occupied farms that sprawled over a 3 mile area. John had Hoskins drive most of Grasslick Road, which meandered pretty much north and south somewhat parallel to Interstate seventy-seven, as he tried to imagine how and when a monastic order would have hidden some artifact or relic here.

John had Hoskins stop the vehicle and he walked down to check out Grasslick Creek. Finding the creek unremarkable, John returned to the car and paused outside the vehicle looking around as he thought.

"Is everything alright?" Hoskins asked?

Continuing to look around, John replied, "Yeah…"

Then shaking his head, he continued. "I don't think this is the place. I'm going under the assumption that the people who committed these crimes were searching for something in the monasteries. These monasteries are hundreds of years old, so I am guessing the thing they are looking for is at least equally as old. If this thing was moved, it would have to have been after the late seventeen hundreds." Finally looking at Hoskins, John asked, "What year was this place settled?"

"1814 I think." Hoskins replied.

"This area has been the same since the eighteen hundreds. There are no Catholic churches here, no Catholic cemeteries,… The monks from back then would not have trusted someone from outside the order, let alone someone outside the religion if they needed to hide something. Nah… when enough of the facts support my gut, I'm usually right."

"So wadda ya wanna do?" Hoskins asked.

"I want to complete my due diligence. I don't want to leave any lingering questions in my head about this place. So, let's go talk to the State Police, and then if you could assist me and take me to go see that Mr. Brammer tomorrow, I can have a chat with him. If I don't turn up anything new, I will be out of your hair after that."

"Sounds good sir. Let's go visit with the troopers. Say, do you have any dinner plans?" Hoskins asked.

"No, not really." John replied.

"Ah know this fantastic BBQ place. Maybe you could join me and a few of the boys for some dinner, and tell us how you track down all them international terrorists."

"Does this place have beer?" John asked.

"Yeah… but I thought I read you was like a priest or something." Hoskins said.

"I'm actually a Novitiate. That's a monk who hasn't taken any vows yet."

"Ohhhh, I see." Said Hoskins "And monks can drink?"

"Who do you think invented beer Lieutenant." John said grinning.

The four men were dressed totally in black, with each of them carrying over fifty pounds of weapons and supplies for their incursion into the United States. The cartel's coyotes were given strict instructions that these high value customers were to be given the best possible treatment, and that every effort to successfully get them across the border must be utilized.

Utilizing a seldom used crossing of the Rio Grande and slipping under some poorly maintained barbed wire, the coyotes got the men across the border undetected and to a jeep waiting on the other side. Donning night vision goggles, the four men left their Mexican guides and struck out across the desert toward Highway Ninety. Once on the highway, they turned east and quickly headed for State Highway 349. Turning north on 349 they traveled for about an hour before finally turning east on Interstate Ten. With the goal of making it to San Antonio before dawn, the group leader did some mental math and calculated that they should complete the three-and-a-half hour trip with a half hour to spare before sunrise.

Reaching San Antonio, they stashed the stolen jeep in an alley near the car rental facility, and having already changed into regular civilian clothing waited with their gear in a hotel that rented rooms by the hour. Using impeccably forged identification documents and a stolen credit card, the group leader rented an SUV for the long drive to New Jersey. Returning to pick up his comrades, the team immediately activated the GPS and followed the directions back to the interstate for their twenty-six hour trip.

Having already chosen the driving rotation schedule, each driver would drive for a six hour stretch, finding the nearest town or rest stop with a gas station as they approached the six-hour mark. While the rest of the team slept, the driver would follow the GPS and make sure to remain at the speed limit and obey all the traffic laws.

Arriving in New Jersey a little less than twenty-six hours later, the team met up with Kim Joo-Won who took command of the men. From notification to their arrival on station, it took the North Korean special forces assault team less than thirty hours to infiltrate, and establish a base of operations in a suburb of the largest city of their greatest enemy. Kim Joo-Won thought to himself, *The Supreme Leader would be proud.*

CHAPTER 13

**Aryphon Corporate Headquarters
Montevideo, Uruguay
Present Day**

"Miss Drussel, what are you doing?" Alvarez asked his son's Executive Assistant.

"I am preparing the board room. Joon Min called out sick today."

"Oh… Well then proceed." Alvarez said.

As the Assistant set up the computer and projector and made sure there were enough water bottles sitting in the tub filled with ice, Alvarez asked, "Do you know how she is doing?"

"Excuse me sir?" Drussel asked.

"Joon Min… Do you know how she is feeling? She so rarely takes time off and she knows how important board meetings are. I was just wondering how she was?"

Drussel said, "I am not sure sir. I can reach out and ask her if you would like."

Alvarez replied, "No, that won't be necessary. We can check in on her later."

As Drussel finished up getting everything set for the meeting, attendees began filing in and taking their seats. Alvarez remained standing, alternately looking out the windows and greeting board members as they entered the room. When the last of the attendees was seated, Alvarez had the Assistant close the shades and then dismissed her. Turning his attention to the members seated around the table, he addressed the Board.

"I would like to thank you all for coming today. I know this special meeting may have inconvenienced a number of you, but I assure you, once all of the information is laid out, you will see the need to modify our plans, and why I have brought you all together today.

We are going to do things a bit differently than our usual board protocol. Rather than complete departmental reports, I will be calling on select individuals to give us updates on their projects, and address questions that we as a group may have. So, I'd like to begin with Emma,…"

Looking over at his daughter with a smile full of pride, Alvarez said, "… who will update us on where things stand with the virus and the vaccine. Emma, if you would please?"

Standing to address the room, Emma Alvarez began, "Thank you papa. As many of you are aware, we were forced to sever ties with the North Korean lab after they inexplicably cut off communications with us. Luckily, ninety-five percent of the work they were contracted to do was complete, and up to that point, they had delivered an excellent product. The modified virus is a Parvovirus, similar to Parvovirus B19 which causes Fifth Disease, a usually mild viral infection, commonly found in children, that causes a red blotchy rash on the cheek. It is accompanied by joint pain, fever, cough, runny nose and headache. In severe cases, it can be accompanied by severe anemia.

Some of you may be familiar with the term Parvovirus, because it also occurs in dogs, giving them similar symptoms with the addition of intestinal distress. We felt this was the ideal candidate for our gain of function research because the viral mutation can easily be attributed to making the jump from canine to human.

The virus given to us by the North Koreans is very stable. We have been doing extensive research on it and it does not appear to be inclined to mutate, therefore unlike with Covid, the vaccine we develop should be able to control the spread without the need for constant tweaking because of multiple variants."

Werner Montana who ran the banking divisions raised his hand and asked, "So the vaccine also won't be like Covid where they only minimized the symptoms but did not truly prevent the spread."

"That is correct." Emma replied. "Once immunized, we estimate you will possess sufficient antibodies to fight the virus for about two years, but we would recommend annual boosters."

Montana continued his line of questioning, "Then once the vaccine is deployed, won't this virus be eradicated in very short order? It does not sound like a long-term revenue stream."

Alvarez interjected, "Werner, let Dr. Alvarez finish and you will see that is not the case."

Nodding his head, Montana said, "I apologize. Please continue."

Emma said, "So, as I was saying, the virus is very stable, however, that does not mean it is without its own tricks for survival. Taking a page from the canine Parvovirus, our Parvovirus,… we are calling it Parvovirus H23 by the way,… Our Parvovirus can go dormant for long periods of time,… up to two years actually. The thing that makes it dormant are temperatures below forty-five degrees Fahrenheit. Actually, temperatures below fifteen degrees Fahrenheit and above one-hundred and six will kill the virus. Once dormant, the virus needs a temperature above seventy-five degrees to become virulent and active again."

Alvarez interrupted again, "The virus was specifically designed that way. Think about it… To combat this virus, we must combat global warming. If we can reduce greenhouse gases that are raising temperatures around the globe, we can reduce the period of time that H23 is virulent. This will be the lever necessary to push most climate deniers over the edge."

With heads nodding around the table, Emma continued. "Like all Parvoviruses, H23 is spread through droplet contact. That means it is airborne and passed by breathing, coughing, talking, sneezing, etcetera. The virus enters through mucus membranes, like when you breathe in, or if you touch your eyes or lips. But unlike Covid, if H23 lands on a hard surface, a table, your hand, anything, it can revert to its dormant state, and live there almost indefinitely until awakened by finding a warm, moist host.

H23 can be transmitted by dogs and cats, and is fatal to canines as well, but not felines. The incubation period is ten to fourteen days, and the patient is infectious five to seven days after exposure. This virus has a nearly one hundred percent mortality rate in canines, and H23 is fatal to primates in ninety-three percent of all cases. Victims will notice a slight cough and possibly a sore throat at first, followed within twenty-four hours by the 'slapped face' rash seen in Parvovirus B19. However, within a day, the rash will have spread to the chest, arms legs and feet. As the virus multiplies in the body, severe joint pain and high fever will be seen, with accompanying anemia and gastrointestinal bloating. Within five days of symptom onset, you will see hypoxia due to the anemia and internal bleeding in the digestive system. Death occurs usually in seven to ten days, depending on care and overall patient health."

The room sat in stunned silence after Emma had concluded, with several Board members actually looking pale. The Cardinal was the first to speak.

"Knowing about the plan, and then hearing it like this… My God… If we do this, can we control it, and is it truly necessary to achieve our means?"

Alvarez replied, "All of Emma's research says yes we can control this, and in order to achieve our goals we must take bold steps." Turning back to his daughter, Alvarez asked, "Emma, how secure is your research?"

"Very secure. The people with access to this project report directly to me, and they are all like us. They believe in our cause and are proud to be playing such an integral part in our plan."

"Good… Very good." Alvarez said. "And how quickly will it spread?"

Emma replied, "Since the virus is transmitted via

droplet, it tends to spread rather quickly. Our plan was to introduce the virus to a number of dogs and let them loose in urban areas. Some of our principle targets… Russia and China… they have a large number of stray dogs in urban areas. In fact, China alone accounts for twenty percent of the total world stray dog population. Korea on the other hand does not have a large stray dog population because… well, people are so desperate for food that they catch and eat any strays. Therefore, our planned methods of transmission would be highly effective on all three of our initial targets. There would be heavy loss of life at all three of our primary targets, and moderate global spread. We would also introduce the virus in similar fashion in select European cities as well as the United States. Once the virus makes the cross species jump, we can expect it to spread at a similar speed and fashion as COVID-19."

"Excellent. Thank you Emma." Alvarez said with a huge smile on his face. "Next, I would like the Board to hear from my son William on the status of our alternative energy plan."

William Alvarez stood up and addressed the room. "Our Lithium-ion battery production is back on track and actually exceeding our original production quotas. Based on our present supply of raw materials, we will be able to maintain this level of production for another fourteen months before our Lithium supply is depleted below levels necessary to sustain current production levels. Despite our best efforts, we have not been able to secure an additional supply of Lithium for our battery production so we will be pivoting our manufacturing to the production of Graphene Aluminum batteries.

After the discovery of the superiority of the Graphene based battery and the potential to cost effectively manufacture mass quantities of the substance, we have been actively seeking the plans for the process that was developed during World War II, along with the cold fusion formula. While we are confident in our ability to secure those schematics, we have learned of two companies that have recently developed a process for mass producing graphene, and are in the process of slowly acquiring controlling interest in one of them as a fallback option. I am confident that we will have sufficient battery production to last us through the impending energy crisis.

Now as to our work to secure the aforementioned schematics, through the work of our research department, we had tracked the plans to America in 1945. The trail grew cold after that, but with the assistance of The Cardinal, we are following a Vatican investigator named John Nowalski, who has tracked down several leads. Currently our team is tailing Nowalski in West Virginia. He is looking for 'The Grasslicked' as he calls it. He actually doesn't know what it is he is looking for, but he feels this 'grasslicked' is the key."

Hermann Alvarez said, "He seems very adept at putting pieces of a puzzle together without needing to actually see the picture. His 'grasslicked' is actually Grosse Licht, the actual name that Wagner gave his discovery."

Nodding his head in agreement with his father, William continued. "This situation is very fluid, and both myself and Mr. Silva are receiving regular updates. Nowalski plans to head to New Jersey next. The Cardinal informs me that he has found some people with the last name of 'Grasslicked."

The senior Alvarez interjected, "Perhaps it would make sense for Mr. Silva to give his report on our overall security as well as on the team following Director Nowalski. Max, if you please?"

Max Silva, President of Donner Global Security stood and thanked both Alvarez and his son. "Ladies and Gentlemen of the Board, our security remains solid as we progress through the phases of our plan. After a brief recovery period from the gun battle the team had in Austria, our team is currently in place and discretely following Nowalski. As of this morning, there was little to report on what was found in West Virginia. I assume they will be heading up to New Jersey if nothing else turns up.

As to the encounter with the other team of operators, we have learned through our DNA analysis of the corpse that the man killed in Austria was from the Korean peninsula, most likely North Korean."

Alvarez leapt from his seat at the news. "North Korean? Are you certain?" He asked Silva.

Nodding his head, Silva replied. "Our test results are Ninety-six percent accurate and the autopsy performed by the Austrian National Police produced similar results. Yes sir, I am certain. Why do you ask?"

"As Emma had reported, we were using resources in North Korea to develop the virus when suddenly they broke the contract and severed ties. Now they have a team operating in Austria interrogating folks and obviously looking for something. It's as if they had… inside information as to our plans. Mr. Silva, could you please get a security team up here immediately, and sweep this room for any listening devices. I would also appreciate it if they could scan every person in this room as well."

A half hour later, all board members were scanned and cleared and the first bug was found in the Board Room. Expanding the search, the team found the bugs in Alvarez's office as well as his phone.

"Max, Miss Drussel informed me that Miss Kim had called out sick today. Could you send a team over to her apartment and collect her for me? I have some questions I would like to ask her." Alvarez said. "And then find out who did her background check, and have them brought to one of the interview rooms on the third floor. I would like a word with them as well."

"Yes sir." Silva replied.

With all of the Board members reseated around the table, Alvarez stood and began walking around the room. "Ladies and gentlemen. It appears that we have had a traitor in our midst. We will get to the bottom of this and will sort out what damage has been done. I apologize for having to subject you all to the scrutiny you just underwent. However, as we near this critical juncture of our plans, and actually contemplate advancing the timetable, we must be certain that we account for all variables in the pursuit of our desired outcome. I was originally going to call for a vote on the acceleration of our timetable. But in light of this breach, I will table that vote until our regular Board meeting at the start of next quarter. That will give us the time needed to assess any security threats and mitigate any potential damages."

Alvarez continued, "We must be deliberate and smart in our actions, and learn from history. Back in 1929,

Germany was in economic tatters. Inflation was out of control, two out of every three businesses were failing and the country's industrial output was running below fifty percent. By 1932, over six million Germans were unemployed. And while the rest of the world was also feeling the effects of the Great Depression, no country felt it more than our beloved Germany. All of this was a result of the sanctions inflicted on the Fatherland by the other European nations after World War I. The Jews capitulated to those sanctions and profited at the expense of fellow Germans, and the rising cancerous influence of communism not only caused Germany to lose the First World War, but added to the country's economic collapse.

The desperation felt by the average German… by our forefathers… was nearly unfathomable. But out of this pit of desperation, rose a single voice of salvation… the great Fuhrer, Adolf Hitler. Hitler showed the people that they had the right to be proud to be German. He punished the backstabbing Jews and Communists. And he tried to punish the rest of the world for their treatment of the Fatherland, but he was too ambitious.

Despite all he did for Germany, Hitler was also either a bit short-sighted or overzealous in his belief that with only a handful of allies, he could change the world when the world did not want to change. And when the world refused to change, he tried to spread his message of order and its accompanying prosperity by force.

Ladies and gentlemen, we will not make the same mistakes. What Hitler failed to realize is that while politics and subterfuge take longer, they are ultimately more effective at moving a populace. Germany was a country in crisis, so it was easy for Hitler to gain the trust of the people. He showed the German people the way out of the crisis. But in 1939, the rest of the world had begun to emerge from their crisis, and therefore was not ready for that much needed change. What we will do in the coming weeks will be to expand on what worked for Hitler. The world is already in crisis. The bomb is primed, and through politics and subterfuge, we will light the fuse and take the world to the brink. And when we are there, and every rational person on this planet is crying out for change… WE WILL BE THAT CHANGE!

We are the children of the chosen. Our parents and grandparents were asked to carry the mantle of the Aryan race and the ideals of National Socialism forward. We have been planning and preparing and waiting for generations. And now, we are on the cusp of fulfilling our destiny. A new dawn is ready to break that will see our Aryan heritage rise from the ashes like a Phoenix, and we will take our rightful places as leaders of this new world. Heil to the Fatherland. Heil to the Fourth Reich. Heil to our Fuhrer… Sieg Heil!"

Standing in unison, the room returned the salute, "Sieg Heil."

With the loss of the listening devices, Joon Min did not hear the speech Alvarez gave the Aryphon Board. However, the plans she had heard prior to the listening devices being found was chilling enough. Aryphon, with the help of her country had developed a biological weapon that could wipe out nearly every living person on the planet. And her country's reward for the work they had done on this was to be one of the first nations targeted by this weapon.

Joon Min was shaking as she drove to the safehouse, not because she feared for her safety, but because of the diabolical nature of the plan she had just heard. She had seen the black SUVs leave the parking garage and speed off in the direction of her apartment. She was sure the place would be totally ransacked, as they searched for leads on both her whereabouts and what information she had obtained. But she was equally sure they would find nothing to implicate her nor North Korea as the sponsor of the espionage. Everything that mattered to her was already moved into the safehouse along with enough clothing to be comfortable for several weeks.

Her next priority was to get this report to Kim Joo-Won. Since he was operating inside the States, it was decided to use Joon Min's mother as a cut-out for sending messages. This way if anyone hacked her email, all they would see were regular messages to her mother. These messages could include photographs or audio files that appeared innocuous enough to even the more than casual observer.

Arriving back at the safehouse, Joon Min typed up her message that talked about how her family's culture continues to amaze her, and included the code words that she needed to speak to Kim. Typing in the subject line *'You HAVE TO listen to this'* indicating the message was of high importance, she attached an audio file of traditional Korean funeral music and hit send. Gertrude Elfmann would decode the message, save it to a jump drive, then forward the decoded message via email to Kim Joo-Won using a different machine with a different email account. While neither incredibly high tech nor time consuming, this process usually presented both parties with at least a one-day delay between sending and receiving messages. Kim Joon-Won would continue looking in the wrong direction for at least another couple of days.

Adam had just returned to the squad room when Captain Benjamin called him into the office. Handing Adam a slip of paper, Benjamin said, "Hey, I need you to head over to this address and take a statement from the homeowner. I got nobody else available and they had a break-in earlier today. I've already called the county crime scene guys, and I'd rather not have them get there before us. Patrol has already responded and cleared the house, so I just need you to take the statement and babysit while the CSI guys do their thing."

"No problem Cap." Adam said as he grabbed the paper from his boss. Grabbing his keys, he headed to the back lot, grabbed his vehicle and headed over to the residence of one, Janine Wagner. Driving the short distance to the townhomes off of Main Street, Adam looked down at the paper again. *"Janine Wagner... Janine Wagner... Why is that name so familiar?..."* he said to himself. Turning off of Main Street on to Kimball Drive, he drove the short distance into the townhouse community before making a right turn on to Byrnes Lane. Parking the car, he walked the short distance up the walkway toward the house. Looking around at the tightly packed townhomes with their parking lots full of cars and children playing, Adam wondered if anyone would come forward with information. Seeing this many people around, he thought that someone had to have seen or heard something.

Adam was greeted at the door by the responding patrol officer who gave him a quick rundown and advised him the homeowner was sitting in the upstairs bedroom down the hall and to the left. Walking into the house, Adam was struck by the level of destruction the perpetrators had caused. The couch and two chairs in the living room were both overturned and from what he could see, it looked like someone had taken a box cutter to both the cushions and the seat backs. The carpeting had been pulled up around all the edges, and every table in the living room had been smashed to bits.

Taking a look in the kitchen, every drawer was removed and the contents scattered across the floor. The same was true for the cabinets and the pantry where broken glass was intermingled with cans and emptied boxes of dried goods. The refrigerator and freezer was open and all the food was thrown across the floor, and the oven and stovetop looked like they had tried to take it apart.

Adam headed up the stairs calling out as he began his ascent. "Hello… Anyone up here? I'm with the police."

A few seconds later, a young woman appeared at the head of the stairs dressed in shorts and a tee shirt that displayed her bare midriff. Her brown hair was pulled back in a pony tail that stuck out from the back of the baseball cap that she wore. She was tan, with some streaks of red on her lower legs where it looked like she had failed to apply sufficient sunscreen. When Adam saw her, he instantly remembered why the name rang a bell.

Reaching the top of the stairs, Adam extended his hand. "I'm Lieutenant Adam Levy. I'm so sorry about all of this." He said waving his free hand around the shattered home.

Taking Adam's extended hand, Janine said, "Thank you." Then cocking her head to the side, she continued. "You look familiar. Have we met before?"

"I ran into you… literally… the other day at St. Luke's. I was headed in to see Pastor Lembrich and…"

Nodding her head, Janine said, "Right, right… I thought you were holding the door for me…"

"I know… I should look where I'm going." Adam said.

"No.. It's Ok. So, what do you think?" Janine asked moving her hands in a sweeping motion across the rooms.

"Well, we have the crime scene people on their way now. They'll dust the place for fingerprints and see if they can turn up something. How did they get in?" Adam asked.

"They broke the glass on the back door and then undid the lock."

"I see you have an alarm system. Was it armed?"

Janine replied, "Unfortunately not. It was such a nice day, I woke up and decided to run to the beach one last time before school starts. I guess I was too distracted getting ready that I forgot to set it."

"Don't beat yourself up. These things happen. Hopefully, the CSI guys will find something or maybe someone saw or heard something. You live in a busy neighborhood and they had to have been here for quite a while to do all this damage." Adam said. "Have you been able to determine what they took?"

Shaking her head, Janine said, "No. I mean, all my

jewelry looks like it's still here, although it's strewn all over the bedroom floor. I had about two hundred dollars in my dresser. I found most of that on the floor as well. I mean, I don't know what they wanted. They actually sliced open my mattress and put holes in my bedroom walls. Do you think it was just kids that got high and trashed the place for kicks?"

"I'm not going to rule out anything at this point." Adam replied.

Just then, there was a knock at the front door as the CSI team had arrived. Adam and Janine joined them downstairs and watched as they went about the process of dusting for prints and looking for other forensic evidence. After completing the first floor, they asked about the upstairs.

"Yeah… The second floor looks just as bad as the first." Adam replied. "You find anything so far?"

Shaking his head, the county CSI investigator said, "Nah. Looks like they wore gloves. You'd think with all this damage, they would leave something, but so far its clean."

An hour later, the CSI team had finished their work. They informed Adam that they weren't able to find anything, but they would send their official report within a day or two.

After the team left, Adam turned to Janine and took two business cards out of his pocket. On the first he wrote a phone number. On the second, he wrote the name of a company and a phone number. Handing both of the cards to Janine, he said, "The first card has my personal cell phone number. If you need any help, day or night do not hesitate to call. The other card has the name of a company that helps clean up things like this. You can use them, or go online and see if you can find someone else, but I've referred these guys to other people and they seem to be reasonable and do good work."

"Thank you." Janine said. "So, what happens now?"

"So now you will go through all your stuff and make a comprehensive list of what was stolen. Once you have that, get me a copy. You can fax or email it… my info is on my card. Next you will need to contact your home owner's insurance company. They will need a copy of that list as well. They will send an adjuster out to look at the damage, and then you work with them on getting a check. In the meantime, I am going to go out now and see if I can speak to your neighbors. I want to see if anyone saw or heard something. I'll follow up in a day or two to see if I can speak to as many people as possible who may have been here. I want to be honest with you however. A lot of times, these types of cases go unsolved."

"I kinda figured that." Janine said. "It's not like on TV."

"No, it's not." Adam agreed. "I'll have my initial report done within a day or so. You may need that for the insurance company as well. I'll reach out in a few days and just give you an update too, but again, don't expect too much. Finally, get someone to replace that glass in the back door… and make sure to set the alarm whenever you go out."

"I most certainly will." Janine replied.

Looking directly into Janine's deep brown eyes, Adam extended his hand again. "I hope the next time we meet, it will be on better circumstances."

"Me too, lieutenant... Me too." Janine replied.

"Please... Call me Adam."

John parked his rental car in the front of Sayreville police headquarters and entered the lobby through the glass front doors. It had been more than twenty-five years since he had been in this building, yet as he walked past the municipal court room on the right, countless memories came flooding back. Approaching the glass window of the Desk Sergeant, he stopped in front of the elevated booth.

Pressing the button that activated the microphone the Sergeant leaned into the microphone and asked John, "Can I help you?"

"I'm here to see Captain Benjamin." John said a bit too loudly as the empty lobby caused his voice to echo off the cinder block walls. Removing his INTERPOL ID John placed it up against the glass.

"Do you have an appointment?" was the tinny reply through the cheap speaker at the base of the glass.

"No, but if you tell him that John Nowalski is here to see him, I'm sure he will see me."

"I'm not too sure. What is this in reference to?

"I'm paying him a courtesy call since he is C.O of the detective bureau and I am investigating a case in his jurisdiction." John said.

"You are working one of our cases?" asked the Sergeant. "You don't have the authority to do that here. Are you carrying a weapon?"

Becoming a bit exasperated, John replied, "No, I am not carrying a weapon and it is not one of your cases. It is a case over in Europe, and I am following up on a lead that is here in New Jersey."

"If you are working on a case here in New Jersey, I think you need permission from either the State Police or the State Department. Have you checked in with them? We are not authorized to grant you that permission."

"Look Sergeant… I used to work here a long time ago. Captain Benjamin and I go way back. I'd like to see him, say hello and tell him that I am here in your town talking to some people about a case I am working in Austria."

"Do you have an appointment? The Sergeant asked again. "Because Captain Benjamin does not see anyone without an appointment. I can give you his card and you can call and set up an appointment, and come back then."

John's level of frustration was reaching a boiling point. What should have been a simple request was turning quite literally into a federal case by this Desk Sergeant. Focused almost exclusively on this human roadblock in front of him, John did not fully process the front door opening behind him and a figure walking tentatively toward him. Attempting one last calm effort to get in to see the Captain, John said, "Sergeant, please. If you could just ring up the Captain and tell him that John…"

"NOWALSKI??!" came out of the booming voice behind him. Turning, John was greeted by Steve Tortorice walking toward him with arms outstretched. "Holy shit. What are you doing here?" Steve asked.

"Hey Steve. It's been a minute." John said through his smile. Returning Tortorice's embrace, John said, "I'm trying to get in to see Benjy, but this…". Looking up at the now scowling Desk Sergeant, John continued, "… gentleman was saying I need an appointment."

"Not a problem. I've got you." Turning to the Desk Sergeant, Tortorice said, "It's OK Bob. He's with me."

Walking past the security door, John and Tortorice made their way to the detective's squad room.

"Hey, just a word of caution… Nobody calls the Captain "Benjy" anymore. He always hated it and has threatened to castrate anyone who even thinks about uttering that nickname again." Tortorice said.

"I remember how he hated it." John replied. "He used to say he was a cop not a dog. But the Captain used to call him that, so that gave the rest of us free reign."

"Well we don't have that anymore, so just watch what you say."

Captain Benjamin was standing outside his office speaking to another detective as John and Tortorice walked in. Looking up as the two men entered, Benjamin took a double take at the sight of John walking toward him.

"As I live and breathe. The prodigal son returns…" Benjamin said in greeting as John made his way to the Captain.

"How have you been, Jake?" John asked as he shook Benjamin's hand.

"I'm good.. good." Looking out across the squad room, Benjamin announced, "Ladies and gentlemen… Let me introduce John Nowalski, formerly Detective Sergeant of the Sayreville Police Department, now… What is it? Director General of the Gendarmerie for the Vatican City State." Turning to John, Benjamin asked, "Did I get that right?"

"Perfectly." John replied. "Except you left out, *And*

Senior Inspector of Interpol, but that title is mostly an honorific."

Benjamin made introductions around the squad room then invited John in to his office. "So, what brings you back home? Is this visit for business or pleasure?"

John replied, "While it is always a pleasure to come home and see old friends, unfortunately this visit is work related. I'm working on the case of the murdered nuns and monks in Austria. I don't know how much of that has made the news here in the States."

"We heard about it. Such a shame." Benjamin replied.

"Well, I've uncovered some leads that have brought me back to America. I just got back from West Virginia, which turned out to be nothing, and now I am hoping to interview someone in Perth Amboy to follow up. It could be nothing, but despite all the forensic evidence we have, we really have little to go on."

"Do you want me to call the Chief over in Perth Amboy? He's a good guy and I know him pretty well."

"I was actually hoping you could do that. Sometimes folks get a little territorial and turn a really simple thing into a whole bureaucratic mess. I'm just gonna talk to a family and see if I can get additional information. It will probably be a bust like down in West Virginia."

"Not a problem, John. So how long were you planning to stay in town?"

"That depends on what I learn. But long enough for us to maybe grab a burger and a beer and catch up." John said.

"That would be great. Maybe we could even invite Steve to join us. There aren't too many of us old-timers left anymore."

Benjamin began walking John out of the squad room, just as Adam was entering.

"G'morning Cap." Adam said as he moved to walk past his boss and John.

"Adam…". Benjamin called out, stopping Levy in his tracks. "Adam, I'd like you to meet John Nowalski. John used to work here and now is with the Vatican police force." Turning to John, he continued, "Adam is our newly minted lieutenant, and quite an amazing detective."

Shaking John's hand, Adam said, "A pleasure to meet you sir. I've heard some pretty amazing stories about you, and the cases you have solved in your day. You have quite a legacy."

"Holy shit Adam…". Benjamin said. "You make it sound like he is a half-step from the grave."

"It's all good, Jake. I'm sure the Lieutenant meant no disrespect, did you, kid?"

Shaking his head vehemently, Adam said, "No sir. I didn't want you to think I was pointing out that you were old. I mean, not old… It's just I have heard about some of the amazing things you have done and… I didn't want to insinuate anything about you being old, I mean, not that you're old and all, but…"

Holding up his hand in front of Adam, John said, "Hold on kid. Since I'm old… Something I have learned from my eons of experience is while salad is good for you, word salad is not. Sometimes a short, direct answer goes a lot farther than getting your tongue tied up in knots. You have to learn how to be careful with what you say so you don't get yourself in trouble, and saying less goes a long way in keeping you safe. A simple 'no sir' would have sufficed in this case. Comprende?"

"Yes sir." Adam replied.

Turning to Benjamin, John playfully slapped him backhanded across the arm. "Look at that Benjy. Now I know why you like this kid so much. He can actually be taught."

The room fell into a deathly silence, and John immediately recognized his error. Looking over to his long-time friend he saw Benjamin's jaw tighten as his eyes became piercing slits on a reddening face.

"It's a good thing you no longer report to me, Nowalski." Benjamin said through nearly gritted teeth.

Patting Benjamin on the shoulder, John quickly grabbed Adam's hand and gave it a perfunctory shake, then waving to the rest of the detectives as he backed out of the room.

"Thanks for the help Captain. I'll touch base later about getting that beer. Great meeting you all." John said as he back pedaled away from his old boss and the squad room.

Making it to the doorway, John turned and quickly headed down the hall toward the front door.

With John beating a rapid retreat, Benjamin turned back to the squad room and said, "What are all you assholes looking at? Didn't anyone ever see a dinosaur put his foot in his mouth before? Get back to work!"

Betty Wagner had spent her entire life living on Deerfield Road in the Parlin section of Sayreville. At eighty-three she had already buried her husband and her eldest son. While she still regularly attended bingo and fellowship meetings at her church, she otherwise remained home, opting to use the grocery delivery service from the local supermarket and online shopping for her other necessities.

Arthritic, and hard of hearing, Betty spent most of her day knitting, watching game shows on TV with the volume turned up, and caring for her two cats. On this particular morning, she was in her bedroom putting away the laundry when there was a knock at her door. The combination of the overly loud TV and Betty's hearing deficiencies prevented her from hearing the nicely dressed Asian man knocking at her front door.

Entering the home by breaking the glass on the back door and then releasing the lock, the four Korean operatives quickly and silently entered the house. Going immediately to the front door, they swung it open, allowing Kim Joo-Won to enter. Seeing the TV on, he immediately instructed his team to clear the first floor, then head upstairs. Working in pairs, the team cleared the first floor in minutes, then silently headed upstairs, finding Betty hanging clothing in her bedroom closet.

Betty was quickly bound with zip-ties, gagged and dragged kicking and struggling into the kitchen. There the operatives took an old kitchen chair and secured Betty to the chair, tying her arms to the arm-rests and her legs to the front legs of the chair. Kim Joo-Won came down a few minutes later, still dressed in his blue business suit.

Giving commands to his team to begin their search of the house, he removed his jacket and tie and pulled a stool up close to Betty Wagner. Rolling up the sleeves of his starched white dress shirt Kim leaned in and said, "Mrs. Wagner, my name is Kim. I am going to remove your gag, and ask you a series of questions. If you scream, I will hurt you…very badly. If you cooperate and answer my questions honestly, this will go a lot better for you. Do you understand this?"

With her eyes wide with fear, Betty Wagner nodded her head. "Good…" Kim said. Removing the gag from her mouth, Kim leaned in so Betty could hear him, "Where is the Big Light?"

The house on Rector Street in Perth Amboy was a triplex, with a brick facade, tile roof and a satellite dish on the overhang to the front porch. While the two end units were single family, the center unit sported two doors in front; one for each of the apartments.

John arrived to find a woman pounding on the door to the downstairs apartment, and shouting out to the person inside. "C'mon Opa… open the door. It's me, Janine. You know who I am. I just want to come in and see how you are doing."

John approached up the front walk-way, unsure about the scene playing out in front of him. "Can I help you miss?" He asked as he stepped onto the first step of the front porch.

"No, I'm just trying to get my grandfather to open the door."

"Is he alright? John asked.

Turning to look at the man standing at the foot of the porch, Janine replied. "Yes, he's fine. He's elderly and I'm just trying to check up on him." Looking John up and down, she scrunched her eyes and nose in a puzzled look and cocked her head to the side and asked, "I'm sorry… Who are you?"

"My name is John Nowalski." John replied, reaching into his back pocket and pulling out his ID and badge. "I'm an investigator with Interpol." John opted to use his status with Interpol since most people in the US had never heard of the Gendarmerie.

"Interpol? What are you doing here, or are you just some nosey eurocop who saw some woman pounding on a door and decided to stick his nose in other people's business?"

"No, actually I'm here on official business. Are you Miss Grasslicked?" John asked

"Wagner…"

"Excuse me?"

"Wagner…" Janine repeated with greater emphasis. "Its next to impossible to teach ninth and tenth graders with a last name of Grasslicked, so I legally changed it. It's also a real show-stopper when it's called out in a packed waiting room."

"OK, so you are not Anna Grasslicked?" John asked.

"No, Anna is my sister. She lives here with my grandfather and claims to take care of him, but in actuality, she just takes care of herself and…" Janine stopped mid-sentence and reached into the bag slung over her shoulder to retrieve the ringing cell phone.

"… And speaking of… here's the bitch now. Hello… Yes, I'm outside the house. I stopped by to check on Opa. I wanted to make sure the house was safe for him… No, I don't believe you… I don't believe… So if you have nothing to hide, why did you change the locks. Yes, I tried to get in… I don't care if you don't want me here unless you are here too. Daddy left this house to both of us… No,… Both of us… Yes, there is a man out here with me. I don't know, some cop. He was asking about you… I don't know… I said, I don't know… I said… Look, just tell Opa to open the door. Anna, tell Opa to… Anna open the fucking…"

"You Bitch!… " Janine said out loud to the sister who had already hung up as she threw her phone into her bag. Turning to John, she said, "I'm sorry. That was Anna. She told my grandfather not to let us in and then hung up on me. My grandfather calls her whenever she's not home and someone is at the door to ask if he should let them in."

Thinking the scene was caused by his presence, John said, "I'm sorry. Had I known my presence would have caused this problem, I wouldn't have come up to the porch."

"No, It's not you. I would have gotten the same response if I was by myself." Janine began walking down the front walkway back toward her car parked at the curb. "My grandfather is elderly and he had a stroke about 30 years ago. My dad moved him in to help take care of him, but then my dad passed away a few years back. He left the house to me and my sister, and I had planned to move in and take care of Opa, but somehow Anna had already swooped in and gotten power of attorney and an advance directive for his health decisions. Then she began living downstairs with him and controlling everything. She controls his bank accounts, his pension, investments, everything. She tells everyone she has had to give up her social life to care for her grandfather, but in reality, she doesn't care for him, she just takes advantage and controls his life… Besides, she never had a social life anyway."

"What about your mom? John asked.

"She passed away a few years before dad… cancer. Dad was never really the same after that. He had a heart attack that severely weakened his heart. He lasted a few days in the hospital before he died. I think he actually died of a broken heart, he missed her that badly. "

"I'm sorry."

"It seems like a lifetime ago. I'm actually doing OK. I just get sad when I talk about it." After a brief pause, Janine asked, "So what did you want to speak to my sister about?"

"This is going to sound strange Mrs. Wagner, but I am not sure."

"It's Miss… Miss Wagner. I changed my own name, I didn't marry to get a new one."

"OK, *Miss* Wagner. My apologies."

Janine said, "So, what do you mean you are not sure why you need to talk to my sister."

"It's a bit complicated. I am working a case that involves the murder of some people. I am following up on some leads I developed. I'm not sure if they will lead me anywhere, but my gut tells me I need to follow up. It would be really helpful if I could interview you, your sister and your grandfather."

Looking at her watch, Janine said. "Unfortunately, I have another appointment in fifteen minutes, so I really must be going. As for Opa and my sister… good luck."

"Perhaps we could talk another time?" John asked.

"I'm free on Friday. Wanna meet at the Starbucks on Rt. 9 in Sayreville?"

"Does ten in the morning work for you?" John asked.

"Ten is perfect." Janine said as she extended her hand to shake John's

Taking her hand in his, their eyes met for a brief instant, and John felt a spark he had not felt in years.

"I look forward to Friday." John said before turning up the block to return to his car.

The burner phone sitting on the living room coffee table buzzed and flashed. It had been three days since Joon Min had sent her message to her mother, and she was beginning to get nervous since she had not gotten either a phone call or return email.

"You said it was urgent that you speak to me, so speak." Kim Joo-Won said on the other end of the phone.

"To begin, I am burned. Alvarez learned the operative killed in Austria was Korean and he sent a team to get me from my apartment. You don't need to worry. I had already swept it clean and there was nothing there to implicate me or our country."

"That is good. How secure are you right now?" Kim asked.

"I believe I am totally secure. I was not followed. I have been using my mobile hot spot to send my emails to my mother, and the cypher while simple is effective."

"What have you learned?" Kim asked.

"Brother, it is worse than we imagined." Joon Min replied.

For the next ten minutes, Joon Min laid out in detail the plan for the delivery of the virus, its anticipated mortality rate and all of the other information she had gleaned from her listening device. She informed Kim about Aryphon's search for the cold fusion plans, and how they were following Nowalski as he tried to track down the missing plans. She ended her report by informing Kim about John's search for 'the grasslicked,' and how he believed he found people living around the Sayreville area with that last name.

Kim Joo-Won chuckled at how John had anglicized the words Grosse Licht. "Leave it to a self-centered American to think that German words should be turned into something in English. That doesn't even make sense… he is looking for a grasslicked?"

"I know." Joon Min replied. "Alvarez mocked him as well. He said for someone who didn't even know what he is looking for, he has gotten so close, yet has stumbled down the wrong path. However, since he found someone with that as a last name, perhaps that might be worth checking out."

"Very well, I concur. Since you are secure in Montevideo, I want you to stay where you are. I am going to reach out to the high command and pass along your report. I will recommend that we complete our mission here and obtain the plans for the cold fusion, and then eliminate the threat from Aryphon. You have done good work Joon Min Kim. The Supreme Leader will be pleased."

"Thank you, comrade brother." Joon Min said.

"We will be in touch." Kim said before hanging up the phone.

John set his phone alarm for six AM, but finally turned it off after hitting snooze for the fifth time. Awakening at eight, he showered, shaved and dressed before heading over to the local IHOP for breakfast. As he sat contemplating both his coffee and the case, John's mind wandered to his encounter with Janine Wagner. Over the course of his career, John had met and interacted with many attractive women yet had always remained true to his vow of celibacy. Despite his decision to not move forward with his official vows, John always felt this one vow was easy to uphold since he was only in love twice in his life.

His first love, Kathy had been taken from him, along with his son when they were murdered by Columbian drug dealers. Believing he would never love again, he was surprised when he fell for the detective he worked with on the Pope Gregory case. In retrospect, he often felt he made the wrong choice when he ended it with her to take his current position with the Gendarmerie. However, at that time, the wounds from the loss of Kathy were still too raw, and he believed his commitment to the Church superseded his personal desires. And despite coming to the conclusion over the past few years that the Church was not as committed to him as he was to it, John had not had a single instance where a woman turned his head, or he had felt a spark of interest.

But that changed yesterday when he met Janine. Her simple beauty intrigued him. Her shoulder length chestnut brown hair framed her pretty face and matched the color of her almond shaped eyes. While she did not have a perfect "Barbie Doll" figure, she was not without curves. But the thing that most attracted John was what he could only describe as her aura. Janine gave off an air of confident ease. She was comfortable in her own skin, and in who she was. This came out in both her personality as she had interacted with John, as well as the expressiveness of her face. John found himself excited and eager to see her again for her interview, yet silently chiding himself for his unprofessional attitude. As he stirred his coffee, he forced himself to focus back on the case, yet he knew in his heart that he looked forward to being distracted again.

Finishing up breakfast, John was back in his hotel room by ten-thirty and pulled out his laptop to begin a day of paperwork and updates. Checking his email first, John saw that Tony had sent him over the report from the Austrian National Police on both the ballistics and the DNA results on the dead operator at the monastery. Reviewing the ballistic and other forensic information first, John learned that including the dead man, there were at least eleven men who had left DNA in the form of blood at the scene. While two of them were coming up as matching DNA in a database, both of these were classified by Washington. This meant that at least two of the perpetrators were most likely former special forces or operators for one of the US intelligence agencies. Despite any official requests made at the highest level to unseal those files, John was certain he was not learning the identity of those individuals through normal channels.

The ballistics identified sixteen distinct weapons that were used at the scene, one of which matched an open INTERPOL murder case in Brussels. From the coroner's report, the monks against the wall died first, with the monk in the chair and the Abbot succumbing to their wounds a few hours later. The analysis performed by Inspector

Altschuler, outlined multiple gun battles moving throughout the monastery over an extended period of time.

Finally, John read the section of the coroner's report on the dead operator. While there was no DNA match in any database, the results conclusively showed this person's DNA heritage came exclusively from the Korean peninsula. When coupled with the coroner's assessment of the quality of the dead man's dental work, the report identified the dead man as most probably North Korean.

"Why would North Korea be looking for a religious artifact." John said to himself.

Taking his yellow notepad out of his briefcase, John began to outline what he knew. Normally, he would use either post-it notes on a wall, or a white board for this exercise, but neither were available in his current hotel room, so John figured just writing things down may help him gain some clarity. After a half hour, John had filled three pages of the notepad and had little more than a concise outline of both the events of the case and the evidence that had been collected. Looking down at his notes, John decided to use them to write his update report to the Cardinal.

Opening his laptop, John began drafting the memo to Sentille. Using his notes, it was easy to logically lay out all of the events from all of the crime scenes, including the 'vandalism' cases that preceded the attacks on the monasteries. He discussed the evidence collected, and what it all meant, as well as the results of the interview with the one monk who had initially survived the attack. Once the report was nearly completed, John re-read what he had written, and reviewed his notepad once again before writing his impressions, conclusions and plan of action.

Despite not having a clear picture of what the attackers were looking for, after laying everything out, John was totally convinced that these people were desperately looking for something they believed was hidden in a monastery in Austria… *'They are systematically going through the monasteries in Austria…'* John thought

John grabbed his notepad and began going through his notes, picking out the dates of the previous attacks and monastery vandalisms and writing them down on the notepad. When he had finished he had a comprehensive timeline of the entire case. Looking over the timeline, John quickly saw that no more than three days went by without a new incident. Checking his watch first, John took out his phone and called Tony.

Answering on the third ring Tony asked, "How are things in America?

"You know… everyone here speaks English with the strangest accent. It's almost like… oh, I don't know it's their native tongue." John quipped. "Hey Tony, I need a favor. Can you double check for me if there have been any more incidents involving monasteries, especially in Austria? I want to make sure I didn't miss a report."

"I don't need to even check, Boss." Tony replied. "I have been keeping my eye out in case anything happened while you were away. It has been real quiet."

"Tony!…" John exclaimed, tongue in cheek. "Have you forgotten everything I taught you? You never use the "Q" word."

"Sorry Boss. I lost my head. But seriously, there has been nothing since that big gun battle. A little strange.

These groups were hitting monasteries like clockwork. It's been more than a week since the last attack."

"You noticed that too." John said. "So, something has changed. Either both teams were too shot up to continue,…"

"Or they found what they were looking for." Tony chimed in.

John agreed, saying, "Yeah… But that doesn't feel right from looking at that last crime scene. If they had found it, why keep the Abbot and that last monk alive. The Koreans would have killed them and just gotten out of there. No, they were still looking when the other team arrived. And I don't think the other team would have stuck around digging through stuff after that gun battle. Based on the blood evidence found, they were all shot up too."

"That leaves the third option." Tony said.

"Which is?…"

"They learned where the Grasslicked is." Tony said.

"I know. John replied. "Or at least they learned it is not in Austria."

"So now what?" Asked Tony.

"Now I continue with the investigation. I am interviewing a Janine Wagner tomorrow. Her last name used to be Grasslicked, but she changed it."

"Good call on her part." Quipped Tony.

"Yeah… Unless she can offer some new information, I got nothin' after that. If I don't turn up anything new, I'll see about getting a flight back this weekend."

"Well, good luck Boss." Tony said.

"Thanks Tony. I'll be in touch."

John hung up the phone and turned his attention to

the nearly finished report on his laptop. He outlined his conclusions, including his most recent ideas about the teams no longer looking in Austria. He informed Sentille about his appointment with Janine tomorrow, and that if nothing new is uncovered from that interview, that he would be home by Sunday the latest.

John had no sooner sent the email and closed his laptop, when his phone rang. Thinking it was Tony calling back, and not looking at the caller ID on the screen, John said. "This is the most handsome, world-famous, protector of all that is good, Director General John Nowalski."

"You left out most modest." Said the accented voice on the other end of the call.

Now glancing at the caller ID screen and seeing the number and ID were blank, John said, "Ari Ben-David… How is my favorite spy with three first names?"

Ben-David held the equivalent rank of Colonel in the Israeli Institute for Intelligence and Special Operations, more commonly known as the Mossad. Over the years, John had worked with Ben-David on several occasions, hunting down terrorists and mutual threats to both of their countries.

"I am good my friend. How is my favorite goy?" Ben-David replied.

"Hey, I told you… I did that DNA ancestor test thing and it said I was six percent Jewish." John said chuckling.

"Which is why I still call you my friend. I am a magnanimous person and can overlook the other ninety-four percent. So, tell me, what are you doing playing with those Aryphon boys. They are a dangerous bunch. You need to be careful."

"What are you talking about? John asked.

"The ballistics report from the attack in Austria. I was reading through the INTERPOL report that some of the casings matched an assassination back in May of Twenty-one. The Belgian Finance Minister was gunned down in a drive-by shooting outside a café in Brussels. We have long suspected that Aryphon was behind it, but could never develop enough evidence to pin it to them."

"OK, hold on a minute…Who is Aryphon and why were you looking into the death of a Belgian Finance Minister? I remember the murder, but the rest of this… Why don't I know about this?" John asked.

"Aryphon Corporation, de S.A. is a multinational conglomerate headquartered out of Montevideo, Uruguay. You probably have never heard of them because they like to travel below the radar, however, they are like an octopus and have their tentacles in a great many things. We are interested in the Finance Minister shooting because he was a major advocate of the cybersecurity system one of our country's corporations was in the process of selling to the EU. However, Aryphon did not want the sale to go through, so they eliminated the Minister, which then just left their people in place to whisper in the right ears and kill the sale."

"Why? John asked. "Do they have a competing product?"

"No, they did it because they are Nazis and hate Israel."

Believing his friend was casting an aspersion John chuckled and asked, "No, really Ari, what was the reason?"

"No, really John. They are Nazis. Aryphon stands for Aryan Phoenix. Aryphon was formed using the Nazi gold that disappeared at the end of World War II. The founding members of Aryphon were all mid-level SS officers who were hand selected by Hitler. As a last resort, if Germany was on the brink of losing the war, these officers were to take their families and accompany the gold to South America and build a power base from which to launch the Fourth Reich."

"Ari, this is all conspiracy theory stuff."

"John, do you think my country would spend millions and millions of dollars chasing down ghosts? Most tall tales and conspiracy theories have some basis in fact. So back in 1945, there was over three-hundred and fifty million in Swiss francs that the Vatican allegedly confiscated for safe keeping. According to the report written by U.S. Treasury Agent Emerson Bigelow, who was tracking the money, one-hundred and fifty million of that was confiscated by the British at the Swiss, Austrian border. The rest, it is alleged made it to Vatican City. But this is only partially true. While about twenty-five million made it to the Vatican, the remaining one-hundred and seventy-five million was stashed aboard a waiting U boat in La Spezia and transported with fifteen families to Argentina. The Vatican, in exchange for the twenty-five million, then gave each of the families new identities. The group laid low for a few years, then relocated to Uruguay where they set up shop with the stolen gold. To give you an idea of what that amount of money was like back then, one-hundred and seventy-five million in 1946 would be like two point five billion today.

Over the decades, they have grown that even more. Aryphon is one of the largest privately held corporations in the world. They have their tentacles in so many places, they make an octopus envious. They own media outlets, lithium mines, medical device manufacturers and countless politicians across the globe. Their security arm, Donner Security, does off the books wet work for governments around the world. And that's in addition to the murders and crimes they commit to advance their own causes."

John asked, "If they are so dirty, why hasn't anyone done anything about them?"

"We have been trying. The problem is that they are fairly compartmentalized. They operate as a corporation with a board of directors and they only come together three or four times a year. Each director is responsible for some aspect of their operation, and runs that area fairly autonomously. The Board is made up primarily of descendants of the original fifteen families. There have been some changes to that due to deaths and certain individuals falling out of favor with the chairman. His name is Hermann Alvarez, and he is one intense individual. Educated in Oxford, he holds a Master's degree in Economics, and oversees all aspects of Aryphon's operations.

The problem is, if we take him out, the corporation still goes on, and our Prime Minister fears that they would exact revenge on our country. And this are not some ragtag terrorist group whose leadership spends as much time bickering amongst themselves as they do anything else. This is a well-oiled machine with a solid succession plan. Their retribution would be swift and furious. No, this is not a snake, this is a Hydra. And if you take it on, you must be sure to cut off all the heads at the same time."

"So why do you think these people are hunting for something in monasteries?" John asked.

"I do not know, my friend. Hitler was always fascinated with ancient religious artifacts. His search for the Ark of the Covenant was real, and not just the plot of an Indiana Jones movie. Perhaps there is something that was stored in a monastery that these people think will give them even greater power."

"That was what I thought at first too, but then I learned today that the body found at the site of the last attack was Korean. Based on his poor quality dental work, the coroner believed he was *North* Korean. And if so, why would they be looking for the same thing. Communists don't believe in God, so they wouldn't care about religious artifacts."

"Very true." Ben-David said. "They are interested in power… anything that would give them a greater voice on the world stage."

"Yeah… I think I need to change some of my assumptions." John said pensively to his friend. "Hey, does Grasslicked mean anything to you?"

"What?" Ben-David asked.

"Grasslicked. Does the word or term Grasslicked mean anything or ring a bell?"

Chucking, Ben-David replied, "No, I cannot say it does. What is it?"

"It is what the monk said they were looking for before he died."

"Looks like you have your work cut out for you." Ben-David said.

"That I do, old friend. Maybe I'll find my answers here in New Jersey."

Ben-David said. "Well, either way, I want you to be careful. Donner Security hires ex-special forces operators.

Those people do not play around. If you learn anything that I might find interesting, please remember me, and if there is anything I can do to help you, always feel free to reach out."

"Thank you Ari. Shalom"

"Shalom my friend." Ben-David said hanging up the phone.

CHAPTER 14

Main Street Townhouse Complex
Sayreville, New Jersey
Present Day

Adam had grabbed Steve Tortorice and had requested a patrol unit to assist him in canvassing the Main Street townhouse complex where Janine lived. After speaking to nearly a dozen neighbors, the most anyone was able to say was there was a well-dressed Asian man knocking on Janine's door early on the morning of the break in. However, the two people who saw him paid little attention, and when they had looked again, he was gone. Both neighbors assumed he had left.

Based on the level of damage to the house, Adam discounted this as not his prime suspect. Especially when a few of the neighborhood kids saw two young males who "looked like drug addicts" in the area earlier that afternoon. Getting nothing else new from the patrol officer,

Adam figured he had all the information he was going to be able to get, and asked Tortorice if he wanted to go to lunch.

Arriving at Adam's favorite pizza place on Washington Road, they ordered a few slices each and grabbed a soda from the display fridge.

"I think we're at a dead end on this one." Adam said dejectedly to Tortorice.

"Yeah, I know. It's a shame. They really trashed the place." Tortorice had seen the pictures from the CSI report. "You seem more upset about this one than usual." Tortorice noted.

"I really hoped I'd be able to help her out. She seems like… you know, a nice person." Adam replied.

"A nice person, huh? And the fact that she is attractive and single doesn't have any bearing on your desire to find these guys?

Smiling at the older man, Adam said, "OK, well maybe a little. I mean,… you should have seen her the other day when she had just gotten back from the beach with those shorts and that just off the beach tan… Holy shit Steve-O, she was lookin' pretty hot."

"Yeah, OK… Calm down there junior." Tortorice said. "Don't go getting yourself all worked up. You need to maintain your professional demeanor. Nothing turns a woman off faster than dealing with someone who gets all creepy with them. Once this case is closed, if you run into her, then maybe you can get something going. But for now, she needs a detective to find the fuckbags that trashed her place, not some cop who's hittin' on her cause he's horny."

"Yeah, I know that Steve. I'm just sayin'. I like the way she looks and she also seems real sweet. You know, I actually ran into her the other day over at St. Luke's. She is helping out with the carnival."

"Look at that… Hot, sweet and civic minded. She's got the whole fuckin' trifecta. You've got to get with this one." Tortorice said.

"Alright, I get it, detective." Adam said.

As the slices came out of the oven, the detectives paid for their lunch and headed to one of the molded plastic tables and benches that lined the perimeter of the pizzeria.

Changing gears, Adam asked, "So you used to work with this Nowalski guy?"

"Yeah. Me and John started out in patrol together. I actually met him right out of the academy. He was always that hard charging type. Always wrote the most tickets, always willing to work overtime… He made Sergeant in patrol first, then transferred over to the detectives when Franks retired. I was already there and I like to joke that I taught him everything he knows. But the truth of the matter is that he has a nose for this shit. I don't know if its luck or skill, but he always is able to latch on to that one special nugget that others don't see. And that winds up being the piece that lets him put it all together."

Adam asked, "Were you guys pretty tight?"

"Yeah, somewhat." Tortorice said. "Like I said, John was the hard charging type. He lived for his work. He put in lots of OT, and was just like a dog on a bone with getting shit solved. I'm not as type A as he was, so he tended to gravitate to people with a similar mindset."

"Ya know Steve, you are an excellent mentor. I mean, you trained Nowalski, you trained me… Why didn't you ever try to become a supervisor?"

"That's just not who I am, kid. I never wanted the headaches. Granted, I never minded taking a newbie like you under my wing as it were, and teaching you the ropes. But I know, after a while you are either gonna get it, or not. If not, you become the problem of the supervisors. If you do, you will be off on your own and I don't have to worry about how you are performing.

Adam, I love my wife and kids. I want to go home to them every night. You have less of a chance of getting hurt on the job here in the detective bureau than on patrol. In my thirty-three years on the job, I have never fired my weapon in anger, nor have I ever missed being home for a birthday or anniversary. I have two more years and then I will retire. For now, I do my job…". Tortorice said through a bite of pizza. "I think I do it pretty well. But there is more to life than the job. So, that is why I never became a supervisor."

"I hear ya Steve. But unfortunately, I don't have a lot else in my life right now."

Nodding his head, Tortorice said, "Yeah, I get it. But, and I don't mean this in a bad way… I see more of Nowalski than of me in you. And I just don't want you to suffer the same fate as he did."

Looking confused, Adam asked, "Why? What happened to him?"

"So, to give you the short version, John was a workaholic. Always was from day one. He gets married… has a kid… and works seven days a week, sixteen hours a day. His wife gives him an ultimatum,… the job or the family."

"So, she left him?" Adam asked.

"No, worse… He swears to his wife he will change. He

actually even came in and talked to Benjamin about how he needed to cut back. Then one night he actually cuts out early and by accident, winds up arresting a Columbian drug lord."

"That was Nowalski? Adam asked. "I kinda heard stories about it. Benjamin brings it up every so often."

"Yeah, that was Nowalski. Tortorice replied. "Then the drug lord escapes, puts a hit on John and his family, and manages to kill his wife and kid while John is at work."

"Holy shit!" exclaimed Adam.

"So, John loses his shit, quits the department, moves into a monastery and becomes like a priest or something. Next thing we hear, a few years later, he saves the Pope's life and is appointed head of the Vatican's anti-terrorism unit. He's been there for like twenty plus years and has foiled a number of terrorist attacks, and tracked down like some big-name bad guys."

"Wow… That's some story. I'd heard about some of the cases he'd solved, both here and when he was at the Vatican. He's got a pretty impressive reputation. And to think, you taught him everything he knows." Adam quipped.

"Yeah…". Tortorice chuckled. "The job has always been John's life, in one form or another. But I really wonder what kind of a life it really was. So just be careful Adam. Don't become like Nowalski."

"I don't plan to, Steve. I just…"

"I know…, don't have much else." Tortorice said.

Finishing up the last of his soda, Adam asked, "Ya ready? Wanna get going?"

"Sure." Tortorice replied. "Hey, I thought you were gonna try online dating. How'd that work out?"

Holding the door to the pizzeria open for his partner, Adam said, "I can sum it up in three words. Blue Polyester Pantsuit."

"Ouch!" Tortorice replied.

"Yeah, ouch." Adam said in a dejected tone. *"But there is always Janine…"* he thought to himself.

Janine walked into the Starbucks on Route 9 and saw John sitting in the corner, sipping on a coffee. Getting on line and ordering, Janine was startled when John suddenly appeared behind her as she approached the register.

"Let me get that Miss Wagner." He said, handing the barista a credit card.

Joining John at the corner table, Janine said, "You didn't have to do that."

"You are taking time out of your busy day to speak to me, when you have no idea what this whole thing is about. The least I could do is buy you a cup of coffee." John replied.

Taking a careful sip of the hot liquid, then wiping the bit that leaked out and dribbled down her chin, Janine said, "You know… I love Starbuck coffee, and I appreciate they want to give me my money's worth, but do they always have to fill the cups to the very top of the brim. They make it impossible to drink without spilling it or having some of it make you look like this is the first day with your new mouth."

"I had the same problem with mine." John replied. "I can't even imagine how you could drink this if you are in a car."

"Right?" Janine said. "So, what is it you needed to talk to me about. You were very cryptic the other day."

John began, "I am working on a case, Miss Wagner, where a number of monks and nuns were killed."

"I heard about that on the news. That was tragic."

"Yeah. You have no idea how bad it was. The news, especially here in the States was probably very cursory. The people were all tortured and interrogated before they were killed. The murders were brutal, but they were not the primary objective of the perpetrators. The killers were at the monasteries looking for something. Our people were killed to leave no witnesses.

Before he died, we were able to speak to one of the monks who initially survived the torture. He kept repeating the same question over and over, which I am assuming refers to what the killers were looking for. We are thinking it might be some religious artifact or antiquity of value and have been following up on this, but so far have not come up with anything. One such avenue of exploration led me here to your family, which is why I was looking to speak to you the other day."

Janine said, "I don't know of any religious artifact that was ever in our possession."

"Would your father or grandfather confide in you… tell you if there was something of great value that they had hidden somewhere?"

Nodding her head, Janine replied, "Our great grandfather was a Lutheran pastor, but I'm pretty sure he never owned a religious artifact. He and my grandfather barely escaped from Nazi Germany during the Second World War, so I don't know how they could have gotten their hands on one, let alone gotten it out of the country. If they had, I'm pretty sure it would have been displayed at the church. My great grandfather was very devoted to his church. I never actually met my Opa's father… actually, not his real father, but that's a whole other story… but in all the family stories I've heard, I've never heard anyone ever talk about something they brought with them out of Germany. However, if you need to be certain, my Opa would be the one to ask."

"Can I speak with him?" John asked. "I know you said he had a stroke."

"The stroke is not the problem. This problem is my sister. I can try to get you to talk to him, but my sister keeps him locked down pretty tight."

John said, "Yeah, I saw that the other day. That was kind of a crazy scene."

"You have no idea, Inspector. My sister is nuts."

John shook his head and chuckled. "There's no drama like family drama. And please call me John."

"OK John. And you should call me Janine. So, getting back to my sister, you have no idea with her. She treats Opa worse than if he were a little child. She controls everyone's access to him, and has to be constantly by his side whenever he goes out in public. She answers questions for him, tells him what he is going to eat and drink and allows the man absolutely no dignity. She initially moved in to the upstairs apartment, but she totally trashed the place and then moved downstairs and is trashing that apartment too."

"What do you mean she trashed the place?" John asked.

"Anna is a hoarder. She throws nothing away. There's newspapers and mail stacked basically on every flat surface going back to when she first moved in. She drags Opa to flea markets and brings back all sorts of crap, and when asked about it, she says he wanted it. There is really no place to store any of that crap, so it sits on the floor and collects dust. She does throw out unfinished food, so at least you don't have half-eaten Chinese food rotting in a corner somewhere, but that really is about as far as she goes with cleaning."

"I'm sorry." John said. "Have you tried talking to her about it, or suggesting she see someone?"

"Multiple times, but she refuses and says that I have OCD and I'm the one who's nuts". Janine replied. "I will admit I may be a bit of a neat freak, but she doesn't clean up at all. The bathroom is totally disgusting. I honestly don't think it has been cleaned since my dad passed away."

"And that was a few years ago, right?" John asked.

"Yeah, I mean, the mold is growing mold. It's disgusting. I'm sure she doesn't pay any rent, and since she has power of attorney, she uses Opa's money to pay all the utility bills and the taxes on the house. She says that since she buys the food it evens out, but somehow I doubt it and I wonder if she is using his money for the food too."

"So, if she is so secretive and won't let anyone in to see him, how do you know all this?" John asked.

"Anna slipped on some ice back in the winter and wound up in the hospital for a couple of days. I had to go over and pick up Opa and bring him to my place to care for him. When I saw the conditions she had him living in, I wouldn't let him go back. I mean, its elder abuse. I told Anna that the only way for him to go back was if she cleaned up the downstairs apartment. She said she was doing it, but somehow, I doubted it. Then one day, right before the school year ended, while I was at work, she came by and took Opa back to the house. She was actually getting frantic because she uses Opa as an excuse to get intermittent FMLA."

"What is that?" John asked

Janine replied, "Anna works at DMV, and since it is a state government job, she is allowed to get up to 180 days of Family Leave each year to take care of Opa…and she can take those days at any time throughout the year. So, whenever she doesn't feel like going in to work, she just calls out and says he has a doctor's appointment, and her job can't fire her."

"That sounds like a pretty sweet deal." John said chuckling.

"The problem was she needs a doctor to certify that she is the primary care giver, and Opa's doctor knew he was living with me at that time, so he wouldn't sign the papers. She needed to get him back, and take him to the doctor and get the papers signed, so she basically kidnapped him. I've tried to get him back but every time I've gone there, she's taken another one of those 180 days and is sitting at home.

She tells people she is living downstairs to take care of Opa, but in reality, after trashing the upstairs apartment and making it so it's actually unlivable, she moved downstairs and has been trashing my dad's place too. She is using our poor disabled grandfather as an excuse to not have to work."

"Wow. That's really messed up. John said, "But you are a teacher. Since you're off during the summer couldn't you just go over during the workday and get him? There has to be a time she is not there."

Janine replied, "That's what I tried to do the other day when you saw me there, but I guess she figured out she couldn't be there every day and wanted to make double sure I couldn't get in, so she had the lock changed."

"And that brings us to where we are right now." John said.

"Exactly." Janine said nodding her head. "

"OK… So, we need to either get Anna's buy in, or find a time that she is not there and convince your Opa to let us in to speak to him."

"That's easier said than done." Said Janine.

John sipped his coffee and pondered the situation for a minute. He wondered if there was actually any additional information he could learn from Janine's grandfather. Based on what she had already told him, it didn't look like the old man or his father had managed to acquire any religious relics. And while it would be nice to speak to the man to confirm this, since the man had a stroke, John wondered if he would be able to actually get anything useful from the conversation. Would the end result really be worth imposing additional conflict on this already divided family?

Finally, John looked up from his coffee and said, "You know Janine, you and your family have been through enough. Your sister sounds like she needs help, and the added stress of us trying to question your grandfather will only make things worse. Based on what you already told me, I don't believe I would be uncovering any additional information that would aid me in solving this case."

Pausing, then shaking his head with a sigh, John continued. "Coming here was a long shot anyway."

"What do you mean?" Janine asked.

"We have a ton of evidence, but no real leads for this case. I have some information on potential suspects, but nothing solid to link to them. I guess I was just grasping at straws when I decided to pursue this investigation here in the States."

"You never told me what led you to my family." Janine said.

"Other than my gut…" John said. "It was what the Monk said on his deathbed. It was what I heard."

"And what was that?" Janine asked.

"How's your German?" John asked.

"Opa made sure we never lost our heritage, so both Anna and I are bi-lingual." Janine replied.

"OK." John said as he took out his phone, and cued up both the original recording of the Monk, and the version with the background noise removed.

"Here… Listen." He said, hitting the play button.

Janine closed her eyes and listened closely, nodding her head as she processed what she heard. Translating as she listened she said, "*Big light… Where is the big light… The man asked where is the big light…Big light…*

"Big light?" John asked? "Grosse licht? That's what you heard? The Austrians all thought he said *The ghastly… das grässlich.* So, you heard the *T* sound on the end of the word as well."

"Yeah. I heard, *Where is the big light?*" Janine replied.

"So, because that poor monk was beaten about his face and everything was swollen, it was tough to make out what he was saying. We ran multiple variations of what we thought he said through the computer, and nothing that made sense came up. But then I heard what sounded like Grasslicked, and when I searched it, a town in West Virginia came up, and so did the obituary for your dad. Since we weren't getting anywhere looking for a thing, my gut said why not check out leads for a person or a place. I went to West Virginia first and didn't find anything, then I came here to follow up on the person part."

"So you thought you heard *Where is the grasslicked?*" Janine said. "That's funny. The same thing happened to Opa when they were coming to America. The American completing the passport paperwork overheard Opa and his father speaking and thought they said their name was Grasslicked when they had said Grosse Licht. He listed Grasslicked as their last name and since it was such a hassle to change it, and people were not too keen on German immigrants back then, they just kept the name. Our running family joke was *Das grosse licht ist das Kreuz das unsere familie trägt.*"

"The big light is the cross our family bears?" John asked.

"Yup. Any time someone in the family would talk about a light, we would say it… You know, like where is the flashlight… The big light is the cross our family bears, or if a lightbulb burns out… The big light…"

"… is the cross our family bears." John said with Janine. "I get it. That's a funny story. So, what was your real last name. What was it supposed to be?" John asked.

"Opa was adopted… well, I don't think it was a legal adoption and all. His real name is Otto Hasselmeyer. Otto's real father was killed in the war and our great grandfather took him in and they fled Germany so Opa wouldn't get conscripted into the army. Great Grandfather's last name was Wagner, but as I said, they figured it was just easier to accept the last name of Grasslicked, and just live their lives letting everyone assume they were father and son.

"From everything I have ever read about that time in history, the period immediately after the war was hectic. Things could easily get confused. They probably made the best choice rather than try to fight the bureaucracy and try to fix it."

Janine said, "As I said, Great Grandfather was a Lutheran pastor. He served in Brooklyn for a while until his English got better, then took a calling here in New Jersey. Opa came with him, and was a carpenter. He got married, had my dad and they just lived a normal life. There was never any talk of religious artifacts or anything like that. Nothing extraordinary or strange… except for maybe my sister."

"And I'm assuming both she and your grandfather would tell me the same thing." John said. "No Janine. I don't want to cause any more drama between you and your sister. I think I've hit another dead end."

Finishing the last of his coffee, John prepared to stand and said, "Guess I'll just thank you for your time and cooperation, head over to police headquarters to say my goodbyes, and make arrangements to head back to Rome."

Standing along with John, Janine said, "If you happen to see Lieutenant Levy at police headquarters, can you ask him to contact me? I have that list of stolen items he was looking for."

"Stolen items?" John asked.

"My place was broken into the other day. Probably a bunch of kids on drugs because they trashed the place, but actually didn't steal very much. Just some cash I had in my dresser. They left all my jewelry, the TV,… everything else. But they freakin' demolished everything."

"They put any holes in the walls?" John asked, trying to maintain a calm demeanor.

"Yeah, in every room." Janine replied. "And they tore up the carpeting and shredded my couch and mattresses. Its nuts. It was almost like they were…"

"…Looking for something." John said finishing her sentence. "I may have to reassess my plans to leave, and I think I actually do need to speak to your grandfather."

"John, what's going on?"

"I'm not sure, yet. Do you have someplace safe to stay?"

"I've been crashing over at a friend's place while mine is being cleaned up and repaired."

"I suggest you head over there. Let me have your cell number, and I'll call you later with more information. This could be just a bad coincidence, or there could be more to this than just a break-in. I'll call you later and let you know. In the meantime, stay at your friends. If you feel you are in any danger, call 911, then text me and I'll come to you right away."

John walked Janine to her car, and then ensured she was not being followed before turning off and heading to police headquarters. Calling Captain Benjamin during his drive, he had him check if there were any similar cases to Janine's that his people were working.

Arriving at headquarters, he was met at the front doors

by both Levy and Benjamin. Extending greetings, they escorted John into the squad room.

"We only noticed it this morning when I was reviewing the new case files from the past few days." Adam said. "Two other break-ins just like Miss Wagner's, all with similar MOs. Nothing but cash taken and the place ransacked with damaged walls, shredded furniture and ripped up carpets. And here's the strangest part. All the victims were named Wagner."

John said, "I've got a bad feeling that my friends have left the monasteries and are looking for something around here."

"Any idea who these people are?" Benjamin asked.

"Actually, we believe it is two competing groups." John replied.

"Oh, great." Moaned Adam.

"We have some working theories on who they are." John said. "One of my sources identified one of the groups as Nazis from South America, and the forensic and crime scene evidence identified one of the other team's shooters as Korean."

"What the fuck..." exclaimed Benjamin.

"Right?" replied John. "I mean, the Korean could actually be part of a Las Vegas crime family, not some kind of North Korean operative. And my source could be dead wrong and the other team be a bunch of pissed off Eskimos for all we actually know. We don't have enough of anything definitive to link this to any person or group."

"But whoever they are, you think they are here." Adam said.

"The MOs are very similar to what we saw in Austria.

All of the sites they hit were torn up like the homes here. The only difference here is there's no trail of bodies." John said.

"Adam, has anyone checked how many people named Wagner live in the borough, or in the surrounding towns for that matter?"

"Not yet boss. I had Tortorice looking into it while we met with Nowalski." Adam replied.

"So what are our next steps?" Adam asked.

"I'd say your people should track down all of the Wagners. See if there are other houses that were hit. I'm going to report in and reach out to my people and see what they can track down on the name Wagner. Janine also listened to my recording of the monk and is fairly certain he was saying, *Where is the big light?*"

"Janine?" Adam said questioningly.

"Miss Wagner." John said.

"I know who you were talking about." Adam replied with an accusing tone. "I was just surprised you were on a first name basis."

Smiling, John said, "I guess my charming personality just lends itself to being on a first name basis."

"Who is tracking down the other people with the last name of Wagner?" Captain Benjamin said bringing the conversation back to the current situation.

"I have Tortorice working on it." Adam replied, as he glared at John.

Turning to John, Benjamin asked, "Do you think this new information will help you in identifying who these groups are?"

"Not really Captain." John said. "It may allow me to

get a better handle on what it is everyone is searching for, but as for pinning this on anyone, that part is doubtful."

"Alright. We all have our marching orders. I suggest we get to it. John, I have your cell number. If anything develops, I'll give you a call. The same goes for you. Remember, you have no jurisdiction here, so please run everything through me."

"Sounds like a plan." John said as he stood to leave.

Adam replied without looking at Benjamin. "You got it boss." Gathering up his papers, Adam continued to give John his best 'stink eye'.

Answering the ringing phone from the comfort of his living room couch, Alvarez said. "Good evening, your Excellency. You are up rather late this evening."

"I was dining with several of my fellow prelates, and then had a few things that needed tending to. I received some updated information today that I thought needed to be passed on immediately."

"Well I thank you for your diligence. Since we had our little chat, you have been more than helpful with our current endeavor." Alvarez said.

"I received some information on Nowalski's investigation today." The Cardinal began. "It seems he is more astute of an investigator than first thought. In his latest report he identified the item that he believes we are searching for as The Big Light, and he ties it to the last name of Wagner. He has his second-in-command following up on this, but I doubt they will uncover anything."

"Thinking for a moment, Alvarez replied, "This is

actually good news. If Nowalski has a better idea what he is looking for, he has a better chance of finding it for us."

"That is true. However, this other piece of news is not as good. His report also stated the bullets from the monastery were a ballistics match to the assassination of the Belgian Finance Minister, and one of his sources has implicated Donner Securities to that killing."

"That is unfortunate news." Alvarez said. "However, if there was any definitive evidence, we would already have people at our doorstep. I am not overly concerned. That being said, I think we may need to add another layer of security to our plan... an insurance policy if you will against Nowalski learning too much."

"What do you have in mind?" The Cardinal asked.

"We have some pull in Washington, and some supporters in their Justice Department. It might be prudent for us to utilize those resources... stage them if you will, in case Nowalski uncovers things that would look damaging to our interests."

"Is there anything more that you would need from me?" The Cardinal asked.

"It might be prudent for you to be closer to the action. Nowalski knows and trusts you. If you were in America, you could be there to intercede if needed. Why don't you make the arrangements to fly to New Jersey. I will have one of our people pick you up. I'm sure you can invent some plausible cover for you to make the trip."

"I can certainly do that, however, that may mean I would not be able to come down for the Board meeting. Ever since the pandemic, the bean counters have been relentless in limiting travel and pushing us to conduct the balance of our international business via Zoom."

"We can accommodate that." Alvarez replied. "I believe it is more important for you to be able to aid our teams if needed. I can make sure we include a Zoom link for our Board meeting."

The Cardinal said, "Very well. I will get started on the arrangements, and let you know when they are complete so your man can pick me up. In the meantime, if I develop any additional information, I will let you know."

"Thank you, your Eminence. Your assistance is greatly appreciated,"

Steve Tortorice slowed the car down to a crawl as he crossed the railroad tracks after turning on to Deerfield Road. Cursing under his breath at how uneven the road and elevated the tracks were at this crossing, he was still surprised that neither the Borough nor the County had ever even attempted to make repairs so that traversing these tracks wouldn't tear up your car's suspension. Proceeding around the curve and down the road, Tortorice searched the mailboxes for a house number.

Finding the address, he pulled up in front of the one-story brick ranch with a small front lawn and a poorly maintained collection of bushes. Getting out of the vehicle, Tortorice walked up to the front door and rang the non-functioning doorbell as well as knocked vigorously on the wooden door. Moving some of the branches of the overgrown azalea bush, Tortorice peered between the slats of the blinds into the front window.

While he couldn't see much more than the movement of light from inside the front room, he could clearly hear the guest being invited on down as the next contestant on the Price is Right from the elevated volume from the TV. Pounding on the door again, Tortorice waited several minutes before he left the front porch and headed around to the back of the house.

Approaching the back door, he could see the glass punched out from one of the door panels. Trying the knob and finding the door open, Tortorice drew his service weapon from the holster, and spoke into the handheld radio requesting back-up from the dispatcher. Completing the radio call, he slowly turned the handle and entered the small mud room inside the back door.

Immediately greeted by the sickly-sweet smell of a decaying body, Tortorice was not surprised when he found the elderly woman slumped over and bound to a chair in the kitchen. Cautiously approaching the woman, Tortorice checked the woman's neck for a pulse just to be sure, then got back on the radio to call in what he had found.

The kitchen was in shambles with every cabinet and draw open and empty, the contents strewn across the floor. The woman's arms and legs were bound to the chair with zip ties, and in addition to the bruising about her face, she had a dime sized hole in the front of her head. As Tortorice made his way into the living room, he could see multiple holes in the walls and the couch and chairs torn to shreds. Aside from the dead body in the kitchen, the scene resembled the other Wagner break-ins they were investigating.

With the sound of sirens growing in intensity, Tortorice pulled out his cell phone and called Benjamin.

"Hey Boss, its Steve. Don't know if you heard. We have a body at Elizabeth Wagner's. The scene looks just like all the others."

"Fuck!" Benjamin swore. "Did it just happen?"

"Nah. This was done a few days ago. In this heat, she's already getting pretty ripe."

"Shit. Well we'll get the forensics guys there, but I doubt we'll learn anything new. I'll reach out to Nowalski, let him know. He'll probably want to come take a look."

Tortorice said, "I gotta hang here anyway. I'll fill him in when he gets here."

"I guess we don't have to wonder if those killers came here." Benjamin said.

"Yeah… I wish we would've been wrong this time."

John had picked Janine up from her friend's apartment and headed up Route 9 headed toward where he had first met her at her grandfather's house. Navigating through the streets after getting off the highway, John was amazed that he still remembered his way around after being away for so long.

"You know, I've been thinking…" Janine said to John as he drove. "…Opa always kept a safety deposit box at the bank. I remember there were a few times my dad would tell me he had to take Opa there to check on the box for some reason. Do you think this thing you are looking for might somehow be in that box?"

"I don't know." Replied John. "I agree with you that it probably would have been hard for your grandfather to have taken anything out of Germany. But if it was something small… like small enough to fit in a safety deposit box?… I don't know. It's something maybe we could ask him about."

Arriving at the South Amboy triplex, John parked the car and joined Janine on the walkway to the front door.

"I'm not sure they will even be awake." Janine said as they approached the front door.

Looking at his watch, John said, "Its nearly one-thirty in the afternoon. They'd still be sleeping?"

"My sister would sleep till six PM if you let her. She stays up late, then goes to sleep and will sleep for like fourteen hours if she isn't disturbed."

"That's nuts." John exclaimed.

"I know. Imagine trying to plan family parties or holidays with that. She shows up three to four hours late for every occasion."

"No she doesn't". John said in disbelief.

"Yeah, she does. I remember one party at a cousin's… It was his daughter's first birthday, and everyone was there. The party started at two in the afternoon, and most people arrived around that time. My cousin tried to keep the food out for as long as they could because, you know, Opa is the patriarch of the family but no one except my sister is allowed to bring him. So of course, he is always late for stuff too.

Anyway, it's now like seven in the evening, everyone is saying their good-byes, all the food is put away, my cousin is cleaning up, and in strolls my sister with Opa. And of course, she is looking for food. My cousin was so pissed off. He didn't want to punish Opa for her behavior, but his daughter was tired after a long day, hell, he and his wife were tired, and the last thing they wanted to do was now have to entertain my sister."

"What did they do?" John asked.

"They let Opa hold a cranky baby, fed them, then I think they kicked them out. They have had a few get-to-gethers since then, and Anna hasn't been invited."

"I feel bad for your grandfather." John said.

"I know." Agreed Janine. "Anna uses him as an excuse for everything." It's her fault for their being late, but she blames it on him. And since no one in the family wants to upset Opa, they all let her get away with it."

Arriving at the front door, Janine rang the doorbell, and began knocking on the door. After about two minutes of no answer, she repeated the knocking, this time with increased vigor.

"Maybe they're not home." John said.

"No, they are here." Pointing toward the street, Janine said, "That's her car. She wouldn't even think to walk anywhere. She's too lazy. They're home. Like I said, she's just sleeping."

After pounding on the door for another minute, Janine's phone began to ring.

"Here we go." Janine said before answering the call and putting it on speaker. "Hello Anna."

The voice on the other end of the phone sounded like they were just awakened from a dead sleep. "Janine? Are you at the front door?"

"Yes Anna. I need to speak to you and Opa. Can you open the door?"

"What do you want?"

"I need to speak to you and Opa. It's important. Can you open the door please?" Janine said.

"Why? What do you want? What is it?"

"We need to speak to you and Opa. It's about his escape from Germany. He may have brought something with him, some relic, and we need to speak to him to see if he did that."

"Who needs to speak to him?" Anna asked. "Who is this we?"

"Myself and a police investigator." Janine replied.

"A Sayreville police officer?" Anna asked.

"No. He's with INTERPOL. You know, the European police agency."

"He's what?" Anna said.

John spoke up. "Anna, my name is Inspector John Nowalski. I am with INTERPOL. I am here investigating the murders of several nuns and monks in Austria. Perhaps you heard about that in the news. If we could come in, I'd like to speak to you and your grandfather about his escape from Nazi Germany. The story of his escape may help inform my investigation. I know that may sound strange but he and your great grandfather may have inadvertently…"

"You are with INTERPOL?" Anna asked cutting him off.

"Yes." John replied

"But you don't have an accent. You sound American."

John chuckled, "I am American. In fact, I'm actually from around here. But for the past twenty or so years I've been working…"

Cutting John off, Anna said, "Janine, you are so naïve. This guy's a fraud. He's probably trying to sell you something… or maybe, he wants to see Opa so he can steal something from him. He thinks Opa's old, he's had a stroke… maybe he thinks he could get Opa to sign over the house or something."

"Miss Grasslicked, I can assure you, I am no fraud." John replied. "If you come to the door I can show you my badge and ID."

Janine said to support John, "Anna, he is for real. I saw his badge and ID. If you won't let us in, can you and Opa just come to the door?"

"You know Janine… Those badges and IDs can be, you know.. they can be forged. I bet you could go online and get that stuff right from like Amazon. You are so gullible…"

"Anna, his credentials are not…" Janine began in an exasperated tone.

"Look, you both need to leave." Anna said cutting her sister off. "If you don't leave, I'm calling the police."

"Yes… Anna, please call the police. John… Inspector Nowalski is working with them." Janine said.

"John?… Since when do we call strangers or people we are dealing with on a professional level by their first name?" Anna said.

"Anna, I've been trying to help him for…"

"You know Janine…That's always been one of your problems. You're boy crazy. You see a cute face and right away you fall for whatever bullshit line they give you."

"What are you talking about?" Janine replied.

"Like back in tenth grade when you thought Bobby McDonald was the hottest thing, and you thought just because he said 'Hi' to you by your locker, he was going to ask you out."

"Anna have you lost your mind? What does that have to do with this?"

Anna said, "You thought he was going to ask you out… It didn't matter to you that I had my eye on him. I mean, he was a senior, like me, and what chance did a little freshman have of getting asked out to the homecoming dance by a senior?"

"Anna… he didn't ask either of us out. He was with that field hockey girl.. what was her name? It doesn't matter… Anna, what does that have to do with any of this?"

"He didn't ask either of us out because he knew we both liked him. He didn't want to cause any family drama, so he did the right thing and went with someone else."

"Anna, you're fuckin' nuts." Janine said.

"No, Janine, you are. You are so desperate to get married, you will believe any story some guy will give you. You are still boy crazy, just like when you were in tenth grade. This… John… is probably just some guy who wants to get into your pants and wants to steal all of Opa's money."

"No Anna… He doesn't want to do either. And as far as stealing Opa's money, he can't do that because you already stole it."

"Fuck you Janine!" Anna yelled into the phone so loud that John heard it through the walls as well as the phone.

Seeing the conversation spinning out of control, John made one last ditch effort to salvage the trip, and said, "Miss Grasslicked, I can assure you I am not a fraud, and I'm not looking to get into anyone's pants. If you want you can call Captain Benjamin at the police department. He is in charge of the detectives, he can confirm who I am. I would really like to speak to you and your grandfather… ask you both a few questions. I promise it won't take long and it would really help…"

Cutting John off again, Anna said. "Is this Captain Benjamin your partner in this charade. You prey on naïve and gullible young women like my sister and steal money from old men and then split it with him. I've heard about you dirty cops. I mean, it's been all over the news… all the poor innocent black people you kill. Well you are not getting the chance with me or my grandfather. Janine, you can go ahead and jump in the sack with him if you want, but don't come crying to me after he hurts you."

Shaking his head, John turned to Janine and said, "This is no use. Let's go."

"Anna, we are going to go. I still want to come and see Opa."

"What for?"

"Because I love him and I miss him… He is my grand-father too."

"If he's feeling better, you can see him in church tomorrow." Anna replied.

"He's not feeling well? What's the matter?" Janine asked.

"His stomach is upset. He has the runs." Anna said.

"It's that shitty diner food you give him. He gets the runs all the time with you. When he was staying with me and I fed him good home-cooked meals, he never had the runs."

"Fuck you Janine. He told me his stomach was upset all the time. And there is nothing wrong with the food he eats here. I eat it, and I'm fine."

"That's cause you're already full of shit… adding more to the pile with what you eat makes no difference. Tell Opa I'll look for him in church tomorrow."

Hanging up the phone, Janine turned to John who was reading a message on his phone. As they began walking down the front walk, Janine growled through partially clenched teeth, "I fucking hate her.." Then seeing the look on John's face, she asked, "What's wrong?"

John replied, almost in a whisper. "I need to get you back, then I have to go. There's been another murder."

John met Tortorice and Adam at Betty Wagner's home within the hour of receiving the text from Benjamin. Viewing the body and the ransacked home, John had no doubt that the same people who killed the nuns in Austria were now here in America.

"Your forensic guys won't find anything here either." John said to Tortorice and Adam. "These guys are professionals." Despite all this carnage, they won't leave even a single hair. The only place we found any real evidence was at the scene of the shoot-out."

"I guess you are less concerned about fiber or DNA evidence when you're being shot at." Tortorice quipped.

"Are there any other families in town with the name Wagner?" John asked.

"No, she was the last one." Adam replied.

"What about surrounding towns… South Amboy, Old Bridge?" John asked.

"There are a handful. We spoke to detectives in those towns, as well as Perth Amboy and South River and gave them all a heads-up. They said they were going to do wellness checks, and then increase patrols in those neighborhoods."

"Good idea." John replied. "You should let them know that if anyone runs into these people, they should call in the cavalry rather than approach. These guys are professionals and they are nasty. The same holds true for your guys, Lieutenant. Tell your people not to approach."

"Thank you for your amazing insight and recommendation, Inspector." Adam replied in a sarcastically condescending tone.

Turning to Tortorice, John said, "You know Steve, I don't know what I've done to offend your lieutenant. I mean, I've been nothing but courteous and professional my entire time here, yet, he treats me with such malice and contempt."

Adam stepped forward between John and Tortorice and said, "Hey, I'm right here mutha-fucker. If you have a problem with me, why don't you address me directly. Tell me face-to face like a man."

"I have learned, in my many years of experience, when assholes like you are this arrogant and belligerent, talking directly to them is like pissing into the wind. You may feel temporary relief, but in the end, you are still full of pee."

"Listen old man…" Adam began stepping forward with clenched fists

Tortorice stepped forward and put a hand on Adam's shoulder. "Let it go Lieutenant. You need to step back and get control of yourself."

"Thank you Steve." John said. "Look, I'm going to remove myself from this situation and go and call my department. I've had them working on some things, and I want to update them on the latest developments here. I would think the other folks with the last name of Wagner should be informed and told they would be safer if they left town."

Turning to Adam he said, "I know you are working the Janine Wagner case. She is currently staying with a friend in Old Bridge. Do you want to inform her, or should I?"

"I got it, Inspector. Go call your people." Adam growled.

"Good enough. Thank you for informing me about this latest development. I'll let you know if I develop anything new." John said.

As John headed toward the street and his rental car, Tortorice looked at Adam and said, "Lieutenant, I say this with the utmost respect... What the fuck is wrong with you?"

"I don't know Steve-O. There is just something about that guy that rubs me the wrong way."

"Look Adam, I've known you since you started with the department, and I respect you as my supervisor. I also like to think of you as a friend. As one friend to another, you don't want to fuck with this guy."

Giving Tortorice a confused look, Adam said, "Really Steve? This guy? He's like a cop for priests. I mean, granted, you said he's been involved in catching some high profile terrorists, but I mean, really, how hard can his job be?"

"OK, so imagine being the head of our Secret Service... but in addition to all the new crazies that are minted every single day, you are dealing with enemies who have hated you for several thousand years. That is what John Nowalski deals with. And in addition to protecting one man like our Secret Service does, you have to actually protect thousands of them across the globe along with hundreds of historical sites. And unlike our Secret Service that has like two thousand agents, you have to do this job with a team of about a dozen."

"How do you know all this?" Adam asked

"Remember a few years ago when we had that missing kid and we were working with the FBI?"

"Yeah…". Adam replied.

"Well one of the agents I had the pleasure of working with used to work anti-terrorism. He remembered that Nowalski used to work here, and asked me about him. I filled him in and since I hadn't spoken to John in like, years I asked the agent to tell me what he knew. Nowalski is highly thought of by police agencies around the world. He regularly gives talks about his ideas on improving police work and anti-terrorist tactics. And don't let that calm, laid back outward demeanor fool you. John is not a dude to mess with either."

"You've got to be shittin' me." Adam said in disbelief.

"This guy is a monk, Adam. That means he doesn't fuck, he doesn't gamble, he doesn't spend his money on nice things. He lives a very simple life devoted to the improvement of his craft, in his case, police work. Monks believe you live your life this way to glorify God. So Nowalski reads, and studies, and trains to be the best cop there is, because he believes that is God's will for him. He speaks like four languages, has multiple college degrees, has black belts in several martial arts, and runs like five miles a day."

"No shit. This guy doesn't get laid?"

"After all that, that's the one thing you dial in on?" Tortorice asked. "No, he doesn't get laid. Monks take vows of celibacy, piety and poverty. Just like Roman Catholic priests."

"Alright. So maybe I should cut this guy some slack." Adam said.

"Yeah, we should be thankful he is here to help. So, stop giving him so much attitude." Nodding his head in the direction of the house, Tortorice switched gears and said. "So, what's our next steps with this case?"

"I guess we go with what Nowalski suggested. I'll go inform Janine Wagner about what happened and tell her to remain with her friend for the time being." Adam said. "Why don't you see if you can get in touch with the other towns with Wagner families and give them the same message. After that, I was planning to head back to the station to write up the report and give Benjamin an update."

"Sounds like a plan Lieutenant." Tortorice replied.

Adam pulled into the parking lot of the garden apartment complex where Janine's was staying. Getting out of the car, Adam wandered around several courtyards before finally finding the correct building. He then made his way down to the apartment door and pressed the buzzer announcing his presence. He heard a window open above him and looked up to see Janine peeking her head out to see who was at the door.

"I'll be right down." Janine shouted from the open window.

Joining Adam outside, Janine said, "My friend is taking an online class. I don't want to disturb her so is it OK if we talk out here?"

"Sure, no problem." Adam said.

"When you called, you said you had some news you

wanted to tell me in person. So what's going on Lieutenant? Is it good news, I hope?"

"Unfortunately, it's not. And please, call me Adam."

"Alright Adam. What's up?"

"There has been a murder." Adam said. "Another resident of the Borough whose last name was Wagner was killed. From the initial investigation, it looks like she was tortured and killed similarly to the way the nuns and monks were killed in Austria."

"Oh my God!" Janine said, bringing her hand up to her mouth.

"It appears whoever was operating in Austria has made their way here and has tied it to the last name of Wagner. So we are asking all of the folks with the same last name to either leave or remain out of town. If these people haven't found what they are looking for by searching the house, they may try to use other means to get that information."

"Well my friend has told me I can stay here as long as I need to." Janine said.

"That's good. Hopefully, we can catch these people quickly and you can return back to your home."

"I hope so Lieutenant. The clean-up and repairs are supposed to be done by mid-week."

Wincing inwardly at Janine's insistence on calling him by his title, Adam said, "We'll do the best we can. In the meantime, I've already spoken to the Old Bridge police. They will increase security by having a car come by several more times a week. And you have my cell number. You can always call me as well."

"Thank you, Lieuten… I mean Adam." Janine said smiling.

Adam and Janine stood looking at each other for several moments, an awkward silence falling over them. Finally, Adam broke the silence. "Janine... Listen, what I am about to say may not be the most professional thing I've ever said, but... well... I... Maybe when this is all over, if you'd like to go out... grab some dinner or just a drink?..."

"Oh, Adam... Thank you..."

"I mean, if you want, we could do it sooner..." Adam said. "We don't have to wait if you don't want to."

Smiling at Adam, Janine said, "That is very sweet, Lieutenant. And under different circumstances, I might consider it. But right now, there is just too much going on in my life. I couldn't even think about a relationship, or even just dating someone new. I'm flattered that you asked, but I must respectfully decline."

Adam's heart sunk. Looking down at his feet and nodding his head, he finally lifted his head to look at Janine and said, "I understand. And I apologize for the bad timing. It's just, since I ran into you, quite literally, at the church, I can't seem to get you out of my mind. Maybe when things settle down, we can re-evaluate and see if it would work then."

"I can't make any promises, but one never knows." Janine said.

"Well thanks." Adam said. By the way, that was the nicest, most polite 'NO' I've ever received. Thank you for being so kind and understanding."

Laughing a little, Janine said, "Well, I've never had anyone thank me for a rejection before."

Chuckling with Janine, Adam said, "What can I say... I'm unique. Look, I'm gonna go now before I embarrass myself any more. Please remember stay away from your home until we advise you it is safe to return. And if you have even a suspicion of a problem, if something just doesn't feel right, call me. You have my number. I promise we'll keep you informed as well."

Janine said, "Thanks Lieutenant. I'm sure I'll hear from you soon."

Adam headed across the courtyard as Janine opened the outer door to the apartment and headed up the stairs. As she got halfway up, her phone began to ring.

"Hello?" she answered.

"Janine? Hi, this is John. I have a quick question. What time does your sister go to church tomorrow?"

"The service is at ten thirty, so she usually leaves around that time and gets there late… I mean, no reason to treat God any differently."

I got an idea. Would you be willing to not attend church and come with me to the house?" John asked.

"Yeah, I could do that. But if Opa's there he won't let us in, and if he's at church, my key doesn't work, remember? What are gonna do? Break in?"

"Let's just say I'm playing the odds and betting on human nature." John said. "I'll pick you up around ten fifteen if that works? And bring your keys."

CHAPTER 15

Middlesex County
Present Day

JOHN PICKED JANINE up as scheduled and headed north on Route Nine toward Perth Amboy. Crossing the Raritan River into the city, the pair turned off Convery Boulevard and headed down toward Janine's grandfather's house. Janine was quiet for most of the trip, and John was a bit preoccupied himself, having received a disturbing call from Cardinal Sentille earlier that morning.

John had been unable to speak to the Cardinal the night before, but had written an update and had sent it before turning in for the night. While John had been able to touch base with Tony, there still wasn't any definitive evidence he could use to tie any of the murders to either Aryphon or the Koreans. John still hoped that by locating the missing artifact he would be able to tie all the information together in a way that would allow him to positively identify the killers and make arrests. This was the information he included in the report he had sent to Sentille, and the reason for the Cardinal's call this morning.

Sentille informed John that the Pope was unhappy with the lack of progress in the case. And while it appeared the attacks on the monasteries had ceased, the pontiff was concerned that the Church's problem had now migrated to the States. If the American media picked up on this, the Pope feared it would show poorly on the Church. Sentille said that he found it a discomforting coincidence that after John had moved his investigation and search for this missing *thing* to the United States, the people committing the murders appeared to have followed him there as well.

John attempted to convince the Cardinal that despite the recent murder of Mrs. Wagner, the fact that the killers were here and searching meant that John was also on the right track. The Cardinal however disagreed, and informed John that he was going to consult with Pinochinio and would get back to John with his recommendations on how John was to proceed.

Looking over to Janine, John noticed she was unusually quiet as well. "Everything OK?" he asked.

Brought out of her daze and back to the present, Janine blinked a confused look off of her face and said, "What... Oh... Yeah... I'm... I'm fine."

Looking at Janine and seeing her eyes glaze back over, John said, "I've been an investigator long enough to know when to call bullshit. What's wrong?"

Turning to face John Janine said, "Nothing... I'm OK. I was just thinking about poor Mrs. Wagner. She was such a nice old lady. She didn't deserve to die that way."

"So, they told you about her death?" John asked.

"Yeah. Lieutenant Levy came by yesterday and told me she was murdered. He warned me to stay with my friend and not to return to my house until this gets resolved."

"Good advice." John said. Did you know Mrs. Wagner well?"

"Not really well. She was a member of our church. I would talk to her upon occasion. She would tell me about what a wonderful pastor my great grandfather was."

"So now how worried are you that these people are coming after you?"

Janine hesitated before she spoke. "I guess I'm a little concerned. I mean, these people obviously have no qualms about killing, and they already destroyed my house... Do you really think they will be looking for me?"

"Janine, there is no question that these are very bad people and they are dangerous. That being said, I don't think they can track you down. Stay away from your house... in fact stay out of Sayreville as much as you can. After we speak to your grandfather and sister, I suggest you spend the rest of your summer relaxing at the shore. I'm hoping to get this wrapped up relatively soon, and then this will all go away."

"And how do you hope to get this all wrapped up?" Janine asked.

"Well, for starters, we are going to get into your grandfather's house and wait for him to get back from church. Hopefully he can give me some insight into what these people are looking for. Then I will find it before they do. I believe finding the Big Light is the lynchpin to solving this whole case."

But first we have to get into Opa's house." Janine said. "How do you expect to do that?… Break in?"

"Nope." John said with a smug expression on his face. "We are going to use the key."

"But she changed the locks. You saw that yourself when we first met there." Janine said a bit exasperated.

"I'll bet she changed the lock… singular, not locks." John replied. "Especially in older houses the front and back door locks were usually keyed to the same key. If your sister never uses the back door, I'll bet she only changed the lock on the front door."

"I don't think I've ever seen anyone use that back door." Janine replied. "In fact, that back vestibule had been used for some storage even before Anna moved in. If the key does work, there may be too much clutter in front of the door. I don't even know if you'd be able to get that door open."

"One hurdle at a time." John replied.

Arriving at the house, the pair made their way into the back yard and up the rickety wooden stairs to the small wooden deck outside the back door. John took the key from Janine, inserted it into the lock, and turned… opening the door six inches.

"Well it looks like we were both right." John said turning to Janine. "Your key still works in the back door, but there is a bunch of stuff blocking the door. I am going to reach up and remove these curtains from the door so we can see what we are dealing with by looking in the window."

Sliding his hand up, John flipped the curtain rod off the bracket, allowing it to fall, then peering through the window, he and Janine could see what was blocking the door from opening.

"It looks like there are several packages of toilet paper stored back here and stacked up in front of the door. I think I can reach in, grab them and flip them out of the way." John said as he began attempting to move the toilet paper.

The first two cases were able to be moved fairly easily, while the third case closest to the floor took a bit more maneuvering. However, even with the toilet paper out of the way, the door still would not open more than the initial six inches. Looking down through the window, John could see what looked like stacks of newspapers lining the floor of the vestibule.

"It looks like there's newspapers down there". John said. I don't think they are bundled, so I should be able to grab them, and pull them out the door. I'm gonna try that, I'll pull them out and hand them to you to get out of the way."

"Sounds good." Janine replied.

John began reaching in and grabbing handfuls of old newspapers, pulling them out and handing them to Janine. He managed to get the first stack out with relative ease. The next stack further in took a little longer, requiring Janine to push on the door as John slid his arm in to grab handfuls of paper. However, after about fifteen minutes, there was enough out of the way that John was able to push the door in a bit further.

"There is a stack of newspaper closer to the door hinge that I can't reach. However, if I lie down like this…". John said as he lay down on his back, feet to the door. "…And push with my legs…" he continued as he pushed the thick wooden door with his legs. "… You should have enough clearance to climb over me and slip inside." He grunted as he strained to push the door open against the trash that blocked it.

Janine deftly climbed over and between John, and slipped inside the gap between the back door and the frame. Releasing the pressure and standing, John said, "If you can move the rest of that stuff over there, I can squeeze in without having to clear out that whole space."

Janine moved the stack of old newspapers that were blocking the door and John pushed his way into the house. The cluttered mess John and Janine encountered in the vestibule was a microcosm of the entire house.

Both the kitchen counter and table were stacked halfway to the ceiling with a myriad of paper, magazines and various pieces of mail. Compact discs, jigsaw puzzles and assorted paperback books completed the collection covering every square inch of both the counter and the table. Several of the kitchen chairs held plastic grocery bags tied off at the top, and filled with who-knows-what.

Off of the kitchen, and blocked by a wall of larger filled garbage bags, was a room that Janine said was the unit's second bedroom. John was unable to determine what type of furniture, if any was in this room because the clutter completely filled the room, front to back and floor to ceiling.

"I swear, I'm going to kill her." Janine said through nearly gritted teeth. "She swore to me she cleaned this place up. This is actually worse than when I was in here the last time."

Looking in the bathroom off of the kitchen, Janine continued, "I mean, look at this. There is black mold all over the bathtub. There is no way anyone is using this shower. The sink is filthy, and I swear I've seen gas station toilets that were cleaner. There's even a quarter inch of dust on the hamper. This is disgusting."

"Well, I mean that's because the hamper is actually out here." John said pointing to a five-foot high pile of dirty clothes sitting in the middle of the living room.

"I can't wait for them to get home. I'm gonna give her a piece of my mind, boy… This shit is just…"

John and Janine both caught the movement out of the corners of their eyes. Turning toward the doorway to the front bedroom, John saw an elderly man, dressed in summer pajamas and leaning on a cane, smiling at Janine.

"Opa!" Janine gleefully exclaimed. "We didn't know you were home. I thought you went to church with Anna."

Walking over to the old man, Janine gave him a big hug and a kiss.

Rubbing his stomach, the man said, "I had the thing in the bathroom… in the night so I couldn't go to the father and the son and the holy ghost."

Looking at John, Janine said, "I told you he had a stroke and it affected his speech. He talks in phrases. Most people have trouble understanding him but Anna and I have gotten used to it and can translate pretty well. He can't say the word 'church' but he can say the holy trinity, so we know what he means."

John replied, "I get it. It's called expressive aphasia. I've seen it before."

Pointing to John, Opa said, "Who is the other one."

"Opa, this is my friend John." Janine said. "John, may I introduce my grandfather, Otto Grasslicked."

Walking over to where Janine stood with her grandfather, John reached out to shake the man's hand.

"A pleasure to meet you sir." John said.

Shaking John's hand with a firm grip, Otto said, "Top of the morning to you."

"That's how he says hello." Janine explained.

"I figured." John replied with a laugh. "It just sounded kinda funny with the German accent."

Looking around the house, Janine said to her grandfather, "Opa, we wanted to come and speak to you and Anna, but seeing this… How can she make you live like this?"

Otto replied, "Oh, It's OK Bobbie. When I was a little girl, I was in worse."

Seeing the confused look on John's face, Janine said, "His wife's name was Roberta. He called her Bobbie. Now it's the only name he seems to be able to say. He also refers to everyone, including himself in the female gender." Shaking her head as she scanned the room again, Janine said, "We need to get him out of here. This is elder abuse, and I can't have him living like this."

"I couldn't agree more." Replied John.

Reaching out to touch John's arm, Janine asked, "John, I wonder if I could ask you a favor?"

"Sure." he replied.

"How many beds do you have in your hotel room?"

"Two double beds. Why?"

"I'd like to take him out of here now, but the problem

is, my friend doesn't have a third bedroom, and I wouldn't feel right asking her…"

"So you are wondering if he could stay at the hotel with me." John said, finishing her thought.

Giving John her best puppy dog eyes, Janine said, "Is there any way you could do that? Please?"

"I don't see an issue with that. It might be better if he stays with you during the day, but he can have the extra bed, and I can help him get ready in the mornings and then bring him to you. That is, if that's alright with him."

Looking at her grandfather, Janine said, "Opa, I am going to take you home with me." Pointing around the room she said, "This is not healthy for you. I think that's why you are always having stomach issues."

"Ja, Ja. It is bad." Otto said in agreement.

Janine continued, "But I'm having some work done on my house and I'm staying with a friend, so at night, we'd like for you to stay with John. Is that OK."

Looking John up and down as if sizing him up, Otto replied, "It is OK. He looks like a nice girl. Strong, with a kind face."

John said, "Janine if we want to have a greater chance of getting out of here without a scene, I think we should probably go before your sister gets home." John said.

Nodding her head, Janine said, "I agree." Turning to her grandfather she said, "Opa, we are going to gather up some of your clothes and go now before Anna gets home."

The old man said, "Oh Bobbie…Oh.. we go now? What about der andere one?"

"I can leave a note and then talk to her on the phone

later." Janine said. Looking at John she said, "*Der andere one* is German for *the other one*, meaning my sister."

John replied. "I got that. Just because I thought big light was grass licked doesn't mean my German is that bad."

Going into the bedroom, Janine saw a three-foot high pile of clothes on the dresser, and mail, papers and other clutter taking up half of the queen sized bed. A folding chair sat on the far side of the bed between the headboard and the wall. Walking up to the pile of clothing, Janine said, "I found the clean pile."

Entering the room, John asked, "How do you know they are clean?"

"Cause they don't stink like that nasty pile in the living room." Janine replied.

Nodding his head, Otto chimed in, "Ja, Ja. Is clean."

Looking at the bed again with all the clutter, and then realizing the only place to sleep in the entire house was on the uncluttered side of the bed, Janine asked, "Opa, where do you sleep?"

"Oh, over there Bobbie." He replied pointing to the uncluttered portion of the bed.

"And where does Anna sleep?" Janine asked.

"Der andere one sleeps there." Otto replied, pointing to the same place.

Giving John a strange look first, Janine asked, "So you sleep with Anna?"

"No, no, no, Bobbie. At night, Bobbie sleeps there, and I sleep there..." he said pointing to the folding chair. "Then when Bobbie goes to... goes to out, I sleep there." He said pointing to the bed.

Fuming at the answer, Janine said, "That bitch makes a ninety-four year old man sleep on a folding chair. And I was concerned about him having to sleep in a hotel room with you."

Walking over to the clean pile of clothing, Janine grabbed several pairs of underwear, socks, two pairs of shorts, a pair of long pants and several shirts. Dumping a plastic bag that contained more old mail on the bed, she shoved the clothing into the bag.

"I think I saw his medicine and toiletries next to the kitchen sink." Janine said. "I'll grab that if you could climb over the shit in the vestibule and re-lock the back door."

"I gotcha." John replied.

After locking up, John helped Otto to the front door and down the steps and walkway to the sidewalk. Opening the passenger side doors, John assisted the old man into the back seat, then closed the door and went around to the driver's side. Climbing in, he looked to Janine and asked, "Where to?"

Turning to face her grandfather, Janine asked, "You hungry Opa? Do you think you could eat something after having an upset stomach?"

"Ja, Ja. I am all better." Otto said enthusiastically.

Turning back to John, she said, "I'd hate to just get him diner food, but it's right between breakfast and lunch. I can't think of anywhere else to go right now."

John replied. "No problem. It might be a good idea to clear out of this area. And in case your sister makes a stop at the local diner on her way home, I know a great diner on Route 18 in East Brunswick we can go to… that is, if it's still there. I haven't been in these parts in a while."

"I think I know which one you are talking about, and it is still there." Janine said. "That works for me."

Thirty minutes later, they were seated in a booth at the diner, looking over the laminated pages of the small novel sized menu. The conversation while driving to the diner was mostly on the lighter side with Janine delicately probing into her sister's ability to care for her grandfather. It became immediately obvious that Otto was trying to be protective of his older granddaughter, while attempting to not lie to Janine. Whenever her questioning touched on a point that he felt painted Anna in too bad of a light, he would immediately take his version of the fifth amendment, feigning memory loss with an, "I don't know Bobbie." This response would then prompt Janine to change the topic to something innocuous like the weather or the latest troubles of Otto's beloved N.Y. Mets.

After the waitress had served everyone coffee and taken their orders, John looked over to Otto and Janine and began, "Otto, I need your help with something."

Getting the nonagenarian's attention, John continued. "Sir, I am a police inspector for the Vatican. I am currently investigating the murder of several monks and nuns in Austria. I believe the people who killed them are now here in New Jersey. They are looking for something called The Big Light, and are killing people after they question them about its whereabouts. Sir, do you know what the Big Light is?"

Otto immediately replied, "Das grosse licht is das Kreuz das unsere familie tragt."

John said, "I understand that is your family saying to explain how you wound up with the last name of Grasslicked, but does it mean anything else?"

"Ja, Ja…" Otto replied enthusiastically. "Father Wagner promised his andere one to… to… watch your fingers."

John looked to Janine to translate, and she said, "Opa uses *watch your fingers* when he wants to say *be careful.*" Then looking at Otto she asked, Who is der andere one?"

"Der andere one. Not.. not like you and der andere one… The other girl. Father Wagner promised to watch your fingers."

John looked over to Janine for help and received a baffled look in reply.

"So, usually Opa can't say sister so he also will always refer to me as *der andere one* to Anna and vice-versa. Looking over to her grandfather Janine asked, "So are you talking about Great grandfather Georg's brother? Great Grandfather Georg promised his brother he would be careful?"

"Ja,… Ja, Father Wagner said der grosse licht… watch your fingers."

"Great grandfather said be careful with the big light?" Janine asked. "To his brother…?"

"Ja, ja." Otto replied

"Opa, why would he tell his brother to be careful. What is it? Is the big light dangerous?" Janine asked.

Otto replied, "It is not made for…" and he gave the Nazi salute, "and it is not made for…" and he gave a regular salute.

"So, both the Nazi's and the Allies were not supposed to have the big light?" Janine asked her grandfather.

"Ja, ja. It is not for them."

"So, the big light is a weapon?" John asked both Janine and Otto. "That's crazy. A religious artifact that the Nazi's and Allies believed to be a weapon?… It's like some Indiana Jones sequel. Do you know where it is."

"No, no no. It is not bang, bang boom." Otto replied. Ich kann nicht sagen until der andere girl kommt."

"It's not a weapon, but you can't say where it is until the other person comes?" Janine said translating her grandfather's aphasic mixed language. "Who is the other person?"

"Der andere girl. Father Wagner asked me to promise Ich nicht sagen until der andere girl kommt."

But Opa, it's important. Lives may depend on us finding it."

Shaking his head, Otto crossed his arms in front of his chest and said, "No. I promised Father Wagner."

Looking at John, Janine said, "He knows where it is, but he promised his father he wouldn't say until someone comes. I can't decipher who that person is."

John said, "Sir, your granddaughter is right. Lives may depend on me finding it before the killers do. If you know where it is, it would seriously help if you could tell us, or lead us to it."

With his arms still crossed in front of his chest, Otto shook his head and replied, "No. I promised."

"Can you at least tell me what it is?" John asked.

Uncrossing his arms and slamming both hands down on the table, Otto said, "Ich kann nicht sagen."

"You can say, Opa, you are just choosing not to." Janine said in frustration. Turning to John, she continued, "Opa has a safe deposit box at the bank. I think we could look there."

Reaching across the table, John touched Janine's hand.

"It's OK Janine." He said. "Your grandfather made a promise and he is keeping that promise." Looking at Otto who was nodding his head, John continued, "Sir, I respect you for your integrity. I apologize if my questioning upset you."

"No, no. All is good." Otto replied.

"But if Opa doesn't tell us, how are you going to find the Big Light?" Janine asked in a voice laced with frustration.

John replied, "Sometimes Janine, when things look hopeless, you have to rely on faith and the power of prayer.

Anna arrived home to find the note Janine left and her grandfather gone, and immediately went into a fit of rage. Since Janine had turned her phone off before entering the diner, the hour and a half of repeated calls that Anna made went straight into voicemail. When the mailbox was finally full and Anna was no longer able to leave scathing obscenity filled messages threatening Janine with grave bodily harm if she did not bring Otto back immediately, Anna jumped in her car and drove to Janine's townhouse and began ringing the bell and pounding on the front door.

Finally recognizing that Janine was not there, Anna went back home and spent the next hour calling relatives and the few mutual friends they had in an attempt to track Janine down. Unable to track Janine down, Anna next turned to determining how Janine gained entry to the house.

She was sure that her grandfather would not have opened the door, so Anna assumed that Janine had somehow broken into the house. Climbing over clothing and clutter, she checked the windows first in the living room, then in the bedroom. Not finding any sign of a forced entry she went down into the basement to see if Janine had somehow gained access through either the Bilko doors or one of the windows.

Climbing over boxes and bins, Anna checked each of the windows and cellar doors before moving the boxes back and returning upstairs. Entering the kitchen, she first checked the window above the sink and then turned and saw the toilet paper moved away from the back door. Going over to the door, she checked the windows to make sure they were all intact, then checked the doorframe for any sign the door was forced open. Not finding any, Anna returned to the living room, trying to figure out how Janine had gotten in.

Grabbing her pocketbook and removing her keys, Anna found the old key on her key ring, climbed over the papers in the vestibule and inserted the old key into the lock on the back door. Turning the key and seeing the door unlock, Anna began smirking. "Clever girl." She said out loud to herself.

Looking at the clock, Anna realized several hours had gone by since she had gotten home and she had yet to even have lunch. Taking her phone out, she pressed the speed dial button for the local Chinese restaurant and ordered a lunch combo to be delivered.

With food on the way, Anna went into the bedroom and sorted through the piles on the bed for yesterday's mail. Going through the various pieces, she sorted out the mail into a pile for bills, a pile for things she might want to consider in the future, and a pile for advertisements and circulars she was not interested in purchasing. Once the mail was sorted, Anna got back on her cell phone and tried Janine again.

On Anna's tenth attempt, Janine picked up the phone.

"Why are you blowing up my phone?" Janine said answering.

"You know very well why." Anna said. "Why were you in my house? I didn't give you permission to be here."

"It's not your house, Anna, it's Opa's and he was really happy to see me."

"Where is he? Where have you taken him? Put him on the phone right now." Anna demanded.

"He's not here right now." Janine replied.

"Well where is he?"

"He went with my friend John to get ice cream." Janine replied.

"What are you doing letting Opa go somewhere with a stranger? I mean, just because you jump in the sack with every swinging dick that looks at you twice doesn't mean you can trust them to look after our grandfather."

"Fuck you, Anna." Janine snarled. "I am not sleeping with John. He is a police inspector for the Vatican for Christ's sake."

"And you are letting him take Opa for ice cream the day after he had stomach issues? Do you want him to get stomach pneumonia?" Anna said.

"What??.. Stomach pneumonia? Anna you're not right in the head. There's no such thing. And Opa was fine. We took him out to eat earlier, and he ate like a horse."

"There is too such a thing…" Anna replied. "He had

a stomach cold yesterday, and now you are putting some-thing cold in there… It's like going outside with a wet head when you have a cold. You wind up with pneumonia."

"All right, whatever… I'm not going to argue about something that stupid." Janine said.

"Where did you take him to eat?" Anna asked.

Not wanting to tell her sister that they went to a diner because of the hard time she always gave Anna for taking Otto to a diner to eat, Janine replied, "We went out to eat. It doesn't matter."

"Well you need to bring him home right away."

"I am not bringing him back to that house until you clean that shithole up. You lied to me when you said you cleaned." Janine said.

"I did clean." Anna said. "I started in the basement and wanted to get that cleaned up so I could move stuff from the main floor down there."

"And what about the bathroom, Anna? It looks like it hasn't been cleaned in years. There is mold all over the shower. How can you let Opa go in there?"

"We don't use the shower." Anna replied.

"You don't shower?" Janine asked.

"No, we use the kitchen sink and take sponge baths."

"What the fuck, Anna?"

"It's fine. We are clean. Taking a shower every day is highly overrated."

"If you think it's fine Anna, I'm not even gonna…

"Oh, listen to miss high and mighty there lecturing me on how to live." Anna interrupted. "I've given up my social life and basically everything to take care of Opa. What have you ever done to help out this family?"

"Take care of Opa? Are you fucking kidding me? You live in his house rent free, you use his money to pay the taxes and utilities. I'll bet you even use his money to buy all that take-out food you get."

"No. Not all the time." Anna said.

"And where does Opa sleep, Anna?"

"In the bed." Anna replied.

"During the day. But at night, you sleep in the bed and he sleeps in a folding chair. A FUCKING FOLDING CHAIR, Anna? You make your ninety-four year old grandfather spend the night sitting in a folding chair."

"It's padded and very comfortable, and besides, he sleeps a lot during the day." Anna said.

"Because he can't sleep at night 'cause you are in the bed and he is in a chair. And when you don't go in to work, which is most of the time, I know you are in the bed sleeping, so where does he sleep then?"

"Fuck you Janine. Listen, you need to bring him back home as soon as he gets back."

"No, Anna, I'm not. He is staying with me so he can sleep in a bed, get home cooked meals, and not have to live in a shithole."

"And what happens when you go back to work? School starts in like two weeks. He has a doctor's appointment in two weeks and I have to take him."

"I can take him, Anna." Janine said. "I'm allowed personal time, and then I'll just make his appointments for later in the afternoon."

No, Anna. I have to take him. You need to bring him back right now." Anna screamed into the phone like a child having a tantrum.

"Why do you have to take him, Anna. Do you need the intermittent FMLA paperwork signed again?"

"Never mind why I have to take him. Anna quickly replied. "You broke into my house. You kidnapped my grandfather. And now you need to bring him back."

While Anna was speaking, there was a knock on the front door. Normally, Anna would have looked through the window to see who was there prior to opening the door, but embroiled in the argument with her sister, she swung the door open to find an Asian man in a dark blue business suit and tie standing on the front porch. He wore dark wrap-around sunglasses pushed up on his forehead, and had a wireless earpiece and microphone in his left ear.

"Miss Grasslicked?" the man asked as Anna opened the door.

"Yes, hold on…I'll be right back. Let me get my purse." Anna replied to the man, assuming he was delivering her Chinese food.

"Anna, I am not bringing Opa back. He is going to be staying with me, at least until you clean that place up, and if you kidnap him again like last time, I am going to report you for elder abuse."

"Fuck you Janine." Anna screeched into the phone. "You bring him back right now."

Calmly, Janine said, "No, I don't think so… Fuck *you* Anna."

"AGGGGGGGHHH…, Shit." Anna yelled as she hung up the phone with her sister.

Grabbing her wallet from her pocketbook on the bed, Anna turned to bring the money to the delivery man and found him standing in the living room.

"What are you doing there? You needed to wait out on the porch. I said I'd be right back."

Anna found it a bit odd that a delivery driver would be dressed in a suit and tie, but she was even more confused by the fact that he didn't have her bag of food.

"Miss Grasslicked, we need..." the Asian man began but was immediately cut off by Anna.

"Look, you should not have come in my house. That was very rude. I told you to wait on the porch. And where is my food? I don't see my food anywhere."

"Miss Grasslicked, I don't have any food for you. I am here to ask you some questions. If you answer my questions honestly, this will go much easier."

"I don't understand. Where is my food? What have you done with my food? I told you, you needed to wait on the porch, but instead you came in here. I think you need to leave right now."

As Anna was speaking, two other men came down the front hallway and entered the living room. Dressed all in black, they also had wireless headsets in their left ear and their wrap-around sunglasses covered their eyes.

"Who are you people? Anna said. "What did you do with my food? You should not be in here. I want you to leave right now."

"Miss Grasslicked, you are not paying attention. I do not know anything about your food..."

With that, a third man came in carrying a bag of Chinese food. He said something in a language Anna assumed was Chinese, and the three other men laughed.

"What did he say?" Anna asked.

The man in the suit replied, "He said you owe him $13.95 plus tip for the food."

"I fail to see the humor in that." Anna said reaching out for the bag. "Look, just give me the food and I'll pay you and then you all can leave. If you go now, I won't call your boss and make a complaint."

While Anna was speaking, one of the men had circled around behind her, and as she reached forward toward the bag, she was violently wrenched back by an arm that suddenly encircled her neck. Unable to breathe, Anna clawed at the arm at her throat while the man in the suit stood in front of her smiling.

A moment later, Anna was shoved down and to the side, and landed sitting in the bedroom folding chair which one of the men had brought out to the living room. Her hands were held down at her sides and were quickly zip-tied to the chair, and as one of the men held her legs, they were bound to the chair as well.

Squatting down in front of her, the man in the suit said, "As I said before Miss Grasslicked, we are going to ask you some questions. If you cooperate, things will go much better for you. Do you understand?"

"What are you doing to me? Anna demanded. "You need to leave right now. I'm going to call the police. You need to leave before…"

Anna was silenced by a sharp backhand to the face that split her lower lip.

"Fuck!" Anna spit out. Now you did it… That's it… I'm calling the police."

"Miss Grasslicked, you are bound to a chair, and I am in control of this situation. Now you will answer my questions or it become very unpleasant for you. Am I making myself clear?" the Asian man asked.

Anna said through a swelling lip, "Look, I don't know what you want but you need to leave…"

Before Anna could finish her sentence, the man in the suit pulled an eight-inch stiletto knife out of a sheath in the inside of his suit jacket and buried it in Anna's right thigh.

Tears formed in Anna's eyes as she howled in pain and fought to break the zip ties holding her to the chair. The Asian in the suit turned to the three other men in the room and said something to them in their native tongue. He then leaned in closer to Anna and said, "I do not understand why you are being so difficult. I asked you a simple yes or no question, and instead of giving me a yes or no answer, you went off on me about leaving. Just so we are clear, I am going to ask you some questions. You are going to answer them honestly. If you do not cooperate, I am going to hurt you. Do you understand?"

Nodding her head with tears streaming down her face, Anna said, "Yes."

"Good. See? You answer my questions properly, you do not get hurt. The sooner you answer all of my questions, the sooner we will leave. Are you ready to get started?"

Anna heard noised coming from both the kitchen and the bedroom that sounded like glass breaking. She had seen one of the other men head to the kitchen and another go into the bedroom. Hearing more noises coming from both rooms, she said, "What are you doing to my house? If they break anything, I will hold you personally responsible."

With cat-like swiftness, the Asian man pulled the knife out of Anna's thigh, ripped open her blouse and deftly swung the blade left and right, inflicting two half inch deep gashes across Anna's upper chest from armpit to armpit. Screaming in pain Anna began to sob.

"I can do this for hours. I know how to inflict countless non-lethal wounds that will leave you praying for death, or you can answer my questions. Which one will it be?"

Between sobs Anna said, "I'll answer your questions."

"Good." The Asian man said. "No more back-talk?

"No." Anna whimpered.

"Excellent. See, when you cooperate and answer correctly, you are not hurt. Now, let's begin. Where is the Big Light?"

Anna replied, "Das grosse licht is das Kreuz das unsere familie tragt."

"FUCK!" the Asian man swore in Korean as he slammed the knife into Anna's left thigh. "What the fuck is wrong with you lady?"

As the man in the bedroom peeked his head around the doorframe to investigate, Kim Joo-Won said, "It looks like this is going to take quite a while."

Five and a half hours later, the four darkly clad men slipped out of the Perth Amboy house and into the waiting SUV. With the leader in the business suit leaving last after firmly closing and locking the front door, he climbed into the front passenger seat and signaled the driver to go.

"That woman may have been the most annoying person I have ever met." Kim Joo-won said. "She was either arrogant or extremely stupid. And while she gave me much of the information we needed, it was almost as if despite the pain, she needed to berate us and hear herself doing it."

The man who was searching the bedroom said to his boss, "There was so much clutter lying around, it was nearly impossible to do a proper search."

"The second floor looked just as bad as the first." The second man said from the back seat. "The only saving grace was that the walls were lathed plaster. There was nowhere to hide anything inside any of the walls."

Kim Joo-Won replied, "I do not believe the Big Light was there. It is close, but it was not stored there."

"So how are we going to find it?" the man in the driver's seat asked.

"The key is the grandfather." Kim answered. "That woman said the grandfather and great grandfather would talk about the Big Light all the time."

"But he is with that Vatican inspector." the driver said. "How are we supposed to find them, and what if the old man tells Nowalski where the Big Light is?"

"Police everywhere exhibit similar behaviors." Kim replied. "They tend to congregate together to brag about their exploits. They either meet in their headquarters or at taverns. Since we do not know where their tavern is, we will watch for Nowalski at the police headquarters. He will show up there to share the news before he goes for the Big Light. Once we acquire him, he will either lead us to the Big Light or the old man. Either way, we are no more than two steps away from our prize."

CHAPTER 16

**Middlesex County
New Jersey
Present Day**

John had just gotten Otto settled in bed when his cell phone rang. Looking at the caller ID, he answered, "You are either up insanely early or burning the midnight oil, Tony."

"I am not doing either, boss. I am in the middle of my shift walking foot patrol around St. Peter's."

"Wait, what? Foot patrol? Tony, what are you talking about?"

"So, me and the guys show up for work at the Information Center this morning, and DiClemente is there and he tells us to go home and report in full uniform to patrol at midnight."

"What? Tony, what is going on?" John asked.

"It seems Sentille met with Pinocchio early this morning and they discussed the case. It was decided that since there are no more attacks on any of our monasteries, that they should close this case and bring you home. They were concerned about the American media picking up on the murder you had there, and wanted to distance us from that as quickly as possible.

"But the case isn't closed." John objected. "The fact that the killers are here too means I am on the right track. I am really close and just need a little more time to nail this down and get some actionable evidence."

"Well that is not how our leadership sees it." Tony replied.

"So, they don't care about justice for our murdered people." John said more as a statement of fact than a question.

"Obviously not." Tony replied. "But it gets worse. Word is that Pinocchio sent you an email ordering you to return to Rome and you failed to acknowledge it. He is saying you are violating direct orders and will be charging you with insubordination."

"I saw the email, but since I have been reporting directly to Sentille on this case, and I spoke to him this morning, I figured the email from Pinocchio was just bullshit, so I ignored it."

"Yeah, well that is not how they are portraying it over here. Sentille is backing up Pinocchio and saying he ordered you to stand down and return home when he spoke to you this morning."

"That lying sack of shit." John exclaimed. And you say Sentille met with Pinocchio this morning before you got in to work?"

"Yeah boss. DiClemente said his orders came directly

from Pinocchio. The department is disbanded… again, we are to work the overnight shift in patrol until we are reassigned, and you are being charged with insubordination and ignoring orders."

John said, "Sentille told me when I spoke to him that he was going to meet with Pinochinio and would get back to me. He never said to return home. But if what you are saying is true, then they had already met when I spoke to the Cardinal this morning, and this whole thing is a set-up to nail me."

"That's pretty much the situation." Tony said. But that is not even the worse part. Supposedly, Sentille is headed to America with some Swiss Guard to relieve you of your command and escort you back to Rome."

"You're fuckin' kidding me." John said in disbelief."

Sitting on the edge of the bed, John was having a hard time grasping the level of deceit he was facing. Angry and dejected, John said, "Tony, I'm sorry I got you guys assigned a shitty detail. You shouldn't have to suffer for their issues with me."

"It's OK boss. Me and the guys talked about it and we are sick to our stomachs about the way you are being treated. We'll be fine. We just gotta work a few shitty shifts for few days." Tony said.

"I'm also sick to my stomach over the total lack of caring about justice being done for those poor nuns and monks. They are more concerned about preserving the Church's image. Do you have any idea when Sentille is coming here?" John asked.

Tony responded. "It's gonna take them a few days to book a flight and get tickets. They have to follow the bean counters rules and get the cheapest airfare available. I'd say you have a little less than a week."

"Yeah, that's what I was figuring too." John said.

"What are you gonna do?" Tony asked.

"Not a friggin' clue right now." John replied. "I'm gonna have to give this some thought. I'm not ready to pull the plug, but now the clock is really ticking." Pausing as he began collecting his thoughts, John concluded, "Thanks for giving me the heads-up, Tony. You be careful over there. I'll touch base soon."

Raul Martinez had been in the employ of Donner Global security for a little over three years. Prior to that he had been known as Chief Petty Officer Martinez, or 'Whopper' to his fellow SEAL Team Seven members. Now parked down the street from the Grasslicked house in Perth Amboy, he watched as the last of the Korean assault team left the house and climbed into the waiting black SUV.

Hitting the speed dial number on his cellphone Martinez called his boss to report.

"They just left the house and are pulling away from the curb as we speak." Martinez said. "No one was carrying anything and they did not look happy. I don't think they found anything there."

"Is the tracker working?" von Alpiner asked.

"It is. Do you want me to follow?"

"Give them some space, then go ahead. These trackers don't have the best range so you don't want to get too far behind, but I don't want you to spook them either."

"Roger that." Martinez replied.

"How certain are you that the Grasslicked woman was in there when they arrived?" von Alpiner asked.

"I watched her walk in, she answered the door, and the last Korean operator made sure the door was locked when he left." Martinez answered.

"OK, I'll send Murphy down to sit on the house in case the sister or Nowalski shows up."

"Yeah, I don' think there is too much of a rush to get someone out here. I doubt anyone is coming to visit at this hour, and she certainly isn't going anywhere."

"Still, I want to keep our bases covered." von Alpiner replied. "We just need to keep our eyes on all the players in this big dance and once the Big Light schematics appear, be there to make them ours."

"I personally don't like all this sneaking around shit." Martinez said. "Especially with the North Koreans."

"I would usually agree with you. Taking them out of the picture would normally improve our odds, but with them already roaming the county tearing up the place and killing folks, an all-out firefight would shine too much light on our operation. No, we do this in stealth mode. We make sure we know where and what our adversaries are up to at all times, and keep a close eye on Nowalski. He'll lead us right to our prize… At least our leadership believes that he will."

"Aye skipper." Martinez said.

"Once you ascertain where the North Koreans are going, report back in. I know how tiring sitting in a car for hours at a time can be, and you've been at it all day and night. I'll get one of our guys to come relieve you. I'm also going to be sending you out to Kennedy Airport to pick up a VIP in the next few days. Give you a little bit of a break from the misery of just sitting around in your car."

"Thanks skipper." Martinez replied as he wondered if his boss knew how thoroughly miserable the traffic made any trip on the Belt Parkway.

John rose at the crack of dawn before his phone alarm went off. Sitting on the edge of the hotel room bed, clearing the cobwebs of a fitful night's sleep, he listened to the rhythmic snoring of the old man in the next bed over. Walking quietly to the bathroom, he shut the door and turning, viewed his image in the mirror. He chuckled as he thought that the bags under his eyes were so big, they looked more like steamer trunks, and he made a mental note that no matter the outcome of this case, when it was done, he needed a vacation.

Turning on the shower, John stripped off his night-clothes and stepped in, allowing the warming water to flow over his head and across his body. Adjusting the shower-head jets to a pulsing spray, he turned and allowed the water to massage his back and shoulders. As the night's fitful sleep dissipated into the steam, John began to focus on his next moves.

While originally, he had wanted to take a soft approach to both Otto and Janine's sister, he now felt his shortened timetable wouldn't allow that. He had already deleted both the calls and emails from Sentille and Pinochinio so that he could feign prior ignorance when presented with his orders to return home. However, with Sentille planning to actually come to America, he could not avoid those orders indefinitely. Based on his conversation with Tony, at best, he had a handful of days, to locate the Big Light and use that to snare his suspects.

As the warm water cascaded over him, John began to formulate an approach that might work. From her behavior the other day, John could see that Janine was bordering on desperate for this case and her current situation to end. She was pleading with her grandfather to disclose what he knew about the Big Light before John actually told her to back off. He also had seen that Janine was not averse to being confrontational with her sister. Perhaps enlisting Janine in a bit of *'Good Cop/Bad Cop'* coupled with a bit of a variation on the *'Prisoner's Dilemma'* may get either Anna or Otto to give up what they knew.

With a game plan taking shape in his mind, John finished showering while he finished devising how this would play out. Drying off, he grabbed his cell phone and sent a text asking Janine to meet him and Otto at the IHOP at 10:30 that morning. His plan was that after breakfast, he would take Janine and Otto back to the Perth Amboy house. If Anna wasn't there, he would have Janine begin 'searching' for the Big Light by dumping over draws and emptying cabinets, all the while forcefully telling her grandfather that he needed to divulge what he knew. John would act as the *'Good Cop'* and calmly explain the urgency in finding the missing artifact.

If Anna were home, he would ask Janine to begin by pushing both Anna and Otto for the information and going through the same actions of emptying drawers. Expecting neither Anna nor Otto to relent, he would then have Janine threaten to call the local police and social services and report Anna for elder abuse. John would step in to defuse the situation if Otto would say where the Big Light was kept.

Finished with his morning routine, John checked his phone and saw that Janine had already replied that she would meet them as requested. Looking at the time on his phone, John surmised that for reasons different than his but still related to this case, Janine was not sleeping well either. With a bit more time before he needed to wake Otto to get ready to go, John decided that since she was up, he could give Janine a call. Selecting her number, John leaned against the bathroom vanity and waited while the phone rang.

"Good morning." Janine said, answering in a voice still a bit husky from sleep. "You are up unusually early."

"I could say the same about you." John replied.

"I haven't been sleeping well." Janine said.

"I can't imagine why." John said sarcastically.

"Yeah, well… So why are you up so early?"

"I didn't sleep well either." John replied. "So, I decided I might as well get up, get showered and get my day started."

"That's pretty industrious of you." Janine chided.

"You're not that industrious?" John asked.

"Not really." Janine replied. "I'm awake but I'm just lying here in bed."

"So you're not up and dressed?" John asked.

"No… Actually, if you saw what I was wearing, you'd say I'm closer to undressed than dressed."

"Well, to that point, I'm actually standing here with just a towel wrapped around myself." John said.

"Mmmmm… Interesting." Janine purred.

"Why?" John asked

"Just trying to picture your description in my mind." Janine replied. "To be honest, I'm not wearing much more."

"Miss Wagner… are we flirting?" John said in tone of mock accusation.

With a little giggle, Janine replied, "I don't know Inspector, are we?"

"Since we are being honest, Janine, I would be ecstatic if we were flirting with each other. However, with all that is going on I think the timing of it couldn't be any worse."

With a bit of a sigh, Janine said, "No John. You're right. While maybe flirting or maybe even more might be fun, I know I am not in a good emotional place right now. Thanks for recognizing that."

"Of course. No thanks are necessary." John said.

"I guess that goes to your maturity."

"Hey… Are you calling me old?" John joked.

"No… no, not at all." Janine quickly replied. "No, I was just comparing the way you are interacting with me with the way Lieutenant Levy… Adam did."

"Why? What did he do? Was he inappropriate? John asked.

"No, I wouldn't say he was inappropriate. He was actually very sweet. He just asked me out, but he backed down right away when I turned him down."

"OK, as long as you don't feel he crossed the line." John said. "Cause if you want, I can speak to his boss."

"No. Please don't. He seems like he's a nice guy. He just… seems a bit uncomfortable around women and has shitty timing."

Smiling to himself, John said, "OK, no problem."

Switching gears he went on, "So,… You wanna hear my plan for finding the Big Light?"

"Sure." Janine replied.

John went on to tell Janine about his conversation with Tony and the impending visit by Sentille. He explained that unfortunately, that meant he needed to take a more aggressive track to finding the artifact. He explained his concern that unless he was able to find it and use it to tie the evidence to the killers, they would still be free to roam the area in their search, thus making it unsafe for Janine and her family. He laid out his plan of pressing Otto and confronting Anna for the information he needed.

"My only concern is that once Opa is back at the house, Anna will totally ignore what we are asking her and divert all her energy into convincing Opa to stay. I've seen her be that manipulative with him before."

"Then if she does that, we use the nuclear option." John said.

"What's that." Janine asked.

"We actually call the cops on her and get her put in cuffs." John replied.

"Oh John. I couldn't do that. They'd arrest her the minute they saw that place, and Opa would be mortified."

Smiling John said, "Not the real cops. Not Perth Amboy, PD. We call your new boyfriend. Anna would never know the difference, and Opa might spill the info seeing his granddaughter in cuffs."

"So we call Adam." Janine said, mulling the idea over. "That might actually work. And by the way, he's not my boyfriend. He's not really my type."

"Oh, and what is your type, Miss Wagner?"

"I prefer the more mature, intelligent, well-traveled and slightly cosmopolitan type." Janine replied, grinning on the other end of the phone.

"Janine, are we flirting again?" John asked in the mock accusatory tone.

Janine replied in a voice best used in the bedroom, "No… I would have been flirting if I said Neapolitan instead of cosmopolitan."

Feeling his face begin to flush, John said, "Ok, well, on that note, I'm gonna wake your grandfather up and get him going. I'll see you a little later at the IHOP."

"I can't wait." Janine replied. "See you later."

Janine met John and her grandfather as planned and after a nice leisurely breakfast, they headed over to Otto and Anna's house. Taking two separate cars, they parked in front of the house and John helped Otto out of the passenger seat and up the front porch steps.

Seeing Anna's car parked across the street, Janine said, "It looks like she's home. So, plan B?"

"Yup. You ready?" John replied.

Nodding the affirmative, Janine knocked loudly on the front door and rang the bell. After several long seconds, she repeated the process, again with no response.

"I know she's here. Her car is there so she didn't go to work. We know she's not in the shower, so she must be sleeping." Pounding even harder on the door, Janine said, "C'mon Anna, open up. I'm here with Opa."

Looking over to John, Janine shrugged her shoulders and said, "Let me try her phone."

After multiple rings, the call went into voicemail, so Janine hung up. "I don't know where she could be." She said to John and her grandfather.

"Let me have the key." John said. "I'll go around back and go in and make sure she's alright. I'll be quiet and if I see her sleeping, I'll quietly open the front door and let you wake her up, this way she isn't startled by some strange man in her bedroom."

"OK, sounds good." Janine said handing John the key.

Walking around to the back, John opened the back door and pushed his way in past the clutter still in the vestibule. He immediately noticed the opened cabinets and drawers dumped in the kitchen amidst the clutter.

"Oh shit." He said to himself out loud as he made his way forward, steeling himself for what he knew he would find somewhere in the house.

Rounding the corner into the living room, he saw Anna's bloody and beaten body, zip tied to the folding chair Otto slept in. Four of her fingers lay on the floor next to her and she had multiple cuts and penetrating knife wounds all over her body, indicating she was tortured for an extended period of time. It looked like the final cause of death was the knife wound to the throat that from the spray and volume of blood, must have severed both carotid arteries.

Careful not to touch anything, John made his way to the front door, undid the lock and carefully opened the door. Stepping outside before Otto or Janine could enter, John reached out with both arms and ushered the pair away from the door. Seeing the look on John's face even before he said anything, Janine knew something was very wrong inside the house.

"You can't go in there." John said to Janine and Otto. "Anna has been killed… murdered. It's way too grisly… I don't want you to have to see it, and it's a crime scene, so we shouldn't go disturbing things.

"My little girl… No… I must…" Otto said as he tried to force his way past John with surprising strength.

"Otto… No." John said, stepping in front of the man and gently but firmly putting his hands on his shoulders and pushing back. "You can't. You really don't want to see her the way she is right now." Looking to both Otto and Janine, he continued, "What is inside is not the final image you want to have of Anna."

Otto stepped back allowing John to remove his hands from the old man's shoulders. Looking down, John saw Janine's tear-filled eyes and he said, "I'm so sorry." and opened his arms up embracing Janine as she buried her face in his chest and began sobbing.

"We need to alert the authorities." John said after several minutes.

Letting go of John and wiping some of the tears away, Janine nodded and said, "You want me to call 911?"

John replied, "No. Let me call Jake Benjamin. See if I can get him down here. He can reach out to the Perth Amboy police."

Pulling out his cell phone, John made the call and informed Benjamin of the situation. Finished with the call, John made his way over to the porch chair where Janine had moved her grandfather. Otto sat silently in the white plastic resin chair with tears streaming down his face. Putting his hand on Otto's shoulder, John said, "I know what you are thinking, sir. If you'd have been here, you would be dead too. There was nothing you could have done to protect her."

Looking up at John and shaking his head, Otto replied, "No,..no. I could. I could."

"I'm sorry. You are wrong, Otto. You must not think that way. These people are trained killers. You could not have protected her, even if you were sixty years younger."

Looking up at John with saddened eyes, Otto replied while tapping his chest, "This is me... My little girl... This is me."

Kneeling down and giving her grandfather a hug, Janine said, "No Opa, this is not your fault. John is right, you couldn't have protected her."

With the growing sound of approaching sirens in the background, John just put his hand on Otto's shoulder as he awaited the arrival of the police.

The first patrol car arrived two minutes later, and two officers warily approached the group, having been dispatched to the scene of a murder, but not sure of the current situation. John identified himself and briefly explained what was going on, then leaving one of the officers with Janine and Otto, accompanied the other officer into the living room.

"I touched the back door and tried to minimize my contact with the front door, 'cause I didn't see any signs of forced entry up here, so there may be prints on the doors." John explained to the officer."

Staring at the body, the officer said. "Yeah, OK. Holy shit. I've seen some shit in my day, but this is fuckin' nuts."

"Yeah. I know. I doubt your forensics guys will find anything. These people are professionals. They killed a bunch of people in Austria too. That's why I'm here. I'm trying to track 'em down."

"Holy shit." Repeated the officer. "OK. Let's go outside. We got detectives already on their way."

John and the officer headed out the door, just as

Perth Amboy Detective Captain Horvath pulled up to the scene, along with three other patrol cars. John introduced himself, and was advised that Captain Benjamin was on his way. As John waited for Benjamin, Captain Horvath went inside to survey the scene.

Benjamin and Adam Levy arrived a few minutes later and came straight to John for an update. Giving Benjamin a brief recounting of what had happened over the past two days, John then returned to Janine and Otto while the two Sayreville detectives entered the house to confer with Horvath.

A few minutes later, Benjamin and Adam emerged and approached the trio. Extending his hand to first Otto, then Janine, Benjamin introduced himself and offered his condolences.

"I am so sorry for your loss." Benjamin began. "When was the last time you saw or spoke to Anna?"

"It was early last night. We were on the phone. We were arguing… Oh my God… The last thing we said to each other was 'fuck you.' Janine said, and immediately burst into tears.

As John stood behind Janine and put his hands on her shoulders to comfort her, Captain Benjamin said, "It's OK Miss Wagner."

Speaking softly into her ear, John also said, "It's OK Janine. Even if you had harsh words for each other, I'm sure she knew you loved her just like you know she loved you."

Composing herself, Janine apologized for her outburst, then said, "What else do you need to know."

"Do you know about what time you spoke to your sister?" Benjamin asked.

"I think it was around five-thirty. We were arguing, then she said something to someone else about getting her purse. I thought she had gotten food delivered or something."

Turning to Adam, Benjamin said, "That's it. That explains the lack of forced entry. They were impersonating the food delivery folks."

"I'll go in and pass that along to Horvath." Adam said.

"Can you think of anything else Miss Wagner?" Benjamin asked. "What about your grandfather."

No. The last time he saw or spoke to Anna was when she left for church in the morning. He's had a stroke that affected his speech, so he has trouble communicating." Janine replied.

"OK. I don't think we need to question him right now.

He looks pretty broken up, as do you, Miss Wagner so thank you for answering my questions. I believe Captain Horvath may have some additional questions for you later though."

"No problem." Janine said. "Captain, can we stay here? John wouldn't let us in to see her. He said it was too grisly. We'd like to see her before you take her away to the morgue. Would that be alright?"

"I don't think it would be a problem. It may take a while. We still need the forensic team to come and gather evidence and the Medical Examiner has also not arrived yet."

"That's fine." Janine said. "We have no place else to go."

John stayed with Janine and Otto as the detectives, forensic team and coroner all came and did their investigations. John overheard several of the forensic team say how difficult it was to gather any evidence since the house was in such a state of disarray. About an hour into the investigation, two Perth Amboy detectives came and questioned them all again. Janine answered the questions with another bout of tears, while Otto sat, stone faced in the chair, not even attempting to add to the answers.

Finally, about an hour after the detectives questioning, the Medical Examiner techs began to wheel Anna's body out the front door. Otto rose stiffly from the chair and walked across the porch to the gurney. Janine asked if they could see Anna, and after Captain Horvath nodded his consent, the tech unzipped the body bag revealing Anna's bruised and blood-caked face.

Janine gasped at the sight of her sister and began to cry, while Otto just stared, then turned to hug and console his younger granddaughter. John nodded to the tech who zipped the bag up, and then proceeded down the stairs and out to their waiting vehicle.

"I will take that as a positive identification of the deceased and not make them go through that again." Horvath said to John.

"Thank you." John replied.

Handing over Anna's pocketbook to John, Horvath said. "You might need this to help with paperwork and making arrangements. Our guys already went through it, so we don't need it any more. And I believe you gave one of my detectives the information where you can be reached?"

"We did, and thank you for this." John said hefting the pocketbook.

"OK. Well, we will be totally out of here in a little bit. We are going to seal this place up as an ongoing crime scene, so if there is anything else they need from inside, maybe you should go in and grab it. It probably wouldn't be good for them to see all that blood."

"I think we are all good, Captain. Thank you." John said.

"We'll be in touch." Horvath said.

"Sounds good. I'll be working with Captain Benjamin, so if either of us develops any information, let's make sure to let the other know."

"You got it." Horvath replied, shaking John's hand.

"C'mon, let's get out of here." John said to Janine and Otto. "We'll take my car. Yours will be safe here Janine."

John took Janine and Otto back to his hotel and the three went into the lounge. Neither Otto nor Janine spoke during the drive over, and John made it a point to leave them to their thoughts. John ordered an appetizer sampler and a pitcher of iced tea for the three of them, then looked across the table to Otto and Janine.

"It will be several days at least before the Medical Examiner will release the body. I can go with you when you want to go make funeral arrangements, but because of the need for an autopsy, I don't think we need to go today or even tomorrow."

The waitress brought over the pitcher of iced tea, and

John poured three glasses. Otto picked up the glass of iced tea, examined it then asked in German what it was.

"Was ist das?" he asked taking a sip.

"It's iced tea, Opa." Janine answered.

Slamming the glass down on the table, Otto shouted, "NEIN! I need ein beer und ein… Ein…". Otto took his thumb and forefinger, brought them closer together to demonstrate 'small,' then made a drinking motion.

"You want a shot and a beer?" John asked.

"Ja, ja. I must prost."

"You want to toast to Anna?" Janine asked.

"Ja, Ja." Otto replied.

John looked quizzically at Janine as if asking if it were OK. Janine answered by saying, "Well it's not like he's under the legal drinking age."

John went up to the bar and ordered three beers and three whiskey shots, which the waitress brought back to the table a few minutes later. Picking up the shot glass, Otto raised it up and said, "To my little girl. Auf wiedersehen. Ich liebe dich."

Janine followed with, "To my sister. I love you." And raised her glass.

John raised his shot glass, clinked it against the others and said, "To Anna. Rest with the Lord."

All three threw back their shots, and then grabbed the beer for a swallow. Looking over to Otto, John saw the man place the beer glass to his lips, tip back and chug the entire glass. Slamming the glass down on the table, Otto looked over to John and said, "Now I fix. Das Grosse Licht ist der kreuz…"

John said, "Yes sir. I know how you got your name…"

"No, no, no. I fix." Otto said emphatically. "My little girl. Der andere one. I could watch your fingers for her, but now ist todt."

"What are you trying to say, Opa? Anna needed to be careful and she didn't so now she is dead?"

"No, no. I could watch your fingers for… for the little girl. But now I fix. Das Grosse Licht ist der… der kreuz…"

Taking a stab at translating, John asked, "She needed to be careful because of the name? The name Grasslicked? That doesn't make sense. These people were keying in on people with the last name of Wagner. How did they make the jump to Grasslicked?"

Shaking his head, no, Otto was about to speak again when Janine interrupted. "Hey, I never thought of that. How did they find Anna?"

"I can only think of two ways." John said. "Either the killers found you and followed us to the house earlier that day, or someone is passing information from my reports on to the killers."

"Both of those are scary thoughts." Janine said.

"Yeah, tell me about it." John agreed.

With John and Janine quiet, Otto tried again. "Das Grosse Licht ist der… der kreuz… Arrrgggh…" Otto moaned in frustration.

"Opa, I'm sorry. I can't get what you're trying to say."

The old man's eyes suddenly got big. He held up an index finger as if to say 'eureka,' then said. "Tomorrow, we go to the money."

"You want to go to the bank Opa? To the safe deposit box? Janine asked.

"Ja, ja." Otto replied and reached into Anna's

pocketbook sitting on the bench next to them and pulled out Anna's keys. Searching the key ring, he held up one of the keys. "Ja, ja. It's good, It's good."

Thinking about what her grandfather was trying to say earlier Janine asked, "The Big Light is in the safe deposit box?"

"Ja, ja."

"Wow. Thank you, Otto." John said. "You may have just given me the key to bringing your granddaughter's killers to justice."

"What are we going to do about the other problem. What if we were followed? Do you think they will come after us now?" Janine asked.

Scanning the lounge, and not seeing anyone that looked like they were paying attention to them, John said, "Here's what we're gonna do. "You stay here with us tonight. I can sleep in the chair and ottoman. I'm gonna go do a little reconnaissance right now and see if there is anyone that looks a little out of place, then I'm going to call Captain Benjamin and see if he can send someone here to babysit. I'm pretty sure we are OK, but I want to make sure you and Otto stay safe."

"Thank you, John. You sure it would be OK for me to stay with you and Opa tonight?"

John replied, "No problem at all. We'll go to the bank tomorrow and hopefully get this wrapped up." Getting up to leave, John said, "Stay put. I'll be back in a bit, and left the lounge to scope out the rest of the hotel.

No sooner did John leave the lounge when his phone rang. Expecting it to be either Sentille or Tony, he checked the screen before answering.

"Bob Whope. To what do I owe this pleasure? How are things at the Bureau?"

Robert Whope was the Deputy Assistant Director of the FBI's Cyber Crime Division. Having previously served as the Unit Chief for the Joint Terrorism Task Force in the New York office, Bob had worked extensively with John on numerous occasions allowing the two to become good friends. Last fall, when Bob and his wife came to Rome on vacation, John had arranged a special tour of St. Peter's for the couple, and had spent several evenings showing them the amazing hidden restaurants tourists never find.

"John, where are you and what are you involved in?" Bob asked, getting right to the point.

"What do you mean?" John asked.

"Your name has come up as a person of interest in a couple of murders in New Jersey and possibly overseas as well."

"What?" John nearly shouted into the phone. "Bob, I am actually in New Jersey, but I'm on the trail of a team of killers who murdered a bunch of nuns and monks in Austria. They are now in New Jersey and I'm working with the local PD to track them down."

"Well this thing came out this morning and it looks like the Washington field office is sending some people down to have a chat with you." Whope said.

"Wait… You said it came out this morning? What time this morning?"

"Looks like it was issued by… Hmmm this is strange…"

"What is strange Bob?"

"This was issued by Deputy Director Walter Bauer at nine AM this morning. Deputy Directors usually never send these out. They usually come from a field office or division like mine."

"You said a couple of murders, too right?" John asked.

"That's right. It says two in New Jersey, and it just says multiple murders overseas." Whope replied.

"I'll tell you what's really strange, Bob. The second murder was only discovered around noon today."

"So how would Bauer know to issue…". Whope began.

"Right Bob. How would he know?" John said.

"Well now…" Whope said.

"This is getting curiouser and curiouser." John said.

"It also seemed a bit strange that they were sending guys from Washington up to speak to you on this." Bob said "John, I can poke around a bit on this, but you need to be careful. I have a feeling there is some political muscle behind this. Bauer is one of those political animals that never really made their bones in the field, but somehow always seemed to be able to climb the ladder."

"Maybe it was his crystal ball that allowed him to climb the ladder… you know, that same crystal ball that allowed him to issue the alert before the body was found."

"Yeah, maybe." Whope replied. "Be careful John. I'll let you know if I learn anything."

"Thanks buddy." John said and hung up the phone.

John spent the night awake, sitting in the upholstered chair with one eye on the door. Having run out to the local big box store after getting the patrol officer to watch Janine and Otto, John had bought a baby monitor. Putting the transmitter next to the chair at the end of the hall where the patrol officer sat watch, John had the receiver in his lap as he listened for any noises that might indicate a disturbance he should be alerted to.

As dawn broke, John was relieved he could still hear the officer outside cough and fart, meaning no one had made any attempt on his life. John made a mental note to ask Captain Benjamin for a weapon the next time they spoke. Hearing movement from the bed closest to the bathroom, John looked over to see Janine quietly pad into the bathroom and close the door.

Despite the drawn room darkening privacy shades, streaks of light were illuminating the room enough that when Janine emerged, she could see John awake in the chair. Wearing one of John's tee shirts and a pair of his gym shorts, Janine needed to hold on to the waistband to prevent the shorts from falling down to her knees as she walked over to John's chair.

Sitting next to John's outstretched legs on the ottoman, she put her hand on his knee and asked, "You didn't get any sleep last night, did you?"

"I wanted to make sure no one snuck up on us. It's OK. I'm used to all night stake-outs. It's part of the job."

"Well I think it's going above and beyond your call of duty." Janine said. "So, what is our game plan today."

John said, "I think we should let Opa sleep as long as he wants this morning. As long as we can get to the bank before three we should be good. He had a very rough day yesterday, and he had a hard time falling asleep last night, so he deserves to sleep in. How are you holding up?"

"I'm all right. I still don't think it has fully sunk in that she's gone. I mean, we fought like cats and dogs all the time, but at the end of the day, she was still my sister, and I loved her."

"I understand. Well, if you ever want to talk about anything, or just need a shoulder to cry on, know that I'm here."

"Thank you, John. That is very sweet of you. So after Opa gets up, what do we do then?" Janine asked.

"We go to the bank, get the Big Light and hopefully use that to nail these bastards.

"That sounds so simple." Janine said.

"I know." John replied, "And the devil is actually in the details. But until I see what the Big Light is, I won't know what those details are."

"Sounds fair." Janine said. "Well, since I'm wide awake now, I think I'm gonna jump in the shower."

"OK. There is a coffee maker and some coffee over there. I don't know how good it is, but I can put some on for you."

"That would be great." Janine said as she headed toward the bathroom.

Janine, and then John showered and got ready for the day. The coffee was terrible, but Janine drank it. While Otto slept, they sat around talking about Anna, life, and the case. Janine asked John about his life, his work and the Vatican. John tried to keep things in a positive light, but Janine could tell John did not want to burden her with whatever problems he was dealing with. They sat softly talking by the hotel room desk until Otto began to stir around eleven in the morning.

John had learned from the previous morning that Otto was fairly self-sufficient with his daily hygiene. John assisted Otto as he stepped over the lip of the tub and into the shower, and then back out again. But other than that, Otto managed on his own and emerged from the bathroom by eleven-forty-five, and asked where they could go for breakfast.

Opting for something other than the IHOP they had been having, John drove down U.S. Route 1 to a diner, and they went in to eat. When the check came, John paid and escorted Janine and Otto back to the car for their trip to the bank. Arriving at the bank, the assistant manager was surprised to see Janine with Otto, commenting that Anna was the person who usually accompanied their grandfather when they came to make withdrawals.

The assistant manager had Otto sign some documents, show his ID and key, then she led him to the vault where they inserted their keys and removed the box. Escorting both John, Janine and Otto to a private room, she closed the door and allowed them to view the contents of the box.

"I'm kinda nervous." Janine said. "I mean, so many people died looking for this."

"I know. I'm hoping this is the piece of the puzzle that ties it all together." John said. "OK Otto. Let's open the box."

The old man opened the metal box and removed a single photograph. It was a picture of the cross he had made for the installation of his adoptive father in the church in New Jersey. On the back, written in old German cursive was the saying, 'Das grosse licht is das Kreuz das unsere familie tragt.'

Looking into the box, John saw it was empty, and the photo was the only thing that had been in there.

"Opa, where is Das Grosse Licht?" Janine asked.

Pointing to the picture, Otto replied, "Das Grosse Licht."

"The picture is the Big Light? Opa, that makes no sense."

"No, no. Das Kreuz… Der Grosse Licht." Otto said, pointing to the picture again.

"Wait a minute." John said. "The cross is the Big Light? I thought the Big Light was something that was brought over from Germany at the end of the war. You made this cross after you were here."

"Ja, ja. Das Kreuz… Der Grosse Licht." Otto insisted.

Shaking his head, John said to Janine, "This really doesn't make any sense. Do you know where this cross is now?"

"Yeah. It's hanging above the altar at my church." She replied.

"Ja, ja. Das Kreuz." Otto said excitedly.

"I wonder if your pastor would mind if we looked at it?" John said

"I could always ask him." Janine replied.

"Alright, let's put this back." John said pointing to the photo. "And maybe you could reach out to your pastor. Then we just need to stop at headquarters and update Benjamin and Horvath before we go take a look at the cross."

As they were returning the box to the vault, John's phone rang. Not recognizing the number, he answered, "This is John Nowalski."

"Inspector Nowalski, this is Captain Horvath."

"Yes Captain. We were just headed to speak to Captain Benjamin and planned to call you to give you an update." John said.

"Oh, well perhaps if you are nearby, you could stop by here first. There are a few additional things we need to speak to you about."

Pausing for a few seconds, John said, "Well, we are really not that close. Is there something I could clear up for you on the phone?"

"Not really. It would be much better if you could just come in and see us. There are some questions about the timeline we want to go over." Horvath said.

"What time will you be there until?" John asked. I could probably be there in about an hour."

"Sure, that's not a problem. I could hang a bit longer if you need me to. Where are you coming from?"

"I'm down in Princeton running down some leads." John lied. "I'm pretty sure I can be there in about an hour."

"OK. Great." Horvath said. "We'll see you in a bit then."

Hanging up the phone, John said, "Shit. We have problems."

With a face looking somewhere between puzzled and concerned, Janine said, "I overheard some of the conversation. We are not in Princeton. Who was that and what's going on?"

"That was Captain Horvath. He has some FBI agents there that want to talk to me."

"What? FBI... what do they want?" Janine asked.

"I don't really know, but I got a call from a friend of

mine in the Bureau telling me they opened a case on me related to Anna's murder, and to be careful."

"But you couldn't have had anything to do with Anna's death. You were with me and Opa the whole time." Janine said.

"I know Janine. And the really screwy thing about this is they opened the case *before* Anna's death was even discovered."

"What? How can that be? Unless…"

"They either witnessed or committed the murder themselves… Right." John said, finishing Janine's sentence.

"So what do we do now?" Janine asked.

"For starters, we are not going to go talk to Horvath and his FBI friends." John said. "Next, I think we need to put that visit to your church off till at least tomorrow. Right now, I need to get a shitload of cash from this bank and buy a burner phone. Then we need to pack up the hotel room and get out of there. We need to find a motel where they take cash and don't ask for identification. Then I need to work the phones a bit to get some information before we take our next step."

"So we need to disappear." Janine said.

Nodding his head, John said "At least for a bit. I'd also love to lose this car."

"We have Anna's keys." Janine said. My car is parked right in front of the house, but Anna's is a bit down the block. I doubt anyone is watching it."

"You are right. I'll bet no one is even giving it a second look." John agreed. "Let's get the cash, then go get the car. We can move forward from there."

John maxed out his cash advance limit on both his

credit cards, and was actually able to get the bank to convert some of the Euros in his checking account to dollars. With nearly twenty-five hundred dollars in cash, John felt he would be able to stay off the electronic grid for a while.

Leaving the bank, John made several sudden turns and timed a number of lights so that he was fairly certain he had lost any cars following them. He then made his way to Otto's house where he dropped Janine off to get Anna's car, and just to confuse the situation even more, he parked his rental and jumped in Janine's car.

After a half hour of more driving designed to shake any tails, John met Janine and Otto at the parking lot of the Home Depot in Piscataway. Parking Janine's car, all three then took Anna's car to the hotel, ran in, grabbed their things and were back on the road again in under five minutes. After another half hour of anti-surveillance driving, John felt it was safe to head north and look for a suitable motel to spend the night.

Checking in to a motel that looked fairly clean, but charged hourly rates and accepted cash, John shepherded Janine and Otto into the room, closed and locked the door and began making calls on the prepaid phone from the list of phone numbers he wrote down before leaving his phone in the rental car.

Finally, after two hours of calls and relentless pacing, John finally began to gain some insight into what was happening, and what to do next. Sitting in the only chair in the room, John ran his hand over his face and contemplated his course of action.

"What's going on? Janine asked, turning down the TV and walking over to John.

"That was a very interesting series of phone calls." John said.

"Good, interesting or bad, interesting?"

"Well, I started out speaking to my friend Bob at the Bureau. He was the one who gave me the heads-up about their interest in me. He did some digging and it turns out that the Deputy Director, his name is Bauer is politically connected and he regularly does favors for select senators and folks on capitol hill. Bob wasn't able to pin down who wanted Bauer to get the FBI to bring some heat, but he did do a bit of an end run around Bauer's crew."

"What did he do?" Janine asked.

"Bob called the Special Agent in Charge of the Newark field office, who happens to be a friend of his. It seems Bauer did this without their knowledge, which, unless it is a matter of national security, is not how things are done in the FBI. Bob also pointed out that the case was opened by Bauer *before* Anna's body was found, so how did he know to open the case. The SAC in Newark is pissed, and plans to send some folks down to Middlesex county to have a chat with Bauer's crew."

"So then we are in the clear?" Janine said.

"Not quite. Things are going to take a few days to sort out, and in the interim, they can still make my life pretty difficult." John said. "But in the meantime, this is a bit more evidence to help tie some pieces of the puzzle together. How did Bauer know about Anna before we reported it? Well, he knew because someone from Aryphon told him. I called my contact at the Mossad, and mentioned Bauer's name and he told me immediately that Bauer and his family are at the very least, sympathizers of the new Nazi party. And the new Nazi party is funded and run by the folks associated with Aryphon Industries."

"Who is Aryphon?" Janine asked.

"They are a privately held multinational conglomerate out of Uruguay. They were initially formed by escaped Nazi's after World War Two, and financed by lost Nazi gold. They are also the people who sent mercenaries to Austria to interrogate, and then kill a bunch of monks as they looked for the Big Light."

"Then they killed Anna." Janine asked more as a statement than a question.

"No, the North Koreans killed your sister." John said. "The MO, the methodology, all follow the murders of the nuns and the second group of monks."

"And how do you know they are North Koreans?" Janine asked.

"At the scene of the third attack, both the Aryphon and North Korean teams were there at the same time which resulted in a major gun battle. We collected lots of DNA evidence including a bunch from the Aryphon team that matched against former members of U.S. special forces. We should be currently going through diplomatic channels to get those records unsealed. We also found a dead Korean operative who we assume is North Korean because the guns and ammunition used in the assault are all standard issue for DPRK special forces. Additionally, I spoke to Captain Benjamin and there was actually some DNA evidence at the scene of Mrs. Wagner's murder, and it came back as belonging to someone from the Korean peninsula."

"So if you know all this, why can't you arrest them?" Janine asked in an exasperated voice.

"Because we need more conclusive evidence to tie this to Aryphon. Based on what we have, I know with relative certainty who the two groups are, but I do not have enough to make arrests or bring charges. And I certainly can't go marching into North Korea and arrest people. Unfortunately, even with a bit more solid evidence, we will have to work through diplomatic channels on both fronts to get any kind of justice."

"Basically, you're saying that we will never see justice done for Anna's murder." Janine said in disgust.

"No Janine, that's not necessarily the case. We are working through diplomatic channels to get the security clearances lifted on the Aryphon mercenaries, and you'd be surprised how persistent the Vatican can be." John said.

"But they didn't kill Anna." Janine nearly cried. "No amount of diplomatic pressure is going to work on North Korea. They are just going to laugh at us."

"Which is why I am using a different tact with them. Which is why I need to get my hands on the Big Light before they do."

Looking directly at John, Janine's deep brown eyes stared deeply into John's as if she was trying to peer down into his soul. John maintained the gaze, and tried to maintain a neutral expression on his face, despite the resolute set of his jaw.

"Because you think it will be the key to tying all of the evidence together…"

"Right." John said. "I've already told you that."

Continuing to stare into John's eyes, Janine began to shake her head.

"No. Bullshit. You know whatever the Big Light is,

it won't tie things back to the killers. You may have once thought that, but now your motivations have changed."

John's eyes began to get big and he slowly inhaled a deep breath as he listened to Janine unravel his game plan.

Janine continued, "You want to get to the Big Light to be able to use it as bait. You want to lure the Koreans out into the open when they go for the Big Light and take them down as they try to get it."

"Janine… I…"

"John, that's insane. You've said it yourself, these people are trained killers. How are you going to manage to capture them, let alone manage to not get yourself killed?"

"It's all a matter of timing. I need to set up any confrontation to be at a time and place that I've chosen, and set up to take them down. That's why this FBI thing is a real fly in the ointment. It throws off the timing and alienates Horvath and his resources I was counting on using."

"John, you can't do this." Janine pleaded. "I couldn't stand to see you get killed. Look… you've started to become important to me. I know we've only known each other for a few days, but… I mean… I've just lost my sister. I can't stand the thought of losing you too."

John's expression softened, and he reached out and softly touched Janine's cheek, then ran his hand past her ear, through her hair and softly caressed the back of her head. "Janine…" He began, "I have been in more dangerous situations than this and come through in the end. Everything is going to work out. You'll see. Everything will be fine."

Janine turned away from John and said, "I don't like it. There has to be a better way." Looking over to Otto, she asked, "Don't you agree Opa?"

Otto had been sitting on the side of the bed, silently listening to the conversation. Now that he was asked for his opinion, he stood up, walked over to Janine and put his hand on her shoulder, saying, "The andere little girl is dead. The other girl…" Making the shape of a gun with his forefinger and thumb, "The bang, bang very bad. They need to show me the money. And der Grosse Licht is not for bang, bang very bad."

"So you think John's idea is good too? I get it that they all are bad and need to pay for what they did, but this plan is insanity." Janine said in a voice filled with frustration. Otto just shrugged and then nodded his head.

"Well, the hell with both of you. I refuse to help you kill yourself." Turning to John she continued, "I'm not talking to Pastor Lembrich, so go see if you can get that cross by yourself."

With that, Janine stormed off into the bathroom, and slammed the door closed, leaving John and Otto standing there. Turning to Otto, John said, "Did we say something wrong?"

CHAPTER 17

**Sayreville Police Headquarters
Sayreville, New Jersey
Present Day**

It took all of breakfast and most of the morning before
Janine would even begin to speak to John or Otto. After
breakfast, John announced he had spoken to Captain Benjamin last night and filled him in on all the details. They
both decided it would be best for everyone to come to
police headquarters first thing in the morning to finalize
their plan. En route, John called Benjamin to make sure
his FBI friends weren't there waiting for him.

John led Janine and Otto into the building where
Adam was waiting to meet them and escort them all back
to the squad room and Benjamin's office. John, Janine and
Otto took seats in the chairs facing Benjamin's desk while
Adam sat on the edge of the desk facing everyone.

"Holy shit Nowalski." Benjamin began. "Does this shit
follow you everywhere you go?"

Laughing a little, John replied, "Not everywhere. I usually don't have any trouble when I go to the bathroom."

With the scowl on her face that she had all morning deepening, Janine said, "What is wrong with you people? People are dead, and John, you are going to use yourself as bait to try to catch the killers… And you're laughing about it. Well, I said it last night and I still mean it. I'm not going to help. I won't ask Pastor Lembrich to let you see the cross."

"Miss Wagner. I understand how you feel." Benjamin said. But let me assure you, I run a tight ship here and have never had an officer killed on my watch. We have a pretty decent plan here that I think is our best chance of nailing these guys."

Looking over to Benjamin, Otto said, "Kein Plan überlebt die erste Feindberührung."

"Thank you Opa." Janine responded.

"What did he say?" Benjamin asked.

John replied, "He said 'No plan survives the first contact with the enemy.' It is a quote from Field Marshal Helmuth Graf von Moltke, architect of Germany's Wars of Unification back in the mid eighteen hundred's. He is considered by many military historians as the one of the most brilliant military minds since Napoleon."

"Well thanks for the vote of confidence, Pops." Benjamin said sarcastically. Switching his focus back to Janine, he continued, "But seriously, I think this idea is the best chance we have of catching the North Koreans, and the Aryphon mercenaries."

"Well you can do it without my help." Janine said.

"I'm sorry you feel that way, Miss Wagner." Benjamin said.

Where are we with the FBI and Horvath?" John asked.

Benjamin replied, "I spoke to SAC Gonzalez both last night and again this morning. She was spitting nails. She is taking this move by Bauer as a racial and gender thing, and plans to make noise up to the top. She was even more pissed when I confirmed that no one outside of the killers should have known Anna was dead before eleven o'clock, and this case was opened at nine that morning. She said she made some inquiries to the Austrian National police and they did not reach out to the FBI with any suspicions about John. She said she's sick of the political bullshit that has been going on in the Bureau, and how it's affecting their credibility. She's sending two agents here today to talk to Horvath and make sure he's good to go. And then, they are going to have a chat with the three clowns who were here looking for you yesterday."

"Good." John said. "What about the HRT?"

"They will be on standby and ready to be deployed when we need them. Gonzalez liked our plan and was more than happy to cooperate. If you can actually find this thing and get those operators out in the open, it will be a feather in her cap if we all bring them down."

"I'm hoping that with an overwhelming show of firepower, this can go off without the exchange of any gunfire."

Benjamin replied, "That is the plan." Then turning swiftly toward Otto and pointing he said, "And you shut up."

"Anything else?" John asked.

"As expected, I received several messages for you from some of your Vatican friends. Cardinal Sentille wanted you to contact him immediately, and he left a local number, and a Cardinal Dietrich wanted to know if I could get you a message to call him."

"Perfect. I will reach out to them later. I guess all that's left to do is retrieve the Big Light, and then we can start the dominos in motion." John said.

Sitting with her arms crossed across her chest, Janine said, "I'm still not calling the Pastor."

Benjamin looked over to Adam who had been quiet this whole time and asked, "Adam, you're fairly well acquainted with the Pastor, aren't you?"

"Yessir." Adam replied.

"Would you mind giving him a buzz and asking if John could come and take a look at that pretty cross hanging above his altar?"

"I have his number by my desk. I'll be right back." Adam said.

A few minutes later, Adam returned and gave everyone the thumbs up. "He said he needs to leave within the next ten minutes, but he will unlock the front doors for us and turn on the lights before he leaves. He said there is a step ladder in the closet on the left, immediately after you enter the church."

"That's perfect. Adam, why don't you drive John over to the church and help him take that cross down." Benjamin said. "It's nearly six feet tall and made of solid wood. It probably weighs a ton."

"Yessir. I'll go grab the keys and bring the car around front."

"Sounds good." John replied.

"And Adam, can you show Miss Wagner and Mr. Grasslicked out to the break room on your way out?

Benjamin asked. Looking over to Janine and Otto he continued, "There's a couch in there, a snack machine and a TV. You'll probably be more comfortable waiting in there. I'll make sure to get you when they return."

"Thank you, Captain." Janine said as she helped her grandfather out of his seat.

With Janine and Otto gone, Benjamin looked over to John and asked, "You think this is really gonna work?"

"What choice do we have?" John replied. "We need to get these players out in the open. The only way to get to Aryphon is to catch these mercenaries and get at least one of 'em to flip. And the North Koreans need to be caught and tried in public so everyone can see how evil that regime is."

"And you think you'll find this thing in the church?"

"That's what the old man said. He was emphatic that the Big Light was the cross. I guess we'll find out in a little bit."

"OK. Good luck." Benjamin said.

"Jake, before I head out… Any way I could get a sidearm? Things are getting a bit dicey and I've had the feeling I might have been followed a few times."

"John, you are not licensed to carry in…". Benjamin began.

"Actually Jake, I usually am. Officially I head the Pope's protective detail when he travels. As such, I am always granted approval by the State Department to carry a weapon, even when I am doing advance work for an upcoming visit. I didn't have time to go through the bureaucratic bullshit of doing the paperwork before I came over, and I certainly don't have the time now."

"John, I'm sorry, I can't. I give you one of my guns and you shoot someone, even legitimately, and I'm fucked. I'm way too close to retirement for that to happen."

Shaking his head, John said, 'You're hangin' me out there, buddy. I'd hate to be in your shoes if I'm unable to protect myself and I'm killed... *I am deeply sorry Mrs. Nowalski... Your husband died because he didn't do the paperwork so I couldn't give him a gun.*"

Shaking his head, Benjamin said, "Fuck you, Nowalski. You're not even married." Reaching down and opening his bottom drawer, Benjamin pulled out what looked like a bulky black handgun in a holster. "Here, take this. Technically, you were trained in its use when you used to work here, and there have never been any mandates on re-qualification."

Picking the Taser up off Benjamin's desk, John said, "Well, I guess it's better than nothing."

"That's the Axon X2 Taser. It holds two cartridges that fire two darts at a time with a dual laser sight so you can see where the two darts are gonna go. With two cartridges it can be fired in a semi-automatic fashion, even at two separate targets. It has a range of fifteen feet, and allows repeated discharges of current by pulling the trigger. It should give you about ten to fifteen minutes of juice when discharging. Try not to take someone's eye out if you have to use it."

"Thanks Dad. Can I get the car keys too?" John quipped.

"Get the fuck out of here." Benjamin said. "Good luck."

John left Benjamin's office and walked into the break room. He pulled a chair up in front of Janine, and gently took her chin between his thumb and forefinger and turned her head to face him. Looking directly into Janine's eyes John said. "I'm sorry I have been glib about what I am going to do. I do recognize the dangers and I think being glib is how I deal with it. This way, I don't have to consider the possible negative outcomes. But I never wanted to cause you any worry or concern, and I certainly don't want to hurt you.

You know, you told me yesterday that you cared about me and I was important to you. When you said it, I didn't return the sentiment. Not because I didn't feel it, but I think it was because it has been so long since I have had these types of feelings. I loved my wife, and when I lost her, I was devastated. I never wanted to feel that pain or loss again, so I threw up walls. I ran away and hid in a monastery. I hid away from the possibility of ever finding love again. But now Janine, I'm done hiding.

I honestly believe, luring them out with the Big Light is the only way to bring this horror show to its rightful end. I need to get these people put away so they can never hurt or threaten anyone ever again. These people must pay for all the innocent people they killed... The nuns, the monks, Mrs. Wagner... Anna. Janine, I also need to give you closure. You need to believe that justice has been served in order to get past the guilt you feel for the way you two fought. I want you to have closure because without closure you won't be able to move on with your life... and I need you to be able to do that... because you are more than important to me too."

Looking deeply into John's eyes, Janine said, "I can't lose you."

"You won't." John replied.

Holding John's gaze for a long moment, Janine finally said, "Go get the Big Light. I'll be waiting right here for you. And please be careful."

"I will." He replied. Winking at Otto he said, "I'll watch my fingers.

Adam was waiting parked outside the front entrance of head-quarters. "About friggin' time." Adam said as John tossed a backpack on the floor and slid into the passenger seat.

"Excuse me?" John asked.

"Nothing. You just took a while." Adam said as he put the car in gear. "I thought you were coming right out"

"I had a few things I wanted to go over with your Captain."

"Anything I should know about?" Adam asked as he turned right on to Main Street, spinning the tires on the bit of sand at the end of the driveway.

"Nothing really. I was just asking Jake if he knew about your raging cocaine habit." John said with a straight face.

"What?… Why would you say something like that to…I have never even tried…"

"Relax Levy." John said laughing. "I'm just being a jerk. I was asking the Captain about the possibility of giving me a gun."

"What did he say?" Adam asked.

"My old pal told me… no fuckin' way."

"Good. I'm glad he didn't betray his principles. You're not authorized to carry a weapon in this jurisdiction." Adam said.

Adam had been so focused on his antagonism toward John he failed to see the black SUV pull out behind him as he left the parking lot. Nor did he see the other two vehicles fall rapidly behind the first.

"So Adam…" John began. "Am I sensing some animosity toward me, or have my keen observational skills failed me?"

"What are you talking about?" Adam replied.

"The glaring, the attitude in your voice. It's pretty obvious you don't like me. The thing I don't understand is why. What have I ever done to you?"

Giving John an incredulous look, Adam said, "For starters, when we first met you gave me a dressing down in front of my boss and some of the other detectives."

"I did? I don't recall." John said

"Of course you don't." Adam snapped.

"Well I apologize. I truly meant no disrespect and was only displaying my bad sense of humor." John said.

"And then there is the whole thing with Miss Wagner."

"What whole thing? John asked.

"I mean, calling her by her first name, the familiarity… Don't you think that's a bit unprofessional?"

"This coming from the guy who asked her out." John said.

"Wait, what? She told you?" Adam asked, as John nodded his head in the affirmative. "Ah shit. Is she pissed? I can't believe she told you. Do you think she's gonna file a complaint?"

"Relax, Romeo. She's cool. She said it's OK." John replied.

"She said it's OK?" Adam asked.

"I think her exact words were something like he's sweet and he seems like a nice guy, but he has the worst timing in the world."

"Really? She said I'm sweet?

"Yeah." John said.

"So… do you think I might have a chance when…"

"No fuckin' way." John said cutting Adam off.

"Oh… Well, it was worth a shot." Adam said.

"It always is, Adam… It always is."

Steve Tortorice was preparing to make a left into the driveway of police headquarters when Josh came shooting out of the other side, spinning his tires. "I wonder what's up his ass." Tortorice said to himself as he watched Adam in his rearview mirror. He was about to turn into the driveway when he noticed the black SUV come speeding out after Adam, and then he saw two other vehicles parked along the shoulder suddenly accelerate into traffic and follow the SUV.

Parking his vehicle in the back, Tortorice grabbed his lunch bag and entered through the back entrance. Heading to the break room, he greeted Janine and Otto, then put his lunch in the refrigerator. Walking to the squad room, he greeted the unit admin and the other detective already there, then sat down at his desk.

"Morning Captain." Tortorice said to Benjamin a few minutes later after Benjamin emerged from his office.

"Hey Steve. How you doin'?" the Captain replied.

"Not bad. Lookin' forward to the weekend. Me and

the bride are gonna pig out on Italian hot dogs and funnel cakes at the fair."

"Sounds like fun." Benjamin said.

"So where was Adam leading the parade to this morning?" Tortorice asked.

"What?" Benjamin replied. "What are you talking about?"

"Levy… I was waiting to turn into the driveway when he came peeling out of the parking lot, and all of a sudden, like, three other cars looked like they were following."

"Are you serious?" the Captain asked. "Did it really look like they were following them?"

"I mean Boss, I don't know if they were actually following, but I got that impression."

"Shit.." Exclaimed Benjamin. "Adam was taking Nowalski to try and actually get the Big Light. John had said he got the feeling that he had a tail. They were headed to St. Luke's. This could be trouble."

Trotting back to his office, Benjamin grabbed his bullet-proof vest out of the closet, and the gun from his desk drawer. Heading toward the door, Benjamin called to the other detective, "Do me a favor and keep an eye on the two people in the break room." Then looking at Tortorice he asked, "Is your vest in your car?"

"Yeah, why?" Tortorice replied.

"Head to the armory and grab a few extra magazines, then grab your car and meet me around front. I'm headed to dispatch to have them send every available unit to the church."

"What's going on boss?" Tortorice asked.

"It might have been the Koreans or the other

mercenaries you saw following Adam. If it was, our guys are in a shit ton of trouble."

Tortorice headed to the armory and grabbed the extra ammunition, then headed out the back to his car. Benjamin went down the hall to the dispatch station and informed the Desk Sargent he needed to send every available unit to St. Luke's church.

"I'm sorry Captain. Every unit is currently tied up, and we are holding calls."

"OK, as soon as anyone clears, send them right away unless you have heard otherwise from me. Got that?"

"Yes sir." The Desk Sargent replied.

Running out the front door, Benjamin got in Tortorice's car and told him to go. "Plug in the teardrop and hit the grill lights, but try to stay off the siren. We need to approach in stealth mode."

"Roger that." Tortorice replied.

John and Adam arrived at the church and parked in the parking lot. Walking over to the front door, they found it open as they had expected. Opening the closet in the church vestibule, John pulled the six-foot ladder out of the closet, and saw a pair of lineman's pliers sitting on the top shelf.

"Grab those pliers, will ya?" John said to Adam.

The cross hung in the sanctuary at the front of the church about four feet above the altar. Hung from two wires that were attached to the back of the cross piece, the cross was a magnificent piece of carpentry. About five feet in length, the main body of the cross was shaped from an eight inch by eight inch piece of dark mahogany with a gold inlay down the front. The cross piece was so finely mitered to the main vertical piece it looked like it was growing out of the sides.

John carried the ladder down the aisle and bowed as he crossed in front of the altar to set up the ladder. Climbing to the top of the ladder John was barely able to reach the eye hooks screwed into the back of the cross piece where the wires were attached.

Looking down to Adam, John said, "I'm gonna disconnect this wire here, which will cause the cross to swing down and to the right. I need you to just stop it from swinging back and knocking me off this ladder."

"Gotcha. Adam replied.

John unwrapped the wire from the eye hook and as carefully as he could, released the left side of the cross. Moving the ladder to the right, he climbed back up and began unwinding the wire attached to the other eye hook.

"Once I free this wire, all of the weight will be on you." John said to Adam who was precariously holding the bottom of the cross with his arms extended over his head. "If you let the top tip towards me, I'll help lower it down."

"OK. I'll try not to have it crash down on you." Adam said with a smirk on his face.

Seeing the smirk, John said "Try real hard, OK?"

"Right." Adam replied, without losing the smirk.

John released the second wire and the cross dropped down a few inches, but Adam, despite his poor positioning, was able to take the weight and control the cross. Slowly tipping it toward John who supported the weight from the cross piece, the two men lowered the cross to the floor.

"Was it me, or was that thing lighter than it looked." John said.

"It was really light." Adam said. "Almost like it was hollow."

"Hollow… hmmmm." John said. Holding the cross upright with one hand, he began knocking on the wooden cross with his knuckles. Starting at the top and working his way down, they noted that while the top half and the cross pieces sounded solid, once John got below the cross piece it sounded a bit like John was knocking on a drum.

"Now why would Otto hollow out the bottom half of this thing?" John said thinking out loud.

Looking carefully at both the front and the back of the cross John could see Otto put a great deal of time and effort into its construction. From both the front and the sides, the cross looked like it was carved from a single enormous piece of wood. Even including the gold inlay on the front, not a single crease or seam could be found. On the back however, upon careful examination, a single seam could be seen directly below the cross piece.

Taking a pocket knife out of his pocket, John opened the folding blade and carefully inserted it into the seam on the back. Surprisingly, it went in with very little effort. Inserting the blade about a half inch, John twisted and pried gently on the knife and the wood on the back of the cross began to move. Twisting and prying a bit more, John was able to move the wood enough to see that the back was a cover to a hidden compartment inside the cross. Getting his fingers inside the void he created, John gently pushed the wooden cover down toward the foot of the cross, exposing a yellow cardboard tube hidden inside.

Carefully, John and Adam laid the cross down on the altar, allowing John to slide the wooden cover down until he was able to remove the cardboard tube.

"The Big Light?" Adam said.

"I don't know." John responded. "It's not what I expected. It looks like a thirty-six inch mailing tube."

"So open it. The Big Light is probably inside." Adam replied.

John pried the end cap off of the tube, tipped it over and shook the tube several times. Several sheets of rolled up paper emerged from the end of the tube. John grasped the pages and carefully pulled them out. Rolling them open over the cross on the altar the men could clearly see the pages were blueprints and plans for some type of machine. Annotated in German and bearing Nazi insignia, John could tell these plans dated back to the Second World War.

"Still not what I expected," John said. "But now I can see why our current day Nazis are interested. "We'd need to find out what these are plans for."

"There anything else in the tube?" Adam asked.

Peering down into the tube, John said, "It looks like there are some more papers stuck to the inside of the cardboard. Let me see if I can shake them out."

Kim Joo-Won had the driver pass the church and park the car on the side street. Sitting in the car, he reviewed the plan of attack with his team. Kim and one other mercenary would enter the church carrying only sidearms and approach Nowalski and the other man. Two of the other team members would wait two minutes and then enter the church armed with their Sterling Sub-machine guns as back-up should Nowalski decide to put up a fight. The driver would remain with the vehicle to provide support should someone approach the rest of the team from the rear, and be available for rapid exfiltration once the mission was complete.

John did not initially see the two Koreans enter the church as he was focused on retrieving the remaining papers from the tube, however, he did catch their motion as they walked up the aisle. Seeing that the two men appeared Asian, he put the tube down and signaled Adam to turn around. With the altar partially obstructing the view of the two men walking down the aisle, John deftly took the Taser and it's holster from behind his back and hid it behind the cross and under the plans..

"Can I help you gentlemen?" Adam asked as he turned to face the approaching men.

"Inspector Nowalski?" Kim asked.

"That would be him." Adam said nodding over toward John.

"My name is Kim Joo-Won." Kim said, steadily walking toward the altar. "And I'm here to collect the Big Light."

Kim and his second-in-command had their guns drawn and aimed at John and Adam before Adam could reach for his sidearm.

"Let me see your hands." Kim commanded as they advanced to the sanctuary with their weapons trained on John and Adam. "I would really hate to see you gentlemen lose your life prematurely."

Walking over to Adam, the second mercenary relieved Adam of his weapon while Kim kept cover from the first step into the sanctuary. With his hands still raised, John walked around the altar and said, "I am not armed. These people won't let me have a gun."

The second mercenary searched John despite his declaration, then allowed John to step back toward the side of the altar.

"What is it you're looking for?" John asked Kim.

"I already told you. I am here to collect the Big Light." Kim replied as the two other mercenaries entered the back of the church and came about halfway down the center aisle.

"I don't have it. We are still looking." John lied.

Nodding over to the other mercenary, Kim took a step closer to the altar as the other mercenary kicked out the back of Adams legs and forced him to his knees. "I said only a moment ago that I would hate to see either of you lose your life prematurely." Kim said. "However, I will not be taken for the fool. I can clearly see you found something. Hand it over or your man over here dies."

With his hands out in front of him making a 'calm down' motion, John said, "OK, OK. No one needs to die. I'm sorry. I do not take you for a fool. Here."

John handed the tube to the mercenary who looked down the tube, then handed it over to Kim.

Dieter von Alpiner and his team made a slow pass in front of the church and continued past without stopping. Continuing down two blocks, the two vehicles turned left into the development, drove two additional blocks, turned left again, then drove down to the street that came out directly across from the front of the church. Coming halfway down the block, von Alpiner parked his vehicles in time to clearly observe Kim and his men enter the church.

Getting on his radio he instructed his team to stand fast. His plan was to wait until Kim and his team emerged from the church, then driving straight across the church lawn, take the opposing team out, secure the Big Light, and be gone before the lookout in Kim's vehicle even knew what happened.

Those instructions disappeared when he saw the police vehicle come speeding into the parking lot, and two plain clothed officers jump out, don bullet proof vests, and run to the front door of the church.

"There is nothing in the tube." Kim said after looking down the open end. Saying something in Korean, the mercenary placed his gun beside Adam's head. Looking toward John, the mercenary replied to Kim before redirecting his attention to Adam, still kneeling on the sanctuary carpeting.

"My associate says there are papers on the altar. Why don't you roll them up and bring them to me?" Kim said smiling. "I wasn't able to see them from this vantage point." Tossing John the empty tube, he turned to face Adam. "What is your name?" he asked.

"My name is Detective Levy." Adam replied.

"Well Detective Levy, it appears we may have found what we came here for, so you are no longer useful as a lever against Inspector Nowalski. Good bye Detective Levy."

Adam heard the hammer being cocked on the FN Hi-Power the mercenary had against the side of his head and expected to briefly hear the report of the gun being fired, before hearing nothing at all. Instead, he heard commotion at the back of the church and the all too familiar voice of Jake Benjamin telling everyone to 'FREEZE' and 'GET DOWN ON THE GROUND.' Then all hell broke loose.

John wasted no time in pulling the Axon X2 Taser from its holster. Recognizing that his targets wore body armor, he sighted on the groin of the mercenary standing behind Adam, and pulled the trigger. With the first two darts away, John aimed the laser sights at the face and neck of Kim who had just turned back to engage John and Adam after briefly looking at Benjamin and Tortorice in the back of the church.

All four darts found their targets and delivered two thousand volts at around only three amps. Causing immediate loss of voluntary muscle control, both men fell to the floor dropping their guns, while the mercenary shot in the groin lost bladder control as well. Retrieving his gun from the fallen mercenary, Adam sprinted off the sanctuary, taking shelter in front of the first pew and joining the gun battle that raged in front of him.

Upon hearing Benjamin's call to 'freeze,' both mercenaries in the back of the church turned to fire at the new threat. Seeing the men turning, both Benjamin and Tortorice fired at the armed men, aiming center mass as their training dictated. Unfortunately, both mercenaries were wearing body armor, and despite taking the shots to the chest, were able to return fire from their sub-machine guns on full automatic.

With Benjamin diving right and Tortorice diving

left behind the last pew, the two men avoided the initial fusillade of bullets. While Benjamin and Tortorice were avoiding the sub-machine gun fire, both mercenaries took similar cover between pews seven rows up. The mercenaries poured full magazines of bullets into the thick wooden pews separating the detectives from their assailants, and Benjamin and Tortorice attempted to time their return fire to coincide with the mercenaries expending their ammunition.

After reloading for the third time, both mercenaries popped up above the pew to unload on the detectives. Needing a better angle to potentially hit their targets, the Korean on the right stepped up onto the pew seat and held his gun above his head, directing the angle of fire down on Tortorice. With bullets splintering the top of the pew, Tortorice hugged the floor as close to the pew as possible to escape the storm of lead. Expending his third magazine, the Korean was about to drop down below the seat when he felt the sharp sting of a bullet pass through his upper right arm. Realizing he was drawing fire from behind him, he turned in time to catch Adam's next shot through the throat. Dropping his weapon and clutching his throat, the mercenary fell to the floor gasping for air as he began to drown in his own blood.

John needed to keep depressing the trigger on the Taser to continue administering the disabling voltage every ten seconds or so, as the effects of the shocks were relatively short lived. Recognizing his upper hand was fleeting, he carefully moved around the fallen mercenary and retrieved the man's gun. While doing so, he looked up to assess the status of the gun battle raging in front of him.

He watched as Adam's shot took down the Korean, and could see that with Adam's suppressing fire, Benjamin and Tortorice were about to perform a flanking maneuver to subdue the other mercenary. With the two in the sanctuary incapacitated, and the two detectives about to surround the Korean in the pews, John was beginning to believe they may have captured this team. Suddenly, a fifth mercenary appeared in the inner doorway of the church, aiming his Kalashnikov-105 at the back of Benjamin's head.

Having seen the two detectives run into the church, the Korean driver shut the engine off, exited the vehicle and ran to the trunk. Removing the AK-105 from under a blanket in the trunk, he ran the one block distance to the front door of the church, and silently slipped inside. Ascending the steps from the door to the main level of the church he reached the top step just as Adam shot his teammate. Assessing the scene, he saw his leader and second-in-command incapacitated by the altar, and his other teammate pinned down. With two enemy shooters in the front of the church and two more a mere six feet in front of him, he took aim at the nearest adversary.

John and Adam both saw the fifth assailant at the same time and called out in warning. Adam fired three quick shots in the direction of the new man, but without careful aim, his shots missed wide left and right.

Temporarily losing concentration from the spray of bullets in his direction, the fifth mercenary needed to refocus his aim on the man in front of him. Sighting down the stock, he squeezed the trigger a split second after getting hit by John's carefully aimed shot. Catching him above and to the left of the body armor's breast plate, the bullet failed to pierce the Kevlar, but the impact knocked the wind from him, broke two ribs, and most importantly, caused his shot to miss the back of Benjamin's head.

Entering Benjamin's left shoulder, the 5.45 millimeter round struck Benjamin's collar bone, shattering the bone and ricocheting downward into the upper lobe of his left lung. Benjamin collapsed into the pew instantly and gasped to catch his breath. He knew he was badly injured when his wet cough produced blood and he felt like a vice was constricting his chest.

Tortorice heard the warning from John and Adam and turned around in time to see Benjamin get shot. Immediately taking aim, he fired three shots at the new shooter, hitting him squarely in the body armor with each shot. The shooter staggered backward, while swinging his AK toward Tortorice and depressing the trigger. In three seconds, he sent thirty rounds toward Tortorice at twenty-eight hundred feet per second. Ten rounds imbedded themselves in the pew in front of Tortorice, and twelve more flew over his head into the adjacent wall and ceiling. However, eight bullets painted themselves across Tortorice from the lower edge of his vest up across his neck and face, dropping him into the pew he used for cover.

While needing to address the shooter in the back of the church, John was forced to stop delivering shocks to the two men in the sanctuary. Realizing his failure, John turned just in time to see both Kim and the other mercenary withdraw secondary sidearms from concealed holsters. Diving for cover behind the altar, John fired three rounds in rapid succession into Kim's second in command. The first shot caught the Korean in the right kneecap, while the second and third shots struck his abdomen below the body armor.

Kim fired three shots in return at John, but John was already safely behind the altar. Hearing shots coming from behind him, Adam recognized that he could be caught in a cross-fire, and leapt over the front pew then immediately reversed his field, firing at Kim. Seeing their leader was himself now caught in a cross-fire, the two mercenaries in the church sprayed bullets at the altar and the pew protecting Adam.

Kim realized that despite the covering fire of his men, his current position crouching down in the middle of the sanctuary left him extremely vulnerable. Seeing the plans still sitting on top of the altar, he made one move toward the altar in an attempt to grab them, and was greeted by a bullet that barely missed the gap in the side of his body armor fired from Adam. Realizing that additional police would probably be only minutes away, Kim rolled backward, and shouted out the order to withdraw.

Popping up, Kim sprinted toward the side door located just outside the sanctuary while his men laid down suppressing fire on Adam and John. Reaching the door, Kim burst through, but then popped back around to supply his own covering fire to support his team's exit. With Kim's covering fire effectively pinning Adam down, the two mercenaries leap-frogged out the back of the church, alternating cover fire with their egress. Upon seeing his men cross the threshold of the rear inner doors, Kim bolted down the seven steps to the side exterior doors, then ran to the SUV parked on the side street nearest his exit.

Arriving at the same time as his men, Kim and the mercenaries jumped in the car and drove off down the side street and into the neighborhood adjacent to the church. Using their GPS, the team avoided the main roads and put distance between themselves and the scene of the gun battle, eventually getting back on a main road to take them to their hotel.

Seeing the Koreans run from the church without anything in their hands except their guns, von Alpiner assumed they were either unable to take the Big Light, or Nowalski didn't find it in the church. He sent his one team after the Koreans, while he remained at the church to see what developed.

With the mercenaries now out of the church, John and Adam ran to the back of the church to check on the fallen detectives. John went to Benjamin and found him uncon-scious with a bullet wound to his shoulder. Ripping his sleeve from his shirt, John applied pressure to the wound as he yelled over to Adam instructing him to contact dispatch and have them rush the ambulance. Within minutes, the first patrol car arrived and a uniformed officer rushed in with his gun drawn. Calling out to him, John had him come and hold pressure on Benjamin's wound as he went over to check on Adam and Tortorice.

John found Adam covered in blood doing CPR on the detective.

"C'mon Steve-O. Hang in there. You can make it. Don't give up…" Adam was saying as he performed compressions on his friend's chest.

John walked over and put his hand on Adam's shoulder. "It's OK Adam… Adam, you can stop, he's gone."

Looking up at John, Adam shouted, "NO… I just have to keep this up till the medics get here. C'mon Steve.. C'mon…

John just stood there next to Adam with his hand on his shoulder while Adam continued his futile attempts to revive the nearly faceless Tortorice. More police arrived on scene, one of which checked on the two mercenaries left in the church. The one in the sanctuary was still alive and he was handcuffed while one of the officers rendered first aid. Finally, the ambulances and medics arrived and scooped up all three victims and raced them off to the trauma center.

John made his way back up to the altar and rolled the plans back up. Stuffing them back in the yellow mailing tube, he then shoved the tube into the backpack he had carried into the church, then walked back down the aisle and found Adam sitting on the steps by the front door.

"That was the scariest fuckin' ten minutes of my life." Adam said as John sat down next to him.

"Amazing how fast that shit goes down." John replied. "You OK?"

"Yeah…" Adam replied at first. Pausing, he then said, "No..No, I'm really not OK. You know, not too long ago I was telling Steve how this job can be really boring and I was hoping for a little excitement. He tried to tell me that boring is a good thing. I didn't believe him."

"What do you think now?" John asked.

"This wasn't excitement. This was pure fucking terror. I never want to have to draw my gun again. I'll take boring every day."

"Smart choice." John said. Looking at how completely drained Adam looked, John continued, "Unfortunately, we are nowhere near done yet."

"What do you mean?" Adam asked.

"Now the real fun begins." John said. "We were just involved in an international incident. Think about it Adam. We were just attacked by Agents of the Democratic People's Republic of Korea. We killed one of them, and sent another to the hospital. This was not just some shoot-out with drug dealers or armed felons. There are gonna be multiple Federal agencies swarming all over this place. And if you think that's bad, wait till you see how crazy the media attention is gonna get."

"Oh fuck. I didn't even think of that." Adam said.

"I figured as much. You don't think about it until it has happened to you."

Adam asked, "You've been involved in stuff like this before?"

"Yeah…". John replied. "Let's just say despite my best efforts, I seem to have had a nose for trouble throughout my career."

"Yeah, I heard a bit about that. Steve and I were talking…" Adam's voice trailed off.

"It's OK Adam. I know. But listen." John began. "You have to try and keep a clear head. Despite the grief and pain, you need to stay focused. This whole thing might become political and you need to try to keep your narrative factual and consistent. Write down your notes and get with your Chief as soon as possible. He will be in the hot seat as much as you will be, but rely on him. Dealing with the political bullshit is his job."

"OK, thanks." Adam replied. "You know, I thought I was dead back there when that gun was inches from my head. I heard that guy cock the hammer... it seemed like it sounded so fucking loud. I waited for the explosion... I expected to die." Turning to face John, Adam continued. "I want to thank you for saving my life. If you had hesitated for even a second, I'm certain that Korean would have pulled the trigger killing me before turning the gun on Steve and the Captain."

"Hey, no thanks are necessary." John replied.

"No, I want you to know I'm truly grateful for what you did. I know I've been a bit of a dick toward you..."

"A bit?" John joked.

"Alright, a total dick. Basically, since day one, I never gave you the respect you deserved, and still, you sit here truly concerned about how I'm doing... giving me advice. You are a true professional. I hope you can forgive me for the way I had acted, and accept my apology with my thanks." Adam said extending his hand to John.

Taking Adam's hand, John said, "Of course Adam. You're a good cop, and a good man. Us good guys need to stick together. And on that note, I actually need a favor."

"Anything. What is it?"

"In your reporting... in your narrative... you can't say we actually found this." John said pointing to the mailing tube. "We don't know what these schematics are for, but obviously they are important enough for North Korea to risk an international incident. Couple that with the warnings that I got from my sources that authorities at multiple levels of government are compromised, and we basically don't know who we can trust. Right now, I trust you, Jake, Janine and Otto. After that, the list gets real short."

"OK. I understand." Adam said.

John said, "Until we know the complete picture, and we expose and catch these bad actors, we play this part close to the vest."

"Gotcha."

Slapping Adam on the shoulder as he stood up. John said, "We got this, Adam. Now C'mon, let's head over to the hospital and check on our guys."

CHAPTER 18

**Robert Wood Johnson University Hospital
New Brunswick, New Jersey
Present Day**

THE SURGICAL WAITING room at Robert Wood Johnson University Hospital had six times the number of people in it than seats, as off duty officers filled the room and spilled out into the hallway. News had already spread amongst the ranks that Steve Tortorice had died from his wounds, and now everyone was awaiting word on Captain Benjamin.

Adam had dropped John off at the hospital, and since there was no news on Benjamin's condition, returned to headquarters to report in and help coordinate the search for the North Koreans. Departments from all over Middlesex and Monmouth counties, along with the State Police were assisting in the search. Adam and Sayreville Chief of Police Dempsey spoke to SAC Gonzalez who was on her way down along with the HRT team to assist in the search. While on the phone with Adam, Gonzalez also mentioned that her agents had not been able to catch up with the three agents Bauer had sent up from Washington, but she was not overly concerned about them being able to cause much trouble.

Janine and Otto caught a ride up to the hospital with one of the officers and headed straight up to the waiting room to see John. Finding him standing in the doorway of the waiting room, Janine ran to John, hugging him. "I was so scared. We were stuck in that stupid TV room and we could see by all the activity that something was happening, but we had no idea what it was. Then you could hear the cops saying that people were shot… It wasn't until Adam came back and told us what happened… Oh John, I'm so sorry." Janine burst into tears and hugged him again.

Letting John go, Janine took a step back and Otto came over and patted John on the shoulder.

"No plans after contact with the enemy." Otto said in German.

Shaking his head and patting Otto's shoulder in response, John said, "You called that one, Opa."

Looking down the hall, John saw a doctor in scrubs walking directly toward the waiting room. Making eye contact, John could instantly tell this doctor was on his way to give everyone an update. Stepping back inside the crowded waiting room, John loudly announced, "Hey everyone… The doctor is here."

All eyes focused on the physician as he entered the room.

"I'm Doctor Daniel Morgenstern. I'm chief of Thoracic Surgery here at the hospital, and I operated on Captain Benjamin. Let me begin by saying the Captain is out of surgery and is resting comfortably. He is in serious but stable condition and I expect he will remain in recovery for a bit longer. The surgery went well with minimal complications. The damage to the Captain's left lung from both the bullet and bone fragments caused considerable damage and we were forced to remove the lung. However, his right lung was undamaged and looks to be in good shape. I expect the Captain to be able to go home in about a week."

The surgeon was barraged by questions from the packed room, and he held out his hand to quiet everyone down. "OK, OK… I understand you are all concerned and have questions." Looking around the room, he spotted a woman sitting in the corner with two young adults crowded around her. "Right now, I would like to take Captain Benjamin's family to my office and speak to them privately. I will send my associate, Doctor Carter in to answer your questions in a little bit."

As the doctor began escorting Benjamin's family out of the room, John grabbed his arm quickly and asked, "Hey Doc. What about the other man?"

Unsure who John was referring to, the doctor replied. "I'm sorry. Both the detective and the Asian man didn't make it."

"Thank you doctor." John replied, clearly shaken.

Seeing that John was upset, Janine put her hand on his shoulder and said, "Oh John. I'm so sorry. I thought you knew Detective Tortorice didn't make it."

Turning to face Janine, John replied, "I did, Janine. It was the death of the Korean that upset me. His death was by my hand."

Hearing John's response, Otto replied, "But that girl… she was bad… very bad."

"I know Otto." John replied. "And I also know that when I shot him, it was in self-defense. However, every life is sacred. The commandment reads, 'Thou shalt not kill,' not Thou shalt not kill good guys. I am pragmatic enough to know that in my line of work, I may be required to take someone's life. However, I'm also spiritual enough to deeply regret when I do."

Grabbing a nurse as they walked past the waiting room, John asked if there was a chapel or somewhere he could go and pray. The nurse directed him and Janine to the chapel, and after grabbing one of the other detectives and letting him know where they were going, John, Janine and Otto headed to the elevator to go to the chapel.

Once in the chapel, John went to one of the front pews, genuflected then entered the pew. Kneeling down, he folded his hands and bowed his head and began his prayers. Janine sat in the adjacent pew with Otto until John finished his prayers, and sat back on the seat.

"You OK?" She asked.

"Yeah. I said a prayer for the man's soul, and asked for forgiveness." John said.

"Do you want to stay here a bit or go back upstairs?" Janine asked.

"I'd like to stay here for a bit if you don't mind. I still want to say some prayers for Jake, and need to refocus. Being here helps me with both."

Looking at the mailing tube sitting next to John, Janine asked, "Is that it? Is that what this is all about?… the Big Light?"

Answering before John, Otto said, "Ja, Ja. Das ist Der Grosse Licht."

"What is it?" Janine asked.

Opening the tube, John pulled out the papers and handed them to Janine. "This is what is in the tube. It looks like some kind of blueprints, plans and formulas. There's a bunch of notes written in old style German, and then formulas and stuff that I also don't understand. You think you could decipher some if it?"

"Let me take a look." Janine replied.

Taking the papers, Janine spread them out on the pew seat while John went back to his prayers. Almost immediately, Janine said, "This looks like a blueprint to manufacture graphene ion batteries, and some accompanying plans and blueprints for a machine that can mass produce graphene."

"What is graphene and is that significant?" John asked.

"Graphene is basically graphite, but it is like only one molecule thick. Because of its structure, it has the ability to absorb, store and then discharge electrical current much more efficiently than even our present lithium ion batteries. The problem with making graphene was there was no easy cost-effective way of mass producing it. In fact, I think even today, there are only one or two companies that have found ways to do this, so being able to do this back in the 1940s would have been very significant."

"So I can see why Aryphon and the North Koreans would want this. It could be worth billions." John said.

Sorting through the papers, Janine said, "There's some other stuff here too. Let me look through the rest of this stuff and see if there is anything more."

John looked up at Otto standing over his granddaughter nodding his head like a bobblehead with a grin from ear to ear. "Ja, ja… more… more." he kept repeating under his breath.

John was about to return to his prayers when Janine exclaimed, "HOLY SHIT!"

With his head snapping around, John asked, "What?…"

"These other papers… these formulas…" Janine began. "No,… this can't be right."

"What is it?" John asked with growing concern, as he saw Otto's head bobbing even faster.

Janine said, "Look John, I have a Masters in Chemistry, but I'm just a high school teacher. We would have to get this validated by some experts…"

"What… What is it?" John implored.

"John, I think these are plans and formulas to create cold fusion."

Otto was nearly jumping up and down in the pew behind his granddaughter, relieved to finally be free of the secret he had kept for three quarters of a century. Hugging Janine, Otto said, "Father Wagner, his other girl, she found it."

"You're saying your father's brother invented it?" Janine translated.

"Ja, ja. Und er sagte, Father Wagner, watch your fingers."

"And the brother told your father to be careful with it… he wanted him to hide it?" Janine asked.

"Ja, ja."

"To keep it from the Nazis". John said.

"Ja, ja." Otto began. "Father Wagner wanted to go to the Father and the Son and the Holy Ghost… To watch your fingers…but the bad ones there."

Janine attempted to translate, saying, "He wanted to hide the plans in the church, but the Nazis were there?"

"No, no…" replied Otto.

"Not a church…" John said. "… A monastery. He wanted to hide the plans in a monastery, but the Nazis were already there waiting for him."

"BINGO." Otto shouted.

"That's why they were tearing up the monasteries. They were looking for these plans. But Wagner must have somehow learned it wasn't safe to go to the monastery, so you escaped and came to America." John said to Otto.

"Ja, ja. We meet…" Otto saluted.. "Captain America. He get us to here."

Janine said, "My dad would tell us stories about how Opa and Great Grandfather escaped over the Alps, and came to America with the help of an American Colonel."

"So now this is all starting to make sense." John began. "Aryphon must have access to archived Nazi records and learned about your great uncle's discovery. The records must have indicated he gave the plans to your great grandfather, and they chased him first to a monastery, and then later to America. Since the archives don't specify which monastery, Aryphon started searching monasteries before somehow learning the plans were here. Once here, they started searching in the homes of people with the last name of Wagner."

"The only part that doesn't make sense is how did the North Koreans get involved, and how did they make the leap from Wagner to Grasslicked?" Janine asked.

"I have a few ideas about both of those, but I want to confirm some things before I speculate." John said. "The important thing right now is that if these plans are what you say they are, there is no way Aryphon or North Korea can get their hands on them."

"So what do we do?" Janine asked.

John was about to answer when the door to the chapel opened and Captain Horvath entered. Walking up to John, he said, "Detective Johnson said you guys came down here."

"What can I do for you Captain?" John asked a bit apprehensively.

"We got a bit of a problem upstairs. Can I speak to you privately?" Horvath said.

"Sure." John said as he shuffled out of the pew. Walking with Horvath to the back of the chapel, he asked, "What's up?"

Speaking in hushed tones, Horvath said, "Our three favorite FBI agents just showed up in the waiting room asking for you. They changed their approach a bit however. Now, instead of wanting you for questioning, they say they are here as part of the task force assisting us in our search for the perps who shot up the church, and needed to ask you some questions about what went down in the church, what you may have found there… stuff like that."

"That's just great." John said.

"Wait, that aint even the worst part." Horvath began. "They showed up with a bunch of muscle… ex-military looking types. It looked like they were fanning out and standing watch for when you come back up."

"You're just chock full of good news. They are probably the Aryphon team. They are looking for the same thing as the North Koreans. You think they got the exits covered too?" John asked.

"I'll bet they got the main exits covered, but this place is a maze. There are lots of ways in and out of here."

"OK, well I still don't want to chat with these guys, so we need to get out of here. Do you know if Adam Levy is still at Sayreville headquarters?"

"I think so, why?" Horvath asked.

"I have an idea." John replied. "I'm gonna give him a call. In the interim, if you have someone here that could run over to Piscataway and pick up a car and bring it here. It would be very helpful."

"I'll see what I can do." Horvath said.

John grabbed the keys to Janine's car and handed them to Horvath, then called Adam. He asked Adam to drive to the hospital, but actually meet him outside the Clinical Academic Building on Paterson Street. He had also directed Horvath to have his people bring Janine's car there as well.

After a brief wait, John gathered up Janine, Otto and the plans and led them down to the foot bridge that spanned French Street between the hospital and the Academic Building. Taking the foot bridge across, they then descended the stairs and out the rear doors on to Paterson Street. Finding Adam, standing near Janine's car, they made their way over to him.

"Thanks for getting here so fast." John said.

"Not a problem." Adam said. "I wanted to get back over here anyway, and the Chief has things under control back at headquarters. So you said you have a plan and need some help."

John laid out his plan to Adam, Janine and Otto. Pulling the mailing tube out of his backpack, John opened it and removed all the documents. He then handed the empty tube to Adam.

John said, "I need you to take this tube and Otto back to the waiting room. Let people see you have it, but *do not* let the FBI or anyone else see that it's empty. Janine and I are going to get the hell out of here with the real plans. Let everyone know that you found us in the chapel, and Janine and I needed to hit the bathroom before coming back up to the room. That will give us plenty of head start before the start looking. Once the FBI and some of the Aryphon goons they brought with them clear out, I need you to take Otto here with you wherever you go. I need for you to protect him for a few days."

Otto began to protest, but John cut him off saying, "Otto, please work with me on this. Janine and I need to be able to move quickly, and you don't do that as well as you used to. I also need you to be safe and right now there are only a handful of people I trust. Adam is one of them. We need to disappear with the Big Light for a few days as I sort out our next moves."

Janine added, "Please Opa. Adam is a good guy. You'll be safe with him and I will be fine with John."

"Watch your fingers." Otto said giving Janine a big hug.

"I'm going to buy a few new burner phones. I'll call you with one of the new ones as soon as I get it so you have the number." John said.

Shaking John's hand, Adam wished him and Janine luck and escorted Otto back into the Academic Building for their return to the hospital. John and Janine got into her car and started the engine.

"I asked Captain Horvath to have his men check the car for bugs and tracking devices. He texted me that they found a magnetic tracking device stuck underneath the back bumper. His guys removed it and stuck it to a nearby lamp post in the parking lot. John said.

"I guess it's a good thing we switched out cars when we did." Janine said. "So what do we do now?"

"We head north for a bit to throw off the scent, then somewhere in Union county, we'll use a credit card to buy the burner phones. Then we get back on the northbound Parkway until I see a place to cross over to the southbound lanes." Talking with his hands to illustrate directional change, John concluded. "Then we bang a U-turn and head south."

"What's our ultimate destination?" Janine asked.

"I want to put a few hours between ourselves and those Aryphon folks. I figure we can start looking for an out of the way place to hide once we are south of Atlantic City."

"Sounds good to me." Janine said.

Two and a half hours later they were checking in to a small bayside motel in Somers Point. Paying with cash, John gave the young front desk clerk his most intimidating look when the young man asked for his ID. After staring the clerk down for several seconds, John was finally handed the key.

"This isn't too bad for a flea-bag, out of the way motel." Janine said upon entering the room.

"It looks fairly clean." John agreed, surveying the room.

Sitting on the bed and bouncing up and down a few times, Janine stated, "The beds don't seem too bad either."

"I know we don't have any of our stuff. We can run out in a bit to get some toiletries and some fresh clothes. I thought I saw a Walmart on our way in here." John said. "I just need to make a few phone calls first."

"OK, no problem." Janine replied.

Pulling out his first burner phone, John called Tony.

"I was starting to get worried when I hadn't heard from you in a few days." John's second in command said.

"Things have been absolutely hectic here. I have been striking out every way I turn. I need to find this Big Light before I talk to Sentille."

"From what we are hearing here, Sentille is pissed." Tony said. "Word is, Pinochinio and Sentille are looking for ways to bring you up on criminal charges. No one thinks they can actually do that, but you are in some pretty deep shit when you get back."

"Thanks for the heads up. They still got you doin' shitty details on the overnight shift?" John asked.

"Nah. I'll be one of the afternoon supervisors in patrol starting on Monday. Today and tomorrow are my days off, and I'm taking some vacation time to be off with the kids this weekend."

"That sounds nice." John replied. "Give my love to Lora. We should get dinner once I get back."

"Sounds good… Boss, I'm sorry I can't be more help but…Pinochinio… he…"

"Tony, don't worry about it. Everything will work out fine in the end. You just gotta have faith."

"OK." Tony said.

"Alright, well, I just wanted to check in. I'll call when I finally find this thing."

"Sounds good. Be careful boss." Tony said before hanging up the phone.

Pressing the 'end' button himself, John dug the piece of paper with the messages he had gotten that morning from his pants pocket. Shaking his head, John thought about how different things were, and all that had happened since just this morning. Dialing the phone, John waited three rings before a male voice answered, "Saint Anthony's rectory. Father Campbell speaking. How may I help you?"

"Good evening Father. This is Director General Nowalski. Is Cardinal Sentille there?"

John was put on hold for a few minutes before the angry voice of Cardinal Sentille filled John's ear. "Director General Nowalski. May I ask where you are?"

"I am in New Jersey, but beyond that, I am not at liberty to say." John replied.

"What do you mean you are not at liberty to say?" Sentille hissed. "Do you recognize that I had to come all the way over here in order to find you and return you to Rome. There you will face charges of insubordination, dereliction of duty, and failing to comply with a direct order. I am looking for ways to bring criminal charges against you as well for your recent behavior."

"So I have heard." John replied.

"So you have heard?… Sentille nearly screamed into the phone. "What do you mean by that?"

"I mean, Your Eminence, that I recently learned that you and Inspector General Pinochinio are looking to hang me out to dry. What you fail to understand is, I have a duty-bound mandate to apprehend the people responsible for murdering our people. To make that happen, I needed to track down what they were looking for, and I have done that. I've found the Big Light."

"You found it?" Sentille asked.

"That is correct."

"And does it tie everything together. Will you be able to solve this case now that you found this religious relic?"

"It is not a religious relic. They are schematics for a machine that can mass produce something called graphene. Graphene can be used instead of lithium in things like cell phone and electric car batteries. As for using it to solve this case, it will help bring this case to a conclusion but I need a little more time."

"Time is a luxury you do not have." Sentille replied. "You will accompany me back to Rome immediately. Once there, we can sort out whether this Big Light you were so obsessed with finding will have any bearing on whether you will be brought up on the charges I have outlined. In the meantime, leave this case to the local authorities. It is their problem now. I will have the St. Anthony's staff book us a flight home for tomorrow."

"I'm sorry Your Eminence. Tomorrow doesn't work for me. How about we look at returning after I apprehend these people. I have already told you, that is what I came here to do and I will not leave until I do it."

"Mr. Nowalski, I will not stand for this insolent behavior." The Cardinal said. "You will speak to me with the respect I deserve. I am a Prince of the Church and you will show me the respect due my office."

"Cardinal Sentille, I show respect to the person, not the office. Your conniving, back-stabbing, petty political behavior barely deserves acknowledgement of your existence, let alone my respect. And since we are setting the record straight, I am not returning to Rome until after I wrap up this case. For one, all the people who were killed deserve justice, and secondly, the Church is irrevocably involved in this. Removing me from it now only guarantees that the Church, and particularly, the Vatican will be seen globally in a very negative light. You pull me out now and I can make sure of that. Your only hope, Mario…" John said, using the Cardinal's first name, "Is that I bring these people to justice and allow the Curia to take the credit for it."

Cardinal Sentille remained silent on the other end of the phone for a long moment before saying, "How will you let the Curia take the credit, and are you close to closing this case?"

"Fairly close." John responded. "And once this case is closed, I will turn over the schematics to you. If this machine works, it could be worth a sizeable amount. You could be the hero that brought in a new significant revenue stream to a Church hurting for funds.

"And you actually have this thing… this Big Light? You actually found it?"

"Yup. I'm looking at it right now." John said.

Pausing to consider his options, the Cardinal finally replied. "I will need you to keep me informed on your progress. And you must get this wrapped up in short order. The Holy Father is very interested in seeing this entire matter come to an end."

"I'll try." John responded, then after a moment said, "And please tell His Holiness that the only way this will end is with the perpetrators behind bars. This does not just go away out of expedience. I'll be in touch."

Kim Joo-Won stood in the shadows of the Robert Wood Johnson University Hospital employee parking lot. Having been dropped off by his men, Kim carried a small backpack and wore a dark tee shirt and black parachute pants, allowing him to blend in to the shadows. After nearly an hour wait, a relatively young Asian doctor emerged from the stairwell carrying a backpack, and headed to his car.

Stepping out between two SUVs as the doctor passed, Kim followed the man at a discrete distance so as to not arouse his suspicion. Upon reaching his Nissan Maxima, the doctor removed his key fob and unlocked the door and popped the trunk. Dropping his backpack into the nearly empty trunk, the doctor closed the hatch and moved toward the driver side door.

Seeing the doctor move toward the car door, Kim rapidly closed the distance, and upon reaching the rear of the car, called out, "Excuse me, doctor…"

Looking up from the open car door, the doctor asked, "Yes, can I help you?"

Before the doctor could even take another breath, Kim was directly in front of the man with the barrel of his silence hand gun angled upward and pressed into the solar plexus of the doctor. Squeezing the trigger twice, the FN Baby Browning fired two hollow point bullets into the doctor's chest, shredding the ventricles of his heart and tearing apart his lungs.

Making sure no one was around, the North Korean operative collected the doctor's key fob and reopened the trunk. Dragging the dead doctor to the rear of the car, he dropped the body into the trunk, grabbing the doctor's wallet, ID and backpack before closing the trunk. Peeling off his tee shirt, Kim pulled a green scrub top out of his backpack, then removed the parachute pants that covered the matching scrub bottoms. Grabbing a fanny pack from the backpack, he stored the wallet, keys and gun in the small bag, then searched the doctor's backpack for anything else that might be useful before tossing it and his bag into the back seat.

Throwing a stethoscope from the doctor's bag around his neck, he attached the ID to his scrub top and headed for the parking deck staircase. Descending to the main floor, Kim used the doctor's ID to gain entrance through the employee entrance and headed up to the surgical waiting room. Impersonating Dr. Michael Park, Kim was able to remain close enough to the waiting room to begin gathering the information he needed.

John ended his call with Sentille and entered another number in the next burner phone. After the third ring the male voice answered, "Ja, hier ist Cardinal Dietrich."

"Your Eminence, it's John Nowalski. I needed to lose my phone so they couldn't track me through it." John said explaining the strange number appearing on the Cardinal's caller ID.

"John, where are you? Cardinal Sentille is looking for you. He has already suspended you without pay and is pressuring me to contact the American State Department to have you listed as a fugitive from Vatican justice."

"I know most of that. I already spoke to Sentille. He is very upset with me."

"That is an understatement my son. Where are you?" The prelate asked again.

Janine Wagner and I are up in Wantage New Jersey. We are staying in a cabin off the grid. In fact, I had to drive five miles away from the cabin just to get cell reception to make this call." John lied.

"So, did you find it?… the Big Light… Did you find it?"

John replied, "I got it your Eminence. It's a bunch of blueprints and plans for some kind of machine. I was able to make out the word graphene, so I am assuming it's a way to manufacture something called graphene."

"Really? Dietrich said. "I thought you said it was some kind of religious relic."

"That was what I originally thought it would be since they were looking in monasteries. But no, it's blueprints for a machine that makes this graphene."

"And you have those plans right now?" Dietrich asked.

"I found it, but it is being kept at the Sayreville Police Headquarters for safe keeping." John replied.

"Good idea. So, what are your plans?"

"I'm going to stay off the grid for a few days… let things cool off a bit, then I'll come back down to Sayreville. I don't know if this graphene stuff is worth anything, but I assume it is since those North Korean's are willing to kill so many people for it. These plans rightfully belong to the Wagner family. They might be in for a windfall."

"You know John, that is not entirely true." Dietrich said.

"What do you mean?" John asked.

"Georg Wagner was really not a Lutheran pastor. He

was actually a Roman Catholic priest. The plans were originally developed by his brother, Peter Wagner. When Peter gave the plans to his brother Georg, in essence he was giving the plans to the Church."

"How do you know all this?" John asked.

"I had some people do some additional research in the Vatican archives. I was trying to lend you some assistance since I knew that Sentille would eventually double cross you and… what do they say in America?… Throw you under the bus."

"I see, your Eminence. Well thank you for looking out for me. You have always been a good friend. But back to the plans… So, you are saying that they rightfully belong to the Church."

"Exactly. So once things calm down and you can catch these North Koreans, you should actually turn the plans over to the Church. Doing so may actually be the only way for you to save your job.

Pausing for a moment as if he was thinking, John then said, "Thank you again, Your Eminence. That's a good idea. I can probably be back at the Vatican in about two weeks. I can give the plans to Sentille then."

Dietrich paused for a moment then said, "Or you could give them to me. I wouldn't want Sentille and Pinochinio to steal the credit you deserve for all your hard work."

"Good point Excellency."

"We can figure it out after you return. Until then, please stay safe, my son."

"Thank you, Excellency. I'll see you soon."

Hanging up the phone, John turned to a very confused looking Janine and said, "Fried shrimp or shrimp scampi?"

"What?" Janine replied.

"We are down the shore." John said, using the New Jersey vernacular for visiting a beachfront town. "There has to be a decent seafood restaurant somewhere nearby, and I'm really feeling shrimp."

"Then you want to go to dinner?" Janine asked.

"Yeah. I thought we could find a place to eat, then hit that Walmart for the stuff we need."

"That sounds OK." Janine said. "But, could I ask you a question first?"

"Sure." John said.

"I wasn't eavesdropping, but I couldn't help overhearing the conversations you just had. You just spoke to three people and basically told them three different things."

"Yup." John said. "One of the things I needed to figure out was how did our bad actors figure out that the Big Light was here, in New Jersey. I stumbled on it almost by accident, but the likelihood that these other guys stumbled on it the same way is nearly statistically impossible. To me, that means they are stealing intel. The three most likely places for leaks would be, one, tapping into my conversations with Tony, or two, getting the information from either Cardinal Sentille or Dietrich. That's why I gave each of them different stories. Depending on what the bad guys next move is will tell me where the leak is coming from."

"Ahhh.. Now I see the method to your supposed madness. I was wondering why did that, especially when you misled your guy in Rome."

"I hated to do that to Tony, but if his phone is bugged, I

needed to know." John said. "I have one more quick phone call to make and then maybe we could get something to eat." Pulling out a new phone, John looked up a number from the paper he was carrying and dialed.

"Shalom Ari. How are things on the other side of the world."

"Good my friend. I hear you had a bit of a dust up with some of our North Korean friends."

"How did you?… Never mind… Silly question." John said. "I temporarily forgot who I was talking to. Hey listen, I need a favor. I believe I found one of those heads on the Hydra we spoke about, but I'm encountering a significant amount of political headwind."

"That's very interesting. Tell me what you need my friend." Ari replied.

Five minutes later, John hung up the phone said to Janine, "Now that this is all done, how about we go get something to eat? I'm starving."

John and Janine found a local seafood eatery within ten minutes, and were seated right away. After a leisurely meal with a carafe of wine, they headed to the store to grab some clothing and essentials. After grabbing the necessary toiletries, a few casual tops, some sweatpants and another pair of jeans each, they headed to the checkout and John paid with cash. Performing a quick mental calculation on their anticipated expenses versus what remained in his wallet, John figured they had about three days-worth of cash remaining. Barring a dramatic change in their situation, he hoped at the very least to be back in Sayreville by then.

"You want any ice cream or something before we head

back to the hotel? John asked. "I forgot to buy, like snacks or something to munch on while we were in the store."

"I'm good" Janine replied. "I'm kinda spent and would just as soon go back and go to bed. Maybe we could put the TV on if you want and just watch from bed, but I really don't want to eat anything else."

"Sounds like a plan to me." John said.

Arriving back at the hotel, John allowed Janine to use the bathroom first while he flipped through the channels on the TV. Settling on a sitcom in syndication, John went in to use the bathroom after Janine emerged in one of the new tee shirts and sweats they had just bought. Climbing into the bed closest to the bathroom, Janine settled in while John headed into the bathroom. When he emerged, he was wearing the same color tee shirt and sweats that Janine wore.

"Hey look… Mommy got us matching PJs. We're twinsises." Janine joked.

"Ha… I didn't even notice we had grabbed the same color stuff." John observed. "I wonder if the rest of our outfits are color coordinated too."

"You know… Our mom used to dress Anna and I in matching outfits all the time when we were little. I don't know who hated it more, me or her."

"I'm sure it was very cute." John said.

"Yeah…" Janine said casually as she stared off into space, her brain going somewhere else. "It's crazy. I still can't believe she is gone. I mean, it's been a few days and with all the craziness, I've pushed her death to the back of my brain. I haven't processed it, and I know I certainly haven't allowed myself to grieve."

"The time will come, and I'm sure it will hit you." John said as he climbed into the second bed. "And, my advice to you is that when that happens, let it happen. Let it come out and allow yourself to go through the grieving process. If you want me to, I can be there for you and help you through it."

"I will, and thank you John. I really appreciate everything you are doing. I mean, here you are looking out for me and Opa, and like… you were shot at this morning. How are you able to compartmentalize? I mean, if I was shot at I would be a mess for days."

"I don't know Janine. Training… Experience… Maybe I just know I need to shift my focus from what happened to me in the past with what needs to be done going forward. Learning from the past is good. Dwelling on it is not."

"So if we are looking to the future, what is our plan?" Janine asked.

"We have a leak somewhere that could ultimately mess up any plans we put together. I laid out some bait tonight and hopefully, depending on what happens next, we can identify where that leak is coming from. My plan is to sit tight for a few days and see if they play their hand. Once we know where the leak is, we can use that to our advantage by feeding them the information that sets them up to take 'em down."

"Then we may be here for a few days." Janine said.

"Yeah, exactly. I will check in with Adam every day, and he has our number to reach out if anything changes on his end. If we have no movement by the end of the weekend, we can head back and go to Plan B, but I have a feeling we won't have to wait that long for them to do something that tips their hand."

Stifling a yawn, John said, "The one constant that is part of Plans A, B and C is we should try to get some sleep. It's been a busy day, and I'm pretty beat."

Shutting off the light, as John grabbed the TV remote, Janine said, "Good Night John. Thank you for everything."

"Good night Janine. And no thanks are necessary."

"Excellency, I am assuming this must be important since you are calling at this late hour." Hermann Alvarez said.

I spoke with John Nowalski a little while ago and I believe he is prepared to hand over the Big Light to me."

"Really? How did you manage that? Alvarez asked.

"We talked about his plans for catching the North Koreans, and about his career and his future. While he may be remarkable at investigating crimes, when it comes to the political game, he is clueless. I was able to manipulate him into believing it would be in his best interest to give the plans to me." The Cardinal replied.

"So he confirmed he has the plans?" Alvarez asked.

"He claims he has found them, but they are at the police headquarters for safe keeping."

"And when did he say he would be turning the plans over to you? Alvarez asked.

"Once he captures the North Koreans and is ready to go back to Rome, he would willingly give me the plans."

"Well, Your Eminence. I must commend you on getting that accomplished, but we cannot wait that long. With that North Korean team still in play, we must take other action to secure our prize. I am speaking to von Alpiner shortly about how to get the Big Light within the next couple of days. Your new information is both timely and helpful. Now that we know where the Big Light is, we can plan accordingly. If our plan fails, we can always use your work as a back-up. I do not feel it is prudent to wait for Inspector Nowalski to call the shots on when to give us what is rightfully ours." Alvarez said.

"Very well, Herr Chairman. We must do what you believe is best. Do you need anything additional from me at this time?"

"Just continue what you are doing, and be there to assist as needed."

"Ja wohl, Herr Chairman." The Cardinal replied.

CHAPTER 19

**Jersey Shore
Somers Point, New Jersey
Present Day**

JOHN AND JANINE rose early the next morning and started what they both hoped would be a less manic day. While Janine showered, John touched base with Adam, getting the update on what was going on back up north. Otto and Adam both spent the night in Headquarters sleeping on cots, much to the chagrin of Adam who had to listen to Otto's incessant snoring. Captain Benjamin had a restful night without incident. He was taken off the ventilator early in the morning and had been doing well with just supplemental oxygen.

SAC Gonzalez arrived late in the evening and met with Adam and Chief Dempsey. Both were unhappy that despite a very serious effort by multiple law enforcement agencies, the Koreans had disappeared without a trace. They discussed next steps in the investigation and drafted a joint press release. A number of regional news outlets had already picked up the story and were clamoring for additional details. When the connection to the murders in the Austrian monasteries was made, Gonzalez was certain the story would go national. Finally, Gonzalez and her team left and promised to return first thing in the morning to pick up where they had left off.

John explained his strategy to Adam and told Adam to contact him immediately if either the Koreans or the Aryphon people made any kind of a move. He asked about the FBI guys from Washington and Adam advised that they rapidly made themselves scarce right before Gonzalez arrived. With Janine finally out of the bathroom, he asked Adam if he could put Otto on the phone so she could speak to her grandfather.

John headed into the bathroom himself after handing the phone to Janine and proceeded through his normal morning hygiene rituals. Finishing up around the same time as Janine hung up with Otto, John asked if she had any preferences for breakfast. Saying she really felt like waffles and syrup, John searched on his phone for a local place that served a broad variety of breakfast fare.

Finishing up breakfast, John asked, "I saw a place back down the road that rents kayaks. Any interest in renting one?

"You think we'd be able to?" Janine asked.

"I don't see why not, unless they need to run a credit card for a security deposit."

Heading to the kayak rental facility, John was able to convince the proprietor not to require his credit card when he showed his INTERPOL badge and ID. The store owner assumed that the likelihood of a cop stealing his boats was relatively low.

Paddling out into the Drag Channel, John and Janine navigated under the Garden State Parkway bridge and circumnavigated Drag Island before heading out into Great Egg Harbor. Paddling with the wind and current, they quickly crossed Great Egg Harbor and viewed the bay front houses in Ocean City. Making sure to not head too close to the inlet and be swept out by the outgoing tide, they beached the kayaks on the bay side of the barrier island and waited for the tide to change.

With the change of tide, the pair paddled back to their starting point and returned the boats. Paying in cash, John collected his badge and ID and returned to the car.

"You up for a bit more shore fun?" He asked Janine.

"I'm tired, but that was the most fun I've had in weeks. What else do you have in mind? She replied.

"Get in. I'll show you."

Navigating by dead reckoning, John headed toward the Ocean Drive bridge. Crossing the bridge, he again used just his sense of direction and pointed the car toward the beach. Once on the beach block, he headed south until they reached the beginning of the Ocean City Boardwalk. Parking the car, John led Janine up onto the Trex decking and proceeded to walk south on the Boardwalk.

"I've never been on this boardwalk before." Janine said. "I usually go to Belmar or Seaside."

"I used to go to Wildwood a lot." John replied as memories of the times spent at that seaside town with his late wife and son came flooding back. "Anything special you want to do? I'm sure they have the standard boardwalk fare."

Janine said with a smile, "Let's just see what they got here."

The couple walked along, stopping in some of the beach wear stores. They laughed as they played a round of miniature golf with Janine cheating at every opportunity. Lunch was boardwalk pizza with a funnel cake desert which John thoroughly regretted after Janine talked him into doing some of the amusement park rides. The walk back was done barefoot on the beach, along the water's edge. Now with the noises of the boardwalk replaced with the sound of crashing waves they were able to really talk.

Janine opened up about her relationship with her sister and continued to express regret about their final conversation. John told Janine a little about Kathy and Michael, his late wife and son. He shared that even twenty plus years later, they are still missed, but assured Janine that in time, the pain would be replaced with good memories. They talked about their jobs and in general, where life had taken them, and somewhere in their conversation, they began holding hands.

When they reached the music pier, they opted to head back up on to the boardwalk and catch a tram back to where they had parked. Without thinking, John put his arm around Janine as they sat on the tram and she rested her head on his shoulder. Arriving at the car, John announced, "I'm kinda hungry, but I'm not... if you know what I mean."

"Sure." Janine replied with a sly grin on her face. "It

means you're hungry, but your stomach is still not speaking to you after those funnel cakes with a Himalaya ride chaser."

"I thought my stomach was gonna file for divorce after I did that." John said with his hand on his stomach.

"Yeah, I've had that happen to me. The stomach usually gives you back your lunch in the divorce settlement but wants to keep your liver and spleen."

Laughing, John said, "I see you've been in a similar abusive relationship."

"Oh… Not just with my stomach, but with my liver as well. My liver's attorney told me that I saw that Jack Daniels character one more time, it was over."

"So then going to grab a drink and maybe some appetizers would be out of the question." John said.

"Oh, not at all." Janine exclaimed. "The attorney forbid me from seeing Jack… He didn't say anything about my new Latin friends Tito or Jose."

John found a nearby restaurant with an outdoor tiki-bar and the couple shared some drinks and appetizers. The conversation turned lighter, with Janine telling stories about some of the kids she'd taught, and John related his version of the worlds dumbest criminals. They checked in with Adam and Otto and were greeted with the news that Captain Benjamin's condition was upgraded from serious to stable and he was doing well. Other than that, there were no new developments. John promised to call in the morning and reminded Adam to reach out immediately if anything happened.

Arriving at the motel, the couple exited the car and headed toward the room. John once again found himself holding Janine's hand. Upon reaching the room, Janine stepped in front of the door blocking John's access to the lock.

Standing behind Janine and holding the key in his hand, John said, "If you could excuse me, I'll open the door."

Janine stepped backward and pivoted causing John to turn sideways to face her as he leaned in to unlock the door. With their faces only inches from each other, both of them leaned in and closed their eyes as their lips met. While only lasting several long seconds, the kiss seemed to last an eternity for John. When it finally ended, John found himself with his arms around her, still holding the key.

Clearing his throat, John said, "Let me just open this door."

Entering the room and closing the door, John and Janine embraced and kissed even more deeply and passionately than the first time. When they finally stopped, Janine disengaged herself from John's arms and said, "Let me use the rest room real quick."

Sitting on the edge of the bed, a million thoughts and questions came flooding into John's brain. *Was this just a stress release?... How much did she drink?... What about the vows I'm supposed to take?... She's so much younger than I am...Where is my future taking me?... It has been so long...*

Janine emerged from the bathroom in only a camisole and her bikini briefs. John excused himself and hurried into the bathroom. Brushing his teeth and doing a quick clean up, he left the bathroom and headed back over to the second bed. Sitting on the edge with his head hung low, he finally looked up at Janine and said, "Can we talk for a minute?"

"Sure John. What's going on?" Janine replied sitting up in the bed.

"First of all, that was the first time I kissed a woman in over twenty years."

"Well you sure have good muscle memory because I certainly couldn't tell you were out of practice." Janine said smiling.

"Really?" John asked.

"Yes John, really. That kiss was amazing."

Feeling his face flush red John said, "Well, thank you. I thought it was pretty hot too." Pausing for a moment to collect his thoughts John continued, "Janine, I really like you. You bring out feelings that I never thought I'd feel again. You are smart, resilient, beautiful, and now I also know, an amazing kisser. I find myself thinking that after this madness is all over, I would want to see if…" John paused as he decided if he could finish the sentence. "…If something more could develop between us. But my life is at a crossroads right now, and while I know I'm done hiding, there are still a lot of questions I need to answer… for myself."

Janine sat on the bed listening to John and nodding her head but not saying anything.

"And then I look at you." John continued. I mean,… you're beautiful and I'm sure you could have any guy you want. And then there is our age difference and…"

Janine cut John off saying, "John, shut up for a minute. In the short time we've known each other, did you ever wonder why I am not married yet?"

"The question did cross my mind, but I didn't really dwell on it." John said honestly.

"I'm not married yet because I haven't found the right person. I've certainly dated enough, and I get asked out all the time. I've had my share of intimate relationships too, but none of them seemed right. I mean, from the beginning, they just didn't seem right. I stuck with them because several times I told myself that I was being too picky, or I was looking to feel a spark that didn't actually exist. But then I met you, and holy shit… from that first day on my grandfather's porch I felt it,… and that kiss a few minutes ago confirmed it." Shaking her head she said, "Woo boy! And as for your age. You are mature, not old. You look like you take care of yourself so unless you go and get yourself shot or something equally as fuckin' stupid, I expect you'll be around for a while."

"Well, that's my plan anyway…" John said chuckling.

"But all that being said…" Janine continued, "I respect that this could be turning your world upside down. You were supposed to become a monk, you live an ocean away… I get all that. I also get that the last relationship you had was stolen from you. So because of all of that, how about we both make a promise to each other that we will always be honest with each other… about everything. And we will never be afraid to communicate and talk about how we feel."

"That sounds like a promise I will not have any problems keeping." John said. "And thank you for understanding."

"Of course, John. But I do have one request."

"What would that be?" John asked.

"I need you to hold me tonight. Nothing else. Just hold me."

"I think I can manage that." John replied.

Janine climbed into bed with John and rested her head on his chest as he wrapped his arms around her. Snuggling his face into her hair, John relaxed and for the first time in months, stopped thinking about work and all the problems in the world.

Kim Joo-Won had been floating around the hospital for almost twenty-four hours. He had learned, much to his actual relief, that his man had not survived surgery. Not that he wanted the man dead, but a live prisoner could potentially be made to talk. And with his team down to only himself and two others, he was somewhat limited in his options to secure the mailing tube containing the plans.

The other detective from the church was carrying the plans with him, and Kim assumed that the man felt them too important to leave anywhere. Constantly surrounded by other officers who now looked at any Asian, man or woman, as a potential suspect, Kim dismissed a frontal assault on the detective to grab the plans.

Over the course of the evening, the waiting room slowly cleared out. The Captain was moved first from recovery to the surgical intensive care unit, then by noon the next day he was moved again to a regular hospital room. Family, friends and other officers came in and out throughout the day to visit, and Kim made sure to stay nearby in order to pick up tidbits of information from the visiting officers.

He learned that an extensive manhunt was underway for him and his team, and that the FBI had brought in their paramilitary unit to engage with his team should they be found. Detective Levy was remaining at police headquarters and was helping direct the search, and several officers noted his new fixation with the yellow mailing tube.

Kim wondered where Nowalski had disappeared to, and no one was talking about him, so he dismissed the thoughts and concentrated on finding a way to gain access to Levy without a cadre of other police officers around. And as he considered his tactical situation, he realized that it may come down to another fire-fight, and in this instance, he would be outgunned. To solve this problem, he sent a message to the only asset he had that was not half a world away, Gertrude Elfmann. Instructing her to fly to New Jersey immediately and be prepared for armed conflict, Kim remembered that Elfmann had originally been trained as an assassin, and her skills could be useful.

Tired, and becoming concerned that his lack of sleep may result in him making a mistake, Kim was about to head for the parking deck and the dead doctor's car when he saw the two attendants, doctor and nurse enter Captain Benjamin's room. Approaching the sleeping Captain, the physician injected something into Benjamin's I.V., then stepped back and stood around the bed with the others for a minute.

"He should be out by now." The doctor said. "Make sure to watch his breathing, and be careful with that chest tube."

Releasing the brakes on the wheels of the bed, the two attendants began pushing Captain Benjamin's bed out the door and down the hall to a waiting elevator. Sensing something was not right, Kim emerged from the room across the hall and sprinted down the hallway calling out, "Hold the elevator please." as the doors began to close. Sticking his hand in, the doors reopened and he was greeted by four scowling faces.

Riding the elevator down to the floor above the Emergency Department, the four pushed Benjamin out of the elevator and allowed the door to close with Kim still in the elevator car before they carefully transferred Benjamin to a waiting ambulance stretcher. Kim meanwhile reached the ground floor and sprinted out the door toward the employee parking deck. Finding the doctor's car, he fired up the engine and sped out of the deck and on to the street, just in time to see the ambulance emerge from the ambulance bays.

Discretely following a vehicle at three AM when there are no other vehicles on the road put every ounce of Kim's trade-craft to the test. Luckily, the mercenary driving did not expect to be followed and was not paying much attention to his rear-view mirrors.

Kim followed the ambulance to a deserted industrial area in the nearby town of Carteret, where the ambulance pulled into an abandoned warehouse. Pulling out his cell phone, Kim contacted his team and instructed them where to meet him. He then parked the doctor's car out of sight from the warehouse and donned his black clothing before moving into the shadows to observe his quarry. When his team arrived, Kim gave them instructions to set up watch over the warehouse and dispose of the doctor's body still in the Nissan's trunk before it began to stink. He then went to the SUV to catch a few hours of sleep. Smiling, Kim thought this turn of events could present the opportunity he was looking for.

John knew something bad had happened, even before he answered the ringing phone by looking at the clock. Freeing his arm from underneath Janine, he turned over and grabbed the Trac phone, pressing the answer button as he brought the phone to his ear.

Clearing his throat, John said, "Hey Adam. What's going on?" as he continued to shake the cobwebs of sleep out of his head.

"They kidnapped Captain Benjamin." Adam said.

"They what?" John asked, unsure he heard Adam correctly.

"They fuckin' kidnapped the Captain." Adam shouted into the phone.

Sitting up in bed, John asked, "When?… and how the fuck did they manage that?"

"At three fourteen AM, security footage shows four people entering Benjamin's room, and a few minutes later, they go wheeling him down the hall, bed and all to the elevator. There was what looks like a doctor in the room across the hall that went running after them, but at three twenty-seven, the four appear in a second floor hallway, transfer the Captain on to an ambulance stretcher, then wheel him out into a stolen ambulance parked outside the ER.

"What about that doctor?" John asked.

"He got off by the ER, and just left the building. I guess he was just running to catch the elevator."

"Were you able to track the ambulance on traffic cameras?" John asked.

"We have the FBI working on that now." Adam replied. "But that's gonna take a little time. These people seemed to really know what they were doing. They disabled the Lojack in the ambulance, and had only stolen it a half hour before from the EMS substation in East Brunswick."

"Any idea which of our friends did it?" John asked.

"They didn't look Asian, but you never get good camera angles or a real clear picture from those security systems." Adam said.

Looking at the clock again, John said, "I know it's only been a little over two hours, but any demands yet?"

"No demands, but a message was called in to dispatch for me that simply said 'We'll be in touch.' The dispatcher didn't really think anything of it, and it actually came in before we even learned of the kidnapping, which was discovered a little after four this morning when a nurses aid was making her rounds."

"Boy, I'd hate to be the staff that was on duty last night." John said

"I know. And his room wasn't even that far from the nurse's station." Adam agreed.

"Alright. We have about a two hour drive back so it may take a bit, but we are on our way up." John said.

"Things might get a little crazy here, so I don't know if I can update you till you get here." Adam said

"Noted." John replied. "Everything OK with Otto?"

"The man snores like a fuckin' bear…"

"I know. Ear plugs help." John said laughing. "We'll see you in a bit."

Northbound traffic turned the normal hour and a half ride to Sayreville into a little over two hours. John stopped at a local bagel shop once in Sayreville and purchased three dozen assorted bagels along with butter and assorted flavors of cream cheese. Handing the bags to Janine he said, "Give these to someone other than Adam who appears in charge once we get there. We'll probably be asking to bend the rules today and believe it or not, this will buy us quite a bit of good will. Besides, we didn't get any breakfast ourselves and I'm hungry."

The detective squad room was a beehive of activity. SAC Gonzalez was already there with her team and it was clear that she was running the show. Walking up to her, John extended his hand and introduced himself while Janine handed over the food.

"Special Agent Gonzalez, I'm John Nowalski." John said. "And this is Janine Wagner. Her Great Uncle invented the Big Light, and she was instrumental in our finding those plans."

Shaking John, then Janine's hand, Gonzalez said, "Ms. Wagner… Director Nowalski. I'm pleased to finally meet you both. Director Nowalski, your reputation precedes you."

"I normally take that as a compliment, but from the look on your face, I feel I should be concerned."

"I actually attended one of your anti-terrorism talks in Paris a few years back. Very insightful and well presented." Gonzalez said.

"Thank you 'mam." John replied.

"And Bob Whope speaks very highly of you. I understand the two of you worked together on a few things."

Nodding his head, John responded, "Bob's a good man.

"All that being said, right now Mr. Nowalski, you are a pain in my ass."

"I don't understand…" John said in confusion.

"Putting aside the whole Bauer business, I have been fielding calls since yesterday from both the Vatican and our State Department advising me that you are no longer a law enforcement officer and if I find you, I should apprehend you and have you extradited back to Rome on charges of sedition, treason and a whole bunch of other things. Now, our friends at State often do things for political reasons rather than legal reasons, which is why they have been buggin' me. But the fact of the matter is that…"

"The U.S. does not an extradition treaty with the Vatican." John finished.

"Correct." Gonzalez said. "So they can all go pound sand as far as that's concerned. However, when it comes to extending any kind of privileges to you as a law enforcement officer, I cannot do that because you have been suspended or fired, or crucified, I don't know what they do over there."

"I can understand that, Agent Gonzalez." John said. "But I think if you check your emails, you'll find that I am still very much in good standing with INTERPOL, and you may even find another special request regarding my status as well."

Gonzalez opened up her email and scrolled through her messages, opening a few until she found another request from the State Department, this time asking that *'on behalf of the State of Israel, she extend every courtesy to Special Investigator John Nowalski.'*

"Looks like you got yourself a new gig pretty quickly." Gonzalez said to John.

"You know… It's amazing what twenty plus years of reputation and relationship building can do for a person." John said with a big grin. "So, now that we have all that bullshit behind us, can we get down to business? Where do things stand?"

"At around three this morning, a team of people abducted Captain Benjamin, transferred him to a stolen Advanced Life Support ambulance and drove off with him." Agent Gonzalez began. "We are still analyzing the surveillance tapes from the hospital, and trying to track the ambulance through traffic cameras, but as of right now, we have no leads as to who the perpetrators are, or where they may have taken him. The Sayreville PD dispatcher received a message at around four-thirty AM for Detective Levy saying they would be in touch. Other than that, there has been no other communication and…"

Adam was sitting at his desk and began waving to Agent Gonzalez and the rest of the people in the squad room.

"Hey. I got something." Adam shouted. As the squad room went silent, FBI, State and Sayreville police officers began approaching Adam's desk.

"I just received an email with a bunch of instructions and their demands. They want the schematics and are look-ing to make the exchange tonight at the fair."

"An exchange?" Gonzalez asked. "That seems odd. Why not a dead drop?"

"I don't know and it doesn't say." Adam replied. "The instructions say to wear some specific clothing and bring the plans to the fair by seven PM. I am to go to the cotton candy trailer and follow the directions I will find behind the trailer's spare tire. Of course it says I should come alone."

"Morgan, Jones…"Gonzalez snapped. "Head over to the fairgrounds now. See if there is anything behind the tire and if not, stake out the area and watch for someone delivering the instructions." Turning next to Adam, Gonzalez said, "Do you actually have these plans… The ones they are looking for?"

Glancing quickly at John and catching the slight nod he gave, Adam replied, "Yeah. We got them from the church."

Looking around the room, Gonzalez said, "OK people… We have all day to plan this and get it right so there should be no problems getting the Captain back and catching these guys." Turning to John, she continued, "Looks like the script got a little flipped but your original concept is still holding true. We will use the plans to flush these people out and grab them when they make the exchange." Addressing the agents and officers in the room she concluded, "Meet with your teams and I want evaluations and proposals to me in two hours. That should give us plenty of time to determine how we are going to do this and get everything set up before seven. Let's get to work."

John walked over to Adam and said, "I am not giving up these plans." Tapping the tube sticking out of his backpack he said, "In fact, they are not leaving my side till this thing is over."

"I'm sure they are going to examine them before they take me to Benjamin." Adam replied. "I can't just go in there with an empty tube."

"You won't." John said. "I have an idea. Can you get me on a computer…" Then turning to Janine he said, "And I'll need your help too."

An hour later John was standing beside the printer as the document he had downloaded off the internet printed out. Gathering up the pages, he and Janine left the building for the local printer John had spoken to a few minutes earlier.

Returning to headquarters at noon, John and Janine walked in as Gonzalez was starting up the briefing.

"Nice of you to rejoin us." Gonzalez said to John.

"Agent Gonzalez, you have already said that I am not here in any official capacity, and I've been involved in enough of these to know that this is your show. Even if I disagree one hundred percent with how you want to run this op, you are gonna disregard my input so I figured I'd put my time to better use." John said waving around the papers in his hand.

"And what is that?" Gonzalez asked.

"These are what we are going to exchange for the Captain." John said. "The Big Light… the real, Big Light is way too important and dangerous to risk letting it fall into the Nazis or North Korean's hands. I downloaded old schematics I found online from Nazi Germany, and Janine here added some chemistry notations in German to them. Then we went to a local printer and had him print them up and help us make the paper look old. I highly doubt anyone examining these at the fair tonight will have a Ph.D. in chemistry or physics, so as long as they look official, we should be fine."

"Ok. But bring the originals with you tonight just in case we need to go to a Plan B." Gonzalez said. "And just so we are clear, you are one hundred percent correct about one thing. You will be on site as an observer only. You will not be actively participating in the op, and Ms. Wagner, you will remain here at headquarters where it is safe. Are we clear?"

"As I said… Even if I disagree, this is your op so I know it's not worth arguing about. So, what's the plan?"

Agent Gonzalez proceeded to lay out her expectations for how the operation would go. The agents she had sent to the fairgrounds confirmed that the first set of instructions were already taped to the back of the cotton candy stand. Gonzalez anticipated that Adam would be directed to multiple locations so that the kidnappers could verify that he was in fact, alone. To account for this, the fairgrounds were divided into twelve different areas, with a surveillance team assigned to each area. In order to minimize suspicion, surveillance teams would not leave their respective areas. Adam would wear a wire and both he and the surveillance team members were to remain in communication with each other and command. Additionally, operations command would have overwatch of the grounds with two high definition cameras mounted on drones which would hover over the fair. Adam was also going to have his pants pockets lined with a clear fluorescent powder. The plan was for him to mark as many of the kidnappers with the powder as possible. While the powder was not visible to the naked eye, it could be picked up by the drone's camera and tracked, or viewed with a UV light. No one was to move in until the Captain was located and secure, and the hope was that between the teams and the drones, the kidnappers could be identified and followed for apprehension after the Captain was safe.

John made several suggestions to the plan Gonzalez

laid out, including giving Adam agreed upon hand signals to use should his communications be compromised. This would allow Adam to provide continued intel to the drones or the surveillance teams if necessary.

"I like your idea about the hand signals." Gonzalez said. "However, as you already noted, this is my operation and I like the plan as it stands, so thank you for your input, but I think we'll go with what we have."

John mumbled under his breath, "Kein Plan überlebt die erste Feindberührung."

"What was that Inspector?" Gonzalez asked.

"Nothing important, Special Agent." John replied. "Just an old German saying."

"Okay then. We have a bunch of work to do before we deploy." Gonzalez said to the room. "Let's everyone get moving so we can be set well before the deadline."

John spoke to Janine, who was not happy about being left behind at police headquarters. He told her that since his role was relegated to only that of an observer, he would be away from the action and safe, so she wouldn't have to worry. And even though observing from the onsite command center was safe, Gonzalez could not allow a civilian to be involved in the operation, even if she did bring everyone bagels.

John made sure Adam was good with the plan, and loaded the counterfeit schematics into the tube. Adam was confident and focused on doing whatever was necessary to get his mentor back. John assured him that he believed Gonzalez's plan was sound, and gave everyone the best chance to rescue Benjamin and catch the kidnappers. He left to let Adam get ready and headed to a quiet corner of the squad-room, and pulled out a phone. Dialing, the phone was answered on the second ring.

"Your Eminence. It's me, John Nowalski. I wanted to give you an update, and I have a question. Do you have a moment to speak?"

"Yes, my son, what can I do for you?" Dietrich asked.

"When we spoke yesterday, you said that probably the only way I could save my job was to turn the plans over to the church."

"That's right. Once you apprehend these North Koreans, giving me the plans should allow me to advocate on your behalf and allow you to return to your former position." The Cardinal said.

"Do you think that is the only way for me to avoid the trouble I am in?"

Dietrich replied, "I believe that may be the case. Why are you asking? What is going on?"

"Captain Benjamin was kidnapped." John said. "The North Koreans are holding him hostage and will exchange him for the Big Light. I believe the operation being run by the police is woefully inadequate, and the schematics may be in jeopardy. They are only placing a limited number of officers and FBI agents at the site of the exchange, and are counting on a radio transmitter and tracking device in Detective Levy's shoes to be able to provide coverage. They are not listening to anything I am saying, and are not even allowing me to be on scene when this is going down. I am worried the schematics will be lost, and they will be difficult if not impossible to re-acquire once the North Koreans have them."

"That is a difficult situation, my son. If they are not allowing you to assist, I do not know what else you could do. I would suggest you do not interfere since you are already in a great deal of trouble. Causing the FBI to be upset with you will not help your cause. If the plans are lost, I will do what I can to help you. In the meantime, I suggest you pray that the American police know what they are doing and can catch these people with the resources they have."

"With respect, there has to be something else I can do other than pray."

"John, sometimes things are just bigger than one man's ability to change them. In those circumstances, you need to trust in our Lord and the power of prayer to allow things to move as He intended."

"I hope you are right." John said. "It goes against my better judgement to sit on the sidelines and let things play out. But if you think it best."

"I do, my son. Let the FBI handle this and I am certain that things will work out as the Lord intends."

"Thank you for your help, Your Eminence." John said. "You have always been a great friend. I will let you know how this all turns out."

"Yes, please keep me posted." Dietrich said.

Hanging up the phone, John joined the teams as they prepared to move the operation to the fairgrounds.

CHAPTER 20

**Sayreville Sports Complex
Sayreville, New Jersey
Present Day**

THE SAYREVILLE SPORTS Complex is an outdoor recreational park located off Bordentown Avenue and adjacent to the borough's Water Department. The fifty-seven plus acres has a softball field, a turf soccer field, and large open fields usually set up with goals for the local recreational youth soccer club. A single road enters into the complex on the east side and curves like a fish hook past the two parking lots that flank the road and ends at a big open dirt field about two hundred feet from the warehouse just west of the complex.

Ordinarily, the fields on any given weekend would be filled with children chasing a black and white ball back and forth between two nets, with parents lining the sidelines in nylon and aluminum camp chairs cheering them on. However, every Labor Day weekend, the fields in the facility host the Borough's Peace Fair. Carnival rides lined the west side of the field and looped around the back of the fields to the north. The tented midway that hosted the various booths assigned to local businesses and non-profit groups ran down the middle of the field from north to south, and the outdoor food court was found closest to the parking area to the east. A band stand was set up on the south side of the field, closest to the main road and served as the reviewing stand for Saturday's parade that terminated at the fair.

The large panel truck that served as the FBI's operations center set up on the grass just off the first paved parking area to the left of the entrance road. As people began to arrive at the fair, plain-clothed officers and agents mixed in with the crowds and proceeded to their assigned sectors. Adam changed into the style and color clothing specified by the kidnappers and donned the sneakers that held the microphone and tracking device. Finally, a technician launched the drones, checked the cameras, and sent the two drones up above the field. By 6:45 Adam was ready to head to the cotton candy truck and the operation would be 'on.'

Kim Joo-Won returned to Carteret after picking up Gertrude Elfmann from Newark Liberty Airport. With two vehicles and four people, Kim now had the ability to field two distinct teams. If the ambulance moved, it would now be easier to follow it without being observed. Kim instructed his people that they would wait for an exchange to be made before making a move on the Big Light. Once the exchange was complete, they would wait for a tactical advantage and use overwhelming firepower to take out the team transporting the plans, secure them, then make their escape. Kim considered using Elfmann to transport the plans out of the country since no one would be looking for an 'American' woman. However, he decided to see what all his options were once the plans were actually in hand.

At 6:20, the overhead door to the warehouse opened, and the ambulance came out. Heading west, the Ambulance turned left on to Roosevelt Avenue and drove south. Making a left on to West Avenue in the town of Port Reading, the ambulance continued on into Perth Amboy before turning west and picking up Route Nine south into Sayreville. Exiting Route Nine on to Bordentown Avenue, the ambulance drove past the Fairgrounds and quietly entered the parking area of the warehouse next to the Sports Complex at 6:55PM.

Pulling in between two parked tractor trailers on the east side of the rear parking lot, the ambulance shut down its engine and two attendants got out of the front. Walking around to the rear of the ambulance, they pulled a large black tarp from one of the exterior compartments. Throwing the tarp over the two containers flanking the ambulance, they pulled it forward till the ambulance was fully covered, then secured it with bungie cords to the container sides.

Kim and his teams carefully followed the ambulance to the warehouse parking lot. Getting out of his vehicle, Kim approached the ambulance on foot to get a better feel for the location and the current tactical situation.

He saw that the ambulance was parked close to the

fair-grounds, partially hidden between two tractor trailers and the tarp. Aside from the ambulance and two other cars parked in front of the nearest truck, all of the other vehicles were just trailers with containers or tractor-trailer rigs. Kim deduced that the two cars may be the escape vehicles for the kidnappers and quickly formulated his plan of attack. Stealthily approaching the cars, he punctured the two front tires of each vehicle. He then called his team of Gertrude Elfmann and his second-in-command and told them to take up a position where they could observe the ambulance and move on the targets when they went to their escape vehicles. He would enter the fair-grounds to see if he could observe the exchange from that side.

Adam arrived at the cotton candy truck precisely at 7:00PM and found the note behind the spare tire. It instructed him to go to the food court and look for a note under the bench of the picnic table closest to the empanada truck. Adam found the note after a few minutes of searching, and saw that he was now instructed to head to the softball field and follow the directions he would find inside the home dugout.

As Adam headed down the road he clearly heard Gonzalez instructing the teams to stand fast, and the two agents assigned to that sector report that they had him in sight. The note in the dugout instructed him to head to the Fun House by the carnival rides and there he would receive further instructions. Reporting the contents of the note to the teams, Adam cut back across the road and towards the carnival rides.

The Fun House ride was actually four trailers arranged side by side allowing for visitors to move through the openings in the sides. The insides of the trailers were a maze of mirrors, moving floors and flashing lights. There was no line to enter as Adam approached, and as he reached the ride attendant, he felt someone put their hand on his right shoulder as they shoved what Adam assumed was a gun into his kidney.

"Let's go inside, and don't turn around." An unseen voice growled in Adam's ear.

Following the man's directions, Adam entered the Fun House. When the door closed, the man who had directed him inside forcibly turned Adam around and pulled the backpack off his shoulder. Patting Adam down for a weapon, the man asked, "Did you bring it?"

Despite the low lighting inside the Fun House, Adam could see the man was about the same size and build as he was and was dressed identically.

"I asked did you bring it?" the man repeated.

"You can clearly see I did." Adam replied, nodding toward the yellow tube sticking out of the top of the backpack.

"Open it. I need to see." The man said.

Taking the packing tube from the backpack, Adam pulled the metal top off the tube and turned the tube over, shaking the schematics out.

"Open them. I need to see." The man repeated.

Adam did as he was instructed, and the man shined a small flashlight on the pages. Adam held his breath as the kidnapper sorted through the pages.

Speaking to someone on his radio, the man said, "Everything looks in order. We are preparing for phase two."

Instructing Adam to roll up the plans, he handed Adam a new tube. "Put the plans in here, and then put on these clothes." He said.

Adam took off his orange tee shirt, blue baseball cap and blue jeans and put on the blue tee shirt, khaki pants and red baseball cap."

"So that's the plan, you become me to throw off anyone watching for me?" Adam said to the man, but for the benefit of the teams and operation center.

"Shut up and change. The shoes too." The man said, throwing Adam a new pair of sneakers.

As Adam went to take off his sneakers, he feigned losing his balance and reached out to steady himself by placing his freshly coated hand on the man's shoulder.

"Hey…" the man said, clearly annoyed by the physical contact.

"I'm sorry. I'm a bit nervous and I needed your shoulder to catch my balance." Adam replied.

Finally finished changing, the man instructed Adam to pick up the backpack and follow him, as he led Adam further into the Fun House. As they entered the next room, Adam saw what looked like a dozen other men dressed either like himself or the kidnapper.

Turning toward Adam, the kidnapper said, "Stick close and follow me."

Adam followed the man and they moved through the Fun House toward the exit. As they moved from room to room, Adam saw even more people dressed the same way.

Upon reaching the exit, Adam was handed a pair of dark wrap-around sunglasses.

"Follow me out the door." The kidnapper said. "We will be going toward the right, back toward the ride's entrance. When you reach the garbage can by the metal barrier, you will be met by someone else who will escort you to your Captain. Once there, we will take the backpack and you can go to your Captain. Try anything funny and you will be the first to die, your Captain will be second. Are we clear on this?"

Adam nodded his head, and the exit door to the Fun House opened and almost as one, the mass of people dressed as Adam and the kidnapper surged out the door. Adam was temporarily disoriented as he was pushed and pulled out the door, but he gathered his feet under himself, regained his composure, and gave his hand signal to indicate he had marked a kidnapper, and he was off comms. As he looked around, he was stunned to see the other 'Adams' performing the same gesture.

"This way. Move it now." The kidnapper urgently instructed Adam, and they began walking toward the entrance to the ride. When Adam reached the trash can, he felt a hand grab his arm and direct him to the left. He was immediately flanked by a second man on his right who told Adam under his breath to keep moving forward.

Gonzalez and the teams were prepared for Adam to come out wearing different clothing, and for Adam to no longer have his tracker or communications. What they were not expecting was for the surge of over thirty people dressed identically as either Adam or what they assumed was the new outfit they made him put on.

The drones and agents clearly saw all of the 'Adams' put their arms over their head giving a signal, but since they each did different things with their hands, they were not sure what the actual sign was.

"Switch to UV." Gonzalez instructed, hoping the drone would be able to pick up something. Immediately, the drone saw the mark on the shoulder of the kidnapper Adam had marked. But other than the one mark, it did not single out anyone else.

"Do you have him?" John asked Gonzalez and the drone techs in the command center.

"We have someone with a marked shoulder, but that must be the kidnapper Adam marked." Gonzalez replied.

"Command to all teams... does anyone have them?"

"Negative Command." came the replies.

"Look for someone dressed in blue tee shirt and khakis being led by someone." John said.

"We got this Nowalski." Gonzalez snapped.

"Are you on the marked kidnapper at least?" John asked.

"I said we got this Inspector." Gonzalez said admonishing John a second time.

"Ma'am, those people are disbursing all across the fairgrounds." The drone tech said.

"Any patterns to that disbursal? Are they headed in any particular direction or staying away from any spot?" Gonzalez asked.

"No ma'am. It looks pretty random."

"And nothing on UV?"

"Nothing ma'am."

Adam was led two hundred feet across the field into a small grove of trees near the back of the fairgrounds and told to sit down under one of the larger trees. The two men leading him communicated with other team members for a few minutes before finally getting Adam back on his feet and walked him through the wooded area toward the complex boundary. They then pushed their way through some additional brush before emerging into the parking lot of the warehouse. Walked around a container, Adam was escorted to the ambulance.

"Gimme the backpack." The larger of the two kidnappers said as he took the backpack from Adam's shoulder. Opening the rear door of the ambulance, Adam could see Captain Benjamin strapped to the stretcher, with two people tending to him seated on the crew bench.

"How do I know he's okay?" Adam asked.

"Look at the monitor, asshole. You can see his heartbeat. He's fine. He's just sedated. Now I need you to climb on in." The large kidnapper said.

Switching places with the people on the ambulance crew bench, Adam checked his boss's pulse. The large kidnapper continued, "I am going to close the door after putting this epoxy in the locking mechanism. It hardens in like five seconds, but if I see you trying to open the door in the next minute, I'll fuckin' shoot you and the Captain. You'll find a cell phone in one of the compartments. Find it, call 911 and get yourself freed and no one else will be hurt. Are we clear on this?"

Nodding his head Adam said, "Yeah, we're clear."

"Good, said the kidnapper as he applied the epoxy to the door mechanism and lock and shut the rear door of the ambulance.

"I can't believe you lost him." John said in exasperation. "Your friggin' ego wouldn't allow you to even hear any of my suggestions 'cause you have to show how in charge you are… Now we are all sitting around holding our asses looking like we're on the corner of Park and 42ⁿᵈ Street, looking for the beach."

"Hey, you need to calm down, Nowalski." Gonzalez shouted. "No one could have anticipated they would have such an extensive plan." Turning back to the drone operator, she asked, "Anything yet?"

"No ma'am." He replied.

"Well keep searching, and make sure the second drone doesn't lose that guy he marked." Then into the radio she said, "Teams one and two… start picking up some of those decoys. We need to start questioning them to try to get some intel."

"Nothing like shutting the barn door after the horses have all run off." John said in his most sarcastic tone.

"That's the last I want to hear from you, Nowalski." Agent Gonzalez said. "It might be best if you stepped out for some air."

"Sounds like a great idea. I'm tired of watching incompetence at its finest anyway." John replied.

Grabbing his backpack, John descended the steps to the mobile command center and headed toward the parking lot.

"Alpha team clear and headed to transport with package in hand." The large kidnapper said into his radio.

"Nice work." von Alpiner replied. "Any problems?"

"Negative. It went smooth as silk. We should be long gone before he even finds that cell phone. Martinez and Grant should exfil if they haven't already. The doc already has the keys to the first vehicle and will take the nurse home. We got the other vehicle and will meet you at the rendezvous."

"Sounds good, Alpha team. I'll get them to prep the jet." von Alpiner said.

"Roger that. It will be good to… What the fuck?"

Von Alpiner paused before responding to the last transmission. "Alpha team,… Say again last message. You cut out… Alpha team?"

Gertrude Elfmann and Kim's second in command saw the Aryphon people arrive at the cars to find the front tires flat. As they stood around the vehicles looking down in surprise, the North Koreans advanced from their hiding spots, firing their AK-105s on full automatic. Two of the kidnappers were able to draw their guns before being mowed down in a rain of bullets, while the remaining Aryphon men, the doctor and nurse were all killed before they could even react. Collecting the backpack with the yellow tube, the North Korean team reported in to Kim while sprinting back to their car.

John left the mobile command center and was walking slowly in the direction of the food court. Crossing over the road he made his way to the second parking lot. Rounding the driveway from the road, he had just gotten into the parking area when a marked Sayreville patrol car came up from behind him.

Lowering the window as he pulled parallel to John, the officer inside said, "I thought you were working with the Feds in the command center."

Turning toward the car, John saw Sergeant Ray Petrowski behind the wheel. A seasoned officer, Ray had joined the force a few years after John. "I was, but after we lost contact with Adam, I was about to bitch slap that Agent Gonzalez. I could tell she was the type who thinks she knows everything, so I was originally laid back about making suggestions about her ops plan. But then, after the shit fell apart, sure enough, she still pretty much dismissed everything I suggested in that condescending tone of hers, and now look where we are."

"I know…". Petrowski began. "I hate it when we have to work with the Feds. They are worse than the State Police with their 'better than you' attitude."

Despite only having to drive the equivalent of two blocks, the traffic heading into the fair delayed Kim Joo-Won's arrival back to the fairgrounds. Forced to park on the grass, all the way in the rear parking area, Kim and his subordinate had begun walking toward the fair on the paved walkway. They were about to follow the walkway toward the fairgrounds when Elfmann radioed that they had just eliminated the Aryphon people and had secured the Big Light.

Kim was about to return to his car when he saw what looked like a familiar figure walking toward him. When that figure turned to speak to the officer in the patrol car, and he saw the yellow tube sticking out of the backpack,

Kim instantly knew the man talking to the officer was John Nowalski. Kim's initial thought was that of vengeance for the teammates Nowalski had killed, but seeing the tube sticking out of John's backpack made Kim begin to wonder... *Why would Nowalski be carrying a tube in his backpack, and if his people had just gotten the Big Light, what was in Nowalski's tube? If the police exchanged the Big Light for their Captain, why was Nowalski here carrying an identical tube?...Unless...*

After everything Nowalski went through to secure those schematics, would he risk losing them as potential ransom for a hostage? Thinking about the situation, Kim weighed the options. He could leave now with what the Aryphon people believed to be the Big Light, or assume that whatever the police had exchanged for their Captain was a fake or a copy, and the actual Big Light was sitting in the backpack Nowalski was carrying. Calling in to his second team, Kim instructed them to get to his location as quickly as possible without arousing suspicion. He then advised his teammate of his hastily conceived plan to take out Nowalski and secure the tube in the backpack.

Walking down the parking lot as if they were looking for their car, Kim pretended to hit the key fob from time to time as if trying to trigger the car's alert. With their guns drawn and hidden behind their legs, the two North Korean operatives began closing the distance between them and their new target.

John first spotted the two men when they were about twenty yards away. When they were about fifteen yards away, he said to Ray Petrowski, "Ray, I think we are in for some trouble. You see these two Asian guys approaching us?"

"Uh huh..." Petrowski replied.

"I'm pretty sure they are the North Koreans we've all been looking for the last few days."

"The ones that kidnapped the Captain?"

"At least the ones that shot him." John said. "I need you to get on the radio and call for back-up."

Releasing his seatbelt and opening the car door, Petrowski said, "No time... We got this."

Stepping back and behind the open patrol car door, John reached around to the small of his back to the automatic pistol he had taken from the North Korean the other day, as Petrowski emerged from the patrol car.

"Can I help you gentlemen?" Petrowski asked as his hand went toward his sidearm.

From a distance now of less than twenty feet, both North Koreans brought their guns out and fired multiple rounds at John and Sergeant Petrowski. John dove for the ground, while Petrowski reached for his sidearm in an attempt to bring his weapon to bear on the targets. While several of the rounds fired at John struck the vehicle door, and two of the North Korean's rounds struck the Sergeant in his Kevlar vest, one round hit Ray Petrowski mid-forehead, killing him instantly.

From his position on the ground, under the cover of the vehicle door, John returned fire at the legs of the man on the right. Striking both ankles with two rounds each, the man collapsed allowing John to place another two rounds in the man's abdomen below his body armor.

As John popped up preparing to fire at Kim, the car door was sprayed by .32 caliber rounds from the Skorpion. 61 machine pistol Kim had slung under the left shoulder. Realizing he was clearly outgunned, John dove into the open patrol car, and threw the gearshift lever into reverse, stomping on the gas. With Kim running after the fleeing police car and firing his machine pistol, John steered the vehicle across the driveway on to the adjacent walkway by barely peering over the back seat. Upon reaching the grass, John spun the wheel, and dropped the vehicle into drive as he planned to transition to forward progress. With all of his attention directed at escaping Kim, John failed to see the approaching SUV and the woman hanging out the window pointing the machine gun at him.

Luckily for John, Gertrude Elfmann did not anticipate John's turning maneuver, and the majority of her shots missed the spinning police car completely. Recognizing the danger to the huge civilian numbers at the fair, John gunned the engine and steered the police cruiser down the access road and out of the fairgrounds.

Kim Joo-Won, tossed Gertrude Elfmann the keys to his vehicle, quickly instructing her to check on their fallen comrade. If he could travel, load him in the car and follow behind. If he could not, terminate him. There could be no prisoners for the evil capitalists to interrogate. Then jumping into the passenger seat of the SUV, the two North Koreans sped down the access roadway behind John's fleeing police car.

Gertrude Elfmann meanwhile found the wounded North Korean, surrounded by a growing crowd. To the crowd's horror, Elfmann chose the latter of Kim's options before calmly walking off in search of Kim's car.

Adam found the hidden cell phone and called for help. Within minutes of his call, the ambulance was surrounded by police and FBI, who also found six dead bodies lying near two vandalized vehicles . Warehouse security footage would later show a man and woman approach the murdered people and open fire with automatic weapons. Then after grabbing a backpack, retreat back into the shadows. The local fire company got the doors to the ambulance open and Captain Benjamin was whisked away in another ambulance to the hospital for evaluation.

Not hearing from his team, Dieter von Alpiner drove into the warehouse parking lot and saw the bodies of his fallen team lying in growing pools of blood next to their vehicles, and knew instantly the Koreans had killed his people and stolen the Big Light. Spinning the car around, he exited the warehouse back on to Jernee Mill Road, and made the green light back on to Bordentown Avenue. He was about to turn into the fairground's entrance when a police cruiser came flying out of the parking lot, followed less than thirty seconds later by a black SUV.

From his vantage point he wasn't sure who was driving the police car, but he was certain the black SUV was occupied by two Asians. Checking that no one was approaching on his right, von Alpiner ignored the hand signals of the officer directing traffic at the entrance, and instructed his driver to swing the Tesla back into traffic and down Bordentown Avenue. Accelerating quickly, he swerved around slow moving cars to keep the North Korean's SUV in sight.

John roared past the police at the entrance to the fairgrounds, and made a left on to Bordentown Avenue attempting to put some distance between himself and the pursuing North Koreans before answering the calls on his radio.

"Six-Four-Three, please respond." The dispatcher called out. "Petrowski, what is going on out there?"

"Six-Four-Three to dispatch. This is John Nowalski. Sergeant Petrowski's dead. Ray and I were attacked in the fairgrounds parking lot by assailants armed with automatic weapons. I subdued one of them but was significantly outgunned. They are now chasing me. I am going to try to lead them away from people and into a place where we can apprehend them. Stand by for updates."

"10-4 Six-Four-Three. I am going to patch you through to the mobile command center as well." The dispatcher said.

Slowing to navigate the 'S' curve by the train trestle on Bordentown Avenue, John accelerated out of the last curve. By utilizing the lights and siren to clear traffic at intersections, John was able to put some distance between himself and his pursuers. However, the big SUV quickly closed in on open stretches of road.

Knowing that almost all of the Borough's police force was at the fair, John figured he needed to take this fight somewhere his backup would be waiting for him, and where there was less of a likelihood of civilian casualties. Trying to recall the town and surrounding villages he was raised in, but had not been back to in years, John decided the best place to stage this confrontation was actually on the other side of the Raritan River in an industrial park section of Keasbey. On the Friday evening of Labor Day weekend, most of the warehouses would be closed and empty, and John remembered a number of the roads ran down toward the river where it was desolate and they could drive right into the trap he wanted to set for the North Koreans.

"Six-Four-Three to dispatch." John said into the radio's microphone.

"Go ahead Six-Four-Three."

"Could we get the State and Keasbey Police to arrange a little welcoming party down near the Exposition Center? It'll take me about ten minutes to get there, so they might be able to get set up, and I think I could lead our guests there."

Agent Gonzalez came on the frequency and said, "Inspector, I've been monitoring. Why go all the way to the Expo Center?"

"It's far enough away that we could get it set up before I get there, and it's out of the way. These people have already displayed a total disregard for human life. We need to take this fight to someplace where we can minimize the risk of civilian casualties." John replied.

"I'm looking at a map right now." Gonzalez said. "I concur. This looks like a good place to trap them in."

'I'm so glad you like my idea… bitch.' John said out loud to himself again.

Gonzalez then proceeded to organize the plan for corralling the Koreans chasing after John. She laid out the route John would take, and coordinated with both the Keasbey and State police in setting up the roadblock John would lead them into.

"Six-Four-Three to Central Command. I will be taking Route Nine north. How about you get Old Bridge to shut down the highway at the Sayreville border, and get South Amboy to block access to the highway, especially from Route Thirty-Five and by the Main Street Extension."

"We are already on it Six-Four-Three." Came the reply.

John had a green light at the intersection of Ernston Road allowing him to sail through. People were regularly moving out of his way when they heard the siren and saw the flashing lights. Checking his rear-view mirror, John could see Kim less than a quarter mile back, swerving around traffic as he sped to catch John.

The intersection of Route Nine and Bordentown Avenue was a conglomeration of on and off ramps mixed in with a cloverleaf that intersected adjoining streets. John changed the mode of the siren to make the other drivers in this spaghetti of streets more aware of his presence, and proceeded into the cloverleaf entrance to the highway at his best possible speed. However, the need to slow down to both avoid other cars and complete the sharp turn allowed Kim to close the remaining distance between the two vehicles. To drive this point home, Kim fired two shots into the trunk of the patrol car.

Merging on to Route Nine, John was pleased to see a significantly reduced amount of traffic. Hoping that the traffic would thin out even more after passing the merge for the Garden State Parkway, John accelerated the police cruiser to eighty miles per hour, with Kim right on his tail. Passing under the Parkway, the two vehicles entered a section of the highway bordered by private residences. Seeing Kim hang out his passenger window and fire off more shots made John accelerate a bit more in order to move clear of the area homes.

Route Nine is a secondary highway that runs North/South most of the length of New Jersey. In some sections it is a major three lane highway, in others it becomes a two lane road with traffic lights, businesses and residences on both sides. In several sections, the highway merges with another road and shares its designation with that road. Such was the case where Route Nine met Route Thirty-Five on the border of Sayreville and South Amboy. At that merge, drivers wanting to continue north on Route Nine must negotiate a sharp exit ramp off their current road and then merge on to the new dually designated highway.

With less than a half mile to that cloverleaf merge, John kept his speed up hoping to rely on the cruiser's brakes to allow him to safely navigate the two-hundred and seventy degree turn.

Swinging from the left lane across the right and on to the merge ramp, John used the angle to allow him to enter the ramp at a greater speed. Praying the South Amboy police had closed off the road south of this merge point, he cut the wheel hard to the right and pumped the brakes, letting his speed and centrifugal force slingshot him onto the new highway. Merging safely, John thanked God for getting the road closed, allowing his fishtailing cruiser a clear shot off of the ramp and on to the highway.

Completing the high-risk maneuver, he now risked a check in his mirror to see where Kim was. While he had gained a bit of distance, the North Koreans were still hot on his tail, and now, Kim was leaning out the window aiming an automatic rifle at John's vehicle. Kim's first burst impacted the trunk of the police cruiser, and caused John to begin swerving from side to side to throw off Kim's aim. Kim's next salvo shattered the rear window and peppered the passenger seat and dashboard. As the two vehicles sped past the Main Street Extension, John saw Kim lean back into the SUV and this time emerge with an M-79 grenade launcher.

Clearly outgunned and running out of options, John began performing a series of erratic turns to prevent Kim from getting a clear shot. However, John knew that with the grenade launcher, Kim didn't need a perfect shot. Anything remotely close would most likely cause severe damage to the vehicle. As the two vehicles began to cross the Raritan River via the Thomas Edison Bridge, John needed a plan to remove Kim's firepower advantage. Looking quickly at the shotgun mounted behind his seat, John figured he would have a better chance in a two-on one firefight than he would being blown up by a grenade.

Moving the cruiser to the right lane, John slowed down slightly. With Kim hanging out the SUV's passenger window, the driver positioned his vehicle slightly behind John's in the left lane. This would allow Kim to clearly line up his shot on John's police cruiser. Knowing both Kim and his driver would be focused on taking their shot, John waited until they were in the center of the bridge, then throwing the steering wheel hard over to the left, he slammed on his brakes.

The police cruiser veered in front of Kim's SUV, and then

braked suddenly, catching Kim's driver by surprise. Unable to brake in time, the SUV hit the rear of the police cruiser at a closure rate of fifteen mile per hour. While not significant enough to cause major damage to either vehicle, the impact jolt was enough to cause Kim to squeeze the trigger on the grenade launcher, discharging the weapon into the macadam to the right of John's passenger side rear tire.

Exploding on impact, the grenade cratered the roadway and blew out the rear tire on John's car. The front right tire on Kim's SUV was also shredded by the explosion and resulting crater. With both cars now spinning toward the guard-railed wall on the right side of the roadway, they struck nearly simultaneously, bounced back from the force of the impact and came to rest straddling the shoulder and the right lane of the highway.

Tossed back and forth against the restraints of the seatbelt, John was temporarily disoriented by the spinning crash. When he regained his senses, he realized both his and Kim's vehicles had come to a stop near the outside wall of the Edison Bridge. John's police cruiser had sustained heavy damage and sat nearly perpendicular to the roadway with smoke coming from the engine compartment.

Kim's SUV sat behind John's vehicle parallel to the highway, and closer to the wall. With its nose facing forward, the vehicle had significant body damage to the driver's side and a missing front wheel.

Kim tried to shake off the effects of the crash quickly, and scrambled out of the passenger seat before John was able to get out of his car. Despite having double vision, Kim aimed his Skorpion machine pistol at John as he emerged from the police cruiser.

"Don't even reach for that shotgun and throw your pistol over this way." Kim instructed John. "After such a valiant fight, I would hate to have to shoot you now because you did something stupid."

As John shook off the effects of the crash, he saw Kim's driver pointing a handgun at him from inside the SUV, along with Kim aiming his Skorpion, John realized he was still outgunned and in a bad tactical situation. Holding out his right hand, he carefully reached into his waistband with two fingers and removed his gun, throwing it on the ground near Kim.

"I must admit, Inspector Nowalski… in all my years in the field, I can't recall ever facing a more worthy adversary." Kim said as he moved toward the front of the SUV. While Kim maintained cover on John, his driver was finally able to get the door open and he exited the vehicle. "With only the clues from this case, you were able to locate the Big Light when two teams with access to intelligence and research were still busy turning over rocks."

"Thank you for your admiration." John said. "But I don't suppose it is enough for you to allow me to put some handcuffs on you and your buddy there and arrest you for the murder of a whole bunch of people."

Laughing, Kim said, "And even in a dire situation, you are still able to maintain a sense of humor. Inspector Nowalski, you truly are a unique individual."

"With all these accolades, I must insist you call me John. So if you won't let me arrest you, can I also assume you won't let me live either?"

"Honestly, I haven't decided yet, John. Probably not, but I'm still weighing the options in that regard." Kim said.

"So now what?" John asked.

"Now, you toss me that tube you've been carrying in your backpack."

"Why don't you just come over here and get it?" John asked tauntingly.

"Because if I do, you will try something stupid and I will either have to kill you or your escape plan might work. I don't like either of those options right now. Therefore, you will reach into that backpack and toss me the Big Light right now before I get upset and just kill you and then come get it myself."

Thinking fast, John said, "Why would you want a decoy?"

"A decoy?" Kim asked.

"The Big Light was used as ransom for our police Captain. I was just at the fair with this decoy in case things went south."

"Inspector Nowalski... John... I was not born yesterday. After all you went through to get that prize, I know you would not risk giving it up to kidnappers. No, the tube in *MY* possession right now, that I took from the kidnappers is the decoy. You have been carrying and guarding the real Big Light this whole time. So toss it over here... NOW." Kim shouted

John's mind was racing. With two guns trained on him, there was little chance of escape. He knew if he made any move to run, he would be gunned down in seconds. Additionally, he didn't think he had much of a chance of grabbing the shotgun mounted to the plexiglass behind the front seats. He considered options for giving the North Koreans what they wanted, then finding a way to take it back, but Kim had already proven to be illusive, so he did not want to take that risk. John knew that help was on its way, but that was still several minutes out, and from the look on Kim's face, John knew he was out of time.

Slowly, John reached into the front seat to grab his backpack, taking another long look at the shotgun only inches away. Resigned that there was no good option for keeping the Big Light, John took the backpack off the front seat, and backed out of the car. With a clear understanding that there was no way he could let the regime in North Korea have this technology, John decided on his only remaining option. With one last look around for any last second alternatives, John withdrew the yellow tube from the backpack.

"That's it. Now toss it over here." Kim said, a grin beginning to form on his face.

Nodding his head, John took the cardboard tube, hefted it to get a feel for its weight, then stepping forward, launched the tube underhand toward Kim.

Things seemed to move in slow motion, as the tube sailed end-over end toward Kim, standing on the roadside shoulder in front of the damaged SUV. With a self-satisfied smile on his face, Kim watched the tube as it arched toward him. Realizing its trajectory would take the tube past him, Kim took two steps backward as he moved to catch it. Kim's smile faded on his second step as he realized, that John had launched the tube with enough force to carry it over the six-foot fence on the side of the bridge, and there was no way to save it. As the tube plummeted over the side of the bridge, Kim turned to watch his long sought after prize fall into the churning water of the Raritan River's outgoing tide.

"Wow… Guess I don't even know my own strength." John quipped.

John saw the rage in Kim's eyes when he turned to face him. Without even addressing John's transgression, he pointed his machine pistol at John and said in Korean, "Kill him."

No one heard the electric vehicle's approach, even when it veered off the roadway on to the shoulder. John and Kim both caught sight of it as it impacted the back of the black SUV. While the driver had managed to reduce the speed down to less than 15 miles per hour at the moment of impact, thus reducing the damage to the front of the Tesla, there was still sufficient momentum to move the SUV forward three feet.

The SUV struck Kim in the side knocking him to the ground and causing his shots to put additional holes in the back of the police cruiser rather than into John. Momentarily distracted by the crash, Kim's second-in-command turned to watch his leader tumble to the ground and missed the Aryphon mercenary aiming his Glock out the window of the car. The three shots fired into the back of the North Korean broke two of his ribs sending him to the ground, but the man's body armor once again saved his life.

Upon seeing his chance, John dove for the front seat of the police cruiser and ripped the shotgun from its mount. Dropping to his knee, John turned to face the second North Korean, and saw the man begin to stand as he prepared to return fire. Aiming for the legs, John fired one round of double 0 buckshot into the backs of the North

Korean's legs. Simultaneously, the Tesla driver fired three more rounds, only one of which struck the North Korean in the left shoulder above the vest.

While John and the driver were engaged with Kim's second-in-command, Dieter von Alpiner had jumped out of the passenger seat and was in a gun battle with Kim, who was now using the rear of the police car as cover. John was about to turn his attention to Kim when a pearl white Nissan Maxima screeched to a halt in front of the police car. Pulling out an AK 105, a woman emerged from the driver's side and sprayed bullets across the entire scene.

John dove for the ground as von Alpiner ducked behind the crumpled fender of the Tesla. Only the Tesla driver without any cover took a shot to the body armor and one to his left shoulder, sending him stumbling back against the electric vehicle.

While Gertrude Elfmann laid down suppressing fire, Kim scrambled for the rear passenger door. Diving in, Elfmann jumped in and stomped on the accelerator, leaving rubber on the road before the car left the scene.

John stood up and quickly brought the shotgun to bear on von Alpiner when he saw the man aiming his weapon at him. Glancing over to the wounded Aryphon mercenary, John saw that he too was pointing a gun his way.

"Well, it looks like we have a bit of a Mexican stand-off…". John said. "Or should I say German stand-off"

"Austrian, actually." Von Alpiner replied. "Your problem though, is that you are outnumbered, and my associate and I are wearing body armor. So in my estimation, it is not a stand-off at all. It means, you lose."

Before von Alpiner could move, a familiar voice called

out from the back seat, "Dieter, NEIN! Schnapp dir einfach das grosse licht und las uns hier raus."

In response, John yelled out, "Great idea, your Eminence…" Turning to point the shotgun toward the back window of the Tesla, John continued, "They should put down the guns and just go get the tube…". As the window to the back seat of the Tesla lowered, John said, "…because, while Dieter may have killed me, my first shot was always going to be through that window. And I assume *you* are not wearing body armor."

With the window fully lowered, Cardinal Dietrich replied, "I didn't know you spoke German."

"And Italian and Spanish and a little Arabic, but then there are a great many things you really don't know about me." John said.

"How did you know I would be in the back seat?" Dietrich asked.

"Well, for starters, I knew you were the one leaking information to Aryphon when we spoke on the phone the other day. You slipped up when you knew all about the schematics and the Wagner history, especially after you said you thought the Big Light was a religious relic a moment before. You are also the only person I told the Sayreville police had the plans. The kidnappers went straight to the heart of that department with their kidnapping and ransom demand. They didn't target me or Janine, or anyone else.

Then there was the fact that you knew who Captain Benjamin was, and you also knew the FBI was involved in the case, so I figured you were more intimately involved. Like on scene intimately involved. Since I don't think Dieter there expected to have to storm into battle, he assumed it would be safe to have you tag along, as I'm sure you insisted on doing."

"I have always known you were a very skilled investigator, my son." Dietrich said. "But now we appear to still be at an impasse. I am willing to give my life for the cause I believe in, which would mean you too would lose your life for my cause. In that case, you and I both lose, but my cause will get the Big Light."

Pausing first, as if weighing his options, John replied, "And what does it mean for me if I opt to let us both live."

"You will most likely still lose your job." Dietrich said. "Sentille and Pinochinio despise you. But since you have caught the killer of our nuns,…" Dietrich nodded his head toward the moaning North Korean lying on the side of the highway. "I'm sure you may be able to negotiate an honorable retirement and the ability to keep your pension. As for any charges you may bring against me, it is your word against mine, and if you go that route, I will side with Sentille and make it my mission to ruin you. John, we have known each other for so many years. Do not push this one. This is when you should stop being a worker bee. Remember, a worker bee always dies after it stings defending the hive."

John looked around at von Alpiner and the North Korean lying on the ground before turning back to Dietrich. "You will support me as I look to retire with my pension from the Vatican?"

"Fully, my son." Dietrich replied.

"And you will take the Big Light and just leave? No more killing? No more attacks? The Wagners can return to their normal lives?"

"All we ever wanted was what is in that tube." Dietrich replied.

"Then take it and get the fuck out of here before the cavalry shows up. I'll see you back in Rome, Excellency." John said, and went to tend to the North Korean's wounds.

Von Alpiner grabbed the yellow mailing tube from the back seat of the SUV, helped his wounded teammate into the back seat, and drove off in the damaged Tesla. With his back turned, no one saw the smirk on John's face as they left.

John controlled the bleeding on the injured North Korean and stood watch until he was taken under heavy guard by ambulance to the same trauma center that was treating the freed Captain Benjamin. John fully debriefed Agent Gonzalez, and after clearing the air on their disagreements, came to a place of mutual respect for one another.

The Sayreville police with the assistance of the New Jersey State Police apprehended Martinez and Grant as they attempted to leave the fairgrounds. After shining a UV light into their vehicle, Adam's handprint on Martinez's shirt was clearly visible marking him as one of the kidnappers. Both men were carrying concealed unlicensed firearms that ballistics eventually matched to the shootout at the monastery, as well as matching Martinez's weapon to the assassination of the Belgian Finance Minister.

Captain Benjamin made a full recovery, however the loss of his lung prevented him from being able to return to work and he retired to spend more time with his family. Adam was given command of the detective unit, and despite the demands of the new role, promised himself he would not allow the job to become the only thing in his life.

John returned to Rome where he originally faced departmental charges brought by Sentille and Pinochinio. However, when both the American and European press picked up the story of John's role in the capture of the 'terrorists' that killed people on both continents, Sentille and Pinochinio were hard pressed to pursue the charges. John submitted his retirement papers and began the process of packing up and transitioning his life.

Aryphon and Donner Security both denied any involvement in either the Belgian assassination or the operations in Austria or New Jersey. To prove this, they produced personnel records showing that both Martinez and Grant had been terminated from the company months before either event.

The wheels of justice turned slowly for Martinez and Grant as both the EU and US, claimed jurisdiction and needed to work out the details of trial schedules and extradition. While awaiting trial, Grant died of a sudden heart attack, and soon after, Martinez committed suicide. Surprisingly, there were major camera malfunctions at each of the prisons on the nights of their deaths, which Agent Bauer of the FBI was assigned to look into.

North Korea denied any connection to the man apprehended on the bridge, and despite numerous interrogations by FBI counterintelligence staff, he refused to say even his name. He was tried as John Doe, and convicted in Federal court on multiple counts of murder and terrorism, and remanded to Federal prison to serve his multiple life sentences.

Deciding that a return to a monastic life was not what he wanted, John left Rome and returned to New Jersey, where he rented a modest apartment in Old Bridge. He and Janine began dating regularly and settled into a steady relationship. When he wasn't working on establishing his new consulting venture, John would regularly spend time with Otto playing chess while Janine was at work teaching.

Janine, while relieved that the whole ordeal was over, repeatedly said that she felt justice was not truly served. In response, John would repeatedly reassure her that God, Karma or someone would see that the true architects of the evil would one day see their day of reckoning. After all, he remained a man of faith, and he had made that promise to her not long after they had first met.

EPILOGUE

Hermann Alvarez called the Board meeting to order. Having postponed the original meeting because of the failed results of their search for the Big Light and the accompanying fallout from the capture of the Donner team members, Alvarez was now anxious to get by-in from the Board to move forward with his revised plan.

"Ladies and gentlemen, thank you all for coming." Alvarez began. "And to those of you on ZOOM…" he said addressing Cardinal Dietrich and his daughter, "…thank you for taking the time to join us.

It has been a challenging few months, marked with a roller-coaster of highs and lows. We thought we had secured our ultimate prize… the Big Light… unlimited power from cold fusion and a revolutionary means of producing the resources to store that energy. But in the end, we found it to be a fraud… a scam perpetuated over decades on not just us, but our forefathers at a time of desperate need.

As you are all aware, the formula did not work, and our

best scientists could not even modify it to where it would work. And the graphene manufacturing schematics were really nothing more than plans to manufacture lithium-ion batteries.

We dealt with some issues in the press, which we were able to squash, and there were some minor hiccups with former personnel. But now, I am proud to say, we are ready to move forward with our ultimate plan, and deploy something that we know does work. Thanks to the work of my daughter, we are ready to deploy our H23 virus. Because deployment will take several months to prepare for, and we would need to launch this for the spring to allow for maximum effectiveness, I am calling for a vote today to launch what I would like to call, Project Phoenix. With this plan we will truly rise from the ashes and reinstate the Aryan race to its rightful position of world leadership."

"Are you sure you want to do this?" Kim Joo-Won asked his sister as they exited their vehicle. "Once we engage, there is no turning back."

"I *need* to do this." Joon Min replied.

Leading her three person team around to the loading dock of the Aryphon building, she pointed out the security camera before they appeared in its view. With a quick shot from his silenced pistol, Kim Joo-Won took out the surveillance camera above the door at the back of the ramp. While her ID had long since been deactivated, Joon Min bet that the key code to the door leading into the building from the loading dock had not been changed.

Entering the 4 numbers, Joon Min turned the handle

and proved her theory correct. Once inside, the team waited for the security staff that they knew would come, to investigate the camera outage. As soon as the man came through the hallway door, Joon Min shot him once in the forehead. Taking the guard's uniform and ID, Kim Joo-Won quickly changed into the outfit, and pulled an Aryphon cap down over his eyes. Navigating swiftly through the halls from the memorized map Joon Min had drawn, Kim headed to the security control room, entered and promptly shot the three security guards stationed in the room. Shutting down the recording devices, he left after inserting a quick drying super glue into the lock. Signaling to Joon Min and her mother, the three operatives converged on the elevator that would take them to the Board room.

Hermann Alvarez had just received his unanimous vote to proceed with Project Phoenix when he heard a bit of commotion in the hallway outside the Board room. Looking over to Max Silva, the President of Donner Security he asked, "Max, could you see what all that noise is about?"

As Silva walked toward the double doors of the board room, the door flew open and three armed assailants entered the room. As Silva reached for his concealed sidearm, he was promptly shot by the older woman as she made her way into the room. With one assailant guarding the door, the older woman worked her way around the left side of the table, while the man worked his way around to the right. Each Board member was shot twice in the head as the shooter advance toward Hermann Alvarez at the head of the table.

As the attackers neared the end of the table, William Alvarez and Werner Montana tried to escape but were easily gunned down, completing the assault. As if for good measure, the male shooter put a bullet into the Zoom camera, shutting out the video portion of the call.

With only Hermann Alvarez remaining alive, the third gunman pulled the doors to the board room closed and advanced to Alvarez. The Chairman's eyes grew wide as he recognized Joon Min.

"Joon Min… What is the meaning of this?" Alvarez asked.

"The meaning? I would think the meaning would be clear." Joon Min said. "The meaning is that we are here to wipe your genocidal asses off the face of the earth." As if to punctuate her statement, Joon Min shot Alvarez in the knee.

Howling in pain, Alvarez doubled over in his chair and grabbed his knee.

"I'm not done talking to you, so look at me" Joon Min snarled, and Kim grabbed Alvarez by the hair and yanked him back to the upright sitting position.

"You have spent a sizeable portion of your life killing and torturing people without giving a second thought to the pain you caused, or the additional lives you ruined. Now, as you are staring death in the face, I want you to experience some of the pain and terror they felt." With that, Joon Min shot Alvarez in the shoulder.

With sweat breaking out on his forehead, Alvarez asked, "Joon Min, please, what can I do?"

"Do you mean what can you do to live?" Joon Min asked.

"Yes, yes… there must be something I can do?"

"I want you to realize, that you were about to wipe out billions of people around the world… entire countries… my home country… I want you to think about how many of those people would be asking that same question as they got sicker and sicker."

"Yes, yes… I understand." Alvarez said in desperation with his head hanging down as he nodded.

Shooting Alvarez in the groin, Joon Min said, "I want you to feel multiple parts of your body shooting messages of pain to your brain, and then realize, that just like those people you planned to kill… your pleas would be meaningless."

Hermann Alvarez looked up at Joon Min's face, just as she pulled the trigger shooting a nine millimeter bullet between his eyes.

Joon Min, Gertrude Elfmann and Kim Joo-Won left the board room and descended the building's back staircase after first pulling the fire alarm. Exiting the building with the evacuating crowd, they made their way to their vehicle and headed to the airport.

"I am very proud of the way you handled yourself in there, hermanita." Kim said in Spanish. "You moved with purpose, never hesitated, and stuck to the plan. I think our little team may be able to add assassinations to the industrial espionage services we will provide.

"Whatever pays the bills, big brother." Joon Min replied. "Isn't capitalism wonderful?"

Cardinal Dietrich sat at the table in the outdoor café and looked around nervously. The name on his caller ID had come up as Hermann Alvarez, but he knew Alvarez was dead. He'd heard the torture and interrogation over the ZOOM audio. In fact, they were all dead… Alvarez, Montana, Silva… or at least he had thought them dead, until he had received that call.

The caller had instructed him to come to this café at noon every day, for the next three days. When it was safe to make contact, they would. They said Aryphon still lived, and would have its revenge. So Dietrich sat at the café as he had the last two days, at noon, and nervously awaited someone to make contact.

The waiter came up behind the Cardinal and said, "Buona sera, signore. Would you like to order something?"

Dietrich thought it strange that the waiter said 'Good Evening, rather than good afternoon, and he turned to look at the man when the waiter nonchalantly put his hand on the top of Dietrich's shoulder. Immediately the Cardinal felt a sharp stinging pain and burning, as if he were just stung by a bee.

The waiter removed his hand and pulled out a chair, sitting down next to Dietrich as the Cardinal rubbed his stinging shoulder. Looking over at the man sitting next to him, Dietrich was about to ask what this was all about when the man leaned in and said in a low voice, "Good Afternoon, Cardinal Dietrich. Allow me to introduce myself. My name is Ari Ben-David. I am an officer with the organization you know as the Mossad."

Dietrich went to speak, but found his mouth did not seem to want to move, and the sounds came out all garbled.

"I do not have much time… or rather, you do not have

much time. You are probably already beginning to feel the effects of the paralytic I injected into your neck."

Dietrich tried to stand, but all he got in return for his effort was a shaking of his arms and legs.

Ben-David continued, "The drug is a little something our scientists invented that shuts down all messages between your brain and your muscles. In very short order, you will begin having difficulty breathing. The really cool thing about this drug, is it does not affect your cognitive abilities, so you will be fully conscious and actually able to feel your heart stop beating. And it is nearly undetectable… But then your religion, like mine believes in the dignity of the human body even in death. Therefore, it will be assumed you just had a heart attack, and no autopsy will be performed."

Dietrich indeed was beginning to struggle to breathe, and he leaned forward in his seat as he willed his muscles to help him draw in air.

"I want you to know, before your soul is taken to Hell, that the State of Israel will not rest until every Nazi is brought to justice. You have just been punished for your crimes in this world. Your eternal punishment will begin shortly. Never Again is more than just a saying, Herr Cardinal. It is a reality."

Ben-David stood up from the table and calmly walked away just as Dietrich stopped breathing. With sheer terror in his eyes, the Cardinal actually felt his heart stop beating moments before his world grew dark.

The lab, like the rest of the building was cold and dark. Aside from the fact that it was nearly midnight, it was the middle of the holiday season and no one was scheduled to be in the building for the balance of the week. The formula had been meticulously prepared, and now sat in a large beaker, with the cathodes and anodes sitting in the solution. Electrical wires ran from a circuit to the beaker, and from the cathode to three dead car batteries hooked up in parallel. Additionally, a digital thermometer was inserted into the solution and hooked up to a laptop to record any change in temperature..

After donning protective goggles over the wrap-around sunglasses they wore, Janine looked at John and asked, "You ready? Remember, do not look directly at the beaker."

Taking John's hand, she counted, "Three... two... one..."

Throwing the circuit, a pulse of electricity charged the solution causing an electro-chemical reaction. Protons and electrons moved, binding to the graphene... Suddenly an enormous flash of light occurred, the thermometer measured a five degree rise in temperature and the voltmeters attached to the previously dead car batteries recorded 14.4 volts before the surge blew out the measuring device.

Ripping off the goggles and turning the lights on in the lab, John and Janine embraced.

"It works... I can't believe it actually works. Janine said ecstatically.

"I always knew you could do it." John replied.

Hugging John again, Janine said, "Not just me. We did it together."

John looked a Janine with a puzzled look on his face. "I

don't see how I had anything to do with this, babe. You're the chemist. You're the one who put the whole experiment together."

Janine smiled at John with a special twinkle in her eyes, and said, "When we were running from the bad guys, it was your idea to buy those more expensive burner phones… You know, the good ones with the sim cards and upgraded cameras. I just took advantage of your wise decision and photographed the documents."